Day of Wrath

Day of Wrath

Iris Collier

PIATKUS

⌘ **Visit the Piatkus website!** ⌘

Piatkus publishes a wide range of exciting fiction and non-fiction,
including books on health, mind, body & spirit, sex, self-help, cookery,
biography and the paranormal. If you want to:

- read descriptions of our popular titles
- buy our books over the internet
- take advantage of our special offers
- enter our monthly competition
- learn more about your favourite Piatkus authors

visit our website at:

www.piatkus.co.uk

Copyright © 2001 by Iris Collier

First published in Great Britain in 2001 by
Judy Piatkus (Publishers) Ltd of
5 Windmill Street, London W1T 2JA
email:info@piatkus.co.uk

The moral right of the author has been asserted

A catalogue record for this book is available from the British Library

ISBN 0 7499 0566 2

Set in Times by
Action Publishing Technology Ltd, Gloucester

Printed and bound in Great Britain by
www.biddles.co.uk

To

Alexander Samuel Arthur

Chapter One

It was almost dark when Nicholas turned off the Eartham road and rode up the long drive leading to Peverell Manor. Above him the bright, crescent moon and a scattering of stars lit up the path, bordered by the great oak trees planted by his ancestor Lord Roger Peverell after the great victory over the French nearly two hundred years ago. His horse, Harry, a strong jet-black stallion with Arab blood in him, needed no urging. Gone was the drooping weariness of half an hour ago. Now he scented a generous supper of oats, a warm stable, and a good rub down by one of the ostlers. Nicholas bent down and patted Harry's sweat-soaked neck. He'd ridden him hard, but Harry had never let him down. Now he, like Harry, needed food and sleep. But first he must see Prior Thomas. The news he'd gleaned from his friends at Court was too important to leave until morning. The King, he thought, was certainly shaking things up. He'd been on the throne for twenty-six years, had grown tired of his first wife, and lost his heart to a dark-eyed beauty who had enticed him with her French manners and sharp wit. And for her he was now turning his kingdom upside down. And he, Nicholas Peverell had to warn his friends.

He reached the main gate, a solid oak door built to keep out undesirables. It was firmly shut. God damn them, he thought. Where were they all? Matthew? Roger? Giles? Hadn't he left instructions that someone had to be on duty when he was away? At all times. He could never be sure when the King would release him from his Court duties. He dismounted and tugged at the bell rope. No one came. He shivered in the cold night air. May, he thought, was a treacherous month. Sunshine by day, then a stab in the back at night when the frost devastated the blossom on the fruit trees.

He tugged at the rope again, more forcibly this time. What was the use, he thought, of keeping a household of servants when they weren't there when he wanted them? It hadn't been like this when Mary was alive. She'd always waited up for him when he came back from Court. She knew how to manage servants. Now the whole lot were out of control. Probably asleep, drunk on the contents of his cellar.

Suddenly he heard the sound of a key turning in a lock, and the huge door inched open. The pale, frightened face of Simon, the under-groom, peered round at him.

'My Lord,' he stammered, 'we didn't expect . . .'

'Open the door, for God's sake. I told you to expect me at any time. Now take hold of Harry. See he's well fed, and give him a good rub down. No short cuts, mind. He's earned his keep today; unlike others I could name.'

Nicholas handed over the reins to Simon, then strode across the courtyard to the great hall of his manor house. A fire was burning in the huge fireplace, and Nicholas went over to it and warmed his hands. The room was still cold. Even though it was May, the solid, stone walls of his house hadn't yet had time to absorb the sun's heat. He kicked over the burning log and turned round to warm his back. At least they'd laid him a place at the table. But where was Matthew? He wanted hot food and a jug of ale before he went out to see the Prior. But nobody came. Had it come to this? he thought furiously. Did he have to get his own food? It was obvious that he'd been away too long. Tomorrow, he'd have to crack the whip. Just as he reached impatiently for the bell rope, Giles Yelman, the under-steward, came scuttling in with a jug of ale.

'Thank God someone's awake around here. Where's Matthew? I gave him orders to wait up for me. No, let me do that,' he said as Giles began to pour the ale out for him, his hand shaking so much that the ale missed the tankard and splashed on to the stone floor. Much as he always tried to be impartial towards his servants, there was always something about Giles which irritated him. Maybe it was his long, narrow face, the sparse, straggly beard, the pale eyes which never met his, and an obsequiousness which Nicholas loathed.

'My Lord,' said Giles, handing the jug to Nicholas. He paused.

'Come on, out with it, man,' said Nicholas, drinking the ale straight from the jug. 'Let me remind you that I've been on the road all day, and I'm hungry. I want meat and fresh bread. Where's Matthew? What's got into the lazy devil?'

'My Lord, there is no Matthew,' blurted out Giles, backing away.

'No Matthew! What the devil do you mean? Is he ill? And what's the matter with you? You look like a hare cornered by the hounds.'

Giles, still retreating, crossed himself. Nicholas's heart missed a beat.

'You don't mean to say he's dead? Don't say the sickness has come to Dean Peverell. People are dropping like flies in London.'

'Yes, he is dead, my Lord. We found him not long ago, lying at the foot of the tower. We think he must have fallen.'

'Fallen? Matthew? Are you mad? Matthew knew that tower like the back of his hand. For God's sake, man, we keep the grain there. Matthew went there daily. Besides, what was he doing at the top of the tower? There's nothing there, and he's not the type to admire the view.'

'We don't know, my Lord. We've only just found him. He was lying there just as if he was taking a nap.'

3

'Where is he now?'

'He's in the store room. We didn't know what to do with him.'

'The store room! For God's sake, man, you shouldn't have moved him. At least not until the Sheriff has taken a look at him. You've sent someone to Marchester to get him, I hope?'

'My Lord,' Giles stammered, 'we didn't think, we didn't know. We waited for you.'

'Well, it's too late now. You weren't to know. Now get him out of the store room, and put him in the chapel. If he is dead, then we'll need a priest. One of you'll have to run down to the Priory and get one.'

'I'm sorry . . . we didn't know what to do. Nothing like this has happened before. We're all shocked.'

'Then it's time you pulled yourself together. Come on, let's take a look at him.'

Giles scurried off, followed by Nicholas. They went down the stone stairs to the rooms under the kitchen where the stores were kept. In the main store room, Matthew lay on the floor, covered by a rough woollen blanket. His round, good-natured face, usually flushed with good living, was now as pale as the stone walls around him. His eyes, unclosed, stared up at the ceiling. At the sight of his stocky body lying there like one of the beasts waiting for the butcher to come, Nicholas's bad temper evaporated. Suddenly, he was overcome by feelings of immense sorrow and he sank down on his knees by the side of the body. Matthew had been his father's steward; he'd been present when Nicholas was born, had watched over him when he was a child, welcomed him home from school. He'd prepared the banquet for his wedding, and the funeral feast when Mary died in giving birth to his son. There never had been a time when Matthew hadn't been there. He was part of the furniture. Memories which he'd tried to suppress over the five years he'd been on his own came flooding back. Life would never be the same again.

4

He stretched out his hand, and gently closed those staring eyes. Then he prayed silently. Time passed and he forgot about the King's affairs and the intrigues of the Court, and thought about the times when Matthew had always been there when he'd wanted him. They had all taken him for granted. And now they would have to manage without him. Suddenly he jerked himself back into the present. There were things to do. First he had to take a good look at the body. He pulled open Matthew's leather jerkin and put his head down on to his great barrel chest. There was no heartbeat. Then he saw the marks round Matthew's thick neck. Purple weals as if he'd been clawed by a wild beast.

'He's dead, but he didn't fall from the tower,' Nicholas said, turning to look at the servants who were crowding into the store room. 'These marks were made by a man's hands. Now, no man can strangle himself, so he was murdered, either where you found him at the foot of the tower, or his body was moved there to make it look as if he had fallen.'

He stood up and looked round at the circle of frightened faces. 'We'll get Landstock over tomorrow. And he'll bring the Coroner. Now get Matthew into the chapel, and you, Dick,' he said, looking at one of the kitchen boys, 'get down to the Priory and ask for a priest for the night vigil. I'll be along later, but first I want to talk to you, Giles, and you, Geoffrey,' he said, looking at his bailiff, a short, thick-set man with a cropped head and a face creased like a bull-dog's. 'Upstairs to my study. Then I shall want to talk to you all. No one, except Dick, is to leave the house. Now get moving. I want Matthew laid out decently on a table in front of the altar. Light two candles. The best ones,' he added. 'The ones we use for Easter. Matthew was a good man, one of the best servants a man can have, and I shall miss him. Now, with no disrespect to Matthew, as I know he'd understand, I need some food. Giles, bring me some cold beef and bread, then after a while, you, Geoffrey, come and join me.'

*

5

Alone in his study, Nicholas wolfed down the food which Giles had brought him. He still felt numb with shock. Matthew of all people! Who could possibly want to murder him? What was the motive? Admittedly he was severe with lazy servants, but on the whole they respected that. They knew where they were with him. It was impossible to hate him, and one would have to hate to kill someone. He'd been generous to his friends, and loyal to the family. He'd been the first to congratulate him on his marriage to Mary – Mary, always delicate, with a pale, fragile beauty like one of the lilies which he grew in his garden.

He finished eating and pushed the plate away. Suddenly, the tiredness vanished. He had a job to do. He had to find out whose hands had been round Matthew's neck, who had squeezed the life out of him and arranged him so neatly at the foot of the tower. And he wanted to bring that person before the justices of the peace and see him sentenced to death by hanging up on Marchester Heath.

He got up and opened the door. Geoffrey Lowe, his bailiff, was standing there.

'Come in, Geoffrey. Now, who found Matthew?'

'Giles did.'

'When?'

'About an hour and a half ago. I remember we were just about to . . .'

'Just answer the questions if you please. Why did Giles go out to look for Matthew?'

'Because we all wanted to know where he was. We missed him, my Lord. We knew you were coming back any minute, and we wanted our orders. Then young Joshua, you know, old Tom's son, he runs the warren when his father's poorly, well, he suddenly piped up.'

'I know Joshua. He'll make a good warrener one of these days. Well, what about him?'

'Well, he thought he heard the sound of breaking wood, and he thought of all those young birds hatching, and we all know there's a gang of thieves in the area. Lots of folk

6

have lost their new hatchlings. So Joshua asked Giles to come out and take a look at the sheds. All was quiet, and Joshua came back to tell us, but Giles wasn't satisfied and decided to take a look round. That's when he went to check on the stores over in the tower and found Matthew.'

'It could be that the thieves were trying to get into the tower and Matthew challenged them and got killed for his pains.'

'It's certainly possible, my Lord. Thieves would want Matthew out of the way otherwise he could identify them later if they got caught. No one wants to end up on Marchester Heath with a rope round his neck.'

'That sounds feasible. But why should the thieves strangle him? Surely, they'd knock him down with something. Strangling's a bit chancey; especially when it's someone like Matthew. He was strong as an ox.'

'Unless their look-out grabbed him from behind and held tight.'

'Could be. Now go and get Giles for me, and then Joshua. And I want you to get off to Marchester and fetch Richard Landstock. This is Sheriff's business, that's for sure. Oh, get along with you man,' he said, seeing Geoffrey's horrified look at the prospect of riding four miles to Marchester in the middle of the night. 'Landstock'll give you a bed for an hour or two. I want you both back here by first light. Take Merlin. He's reliable. There's a good moon tonight, and the stars will light you on your way. Now, be off, man. There's been a murder here, and possibly thieving. We'll have to move fast if we're to catch the devils responsible.'

'We'll catch them, sir. Someone will know who they are and spill the beans. Everyone liked Matthew. He treated us fair. It's not right he should be bumped off by common thieves just because he got in the way.'

Giles and Joshua confirmed what Geoffrey Lowe had said and Nicholas ordered everyone off to their beds. Tomorrow, when the Sheriff of Marchester came, they'd

7

all have to make statements. But he wasn't ready for sleep. First, he had to look at the place where they'd found Matthew's body.

Outside in the courtyard he shivered. This tragedy was going to affect them all. It would be impossible to replace Matthew. He turned to look at his sturdy manor house, built in the Norman style, which the first Lord Peverell had built after Duke William conquered the land and parcelled out the various manors to his followers. It looked more like a castle than a house, but over the years the harsh outlines had softened. The surrounding wall was still turretted, and the moat, which in early times was designed to keep out attackers, was now stocked with fish for the table. Mary had done that. She wanted to build a fine, modern house, furnished with chairs and tables bought in London, and she'd wanted to cover the cold, stone walls with Flemish tapestries. But it wasn't to be; she'd died too soon. She'd left the vision behind her, though, and one of these days, when times were more settled, he'd get down to it and build the sort of house which she would have approved of. Meanwhile, there was her garden, and that gave him immense satisfaction.

He walked over to the tower, which in earlier times was the last stronghold when the place was under attack. Now it loomed up in front of him, looking sinister in the moonlight. An owl hooted. All around, he could hear the rustling sounds of small creatures which had drifted in from the surrounding fields and were settling down in the piles of straw scattered over the courtyard. He tried to visualise where Giles had found Matthew's body. It couldn't have been thrown from the tower, Nicholas thought. The body was intact. No broken bones, no bruised skin except for those deep claw marks. Whoever murdered him must be very naive to think they could cover up their crime by making it look as if Matthew had accidentally fallen from the tower. Those tell-tale marks round Matthew's throat were a give-away. There was no doubt that he'd been

8

murdered. Most likely he'd interrupted thieves. They had then compounded robbery with murder and were destined for Marchester's Heath. And he'd catch them, sure enough.

He went back to the house, stopping to look in the chapel. Matthew had been laid out in front of the altar; a lighted candle had been placed at his feet and head. One of the monks who was also a priest was kneeling beside him saying the prayers for the dead. Nicholas recognised him. Father John. He'd been a member of the community at the Priory for a long time. Nicholas remembered him from his boyhood. He nodded to him, but the priest, wrapped in his prayers, didn't look up.

Nicholas walked over to the body. 'Rest in peace, Matthew Hayward,' he said, looking down into the waxen face. 'I promise you that I'll not rest until I catch whoever did this to you. Goodnight, Matthew, the best of stewards.'

Chapter Two

Next morning, Nicholas woke up late with the sun streaming in through the window, caressing his face. He opened his eyes and slowly his brain clicked into life. Then he remembered. Matthew lying in the chapel, his demoralised household waiting for instructions, and Landstock on his way from Marchester. And then there was also that urgent news he had to tell Prior Thomas.

He jumped out of bed and reached for his breeches. It was a relief to be back in the country. At Court he had to look his best in velvet doublet, slashed breeches and fine silk hose, but now it was leather breeches and doublet, woollen hose and a warm cloak for outdoors. He pulled on his long boots, still covered in the dust of the execrable Sussex roads and ran his fingers through his short beard, trying to smooth out the tangles in his unruly fair hair. It was always in the mornings that he most missed Mary. She used to lie back on the pillows and watch him dress. Sometimes she would call him over and gently tied the laces on his doublet for him. She enjoyed looking at him, she said, as much as he enjoyed looking at her.

She liked him clean, too, he thought with a guilty start. She always ordered the servants to bring up pails of hot water, saw that the tub was filled and checked the temperature. Then she used to sprinkle herbs in it too, herbs fresh from the garden which they had created together. Their sweet, pungent scent used to fill the house. Impatiently he reined in his imagination. Self-pity was an indulgence and led nowhere. Mary was safe with God. Soon, the chantry chapel he was building in the Priory for both of them would be complete. One day they would lie together under the chapel in the church of which he was patron, in sight of the high altar. He wanted the chapel to be carved with angels – angels playing harps and viols, angels singing and angels blowing trumpets and pipes. The best craftsmen in the county were working on it.

But now, he thought, as he splashed cold water on his face, what was going to happen to the Priory? His interview with Thomas Cromwell, that dour, enigmatic servant of the King, hadn't been reassuring. The King wanted the monastic revenues, that was for sure. His Priory was small in comparison with the great monasteries of Glastonbury and Malmesbury, but, all the same, the plate, the lead on the roof, the lands which the Priory owned were not inconsiderable. Prior Thomas had to be warned. They were friends, and Nicholas knew that the Prior would expect him to save them, but Nicholas knew he could not oppose the King. No one could. Not now, with the print scarcely dry on the new Treason Act.

He went down into the great hall, and ate the bread and honey which had been laid out for him. The honey was of the best quality and tasted of clover. The ale was freshly drawn. Life was going on; Giles was taking over from Matthew.

He went to find his servants, and found Giles in the kitchen, extracting goose grease from a jar. He looked nervously at Nicholas as if expecting a rebuke. Nicholas checked his irritation. Giles was only trying to do his best.

'Landstock should be here any minute now, Giles. Have the servants assembled in the hall. Landstock can use my study for the interviews. Oh yes, one thing did occur to me this morning. When I got back last night, the main gate was locked. Now if the thieves murdered Matthew, and then

11

dragged his body over to the tower, how the devil did they get into the courtyard in the first place? No, don't say it . . .' he went on, as Giles's face flushed with embarrassment. 'You didn't lock the main gate yesterday, did you? You forgot. Then Matthew was found, and you locked it. That's it, isn't it? The thieves just sauntered in and left at their leisure.'

'My Lord, we fully intended to, but what with Matthew disappearing, and all the commotion over Joshua hearing things up in the warren, we forgot all about locking the gate.'

'And how many times did you forget to lock it whilst I was away?'

'We always locked it before we went to bed.'

'Too late, too late. What a pack of incompetent oafs I am cursed with for servants! That gate must be locked at all times. And someone must be there to act as gatekeeper. We live in unsettled times and there are desperate men around. But it's no use crying over spilt milk. Get someone to run down to the Prior and tell him I shall be coming to see him shortly, just as soon as Landstock gets on with his business.'

The servants were beginning to drift into the hall. They looked dejected, mumbled their morning greetings, and dropped their eyes when he spoke to them. Nicholas hated to see them like this. He liked a happy household. Peverell Hall had always been a place where he could relax, study the new books which he'd bought from bookshops in London and add to his growing library. But now it seemed that Matthew's murder had contaminated the whole place, making everyone suspect his neighbour.

He didn't for one minute think that Matthew's murderer was a member of his own household. He knew them all. Some, like Geoffrey Lowe, had worked for his father, and their loyalty was unquestionable. Geoffrey's responsibilities were enormous – he supervised everything round the estate from the growing of corn and barley to seeing that the

12

grazing was sufficient for the cattle and the sheep. He organised the shearing of the wool and sold it at the best prices; he saw that the warren was always well stocked with plump rabbits and game, and that the fishponds were full of carp. He handled money and paid the workers. Yet he had never given Nicholas cause to mistrust him.

He didn't know the other servants as well as he knew Geoffrey and Matthew, of course. One of them might have harboured a grudge against Matthew. Maybe he'd been wrongly accused, or punished too severely. But that didn't usually turn a man into a murderer. However, a motive would no doubt emerge and it was Landstock's business to interview everyone and check on their alibis. He, Peverell, would take over when the wretches were brought before him at Quarter Sessions.

Suddenly, the door swung open, and Sheriff Landstock came in, followed by Geoffrey Lowe. Nicholas walked over to greet him. He liked Landstock, although they didn't always agree. But they'd worked well together in the past, and no doubt would continue to do so now. He'd not rest until he'd tracked down Matthew's killer.

Landstock looked his usual pugnacious self. He was a short, stocky man, bristling with indignation and radiating energy. His weather-beaten face, bushy eyebrows, short, thrusting ginger beard and hair that stuck straight up like a stiff brush gave him a foxy look which most people found intimidating. He had an extensive knowledge of the local criminal fraternity, who were terrified of him, and he had a keen nose for smelling out the liars and cheats.

'This is bad news, my Lord,' Landstock said, giving Nicholas's hand a vigorous shaking.

'It is indeed. I've lost a good friend and a trustworthy steward.'

'Where've you put him?'

'In the chapel.'

'A pity your servants moved him. You know I always like to see where the body was found. Remember that next

13

time you find a corpse on your premises,' he said, poking Nicholas in the ribs, and giving a loud bray of laughter which he checked when Nicholas glared at him. 'Oh well, let's go and see him, then. The Coroner's on his way. Your bailiff tells me that the cause of death is obvious. Is that so?'

'Just take a look at the marks on his neck.'

'Really? Then I'll not take long. I'll need to see all the servants, of course. One at a time. Have a room ready for me. Oh, a jug of your mulled ale will be welcome.'

'Giles will see to it. Meanwhile, if I'm not wanted for the time being, I must get down to see Prior Thomas. Bad things are coming to the Priory and I must warn him. Not that he'll take a blind bit of notice. He's seen it coming for years and has done nothing about putting his house in order.'

'What's up? You've heard something at Court? Mind you, I'm all for change. Especially where the clergy's concerned. Bloody parasites the lot of them, especially the monks.'

'That's a matter of opinion. But we're talking about matters of state here, Richard. I'm just back from Hampton Court – the King's gone there to avoid the sickness – and I was able to talk to Thomas Cromwell. He's holding the reins of power at the moment; it won't be long before he's made Lord Privy Seal.'

'What does the King see in him?' said Landstock, as they made their way to the chapel.

'Oh, he's useful right enough. Knows which side's his bread's buttered. When the good Sir Thomas More is condemned, as condemned he will be, and soon, there'll be no stopping Cromwell. But he'll not last long, mark my words. He's making too many enemies.'

'These are dangerous times, my Lord.'

'You can say that again. But I thank God that we've got a strong King. He'll never let the country sink into civil war as it did in my father's time. But he's self-willed, and more to the point, he's short of money. And that's where our friend Cromwell comes in. He knows how to keep the King happy – provide him with enough money to pay for his lavish life-style and his fleet of warships out on the Solent.'

'If he thinks he'll get enough money by kicking out a lot of lazy monks, then good luck to him, say I.'

'Richard, Richard, how can you say that? Haven't you any feelings for the Priory? Haven't you any sense of tradition? Our Priory's been here for centuries. Remember it was my ancestors who founded it. The Peverells have always been its patrons. Just stop for a moment and think of what the monks do. They run the only school in the district. Their hospital is overflowing at the moment because of all the sickness around. They hand out alms. They're good employers. Take away the Priory and you take away the village of Dean Peverell.'

They paused at the chapel door. 'That's how you see it, my Lord. I see a collection of lazy men living on the money which our people can ill afford. I see gold and silver plate used in their services whilst most people round here live in poverty. I'm told that my Lord Prior even uses silver plate at his table. I see wealth in the midst of poverty, and exploitation of humble people – for instance the prices they charge for the use of their mill in Marchester are higher than any one else's. As for prayer, I'm told Thomas Rymes enjoys archery contests rather more than saying his prayers and a good meal rather than fasting. No, my Lord, I'm not with you on this one. Kick the lazy bastards out, I say. Let them work for a living for a change.'

'You and Guy Warrener make a fine pair. He thinks the same way as you do.'

'I know, and I admire him for speaking his mind. He's a realist, like me. We must move with the times, my Lord. As for the monks, their days are over. Now let's have a look at your unfortunate steward.'

Later, when the Coroner had arrived and the cause of death

15

had been confirmed, the Sheriff and his clerk started on the lengthy process of taking statements from the servants. There was no obvious need for Nicholas to stay at home. He'd only get in everyone's way. Meanwhile, he had to see the Prior. For once, Nicholas dreaded the interview. Thomas Rymes was a stubborn man. He lived in the past, that was his trouble, thought Nicholas, as he went over to the stables. Now Landstock, insensitive and brash as he was, was typical of the new type of man emerging. Pragmatic, materialistic, always chasing after new ideas coming over from the Continent, always looking for the main chance. He'd survive, though, as long as he kept his nose clean, and that was more than you could say about idealists like Sir Thomas More, locked up in the Tower preparing to meet his Maker, and Prior Thomas, refusing to see changes coming until he was overwhelmed by them.

Harry greeted him with a joyful whinny. He was fully recovered after yesterday's gruelling ride. The grooms had fed him well, and his black coat shone like a mirror. Nicholas loved all his horses, but he favoured Harry more than the others. There was a big dash of Arab blood in him, which, coupled with the strength of the English war horse, made a formidable combination of beauty, swiftness and strength. Once again, Nicholas sent up a prayer of thanks to his crusading ancestor who had come back from the wars against the Infidel, bringing with him a pair of Arab horses. From these two he'd built up a stock of horses which were the best in the county.

He saddled Harry himself, mounted, and one of the grooms opened the main gate. Then he rode down the long drive towards the village of Dean Peverell.

The first Lord Peverell had built his house at the foot of the South Downs from where he could see the five channels of Marchester harbour shining like bright swords in the summer sunshine. The village was just a single street with cottages on either side. A track led up to the Priory which the first Lord Peverell had founded, bringing the first

16

monks over from his local abbey in Normandy. As the low tower appeared above the surrounding trees, Nicholas reined in Harry. Suddenly, he saw the Priory as if for the first time. It was doomed. King Henry was set on its destruction. And he was going to justify his act of vandalism by trumping up charges of licentious behaviour against the monks. Charges which, he knew in advance, would be grossly exaggerated. Admittedly the Prior was over-fond of the pleasures of the table and drank too freely of the fine Bordeaux wines which he bought from the French vintners. But there was no harm in that, thought Nicholas as he rode up to the gatehouse of the Priory. After all, most of the other pleasures were denied him; surely he was entitled to one harmless indulgence.

It was unfortunate that the Priory, even if it was small, represented a great deal of wealth, he thought. There were only seventeen monks but over the centuries they had acquired lands in other parishes and collected rents from mills and quarries all over the county. Also there was a fine collection of church furnishings – a gold altar frontal, silver candlesticks, a jewel-encrusted icon of the Virgin and Child brought back from the East after the sack of Constantinople. And then there was the chalice, solid gold and encrusted with rubies. Now that was beyond price. He had to warn Prior Thomas about that. Cromwell's inspectors must not set eyes on it. Even if he couldn't stop the King from closing the Priory, he could urge the Prior to hide its treasures.

The gatekeeper welcomed him and took Harry's reins.

'The Prior, my Lord, is in his house. We are all pleased to see you back safe and sound.'

'Thank you, Brother Ambrose. Peace be with you.'

As always, the tranquillity of the Priory moved him as he walked across the cloisters where some of the Brothers were at work on their manuscripts, making the most of the fine day. The Prior's house stood apart from the main monastic buildings, because it also served as a guest house and it was undesirable that the monks should be in too close a proximity to the visitors from the outside world. Built at a later time than the rest of the buildings, it stood in its own grounds, a large three-storeyed building, built of local flint-stone, its thick walls pierced by elegant windows with pointed arches. The entrance door stood open, and he went into the kitchen area where a fire burned in the great fire-place, and a pig rotated on a spit in front of the flames. Brother Cyril, the Prior's steward, smiled a greeting and took him upstairs to the first floor, where Prior Thomas had his study. The door was open, and Nicholas went in.

Thomas Rymes was a big man in the prime of life. His good-natured face radiated health, the result of a good digestion. He was wearing a black robe, belted round his ample girth with a cord. A large, silver cross hung down on to his expansive chest.

'Welcome home, Lord Nicholas,' he said glancing up from a document he was reading. 'What news of the King?'

He indicated the jug of ale beside him on the desk, and Nicholas helped himself. He was at ease with Prior Thomas. He approved of his philosophy, which was that you gave due respect to God, worked hard at whatever work God sent you, and then you celebrated with your friends when work was over. And celebrate they did. Nicholas had enjoyed some fine dinners in this house. The Prior liked prime-quality beef and on fast days he made full use of his stock of fat carp in his fishponds. Now, thought Nicholas, this idyll was going to be shattered. It was heart-breaking.

'The King, Prior Thomas, thrives, as always.'

'Thanks be to God. If the King thrives, the kingdom thrives. There's nothing worse than a sickly king, espe-cially when the heir to the throne is a mere girl.'

'The Queen's infant daughter, Elizabeth, is a healthy lass.'

The Prior looked puzzled, then, when he understood, his expression turned to one of disapproval. 'The Queen, my

Lord? Surely you mean the King's whore, Mistress Anne Boleyn?'

'For God's sake, Prior, guard your tongue. I mean Queen Anne. Catherine lives in retirement, poor lady. In bad health, so they say, with her daughter ignored by everyone.'

'It's monstrous, monstrous,' roared the Prior, his face flaming with anger. 'I will never call that whore, Queen. How can King Henry flout the Pope's wishes! Nothing good will come of this illegal, adulterous liaison. Some say that she's a witch.'

'Prior, hold your tongue. It's dangerous to say such things. Henry divorced his first wife. Thomas Cranmer married him to Anne Boleyn, and there's an end to it. One day their daughter might be Queen of England. Do you want to end up in the Tower of London?'

'The King'll not dare to touch me.'

'Not dare! Are you mad? He dared to arrest Cardinal Wolsey and seized his house. He dared to arrest Thomas More, and he's been in the Tower for thirteen months now. He will sign your death warrant without a second thought should he hear what you've just said. It's just as well that I'm a good friend of yours.'

'The King over-reaches himself,' said Prior Thomas, sinking back into his chair. 'He should be made aware of his own mortality.'

'And who's going to do that? Not me, that's for sure. No one can tell the King he's only a man.'

'We're all only men, my Lord,' said the Prior wearily. 'One day we'll all have to face our Maker.'

'And I don't intend to do that just yet. Not if I can help it.'

'Amen to that, Lord Nicholas. But come now, let's talk of other things. I am sorry to hear about your steward. He was a good man. Your stock cupboards are almost as good as mine. Your honey's certainly better than mine. One day I'll come and take a look at that garden of yours and see what's growing there. Your lamb is excellent, also.'

'I'll see Giles sends some cuts, Prior, when we do the slaughtering. Yes, it's bad news about Matthew. I shall miss him.'

'Killed defending your warren, I've heard. A dreadful thing. There are far too many thieves around. That Sheriff fellow ought to be more vigilant. They're always trying to get into our barns.'

'Strangely enough, we've got no signs of a break-in.'

'Really? Then what's the motive?'

'That's what Landstock's trying to find out at this very moment. I've left him to it as I had to come and warn you.'

'Warn me? About thieves? I don't need to be warned about them. We're always on our guard. As you should be. You mustn't let things slip when you're away, Lord Nicholas.'

'I'm not warning you about guarding your warren, Prior. There is another matter . . .'

There was a knock on the study door, and Prior Thomas sighed irritably. 'Come in, come in,' he called out impatiently.

The door opened and a monk came in. He was tall, gaunt, with a long, melancholy face. His black robe hung loosely on his bony frame, and, unlike the other monks, his head was untonsured because he was completely bald. Brother Michael. Nicholas knew him well. Once again, he reminded Nicholas of one of the gargoyles which spouted rain-water from the gutters on the tower.

'Brother Michael, I've given orders that I'm not to be disturbed when Lord Nicholas is with me.'

'I'm sorry, my Lord Prior, but Hobbes insisted that I should tell you the news immediately.'

'The Vicar? Giving orders? What impertinence! Well as you're here, you'd better get it out.'

'The King's Commissioners have arrived in Lewes. It won't be long before they're here.'

'Is that all? Stop your fussing, Brother Michael, and get

20

back to your patients. There've been rumours flying around for months now.'

'This time it's true,' interrupted Nicholas. 'At last we're getting down to business. Brother Michael is quite right to take this matter seriously. How did Alfred Hobbes hear about the King's Commissioners?'

'Oh you know Hobbes,' said Brother Michael with more than a hint of disapproval in his voice. 'He always loves a gossip. A babbler. A frequenter of ale-houses if I didn't keep an eye on him. He was up at Mortimer's place to complain about his tithe, as he always does, and Sir Roger told him.'

'Then Sir Roger is right for once. The King's inspectors are in Lewes and they will be coming here. This is what I was going to tell you, Prior. The King is set on closing down the monasteries, for reasons of his own. Your only hope of escaping closure, Prior, is to see that everything is in order when they come. See to it that the monks observe the Rule strictly. There must be no grounds for criticism on that front. Restrain your enthusiasm for archery competitions, keep a modest table, and keep the dairymaids out of the monastic buildings.'

'I'll do no such thing,' said Prior Thomas, rising to his feet. 'No one, not even the King, has the right to tell me how to run my own Priory.'

'We could, however, observe a fast ...' said Brother Michael tentatively, 'and stop the secular music.'

'Over my dead body,' shouted the Prior. 'Fasting's for Lent. Now's the time to give thanks for the fresh food. You can eat your gruel and vegetables, Brother Michael, but don't expect us all to live as frugally as you do. Good God, Brother, you could do with some red meat inside you. Do you bleed yourself when you bleed the other brothers? You look like a model for Brother Alfred's painting of the dance of death. Now, go away and read the Rule. St Benedict didn't disapprove of meat.'

'Only for the sick and old,' said Brother Michael meekly.

'And you fit the bill on both counts. Now get out, and don't come back here again with your miserly comments.'

'But the music, my Lord Prior. I was told you had a singer here the other night. Brother Benedict, playing a lute and singing about the joys of love.'

'And very beautifully he sang, too. There's nothing wrong with love, Brother Michael. It's God's greatest gift to man.'

'But it could be misconstrued.'

'Evil, they say, is in the eye of the beholder. Brother Benedict is a gift from God, sent to bring us all joy. This Priory has a musical tradition, as you well know, Brother. I intend asking Lord Nicholas over to hear our beloved Benedict sing. Tonight, my Lord? The young suckling pig will be delicious.'

'I should be delighted, Prior, if the Sheriff doesn't need me. But you mustn't ignore what's staring you in the face. The Commissioners will soon be here. They won't like suckling pigs and won't take kindly to love songs at meal-times. They'll use it against you. Don't make it easy for them. For a few weeks you would do well to observe the Rule of your founder. The King wants the monasteries closed. Let me make myself quite clear. Thomas Cromwell has been instructed to deal with the matter. Don't give his Commissioners any grounds for criticism. Listen to Brother Michael.'

Brother Michael's gaunt face creased into a satisfied smile. Although Nicholas couldn't go along with Brother Michael's views on the joys of the ascetic life, he wished heartily that the Prior had some of his qualities. What a pair they made! The Prior, smooth and fat with good living, Brother Michael, lean and gaunt, his breath smelling sour with fasting. The Prior, good humoured and easy-going; Brother Michael, bitter and censorious.

Nicholas walked across to the window and stared out at the surrounding fields where sheep were grazing, and the outhouses where cows were being milked and cheese was being made, and ale brewed. Over in the church, the monks were assembling for the morning Mass.

'The King wants all this to end, Prior. You, and others like you, are thorns in his side. You may have taken the Oath of Supremacy, but you take the Pope's side in the matter of his divorce and marriage to Anne Boleyn. You didn't make a stand like Sir Thomas More; as you said, you're not made of the stuff of martyrs. No, don't speak,' he said, as Prior Thomas opened his mouth to protest. 'You'll only say too much. You've got an enviable establishment here, Prior. There are only a dozen or so of you but just think for a moment of your church. Forget Hobbes's parish church. There's nothing much there to tempt the King, but in your monks' choir you have silver plate, candlesticks, priceless vestments and a solid gold chalice.'

'Given to us by one of your ancestors, my Lord.'

'Aye, and God knows where he got it from. But I hope the King never sets eyes on it. What he sees, he wants, as Wolsey knew to his cost. And he'll want your treasures, Prior. He'll not be interested in the buildings, except for the lead on the roof – he'll know he can get a good price for that. The stones he'll sell to local people like that jackal Guy Warrener. Cromwell told me that this Priory, although small, is one of the richest, and after the monasteries have been closed down, and their goods confiscated, he'll be able to clear off the King's debts in one go and still have plenty over to furnish the King's fleet. It's not now a case of "if" he closes down the monasteries, but "when".'

There was silence as the Prior and Brother Michael digested this information. Then the Prior began to pace restlessly up and down the room.

'Lord Nicholas, I don't doubt for a minute that what you are saying is true. You are a man of the world, and Brother Michael and I are men of God, living quietly in the country, knowing nothing of politics and the ways of the Court. Yet we do know all about human nature and we

23

know that men are capable of every wickedness. Yes, I see now that the Commissioners will come here and they will want our treasures. I shall be sorry to see those priceless things go, but what I am more worried about is my brethren. What's going to happen to them? Some of my monks, Father John, for instance, have lived here all their lives. He couldn't survive for long if he was turned out of here. It would be pure wickedness to inflict that on him.

'And what about the people who work on the estate?' he said, turning to look at Nicholas, as if he was responsible for the fate of the Priory. 'And the children in the school, and the poor people in the hospital? Are they to be turned loose to fend for themselves like common vagabonds? It can't happen. The King couldn't be so cruel.'

'Take care what you say, Prior,' said Nicholas in alarm. 'You must control your anger, or else you'll say things you'll regret. Your brethren will need all your strength and subtlety if you're going to survive. The King can do what he pleases. Parliament will pass the legislation; there's no doubt about that. It's full of greedy people licking their lips over the promise of rich pickings. There is talk of giving the monks pensions. There's nothing to stop them from joining the secular clergy. They're not suggesting that the parish churches should be closed. They'll continue and they'll need clergy to run them just as they always have. But I do advise you to hide your treasures. I'll help you all I can. I could make the King an offer to buy the bells myself. Come to think of it, I could offer to buy the Priory and in that way we'll keep all our treasures for posterity. I'll also preserve my chantry and Mary can be laid to rest there in peace with no threat of disturbing her. The King would bite if I offered him a good enough price. But this won't save you, Prior, nor your monks. We shall have to get used to an England without monks.'

'To think that we welcomed King Henry as our anointed Sovereign when he came to the throne. Now he's forfeited that right. He's the devil emissary,' said Brother Michael,

24

scarcely able to control his anger.

Nicholas turned to look at him. Brother Michael looked calm, but his eyes glowed with a deep anger. There was passion in that man, he thought. A deeper, more dangerous passion than the explosive anger of the Prior.

'You must both control yourselves,' Nicholas said. 'Never again repeat what you've just said to me in anger, otherwise you'll both suffer a terrible death. You know the penalty for treason. What use will you be to your brethren or the children in your school or the sick in your hospital if you are dragged off to Marchester Heath to be butchered there as an example of what happens when the King is crossed? Look to yourselves and your brethren. I will do my best to help you. If we work together, we shall survive. But hide the Priory treasures. Let's try to keep something of our time to pass on to posterity.'

'This can't happen. It must not happen,' said Brother Michael furiously.

'Face the facts, both of you. It is going to happen. Now you must work to save yourselves and this community.'

'Are you telling us to give in to the King and save our own skins? That's telling us to do the devil's work for him!' exclaimed Brother Michael.

'Hush, Brother,' interposed the Prior, 'Lord Nicholas knows the King's mind. Surely, my Lord,' he went on, 'you could speak to him, tell him how we pray for him daily, and for his family and his kingdom. Surely he will listen to you.'

'Nothing I do or say, Prior, will make him change his mind. I cannot save you and your brethren from being evicted. Neither can I save your treasure if the Commissioners set eyes on it. I shall be seeing the King again soon. I'll see what I can do about finding benefices for you all. I expect there'll be a cathedral appointment for you, Prior. With your musical talent, you'd make a fine Precentor.'

'Lord Nicholas, you go too fast. Here am I just trying to

25

grasp the fact that we are to be evicted and you're talking about cathedral appointments.'

'Time is just what we haven't got. Now give me your blessing and I must get back to Landstock. Remember that I've got a murder investigation on my hands.'

Nicholas bowed his head for the Prior's blessing. He felt immensely sorry for his friend. Impulsive and arrogant as he might be, he had a sincere compassion for all the members of the community in his charge. He was also a devoted friend, and at the time of Mary's death his support and advice had been invaluable. Hard times were coming, but he might just possibly be able to help them. As long as Prior Thomas guarded his tongue. And Brother Michael controlled his anger. Extremists would get nowhere at all in these times. And the King had a swift way of dealing with them.

Chapter Three

Nicholas rode back to Peverell Manor, checking Harry, who fidgeted, wanting Nicholas to give him his head. But Nicholas was in no mood for a joy-ride. All around him the countryside was bursting with life – the hedgerows buried under a haze of cow-parsley punctuated with the bright faces of ragged robins. The coppice, where pigs rooted around for acorns, was carpeted with bluebells, and above him the birds were urging their mates to greater efforts to find food for their demanding fledglings. But all this was lost on him today. His steward had been murdered, his Priory was doomed. His friend, Thomas Rymes, faced an uncertain future. The monks and lay workers would soon have to find work in a cold and unsympathetic world.

He rode on, scarcely aware of the villagers, most of whom were his tenants, who called out cheerful greetings to him, glad to see him safely back from Court. At any other time, this ride would have given him great pleasure. But not today.

Ahead of him, walking along the side of the road, was a girl whom he'd often seen before – Jane Warrener. She was young and slim, dressed simply in a plain linen dress, her long, chestnut-coloured hair hanging unbound down to her waist. As he rode up, she turned round. The sight of her young face, glowing with health and vitality, always had the effect of lifting his spirits. Her skin had a satin sheen to it which reminded him of the petals of his favourite roses. Her eyes, which met his without flinching, were the same colour as the sky on that May morning.

He forced Harry to stand still whilst he dismounted. Not for the first time he marvelled at the trick of nature that such a beautiful girl could spring from old Guy Warrener's loins. Warrener was an irascible and greedy rogue, wealthy, it was rumoured – certainly he lived in one of the largest houses on the edge of the village. His gardens were brimming over with produce and the honey which his bees produced was even more famous than his own. Jane was his only child, and he poured into her all his own pent-up love which had been frustrated ever since his wife died at her birth, eighteen years ago. Work was his consolation and it was said that he had already set his eyes on the stonework of the Priory when the monks were sent packing. When that happened, thought Nicholas ruefully, Warrener would be the first to arrive at the Priory armed with a pickaxe and pushing a wheelbarrow. He'd rebuild his house, and in a few years he'd have a fine stone house which would rival his own and that of his neighbour, Sir Roger Mortimer. How could Jane cope with such a father? he thought, as he walked beside her in companionable silence, leading a resigned Harry. Admittedly, Jane was her father's pride and joy. He'd heard that she was well educated and could read Greek and Latin fluently whilst her father still signed his name with a cross. She could read French also, and made a point of reading all the works of the Protestant reformers she could lay her hands on. Now, at eighteen, she was a beautiful and accomplished young woman, able to entertain her father's guests with a variety of musical instruments. And she had a mind of her own, and wasn't afraid of anyone.

Now she seemed to symbolise that spring morning. She reminded him of the fields full of daffodils, cowslips and wild roses. She was looking at him shyly, too, and he noticed the flush of colour on her face which was spreading

28

down her neck to lose itself in the soft folds of the linen cloth which filled in the square-cut neckline of her dress. It pleased him to realise that she wasn't indifferent to him.

'Not riding Melissa this morning, Jane?' he said, remembering that her father had bought a white mare from his stables for her sixteenth birthday.

'No, my Lord. I haven't far to go, and I enjoy the walk. Later, I'll take her out.'

He'd seen her once, cantering Melissa over the springy downland turf and he'd thought he'd never seen anything so beautiful. She rode astride, despising the more seemly side-saddle which ladies of quality were supposed to adopt.

'She still serves you well?' he asked.

'She's the darling of my heart,' said Jane, laughing gaily. 'And Harry looks full of beans, this morning.' She reached out and stroked Harry's velvety nose and he nuzzled her hand appreciatively.

'Yes, surprisingly, he's raring to go. We got back from London only last night, and yet he was as bright as a button this morning.'

'Have you been to Court? Did you see the King? And Queen Anne? Is she as beautiful as they say she is? And the young princesses? Did you see them?'

'Hold on, lass. One thing at a time. Yes, I spoke with the King. I'm a member of his Council, remember. Yes. I saw Queen Anne. She's not beautiful, but striking. I think she pushes the King too far. There was a nervousness about her that I haven't seen before. The King has a roving eye and she'll have her work cut out to keep him interested, especially if she doesn't give him the son which he wants so desperately.'

'Do you think she's a witch?'

'Well, she enchanted the King once. You could call that witchcraft, I suppose.'

'I don't envy her. She must be surrounded by enemies.'

'Yes, you could say that. Thank God you live here in the peace and tranquillity of the Sussex countryside. You'd have a rough time at Court. Some old and crabby courtier would snap you up as soon as you arrived, hoping you'd provide him with vigorous heirs.'

'Oh, they'd take no notice of me,' she laughed. 'I'm not rich enough. Father says he's not providing me with a huge dowry. Besides, I'll not marry anyone I don't love.'

'You don't need a dowry, Mistress Warrener. Not with your beauty. You are all the dowry a man could need.'

They'd reached the outskirts of the village, and ahead of them stretched the avenue of oaks which led up to his house. Jane stopped. 'I have to turn off here to see Agnes Myles, my Lord.'

But Nicholas didn't want her to leave. 'Why are you going to see that old woman?' he said, scowling. 'On a day like this you shouldn't be mixing with cantankerous old biddies like Agnes Myles. Come and look at my garden.'

He saw her hesitate, then she shook her head, and turned away. 'I need some juniper berries,' she said. 'My father's chest is bad again. He coughs at night and now after weeks of nagging he's agreed to let me help him. Juniper berries work wonders for people with chest trouble, but we've used up all our supplies. Agnes always has plenty in stock.'

'Say no more,' said Nicholas with a sigh of relief. 'We've got plenty in our stores, I'm sure.'

'That's very kind of you, my Lord, but . . .'

'No buts, Jane; and I insist you stop calling me "my Lord". From now on I'm going to call you Jane, so you must call me Nicholas.'

'Oh no! My father wouldn't approve.'

'Your father's not here, is he? And no one's going to tell him, are they? Come on, jump up on Harry. He's dying for a gallop. Ride up to the house, and then stop at the small gate over to the right. It leads into my garden. I'll follow. The walk'll do me good. Come on, lass, I'm sure you'll enjoy riding Harry.'

Jane hesitated, but only for a moment. She hitched up her skirts like a dairymaid, revealing slim legs covered by

30

white stockings, and jumped nimbly up on to Harry's back. She looked enchanting perched up there, Nicholas thought. Harry immediately began to show off, tossing his head and swirling round in circles, and Nicholas began to regret his impulsive action. But there was no need to worry. She sat there firmly until Harry calmed down, then she gave him a hearty kick and he was off up the drive like a black demon. With a sigh of relief, Nicholas ran after them.

When he caught up with her, she'd tied Harry to a tree outside a small gate, and together they went into the first of the gardens. The wall which surrounded the garden had mellowed since he'd built it eight years ago, and today it was bright with valerian and the delicate white flowers of climbing bedstraw which grew profusely out of the crevices.

'How beautiful,' she said. 'How perfectly beautiful.'

'I suppose it is,' he said, suddenly seeing the garden through her eyes. 'I call it my "pleasance". Mary designed it and I simply tell the gardeners to keep it as she would have liked it. They seem to have done just that.'

He saw the smoothly cut turf, sparkling with daisies and buttercups which the careful scything of his gardeners had not been able to eliminate, and the neatly trimmed hedges round the rectangular beds. In these beds every type of herb was growing in profusion, including great clumps of lavender whose shafts of purple were just about to burst into bloom. Sage bushes, with their delicate grey-green leaves creating their own back-drop for their purple flowers, scented the air. Thyme grew out of the sanded walks, and rosemary, mint, marjoram, birthwort, tall heads of fennel and dill, lovage and a mad riot of marigolds burst over the confines of their beds and made a jewelled carpet for them to walk on.

Dizzy with the mixture of intoxicating scents, brushing aside the swarms of butterflies, they walked across to the far wall where another door led into another garden. Nicholas opened it and beckoned Jane in. He watched her

31

face light up in wonder, and he thought how happy he was at that moment. He pushed out of his mind affairs of state and the Sheriff's sad investigation, and wanted only to look at Jane's lovely face glowing with pleasure.

The second garden was part orchard, and part wild garden where the grass had been left uncut and ox-eyed daisies and scarlet poppies grew beneath the fruit trees now in full blossom. Honeysuckle hung over the surrounding walls, the lush apricot-coloured flowers filling the air with their sweet scent. Gently, Nicholas shook the low branch of a cherry tree and the delicate blossoms showered down on Jane, spattering her hair and dress with petals.

'What a wonderful place,' she said.

'There's more. Come with me through the next door.'

Reality receded. He forgot about Matthew, the Sheriff and a household waiting for his orders, and, feeling as if someone had waved a magic wand over them and they had become an enchanted couple in a mediaeval romance, he took Jane into the third and last garden. Here nature had been tamed and ordered. In the centre was a square of smoothly cut grass, and in the centre of this was a marble fountain shaped like a great fish arching out of the sea, with water spouting out of its mouth. The water trickled out of the basin and into a second pond where fish fled for shelter under the flat leaves of water lilies at their approach. Behind this was an arbour which contained a seat with vines trailing over it, which met in the centre with climbing roses and honeysuckle. There was another pond to the right of the arbour and standing in the centre of the pond was a marble statue of a woman carrying a water pot on her shoulder. Fronds of hair drifted over her delicate breasts, and her eyes were modestly lowered. Between the arbour and the end wall were rows of vines, now vigorously sprouting delicate green leaves.

'There, Jane, do you like my gardens? They are my chief joy now that Mary's gone. After all the horrors I've seen around me, the filth and the pestilence in the streets of

London, the selfish greed of powerful men, the agony of Tyburn, I come here to wander round and relax in the scent and sight of so much beauty. And you, Jane Warrener, are the fairest flower of them all.'

She blushed, and dropped her eyes. Not wanting to embarrass her, he took her arm and led her back into the orchard garden. 'You can come here, Jane, whenever you like. Help yourself to whatever herbs you require, and if I'm not here, find Giles and he'll give you what you want. Mary always gathered herbs and dried them for winter use. She and I went to Italy, you know, and we bought that statue, and the fountain. Poor soul, she was never strong and she found the journey very tiring. Then she became pregnant and it was all too much for her. She wanted so much for us to enjoy these gardens, but I haven't much time these days. We brought the water for the ponds and the fountain down from the spring and I love the sound of water. Paradise, according to the Arabs, is full of fountains and rivers, and I can go along with that. I want to do nothing else with my life but to tend these gardens and plan others like them. I wish to God that we lived in some other, less troubled times.'

'My Lord . . . I mean Nicholas, you've made a paradise here, but you can't escape from reality. Terrible things have happened. I've heard that your steward's been murdered. Do you know who did it, and why? We all respected Matthew. Now you must turn your mind back to him. There'll be a time for enjoying your gardens when we find out who murdered him and why.'

She was right, of course, thought Nicholas. He was as bad as the Prior. He was living in the past. Time to wake up. He had forgotten Matthew. He'd lost himself for a few moments in the beauty of a young woman and a garden in May.

'I'm sorry, Jane. You're right. This is no time for dreaming. No, I don't know who murdered Matthew. And I ought to get back to see Landstock. We think at the moment that Matthew probably disturbed thieves and they decided to kill him rather than let him live and to witness against them.'

'Thieves, you say? I don't believe that. Matthew was murdered because he knew too much. He had to be silenced.'

Nicholas turned and looked at her in astonishment. There was a firmness in her voice that took him by surprise. She looked so demure standing there covered in cherry blossom, and yet she was expressing opinions about a murder with all the certainty of a criminal investigator.

'Jane, what are you saying?'

Jane shrugged her shoulders and her eyes met his unwaveringly. 'Only that Matthew was a frequent visitor to Mortimer Hall.'

'So? You're not suggesting that Sir Roger . . .?'

'No, not that. Matthew was courting Bess Knowles – Lady Mortimer's personal maid. Bess and I are good friends. Now Bess said that she and Matthew were talking together in the parlour when in came some friends of Sir Roger's. Bess and Matthew ducked down behind one of the big settees and heard things that they shouldn't have. You know, political matters about Sir Thomas More and the King's plan to close down the monasteries. Matthew was very upset when he heard this and I had to tell him to keep his opinions to himself. You see, he was very loyal to the King, hated the monks and wanted to see the Church reformed. Bess said he went to see Sir Roger and asked him, as a Member of Parliament, not to oppose the King's legislation. I think it was then that Sir Roger decided to get rid of him in order to shut him up. As you know the Mortimers are very traditional, and don't want any changes. The conspirators must have . . .'

'Jane, for God's sake, stop,' said Nicholas thoroughly alarmed. 'Don't say another word. Thank God we're out here in the garden where we can't be overheard. Don't ever mention the word conspiracy again. Think of Sir Thomas in

34

the Tower, facing execution on Tower Green. And why? Because he opposed the King over the matter of the Royal Supremacy. If you say or do anything against the King's wishes you run the risk of being arrested and I will have to sentence you to a terrible death up on Marchester Heath. And that would break my heart. Now, if what you say is true, and there is a conspiracy abroad in West Sussex, and Matthew got mixed up in it, then you must steer clear of it. We have a ruthless King on the throne, Jane, with a ruthless servant only too eager to carry out his wishes. Don't ever say that word again. Don't even think of it.'

'Nicholas, I value my life as much as anyone, but I must speak up if we are to get to the truth. As a woman, I can do and say things that men cannot do. No one expects me to understand politics. I'm regarded as a non-person when I go up to Mortimer Hall to see Bess. They don't think Bess has got any brains either, but she's sharper than me, and always tells me what's going on. She loved Matthew. She was seriously considering accepting his offer of marriage. He would have given her all the love and security she was looking for. Now she's certain that Sir Roger wanted him dead to stop him talking. She wants him avenged and she'll help us.'

'Us? So you're with me then, Jane Warrener?'

'Of course. I want to know who killed Matthew. And I want to stop anyone else getting killed.'

'Anyone else? What have you heard?'

'Only that there is a conspiracy – yes, I must say the word – here in Sussex against the King.'

'Jane, you must tell me everything. It's your duty.'

'Only if you'll take me on as your assistant.'

'Are you mad? You could end up like Matthew. And so could your friend, Bess Knowles. Keep away from this, Jane. Stick to looking after your ailing father. Ride your beautiful mare, marry someone worthy of you and rear a clutch of splendid children. Don't, I beseech you, meddle in politics.'

'Is that how you think of me? Then you're no different from all the other men, including my father. I might be a woman, I can't help that, but I can think like a man, and I want to help you.'

He looked into her candid blue eyes, and saw that she was serious. Feelings which he never expected to feel again after Mary's death flooded through him. Jane, his beautiful spy. Jane, the beautiful lady of his garden. No, it wasn't possible. Unthinkable. She was not made for political intrigue. She was made for pleasure and childbearing, and the management of a great household.

'I won't have you risking your life, Jane. Come, let's pretend this conversation's never happened. You came for juniper berries, and juniper berries you shall have and anything else you want. And then you must go back to the safety of your father's house.'

'How old-fashioned you are, Nicholas. And how short-sighted. Don't you see how valuable a woman assistant could be to you? I wouldn't draw attention to myself. I'll report back here to you in this garden when I've got anything to say. If anyone asks me what I'm doing, I can always say I'm collecting herbs.'

She looked at him so seriously, with just a hint of a twinkle in her eyes, that Nicholas found himself wavering. If there was a conspiracy against the King in this part of Sussex, then it was his job to find out about it and nip it in the bud. Much as he disapproved of the King's policy against the monks, he'd never be part of a conspiracy to rid the country of a lawfully anointed king. To do that would be to plunge the country back half a century into bloody civil war when Yorkists fought against Lancastrians. But to use a woman . . . And a young and beautiful one like Jane . . . No, he couldn't do it. Except . . .

'Come on, Nicholas. Why are you dithering like an old woman? You know it makes sense.'

'I suppose you could be useful, but this is *my* investigation, remember. You will only do what I ask you.'

'My Lord, would I presume to do anything else?'

He looked at her sharply, but she lowered her gaze demurely. 'I don't trust you, Jane. There's more to you than meets the eye. But if you're going to be my spy, we must trust one another. Has this conspiracy got a name?'

'I think it's called Day of Wrath. But usually they use the Latin words, Dies Irae.'

He suddenly felt a surge of fear. This all sounded uncomfortably real. 'They, Jane? Who are they? You must tell me. My God, Jane, I don't like this. You should never have got involved in this.'

'Me? Involved? Oh no, Nicholas, spies never get involved. They only make reports. Don't worry about me. Besides, I don't know who the "they" are. I am only telling you what Bess told me.'

'Then I must talk to Bess Knowles. But be careful, Jane. Make sure you only speak to me about these matters. Now, I must ask you this, where do you stand regarding the King's plans? Are you for the monks, or do you, like your father, want to see them turned out?'

'I share my father's views on reform of the Church. But I shall never agree to the eviction of the monks and the pulling down of their buildings. The Vicar and my father want that to happen. But I respect the monks, and consider Prior Thomas my friend. And of course I am loyal to our King. He might be selfish and ruthless, but he keeps the peace, and who knows, out of all this, something good might happen. Change isn't always bad. No, I'm for King Henry and I think that in the long run people will look back on his reign and judge him favourably.'

Nicholas stared at his new assistant in amazement. He'd never heard a woman talk like this. Mary had never expressed any opinions, political or otherwise. She'd always followed his lead, and had never once opposed him. But Jane was different. She'd make a deplorable wife, but as a second-in-command in a murder investigation, she might have her uses.

'Then I am glad we agree on something. Now I must get back to Landstock, and you must return to your father, otherwise he'll be getting suspicious. I don't want him to upset our plans.'

'Father? He'll do as he's told. He doesn't want me to go to the Prior's supper tonight, but I'm going.'

'Then I look forward to seeing you there. But you'll not go on your own?'

'No, Prior Thomas is sending his carriage for me. Father won't like it, but his chest is too bad to allow him out at night. The Prior'll go mad if he disturbs the music with his coughing.'

'What's the Prior asking an attractive woman like you to supper for? That man's the limit.'

'Because I'm good value, I'd say.'

'Good value? What the hell do you mean?'

'I can sing. And he's got some new songs composed by Josquin Després which Brother Benedict brought over from France. Prior Thomas thinks together we'll make fine music. I'm looking forward to it.'

'Why not let me come and collect you?'

'Because my father will have a fit. He'll think you've got designs on my virtue. He can't object to me going in the Prior's carriage.'

Nicholas looked thoughtfully at his new assistant. 'You're an amazing woman, Jane, and I shall enjoy getting to know you better. I look forward to hearing you sing tonight. Now let's see if we can cure your father's cough. You must look after him, you know; he so obviously cares for you.'

'I'll always look after him. Difficult as he is, I love him. And he's all I've got.'

'From now on Jane, consider me your friend.'

'Thank you, my Lord, I'm honoured,' she said as she dropped him a curtsy.

Back in the house, Landstock had come to the end of the

38

servants' interviews. He was deep in conversation with the Coroner when Nicholas came into the study. Nicholas knew the Coroner well. He was an elderly man, with a scholarly stoop, and a long, thin face with the lugubrious eyes of a bloodhound.

'We've done all we can, for the moment,' Landstock said briskly. 'Nothing much has come out of the servants' statements. They all agree with Giles that Matthew must have heard a disturbance and went out to see what was up. He never came back. Hardcastle,' he indicated the Coroner, 'has reported a verdict of murder by person or persons unknown, and it's my job to catch the thieves and present them to you for the preliminary hearing. Then it's off to Marchester Assizes and a swift death up on the Heath.'

'You make it sound quite straightforward, Sheriff. Has anyone found signs of a break-in?'

'No, but Joshua and Giles definitely say they heard something.'

'Hmm . . . not enough to establish a motive. However, at least we can rule out the servants. They all have water-tight alibis and can vouch for each other, I suppose?'

'Oh yes. They all seemed to be where they should be. This is an outside job.'

'There's one other thing that bothers me,' said Nicholas thoughtfully, 'it might not be important, but I'm puzzled by the way Matthew was killed. Would common thieves bother to strangle someone who'd interrupted their work? It seems more likely to me that they'd turn round and hit him over the head. Strangling someone as strong as Matthew wouldn't be easy. Matthew was a tough man, and he'd go down fighting. Strangling implies premeditation. I think someone was lying in wait for him. Someone jumped out on him and seized him round the throat.'

'I'm inclined to agree with you, my Lord,' said the Coroner, coming to life. 'But why should anyone want to murder someone as harmless as your steward? If we rule out thieves then we are without a motive and that's very

39

undesirable. The Sheriff'll get nowhere without establishing a motive.'

'It seems to me that you want to tidy this case up just too neatly,' said Nicholas severely. 'First, find the facts, then establish the motive. Not the other way round.'

'Oh yes, my Lord. Certainly, my Lord. I shouldn't have spoken.'

'Well, forget it. And now I expect you could both do with some refreshment. Something to drink? And a slice of ham to go with it?'

'If it's no trouble, my Lord.'

'No trouble at all, Coroner. You've had a long, hard morning's work and there's a brisk ride ahead of you. Now when can I bury poor Matthew? I can't keep him in the chapel for ever?'

'As soon as you can make the arrangements,' said Landstock. 'We've finished with him. Now we've got to get on and find the thieves. Shouldn't take us long. Someone, somewhere, always seems to see something suspicious and is willing to spill the beans. Particularly when there's a reward offered.'

Chapter Four

A pity the King wasn't here to enjoy this meal, thought Nicholas, as Brother Cyril plunged his knife into the rich suet crust of the great pie, releasing a delicious aroma of rabbits and chickens stuffed with dried plums and raisins, cooked slowly in red wine. He would have enjoyed it enormously. Nicholas was hungry. It seemed a long time ago since he'd eaten his last proper meal at Court, and yet it was only yesterday. And now he was drinking the King's health in a fine claret, polishing off the pie, and gleefully anticipating the arrival of the suckling pig.

He loosened the fastenings of his doublet and turned to the monk who was sitting next to him.

'You keep a well-stocked cellar, Brother Jeremy. Do you personally sample all the casks before you buy?'

'If I did, my Lord, I wouldn't be sitting here at this moment reasonably in command of my wits. No, I leave the sampling to Prior Thomas. He's a better judge than me. I just place the order. Do you like this one?'

'It's one of the best I've tasted. It complements the pig to perfection.'

'Then I'll have a word with the Prior and see that you get a cask in time to celebrate the feast of Corpus Christi. Brother Benedict brought us over some casks of a new wine from the vineyards of Rivières. They are a present from his abbot.'

Ah, Brother Benedict, thought Nicholas, as, through the steam from the pie and the smoke from the woodfire burning at one end of the great hall, he looked across to the other side of the table where a young monk of outstanding beauty was sitting next to the Prior. Prior Thomas had draped an arm affectionately round the young man's shoulders, but Brother Benedict's dark eyes were fixed on Jane Warrener, who had left the table and was busy tuning a lute in one of the alcoves at the far end of the hall. Suddenly, Nicholas felt indignant. No monk should look at a woman like that, he thought. The Prior would have to get rid of that young man before the King's inspectors arrived.

The arrival of the suckling pig put an end to such thoughts. Brother Giles had cooked it to perfection and Nicholas tackled his plateful of steaming meat with gusto. One of the steward's underlings brought in jugs of a different wine, a full-blooded claret from the vineyards around Bordeaux, and Nicholas gave himself up to the pleasures of the table. The pig was soon demolished, the bones thrown down on the rush-strewn floor, where the Prior's lapdogs snapped and snarled at each other as they fought over the scraps with glee. Later, when the tables had been cleared, the servants would let in the most favoured of the Prior's hounds to clear up the remains.

By the time Brother Cyril brought in a great tray of sweetmeats, honey cakes filled with walnuts and lightly dusted with cinnamon, and marzipan fashioned into the shapes of small birds and woodland creatures, Nicholas's head was spinning. He looked round at the flushed faces of the monks and the thought entered his head as to what their founder, St Benedict, would have thought of these proceedings. And he also thought how oblivious they all were to the sword of Damocles hanging over their heads. No wonder the reformers regarded the monasteries as fair game.

The servants were removing the empty dishes. Prior Thomas pushed back his chair and stood up.

'Come Benedict, my beloved guest from distant France, finish your wine and let us hear that fine voice of yours.'

Benedict forced his attention away from Jane and back to the Prior.

'No, my Lord, my singing is nothing but the croaking of a frog in comparison with Jane Warrener. She has the sweetest voice I have ever heard. Don't you agree with me, Brother Oswald?' he said, addressing one of the monks, whose black habit was tightly stretched across his pendulous belly, his huge moonface glowing with good living. Brother Oswald pursed his lips and considered his answer for a few moments.

'Mistress Warrener sings well – for a girl. But there is nothing to beat the purity of the male voice; especially a light tenor, Brother, which you possess.'

'You've hit the nail on the head, Brother Oswald, as usual,' said the Prior, patting Benedict's head approvingly. 'The male voice wins hands down. It has a special purity which the female voice with its emotional undertones cannot compete with.'

'But when the two are in harmony,' said Nicholas smiling across at the Prior, 'they are incomparable.'

'Then let us settle the argument by putting it to the test,' said Prior Thomas genially. 'Come, fill up the tray of sweetmeats, Brother Cyril, and bring us some more jugs of wine, and tune up the instruments. Come, my Lord,' he said turning to Nicholas, 'we'll go and sit over by the fire and let the young entertain us.'

He walked unsteadily over to Brother Oswald and helped him out of his chair. Then, clutching a jug of wine each, they staggered over to the fireplace at the far end of the room where some finely carved oak armchairs had been arranged on both sides of the crackling log fire.

Nicholas hung back for a moment, watching Benedict join Jane in the alcove. She greeted him with a broad smile and handed him a lute which she'd been tuning. Nicholas scowled. Fighting down a feeling of resentment, he turned to

43

Father Hubert, the elderly Sacristan who acted as sub-Prior when Prior Thomas was incapacitated. Hubert had not touched the sweetmeats and had eaten only a small portion of the pie. He had only exchanged a few words with Nicholas during the meal and had passed him the jug of wine when his glass was empty but hadn't touched a drop himself. Now he made no move to join the others round the fire.

'Where are the rest of the brethren?' said Nicholas, forcing himself not to look at the two in the alcove, where Brother Benedict was taking off his monastic habit to reveal an elegant doublet and hose underneath.

'They'll have said Compline, and will soon be in their beds,' he said. 'And that's where we should be shortly.'

'Yet it appears that the evening's just started,' said Nicholas evenly.

'For you, yes; but not for me. I'd like to hear that young lass sing, but Brother Benedict's got no business to sing here. His place is in the choir with the others, not entertaining the Prior as if he were at the royal court.'

'But I thought the Abbot of Rivières sent him here to sing to the Prior, Father?'

Hubert snorted, his small, pinched face flushing with anger.

'Not to entertain the Prior, my Lord, but to sing to the glory of God in the right place and at the right time. That's what a monk's for. It seems to me that sometimes my Lord Prior forgets this simple fact.'

He made no attempt to lower his voice and Prior Thomas, ensconced in the best chair by the fire, glanced across at him.

'Come, come, Father Hubert, you're worse than those kill-joy reformers. Music, as I'm sure Lord Nicholas would agree with me, is sent by God to give us a foretaste of heavenly delights. When you get to heaven, Father, you will be surrounded by choirs playing harps and singing the divine praises. You may as well start getting used to the idea here and now.'

44

'I shall sing the divine praises, my Lord Prior, in the church with the others. I have nothing against music – as you say it is one of God's gifts to us – but to listen to a young monk singing about earthly love accompanied by a girl strumming a lute is not what the Creator intended us to do.'

'Yet we can worship God in the beauty of his creation and the exquisite music of the Flemish composers. Be off to your choir stall, if you must, Father, and do not judge others lest they judge you.'

Father Hubert stood up, bowed his head in submission, nodded to Nicholas, and left the great hall of the Prior's house.

There were just the seven of them: the Prior, Brother Jeremy, Brother Oswald, Brother Cyril, himself and the two performers. An exclusive gathering, he thought. No sign of Brother Michael; he was probably waiting for Father Hubert to join the rest of them in church. He stood up and walked across to join the others round the fire, forcing himself not to look towards the alcove where the two musicians were getting ready.

At last the instruments were turned to Jane's satisfaction, and they walked across to join the company. She was carrying a reed instrument which Nicholas remembered he'd recently seen at Court. Benedict walked behind her, carrying a lute. They were a well-matched pair; well matched in beauty as well as being well matched musically, he felt sure. Jane was looking enchanting in a full-skirted cream dress shot through with gold thread, which glowed in the soft light of the candles which Cyril had placed round that corner of the room. Her copper hair was drawn back gently from her face and held in position by a garland of spring flowers, ox-eye daisies, cowslips and forget-me-nots. The bodice of the dress was tight fitting and cut squarely across her young breasts, revealing a pink satin skin which gleamed in the soft light. She wore no jewellery, and needed none, Nicholas thought.

45

Benedict had put aside his monk's habit and was now dressed in a richly embroidered doublet and a dark coloured hose which showed off his well-honed figure to perfection. He wore soft leather shoes, and, had it not been for his monk's tonsure, almost hidden by his thick curly dark hair, he could have passed as one of the King's courtiers. Nicholas glanced at the Prior and saw that he was enthralled. His heart sank. One thing was for sure; they would have to hide Brother Benedict when Cromwell's Commissioners made their inspection. He was sure the Prior led a chaste life – there had been no rumours to the contrary – but Benedict would tempt the Archangel Gabriel himself.

Jane sang first, Benedict accompanying her with his lute. She sang a simple song about spring and joy in God's creation. Her sweet, soprano voice had a bell-like quality and as she sang a satisfied smile spread over Brother Oswald's face, and when the song finished he applauded more enthusiastically than anyone else.

'I wrote that,' he said, turning to Nicholas.

'Beautifully composed, and beautifully sung. But as you are Precentor of the Priory, I would have expected nothing less. Have you composed many songs like the one we've just heard?'

'Volumes of them,' roared the Prior. 'He keeps all the brethren up to scratch by making them copy out his manuscripts. You should take a look at our library; it's bulging with all his compositions.'

'All to the glory of God, my Lord,' said Brother Oswald with a smug smile of satisfaction. 'And I thank Him for giving me the talent.'

'And we thank Him for sending you into our midst. But come now, another song. Let Benedict hand the lute over, Mistress Warrener. Let's hear one of the chansons of the divine Josquin. He's a Flemish composer,' the Prior said pedantically to Nicholas. 'Benedict brought some of his songs over with him.'

Jane picked up the lute, and nodded to Benedict when she was ready. He sang a beautiful song about the Virgin Mary, 'Ave maris stella', and his honey-sweet tenor voice flowed seductively over them and brought tears of pure joy to the Prior's eyes. He was indeed a charmer, thought Nicholas; and wouldn't be out of place at the Court of King Henry.

After the applause, Jane picked up the shawm. Nicholas, who knew it was a difficult instrument to play, felt nervous on her behalf. But he needn't have worried. From the first plaintive note which echoed round the great hall, she proved herself an accomplished performer. The instrument had an eerie quality to it, and Benedict sang a song about war and death and the futility of human conflict. It made Nicholas think of the horrors he'd seen in the streets of London, as the plague took its toll of the citizens. He remembered the scenes at Tyburn where traitors were butchered and put on public display, and then, as the song went on about the sadness of losing a loved one, his mind turned to his beloved wife and the child who'd only lived for a few hours. When the song came to an end, and Jane put down the shawm, the group was silent, everyone lost in his own thoughts.

But not for long. The next song was a duet, and they sang about happier things, the love of a man for a maid, comparing the joys of human love with the bliss of divine love. The couple were indeed perfectly matched, and Jane's pure soprano blended with Benedict's mellifluous tenor, creating a glorious harmony. Nicholas could have stayed there all night listening to the pair, but the end came abruptly. There was a sound of footsteps coming up the stone stairs to the hall, the door flew open and Brother Michael stood there, his lean face stern with disapproval.

'What is it, Brother Michael?' said the Prior impatiently. 'I told you not to interrupt us. We have been in the company of the angels and your long face is the only discordant note we've had this evening.'

'My Lord, the brethren are waiting for your blessing.

Compline's finished and they are ready for sleep.'

'Tell them I'll join them for Matins. Father Hubert can bless them tonight.'

'But you always . . .'

'Well, just for once, I can't come. Be off with you, man, can't you see we're busy?'

'I can see that you're enjoying yourselves. And what's Brother Benedict doing here? In secular dress too, I see. This is outrageous. Brother Benedict is a monk, my Lord, a holy man of God. He should never put aside his habit. St Benedict . . .'

'Don't you dare lecture me about St Benedict,' shouted the Prior, hauling himself to his feet. 'Just for one night our guest has put aside his habit to put on clothes more appropriate to the occasion. There's no harm in that.'

'Not yet. But evil, my Lord, is insidious. It could quite turn the head of a young monk to sing in the company of a woman and receive the adulation of his superiors. What looks harmless at first sight, could be the beginning of our own damnation.'

'Oh, be off with you, you sanctimonious old misery. Get back to your bleak dormitory and pray for forgiveness. Remember, Brother Michael, that once you took a vow of obedience.'

Scowling his disapproval, Michael retreated. The spell was broken. Jane said she should go back to her father, and Nicholas said he would escort her to the Prior's carriage. He thanked the Prior for his hospitality, and went over to Benedict.

'You sing most beautifully, young man. The King, I'm sure, would love to hear you.'

'He's not likely to, my Lord. I haven't got permission to leave the Priory.'

'Then maybe you will come and sing to me? I'm sure Prior Thomas would release you for a couple of hours.'

'That would give me great pleasure,' said Benedict in his soft voice with its pronounced French accent.

48

Nicholas shook his hand, and left the hall with Jane. Once outside, she stopped and suddenly became serious.

'Nicholas. I've found out something that might be relevant to your murder investigation. Landstock's not made an arrest yet, has he?'

Nicholas, who could think of nothing else but the beauty of the music he'd just enjoyed, gave a guilty start.

'Jane, I'm sorry. We've all experienced a glimpse of heaven and now you talk about murder.'

She looked at him impatiently. 'Of course. You've got to get your priorities right, Lord Nicholas. You've got a murder investigation on your hands. Don't say you've forgotten all about it?'

'There's nothing we can do at the moment, Jane. Don't be so censorious. It isn't becoming in a woman. But out with it, what have you found out?'

'It seems to me, my Lord, that women have a better idea of what's important and what isn't. Anyway, I've learnt that Giles Yelman has been a frequent visitor to Mortimer's place. But he wasn't courting Bess Knowles; or anyone else for that matter.'

'Then what the hell was my under-steward doing at Roger Mortimer's house?'

'That's for you to find out. I can't start asking those sorts of questions. It's not becoming in a woman. I'd be sent packing in no time.'

'Then I must get over there first thing tomorrow morning. But now let me talk about pleasanter things. You sing divinely, Jane. Perhaps one day you'll come and sing for me at my house.'

She turned and smiled at him demurely. 'I'd love to, but my father would never let me come.'

'Yet he lets you come and sing for the Prior?'

'He thinks he's safe.'

'But surely . . .'

'There's no surely. My father doesn't like the gentry. Or rather he doesn't trust them. However, he might just

49

possibly change his mind; but I doubt it.'

'Then let me talk to him. He can't keep you locked up like a caged song bird.'

'He worries about me, that's all. I'm all he's got. But now here comes my carriage. It's very good of the Prior to let me use it. Goodnight, Nicholas.'

And with a sweet smile she jumped up into the carriage, and Nicholas watched the driver urge the horse forward. A young monk fetched Harry from the stable, and feeling suddenly overwhelmed with loneliness, Nicholas climbed into the saddle and rode slowly back to his house.

Next morning, Nicholas ordered Harry to be brought round to the main door. Harry was in excellent spirits. A slight pressure of Nicholas's heel and he was off across the fields where the ewes indignantly gathered their lambs together as he romped past them. Then into the wood where Harry's flying hooves slashed into the succulent bluebells, disturbing a family of woodcock who, uttering shrill cries of annoyance, rose into the air with a frantic whirring of wings. Harry shied skittishly off the path and made for the beech trees, nearly decapitating Nicholas as he bounded under some low branches.

At the far side of the wood, Nicholas reined him in. Already he felt better. The demons which had disturbed his sleep last night had been dispersed by the bright sky and the clear, cold morning air. Ahead of him was the stretch of common land which separated his estate from Sir Roger Mortimer's, and at the far side was Mortimer Lodge, a solid, low, stone building which crouched at the edge of an artificial lake which Sir Roger's grandfather had constructed to serve as a moat to separate his property from the common. With difficulty, Nicholas eased Harry down into a walk. For some reason, Harry had taken an instant dislike to the villagers' pigs, who were rooting around for acorns. With a snort of disdain and an exaggerated toss of his head which sent his mane flying and his bit jangling, he danced over the short turf, narrowly missing the rabbit burrows.

'Stop it, you fool,' shouted Nicholas, 'you'll have me off. Behave yourself or else I'll trade you in for a sensible gelding.'

Harry snorted and danced daintily round the edge of the lake towards the main entrance to the house. In the court-yard, Sir Roger was supervising the grooming of his own horse, a splendid bay called Galliard. It was ages since he'd been to Mortimer's place, Nicholas thought, as he dismounted and handed Harry over to a groom who suddenly appeared out of nowhere. Mortimer was still the same surly devil. Couldn't be bothered to look up from grooming Galliard's glossy flanks. Nicholas walked over to him and stood there fuming until Mortimer decided that Galliard's coat needed no more attention. Then he put down the brush he was using, and stood up.

Mortimer was in his early forties. He had a short muscu-lar body, a dark, lugubrious face which Nicholas had never seen creased in laughter, a shaggy dark beard, and long, straggling black hair. He could never understand why Lady Margot, a lady in her own right, had agreed to leave her father's estate in East Sussex and come here to look after this gloomy individual. But they'd been married for twelve years and had produced three children, one still a babe in arms.

Sir Roger could ignore Nicholas no longer. His bay was glaring at Harry, who was pawing the ground in eager anticipation of a fight. He handed his horse over to a groom, and looked morosely at Nicholas.

'So, Henry Tudor's decided he can do without you for a few days. Now you come to seek out your neighbours. I'm afraid we can't offer you the sort of hospitality you've enjoyed at Court, but you're welcome to come inside for a jug of ale, or mead if you prefer.'

'Thank you, ale will do me fine.'

They went into the house, through the hall and into a

51

small room dominated by a large oak desk covered with documents. Tall, narrow windows which seemed designed to let out archers' arrows rather than let in the sunshine, gave a glimpse of the gardens beyond.

'So Court life suits you, my Lord,' said Mortimer as the servant brought in the tankards of ale.

'I do my duty, Sir Roger, that's all. Given the choice I'd prefer to live the life of the country gentleman, but the King needs counsellors, and he won't come to us, so we have to go to him.'

'A pity he doesn't choose more wisely.'

'I'm sorry you think me incompetent.'

'Nothing personal. I'm sure you're like all the others who surround the King; courtiers, all of you. Wouldn't say boo to a goose, one eye on your own advancement, and let the country go to the devil.'

Nicholas placed his pewter tankard carefully down on the desk. With difficulty he controlled himself. No use matching insult with insult. 'I can't see any signs that the devil is up to his tricks; no more than usual, that is.'

'The King, my Lord, is plunging England into anarchy, heresy walks abroad unchecked, and he does nothing. And you, and those who are supposed to advise him, also do nothing.'

'You use strong words, Sir Roger. Watch out that the King doesn't hear them.'

'I don't care if he does. Someone's got to tell him. I've heard that he's going to close down our monasteries and turn the holy monks out to beg their bread in the street. He's already severed us from His Holiness the Pope – soon he'll close down the churches, and we shall be excommunicated and left to rot. These are terrible times, terrible times, and no one tries to stop the King.'

'The King, Sir Roger, goes his own way. No one can stop him. But I promise I shall do my best to try and save our Priory.'

The door opened and a lady came in, carrying a baby of

about ten months old. Nicholas watched as Mortimer's severe face softened. There was no doubt about it; he loved his wife, Margot. She smiled at Nicholas and not for the first time he was struck by her placid beauty. She was still in her twenties, but her body was matronly with childbearing. Unlike her husband's, her face was smooth and pink; her sleek brown hair was drawn back tightly from her face and held in position under a neat cap. She was wearing a dark-coloured dress made of fine linen, and she handled the baby with the competence which comes from long practice. Nicholas felt his annoyance evaporate. Margot had been so kind to his wife, Mary, who had been the opposite of her in every way. Mary with her slender body not designed for childbearing. Margot had given her strength throughout the troubled pregnancy, and had been there at the birth, and supported him when both Mary and his son died, and he felt that life was not worth living.

'It's good to see you again, Margot. How well you look, and how beautiful your little girl is,' he said, going over to kiss her on the cheek and lift back the edge of the shawl which was wrapped around the child.

'Yes, she's a joy. A good child, I'm delighted to say. But I heard you arrive, and I just wanted to say how sorry we were to hear about the death of Matthew. He was always welcome here, you know, and Bess was very fond of him. In fact, we hoped to see them both wed in the near future. What happened? I've heard he was killed by thieves, is that so?'

'Landstock and the Coroner say he was murdered, but we don't know who by, and for what reason.'

'Murdered?' said Mortimer, rousing himself from his gloomy introspection. 'I am surprised. Who'd want to murder your steward? I would say he was a man absolutely without enemies. He must have disturbed thieves at work and they attacked him. I've suffered from break-ins too. Only recently they emptied my lake of carp. Prime carp, too, ready for the table. I've had to re-stock. The Prior kindly gave me permission to help myself from his own fishponds. I'm most grateful to him. Fortunately he always keeps a good supply; he's very partial to a fat carp.'

'Yes, you're probably right. He could have disturbed thieves and tried to stop them. I shall miss him. He was a good man, and I'm glad he found some happiness in your household.'

'He loved Bess,' said Margot moving the baby from one shoulder to the other. 'She's now quite beside herself with grief. She keeps to her room and won't see anyone. I've tried to persuade her to come down into the garden for some fresh air, but she refuses. I've sent for Mistress Jane to come and see her this afternoon. She's the only person Bess lets near her.'

'Jane Warrener coming here?' said Nicholas, feeling his heart miss a beat at the mention of her name.

'Yes. Jane's been a good support.'

'I can't think how that misery of a father produced such a delightful girl,' said Mortimer. 'He and that devil of a Vicar are a real menace, praising the King to high heaven and stirring up the villagers against the monks. As soon as the monks are kicked out, Warrener will be up at the Priory with his wheelbarrow and pickaxe. It's monstrous, Lord Nicholas. You must stop it. You've got the ear of the King.'

'I'm sure Lord Nicholas is doing his best,' said Margot evenly. 'Your family's been patron of the Priory since Duke William came over from Normandy. You'll not see it pulled down without a protest.'

'I shall certainly try to dissuade the King when next I see him. But he's a very determined man.'

'Then if you don't succeed we shall have to take action ourselves.'

Nicholas looked at him sharply. 'Have a care, Sir Roger. The King doesn't like criticism. It's a small step from opposition to treason as far as he's concerned.'

'So we should all submit to the tyrant's will?'

'I refuse to listen to any more of this. Remember my

54

position as a Justice. Do you want to be arrested?'

'Are you threatening me?'

'Just warning you. That's all. Now, Lady Margot, is it possible to have a word with Bess? She might be able to tell me more about Matthew. Whom he associated with – that sort of thing. Everything can be helpful in a murder investigation.'

Nicholas saw a look pass between Mortimer and his wife. She shook her head. 'Not yet, my Lord. She's still in a state of shock.'

Nicholas saw Margot's face close down, and he knew he wouldn't see Bess that day. But the Mortimers knew more than they let on. How much did they know? And how could he find out?

'The funeral's tomorrow. Bess will be there, of course? Maybe I can speak to her then.'

'I'll see to it that she's there. But she'll not be up to any questioning,' said Margot firmly.

'I wouldn't want to upset her any more. But there is one thing that puzzles me. I understand my under-steward, Giles Yelman, has been coming to see you. Now why does he come? Is he courting one of your dairymaids?'

'Your under-steward, Lord Nicholas?' said Mortimer. 'He's never been here, not to my knowledge anyway. Have you seen him, my dear?'

'Your under-steward? No, he's not been here, I'm sure of that,' said Lady Margot, looking down at her baby, who was becoming fretful.

They were lying, thought Nicholas, as he picked up his riding gloves. Jane had told him that Giles had been here. Jane wouldn't have made it up. Now what were the Mortimers trying to hide? He must talk to Giles.

Outside in the courtyard, the groom brought Harry out of the stable. Mortimer looked at Nicholas.

'We must talk some more about these things, my Lord. Come and dine with us soon. We are all interested to know the King's mind.'

'If I knew that, Sir Roger, I would be a magician, not a man. He goes his own way.'

'But I'm sure he'll listen to you. After all, you come from one of the oldest families in the land. Your ancestors have always been close to the King. As for myself, I'm only a nonentity. My family only goes back to the days of the Black Prince.'

'And by all accounts, your ancestor did him a great service at the Battle of Poitiers?'

'He saved his life, yes, but it only earned him a knight-hood.'

'And he was given this house. One of the royal hunting lodges. Not a bad reward for services rendered.'

More to the point, thought Nicholas as he rode away, your wife is related to the Yorkist King Edward. And it's best to keep quiet about that. Henry Tudor doesn't take kindly to anyone with Yorkist connections.

Chapter Five

'She's in her room, Jane, my dear,' said Lady Margot, who was in the kitchen supervising the stuffing of a brace of woodcock. 'She's very upset. Nothing we can do or say seems to have any effect on her. I'm glad you've come; you might be able to rouse her. She won't eat anything. Hannah takes her up some water in the morning and she only takes a tiny sip. You might be able to persuade her to eat something. Matthew certainly wouldn't want her to starve herself for his sake. She'll listen to you, I know. You've always been such good friends; she's waiting for you to come.'

Jane went upstairs to the small room tucked under the eaves which had been Bess's room ever since she'd come to Mortimer Lodge with Lady Margot twelve years ago. She knocked and went in.

Bess was sitting in a chair by the casement window, which looked out over the commons to the manor of Dean Peverell. Jane was shocked at her appearance. Bess had always been slim but that morning she looked gaunt, and her sweet, oval face was haggard. Her dark eyes, her best feature, usually glowing with mischief, were dull and lifeless. She looked the picture of desolation, and Jane went over to her, wrapped her arms round her painfully thin shoulders and buried her head in her dark hair.

'Bess, my dear Bess, I am so sorry. I know how much

you loved him. But please don't give up. He wouldn't want to see you like this. Is there anything I can do to help? Forgive me, I know that sounds stupid but we're all so worried about you.' Bess shook her head, but Jane could feel her begin to relax. She pulled over a footstool, put it beside Bess's chair, sat down and waited.

'Yes, I loved him, Jane,' Bess whispered. 'We were planning to get married, you know. Lady Margot was happy about it. Next month, after the feast of Corpus Christi. Our baby would be four months by then. Yes, I am carrying his baby,' she said as Jane looked up at her in surprise. 'What's wrong with that? We loved each other. Why should we have waited for a priest to make us man and wife? I was so glad when I knew, but now . . . I think I ought to leave this place, and go back to Guisborne. There's nothing for me here. I'm sure Lady Margot wouldn't want to be bothered with an unmarried mother with a fatherless child.'

'I'm so pleased about the baby, Bess, and I'm sure Lady Margot will be very supportive. After all, she's like a mother to you. Have you told her yet?'

'She's guessed. I've been very sick in the mornings and haven't been much use in supervising the children's breakfast.'

'Then nothing's changed. Lady Margot will love your child. So why go back to Guisborne? Those days are over. You've been here twelve years, ever since you were a child. You were just six years old.'

'It's where I was born. Someone will remember me and take me in.'

'But you told me you never knew your father, and your mother's been dead these five years. We all love you and if Lady Margot dismisses you, which I'm sure she won't, then there will always be a place for you and your child with us.'

'Jane, how wonderfully kind you are. But I'm sure your father . . .'

'Oh, he'll not mind. Besides, he always does as I say.'

58

A smile lit up Bess's wan face for a brief moment. 'Jane, you're wicked. But I love you all the same. I don't want to be a burden to anyone. Just look how weak I am.'

She stood up slowly, levering herself up out of the armchair like an old woman. Then she tottered over to the bed, and sat down on the edge of it, breathing heavily.

'See how it is? I couldn't possibly go downstairs. I can hardly walk. Jane, what's the matter with me?'

'You're weak, and ill. I'll tell Lady Margot you need a doctor, some fortifying soup and a long, sound sleep.'

Gently, Jane eased Bess back on her pillow, and pushed the strands of her dark hair back from her face.

'Please don't trouble Lady Margot any more. One of the monks has already been to see me. He brought me a fortifying potion yesterday and he said he'll be back today. It hasn't done me much good so far, but I'll probably feel better later on today. But Jane, I feel so frightened, and I don't know why. I don't seem to understand anything. Why should anyone want to murder Matthew? They tell me thieves did it, but why are they so sure? Sir Roger refuses to discuss it with me; he just frowns and walks away, and Lady Margot changes the subject when I ask if the thieves have been caught. Something's horribly wrong, Jane; and it's all so confusing and my brain goes round and round in circles.'

'Don't worry about catching Matthew's murderers, Bess. Lord Nicholas is leading the investigation and he's doing all he can. The Sheriff will soon catch them. He knows all the rogues in the district. He'll soon have them under lock and key. But it's you I'm worried about; even more so now that I know you're carrying Matthew's child. You must get better so that you can give birth to a fine, healthy baby. Think how much Matthew would have wanted this child. I'll see if Agnes Myles has a strengthening tonic for you.'

'Oh you and your old witch! I don't expect she can do anything for me.'

'Hush, Bess, she's not a witch. She's a herbalist and

59

knows more about how our bodies work than all the apothecaries in the south of England.'

'Then I do hope she can do something for me. I really don't feel well; and I have a feeling that the child's not well either. Can a baby share his mother's grief and die in the womb, Jane?'

'I'm not a doctor, Bess, but as far as I know, babies survive most things. He's quite safe in there,' she said, patting Bess's abdomen which was still flat as a board. 'But now there's even more reason why you must start eating again. Let me get you some bread and soup.'

Jane left Bess and went down to the kitchen where Mary, the Mortimers' stout cook, was stirring the big iron pot which always hung over the fire. She asked if she could have a bowl of soup and some bread, and Mary, her large, plain face flushed and perspiring, scooped some soup out of the pot with a huge iron ladle and told her to help herself to bread.

She took the food up to Bess, who'd curled up on to her side, and seemed to be asleep. She put the bowl down and roused her. Then, after propping her up on a pillow, she gave Bess the spoon, but Bess was too weak to hold it so Jane fed her like a child. After only one mouthful, Bess pushed the spoon away.

'It's no use, Jane. I can't eat it; I'll only be sick, and that makes me even weaker. I really would like to go to sleep, so don't stay with me much longer. You've got your father to look after and a house to run. By the way, when are they going to bury Matthew?'

'Tomorrow; but unless you're a lot stronger, you shouldn't even think of coming. It would only upset you. I'll tell you everything when it's all over. But now, sleep well and I'll come back later on this evening.'

'Jane, you're such a comfort to me. You'll take me to the graveyard, won't you, when it's all over, and show me where they bury him?'

'Of course I will. Sleep now. Don't think about anything,

except the child you're carrying.'

'I'll try not to worry, but things go round and round in my head. That day when Matthew and I hid behind the sofa and we heard all those terrible things about the King, what did it all mean? And now Giles Yelman has been coming here and he talks with Sir Roger for a long time, locked away in the study. What are they talking about, Jane? And why does Lady Margot turn away when I ask her?'

'Has Giles been here lately, Bess?'

'I don't know. But he was here on the day Matthew died, when Lord Nicholas was away.'

'Perhaps he came to complain about something; Sir Roger's cattle straying across to Lord Nicholas's land, for instance.'

'Then surely the bailiff would come, not Giles. He's nothing; just a slimy toad of a man, always peering under stones. Jane, I'm so frightened. What will become of Lady Margot and the children if anything should happen to Sir Roger?'

'I'll speak to Lord Nicholas, Bess, when I next see him. He'll soon sort this out. But now you mustn't think about Giles Yelman. Just close your eyes and sleep.'

The effort of talking had exhausted Bess and she sank back on her pillow and closed her eyes. Jane watched as Bess's body relaxed and she sank into a deep sleep. Then she picked up the bowl of soup and the bread and went down to the kitchen.

Mary looked at the uneaten food and shook her head. 'She can't live on air, Mistress Warrener. The poor child's already as thin as a reed.'

'She's very weak, Mary, and I'm worried about her. She was always so full of life; it's dreadful to see her like this.'

'I can remember you both as small girls playing together out in the garden. You picked peas for me, and shelled them, eating more than you put in the bowl. You helped yourselves to strawberries, too, stuffing them into your mouths until the juice dribbled all down your smocks. You

61

were always the forward one, mind. Bess got all her ideas from you.'

'I can't remember Bess having a shortage of ideas. But we did have some good times, didn't we? We're two of a pair, and that's why I'm so sad to see her like this. Bess was six when she came here with Lady Margot as her ward, and we've been the best of friends ever since.'

'Ward, you say?' said Mary giving the soup a hearty stir. 'Well, I suppose that's one way of putting it. Though why a daughter has to cover up for the sins of her father, I don't know.'

'Mary, what are you suggesting? Everyone knows Lady Margot adopted Bess when her father disappeared and her mother couldn't cope on her own.'

'I'll say no more, Mistress Warrener. Bess earns her keep. I'm sorry for her sweetheart's death and I hope she gets better soon.'

Then she banged down the spoon on the table and gave the spit a vigorous turn, sending the fat from the roasting chickens flying on to the flagstones. 'You'll not be staying for dinner, I take it?' she added.

'Thank you, no. I must get off home. You could take Bess some of that chicken later, when she wakes up. She might be ready to eat by then.'

'Let's hope so. She needs feeding up, the poor lass. Good day to you, Mistress Warrener. My regards to that father of yours.'

Jane left Mortimer Lodge, and walked quickly along the road that led to the village. She didn't like leaving Bess. Something was telling her that things were not right. Of course she would be shocked and grief-stricken by Matthew's death, but she had always been physically strong. She'd never even seen her so thin and lethargic. She was also worried about the child. Maybe it was the cause of Bess's weakness. She had to talk to Agnes Myles; there was nothing she didn't know about babies. She used to be the village midwife for years before she got too old.

As she walked along the road where, on either side, the hedgerows were radiant in their bridal veils of white hawthorn flowers, and ragged robins and celandines made a bright patchwork quilt along the verges, she passed a young monk walking in the opposite direction. She nodded to him and he lowered his eyes. She remembered seeing him around. He was Brother Martin, assistant to Brother Michael, the Prior's Infirmarer. Good, she thought, maybe he was taking some fortifying medicine to Bess. The monks were experts in healing herbs.

'I thought I'd caught the buggers, Lord Nicholas, I really did. Got them last night breaking into the Bishop's wine stocks. However, it turned out that I'd picked up the wrong lot. It seems that they were nowhere near your place on Monday night when Matthew Hayward was murdered. Not if I believe all the rogues who've crawled out of the woodwork to swear that the Bishop's thieves were with them in the Fox and Hounds on the Portsmouth road. I've no reason not to believe them, so I can't charge anyone for murder. Pity. I'd like to clear this case up good and proper.'

Nicholas turned round and frowned at the Sheriff. They were in his house in Marchester, and outside, in the main square, the stonemasons were just putting the finishing touches to the new market cross, built and paid for out of Bishop Radcliffe's privy purse. Already it was in use, and the farmers were just packing away their produce at the end of another busy market day.

'What are you saying, Landstock? You can't charge people without incontrovertible evidence. This is England, not France. People here have long-established rights.'

'Only wishful thinking, my Lord. My job is to clean up all the lawless scum in the county. Bang 'em all up, say I. They're all the same, thieves, murderers. I hate the lot of them.'

'You still need evidence, Landstock; otherwise I can't pass them over to the Assizes. However, you know the score; I'm not teaching you to suck eggs. But let's get down to business. I can't altogether go along with you that Matthew died defending my property. I'm beginning to think that his death's part of a much wider plot. Come on, man, you're in touch with what goes on around here. Have you heard any rumours? Anyone discontented? Any talk of conspiracy?'

'Conspiracy? Damn me, that's a dangerous word. No one in his right mind would talk about conspiracy today. Mind you, there are lots of discontented people about – there always are – but not many of them are prepared to do anything about it. Now where's that servant of mine? I told him to bring in some beer – some of my own brew, made with Lord Gilbert's hops; much better than that piddling stuff which the monks make.'

He strode over to the door, and wrenched it open. 'Here, John, where are you, damn your eyes? Lord Nicholas here is dying of thirst.'

A servant came in with two tankards of foaming beer. Then he backed out hastily. Landstock took a gulp of his and beamed at Nicholas.

'Not at all bad. Goes down like a treat at any time of the day.' And he wiped his foam-flecked ginger beard with the back of his hand. Nicholas took a gulp of his.

'It's good, Landstock. It's from Gilbert Fitzroy, you say? I didn't know he grew hops on his estate.'

'Didn't you? Well, he's got a prime site at Arundel. Keeps me stocked up. I did a small favour for him once upon a time, and he's still damn grateful. I hope he stays that way.'

'A sensible man, Lord Gilbert Fitzroy. Likes to live quietly. He does what his ancestors have always done, looks after the county and supports the King when called upon to do so. And his stewards don't get murdered.'

'He keeps his head down and his nose clean,' said Landstock, draining his tankard. 'Mind you, he doesn't have to go to Court like you do.'

'Lucky man. I wish I could live peacefully in my manor and grow hops. But the King seems to like me around at the moment. I can't think why. Lord Gilbert's a much bigger fish than I am.'

'He's probably saving him for later; when he's finished with you. The King's after something, that's for sure. He wants your Priory for starters. Watch out he doesn't take your house. Look what happened to Wolsey.'

Nicholas laughed. 'Peverell Manor's not quite up to the splendour of Hampton Court. Now tell me, Landstock, from your experience, what does it mean if someone's caught out telling lies?'

'That someone's hiding something, that what he's doing. Who's been lying to you, Lord Nicholas?'

'My under-steward, Giles Yelman. You probably don't know him; small, insignificant, a bit shifty. Makes himself useful, so I can't complain. Now I've heard a report that he's been seen up at Mortimer's place. I had a go at him this morning, but he swears he's never been there. Now what do you make of that?'

'Who's your informant?'

'Jane. Jane Warrener.'

'Mistress Warrener? Now I can't see her telling lies. She's a bright lass. Sharp tongue, mind. She'll have to control that or else she'll turn into a right shrew. I pity the man who marries her.'

'That's as may be. Now she told me that Giles has been visiting Mortimer's house. Now why should he do that? And why should he deny it?'

'I suppose he's every right to go to Mortimer's place.'

'Not without my permission, he hasn't. Apparently he was there the day Matthew died. I don't like it, Landstock. There's more to Matthew's murder than a chance encounter with thieves.'

'Now you're back with your conspiracy theory again. I hope you're not going to accuse Sir Roger of treachery. Mind you, I find him a surly bugger. Nice wife though, and three nice children. He wouldn't want to see them come to any harm, would he? What are you implying, Lord Nicholas? That Sir Roger told Giles Yelman to bump off your steward? Doesn't sound likely, does it?'

'Yelman's no murderer. But he could have let the murderers into my manor house.'

'On whose orders? Mortimer's? Come off it, Lord Nicholas, I don't expect Mortimer even knows what Giles Yelman looks like. In any case, why should Mortimer want to get rid of your steward?'

'Matthew was friends with Bess Knowles. The two of them could have overheard something.'

'And Mortimer wanted him silenced? Sounds a bit far-fetched.'

'Depends what Matthew overheard.'

Landstock looked keenly at Nicholas, his eyes suddenly alert. 'Well, I suppose we ought to take a closer look at Master Yelman. You say you've spoken to him?'

'I cross-examined him this morning, but got nowhere. He denied going over to Mortimer's place.'

'Then let me have a go at him. Hold on to him tonight, and I'll come over to your place tomorrow after the funeral. As you say, someone's lying; and I don't think Mistress Warrener's the lying type. Incidentally, how is Bess? I'm very fond of her.'

'She's taken Matthew's death very badly. They were going to be wed, you know.'

'So I heard. It's hard on the lass. It would have been a good match. She's got no dowry, but she's a good-looker and has the support of Lady Mortimer. Hayward had a good position in your household. Now she'll have to look elsewhere.'

'Has she no family to go to?'

'None that I know of. They say she's old St John Pearce's daughter by one of his servants. He and his wife brought her up with their only daughter, Lady Margot, and she brought her to Mortimer's place when she married him; God knows why! Bess was lucky. Not many ladies of the manor look after their husband's bastards. My wife wouldn't, that's for sure. She'd throw me out as quick as greased lightning. Not that I own a manor, nor ever likely to. But then the St John Pearces are the sort who close ranks.'

Nicholas left the Sheriff's house and rode the four miles back to Dean Peverell. The road was a good one, running straight as an arrow along the edge of the Downs towards London. Built by the Romans and designed to last.

He arrived at his house and a groom took Harry away. Then he shouted for Giles Yelman and his bailiff, Geoffrey Lowe, came running out, looking more worried than usual.

'He's gone, my Lord. We can't find him anywhere.'

'Hell's teeth, I should have anticipated this. Damn! Damn! Get a search party going, Geoffrey, and be quick about it. And for God's sake, when you've got him, don't let him go.'

Chapter Six

'*Requiem aeternam dona eis, Domine.*' The sonorous chanting of the monks sounded like a choir of angels bringing Matthew home to rest. Nicholas, sitting in his place of honour at the bottom of the sanctuary steps in the parish church, looked through the open doors, one on either side of the altar, to where the black-robed figures, their hoods pulled down over their faces, sat facing each other in their choir, and he thought how privileged he was to be the patron of this Priory church. He remembered how seriously his father had carried out his responsibilities, how he'd looked after the monks, and given the parishioners of Dean Peverell a new roof to their church with a vaulted ceiling so that they could worship in a building that was not only spacious, but dry in wet weather.

And then Nicholas wondered what would happen to the monks if the King ordered them to leave. Some of them, like Father John for instance, had spent their entire lives here. How long would he survive if he had to rely on people's charity? He didn't deserve to die like a stray dog in the bottom of a ditch. The image was an uncomfortable one, and Nicholas knew that he couldn't let that happen; he had to do something. If he couldn't stop the King, then at least he could look after the monks.

At the top of the sanctuary steps, Matthew's body, wrapped tightly in its woollen shroud, rested on a bier, behind which stood the diminutive figure of the Vicar, Alfred Hobbes. Usually dressed in a threadbare cassock, today he was wearing the cope that Nicholas's mother had given him. It was made of black velvet and she had embroidered with her own hands the elaborately entwined flowers which decorated it, using expensive gold and silver thread which she'd ordered from a London haberdasher's. Today, Hobbes's face was glowing with the satisfaction of knowing that this was his church, his service, and that the monks were confined to their own part of the church behind the screen that separated them from the parishioners, and that, for once, the Prior was no longer centre stage. He needed the monks' voices, though. Matthew couldn't be laid to rest without the appropriate chanting of the requiem Mass.

Nicholas raised his eyes from the figure on the bier and looked round. People were pouring in and soon there would be standing room only. Matthew had been popular and friends and relations were coming from Marchester and neighbouring villages; some had arrived before dawn bringing their bundles of food with them. They were perched on benches along the side of the nave like a row of roosters determined not to be removed from their perches.

Sheriff Landstock came in, nodded to Nicholas, and sat down on one of the benches which the verger had placed at the front of the church for the use of the gentry. Then Guy Warrener pushed his way to the front, and pointed to a place just behind Nicholas, where the verger set down his bench. Nicholas smiled a greeting and was treated to a scowl in return. Guy Warrener's large, flat face was criss-crossed with lines of disapproval and he rarely smiled. However, his face softened when Jane came to sit next to him. She looked cool and elegant that morning. She was wearing a grey dress of some soft material with lace at her throat and encircling her cuffs; her hair was covered by a fashionable, square-shaped cap, fringed with starched white lace, that framed her face to perfection. Master Holbein ought to see her now, Nicholas thought, and paint her just

69

as she was, sitting on a rough bench next to her father in a country church; and he'd be the first person to buy the picture. She smiled at Nicholas and he forgot the solemn chanting of the monks and heard only the chorus of the song birds outside in the churchyard, filling the brilliant May morning with their joyful hymns to the spring.

He watched whilst she helped her father settle himself down on the uncomfortable bench, and then she leaned across and straightened out his leather jerkin, which had seen better days. It was an affectionate gesture which made Nicholas's heart miss a beat. She really loved that cantankerous old devil, he thought.

The choir stopped singing, and Alfred Hobbes, in a surprisingly powerful voice for such a small man, recited the prayers for the dead. At the back of the church people shuffled their feet in the loose straw, coughed and pushed forward for a better view. Then the monks began to chant the Dies Irae, the great sequence for the soul of the departed facing God's judgement. At the words, Dies Irae, Day of Wrath, something clicked in Nicholas's brain. Jane had talked about a conspiracy and given it that name. At the words, 'Oh what trembling there shall be when the world its Judge shall see, coming in dread Majesty,' he turned to look at her, but she was listening to the music and her face was set in sadness. Guy Warrener gave him a disapproving look, so he quickly turned back to face the altar and tried to concentrate. But he could not pay attention. The word 'conspiracy' lingered in his mind. Dear God, he prayed, what sort of a conspiracy was she hinting at? Let it not be a rebellion. Not here in peaceful Sussex. Rebellions only took place in the wild and lawless north of England. The people of Sussex had always been easy-going, traditional, content with the *status quo* as long as there was a plentiful supply of bread and ale.

The bier was censed on both sides, each time beginning from the head and proceeding to the feet in the age-old tradition established by the Salisbury rite; Matthew was not

70

to go on his journey without a proper send-off. The Mass proceeded along its well-ordered path, and Nicholas found his thoughts wandering. Through the open doors which linked the parish church to the monks' choir, he could see his chantry chapel, which he had had built for himself and his wife. It wasn't quite finished. The stonemasons still had some finishing touches to do and the figures of the saints which he'd ordered to be placed in their niches round the top part of the chapel weren't yet in place. But the crafts-men had done a beautiful job, he had to admit. The tiny chapel stood there like a beautifully sculptured casket; a church within a church. It took up one bay of the arcade, near the monks' high altar, and with its rich carvings of cherubs acting as shield-bearers, and angels singing praises to God, it would be a fitting memorial to his wife and his family. When Mary's body was removed from the church-yard and placed in the vault underneath the chantry chapel, he would order the monks to sing masses there daily for her. And when the time came and he was laid to rest beside her, they would sing masses for him as well. But was this all a dream? If the monks were driven out, what would happen to their building? Would it be torn down by the likes of Guy Warrener so that he could use the stones to build an even bigger and better house for himself? And he'd be one of many – vultures, waiting for the opportunity and getting ready for the kill. No, it mustn't happen, he thought, as the choir reached the 'Libera me, Domine, de morte aeterna', and the congregation began to get restless, and those near the back started to leave the church and drift across to the place in the churchyard where the sexton had dug Matthew's grave.

Out in the brilliant May sunshine, with the air crisp and cool like fine white wine, Nicholas stood with the others whilst Matthew was lowered into the grave, and the final prayers were said.

The Prior had offered the use of his solarium for the mourners to partake of some refreshment before they made their way home. The solarium was a fine, south-facing room, attached to the Prior's house, and built by him to house his important visitors. When the service was finished, Nicholas made his way over to the Prior's house, accompanied by Sheriff Landstock.

'A good send-off,' said Landstock. 'Matthew would have approved.'

'A pity there wasn't time to consult him. He wasn't prepared for an early death; and he didn't deserve one. But, down to business, Giles has disappeared,' said Nicholas. 'I've got a search party looking for him.'

Landstock stopped in his tracks. 'Then I'll search the county. When a man tells lies and then bolts, it's serious.'

'You might find him, but he'll not talk.'

'I'll make him talk all right. Just leave that to me, Lord Nicholas. A few nights in my gaol will soon make him change his mind about not talking.'

'We might be barking up the wrong tree, Landstock. After all, what have we got so far? A man's murdered. We don't know why. And my under-steward decided to pay my neighbour a visit. What's wrong with that?'

'But he's run off without leave. And Mistress Jane's been hinting about a conspiracy. That's enough for me to take action.'

They'd reached the solarium where the lay Brothers were handing round tankards of beer and platefuls of cakes baked in the Priory's ovens. Alfred Hobbes, divested of his elegant cope and back in his scruffy cassock, came over to join them.

'The Prior does us proud,' said Nicholas conversationally.

'And so he should. His house is big enough to house an army, whilst I've only got a miserable room over the entrance porch.'

'The Prior needs a big house. After all, he's expected to offer hospitality to all and sundry.'

'And don't I have to look after the souls of all these

parishioners? No one bothers to think about building me a house to live in.'

'Then you're in the wrong job,' said Landstock jovially. 'You should have been a monk; better food, better accommodation, a quieter life.'

'Not for much longer, though. They've got it coming to them.'

'And about time, too,' said a deep voice behind them. Nicholas groaned. It was Guy Warrener. 'Parasites the lot of them,' he said, as he took a gulp of the beer which the lay brother had just given him. 'Kick them out and let them earn their keep. But I can't see Brother Oswald behind a plough or building barns.'

'Come, come, Warrener,' said Nicholas impatiently. 'We've been down that track over and over again. Don't keep talking about when the monks leave. There's legislation to be passed. It might not get through.'

'Of course it will,' said Warrener belligerently. 'What Harry Tudor wants, he gets. And you'll see to it that he does get it. So here's to him,' he said, raising his tankard. 'Long live the King; and the devil take his enemies.'

'I'll drink to that,' said Landstock taking a gulp of beer. 'Not bad, not bad at all,' he said to Prior Thomas, who'd sauntered over to join them. 'Mind you, it would be greatly improved if you'd added a few hops. Then you'd get a really excellent brew.'

'I've heard that you serve a fine beer, Sheriff,' said the Prior. 'I'd like to try some.'

'It's good enough for me and Lord Nicholas. But I'll send you over a barrel or two, if you like.'

'And don't forget me,' said Hobbes querulously. 'Why should Prior Thomas get all the perks?'

'Oh stop moaning, Vicar. You do very well. Look how you help yourself to my vegetables.'

'It's my right. The Bishop says so,' said Hobbes, hopping up and down with annoyance.

'You made enough fuss about it. You shouldn't have

73

taken it to the Archdeacon's Court. It made me look a right fool. You know you can help yourself to as many vegetables as you like. Personally I can't stand the damn things.'

'That's not what Brother Cyril says. He threatened me, Prior, said I was stealing the brothers' cabbages and I should go to gaol. Called me a common thief. Me, Vicar of the parish church of Dean Peverell, called a thief. Now I'm reduced to grubbing around in your vegetable garden to find a few cabbage leaves that you lot haven't eaten. It's not right and it's not fair. Of course I took it to the Archdeacon.'

Hobbes had raised his fists and was hopping from one leg to the other like a lightweight boxer in the ring. His face was flushed with anger and he would have punched the Prior had Nicholas not restrained him.

'Calm down, Vicar. We shouldn't quarrel on a day like this. My steward's just been laid to rest, the sun's shining and we have all this food and drink to enjoy which you have so generously provided, my Lord Prior. Don't keep raking over dead ashes, Vicar. You look very well on whatever you eat, and no doubt the parishioners look after you very well.'

'I get by,' said Hobbes, controlling himself. 'Nothing to spare, though. Not like the brethren here. Still, I know my place; baptise, marry 'em, bury 'em. The monks only pray for 'em. And do you know, Lord Nicholas, I'm going to be here long after this lot've all been turned out. One day I'll come into my own.'

'And what do you mean by that?' shouted the Prior, his thick eyebrows knitting together into a scowl. 'Surely you're not turning into one of these reformers I hear about. You don't want to change the system, surely? You'd be out of a job.'

Nicholas turned away impatiently. He was sick and tired of the bickering and squabbling that went on between the Vicar and the Prior. If they couldn't live together peacefully side by side, then who could?

74

Jane was walking across the grass towards him. His spirits lifted and he went to meet her.

'What's up, Jane? You look anxious.'

'I've just heard that Giles has disappeared. Nicholas, I'm worried. Did you notice that the Mortimers didn't come to the funeral? They should've been here because they knew Matthew. And Bess couldn't make it. She's ill, Nicholas, and I think it's serious. I know her health's not good and she's grieving for Matthew, but she gets weaker and weaker by the hour. I'm worried about her. She was very close to Matthew. They shared things.'

'You still think Mortimer's got something to do with Matthew's death.'

'I'm sure of it. And I think Giles was paid to let the murderers in to your house.'

'These are wild accusations, Jane. There simply isn't any proof. We can't ask Landstock to arrest Mortimer without proper evidence except the suspicions of his wife's maid and her friend. Let's get on with finding Giles and hope he'll tell us more.'

'And meanwhile Bess is going to be the next victim.'

Nicholas was conscious that Guy Warrener was watching him closely. Damn the man, was he going to be his daughter's gaoler? Suddenly, he saw one of his servants running across the grass towards them.

'What is it, William? What's happened?' he said, going to meet him.

'A messenger's arrived up at the house. From the King, my Lord. You're wanted at Hampton Court immediately.'

'Tell him to wait and I'll be back as soon as I can.'

'He says you're to come at once. That's what he said, my Lord. I told him you were at a funeral but he said it was urgent.'

'Then tell Geoffrey to pack my bag, and get Harry ready.'

'The King keeps you at his beck and call,' said Jane, who'd followed him.

75

'Yes, damn him. I can't think what's so urgent that he wants me to leave immediately.'

'Then tell him to wait; at least until Giles is found.'

'Tell him to wait, Jane? Are you out of your mind? I want to keep this head on my shoulders, you know.'

'But you can't go now. What with Bess ill and Giles still at large.'

'I can do nothing about Bess, Jane. I'm not a doctor. And Landstock will see to Giles. I can't keep the King waiting.'

'Then you don't care what happens to us . . .'

'Nothing's going to happen to you. Landstock will look after things, and you must keep your ears and eyes open whilst I'm away and report to me when I return. I'll be back as soon as I can.'

'It'll be too late. I know something terrible's going to happen,' said Jane bitterly.

'Leaving us so soon, my Lord?' said Warrener, coming up to join them. 'I'm glad someone's doing something about this lot of parasites. Now get the legislation through Parliament. I can't wait to see them go. But let's drink up their beer and finish up the cakes before you leave. Make hay whilst the sun shines, I say.'

'I hope to God, man, that the monks will be here long after you and I are dead.'

'Times are changing, my Lord. New ideas, new men at Court. I'm all for it. It's about time there was an end to all this superstitious nonsense. No more prayers for the dead, no more services in Latin – what's wrong with English, I say? I'm all for this man Martin Luther. He might be German but he's got the right ideas. Down with the Pope. Let's have an English Church with an English King at its head.'

He stopped as a fit of coughing racked his body. Jane came up and took him by the arm. 'Come home, father. Lord Nicholas has better things to do than to listen to your ranting. The King calls, and he must fly to his side.'

'Jane, that's unfair. You know that I've got to go.'

76

She led her father away without another look at Nicholas.

'Damn! Women! Why are they always so unreasonable?' he said out loud.

'Because it's their nature, my Lord,' answered Landstock. 'They're not like us men. I'll say they're unreasonable; you've hit the nail on the head there. And stubborn. And Mistress Warrener's the stubbornest of them all.'

Chapter Seven

'It's good to see you, Peverell. You shouldn't keep dashing off to that country retreat of yours. Your place is here in the centre of things. You ought to slow down a bit. All this coming and going does you no good; no good at all. Anyway, you're here and just in time for a game of tennis. Come along, man, relax, don't you want to have a body like mine?'

Henry Tudor pulled in his stomach and drew himself up to his full height, three inches shorter than Nicholas. He was dressed for sport – a white shirt, open at the neck, loose-fitting breeches and close-fitting stockings which revealed his well-honed calf muscles. Nicholas, having ridden hard through most of the night, except for a brief nap at Merrow, sighed in resignation.

'Your Grace, as always, looks in peak condition. But I'm sorry to say that I have ridden seventy miles with just brief stops to change horses in answer to your Grace's command, and I'm a bit stiff, to put it mildly.'

'Then it's time to loosen up. You're out of condition with all that soft country living. Come along, man, don't bother to change. Plenty of time for all that later.'

King Henry strode off in the direction of his newly built tennis court, of which he was inordinately proud. Nicholas knew there was no escape. Reluctantly, he handed his cloak to a waiting servant and followed the King towards the walled tennis court.

Henry's energy was legendary. He played hard and he liked to win. But Nicholas had the advantage of being younger than the King by ten years, and he was fitter. Also the physical results of an over-keen appetite were taking their toll on the King. After half an hour's hard play in which Nicholas held his own, the King stopped suddenly, threw down his racket and beckoned a servant to bring over warm towels.

'I think we're well-matched, Peverell,' he said, mopping his face. 'But I can see the journey has taken it out of you. I don't want to risk ruining your health. Here, have a drink,' he said, handing Nicholas one of the tankards which another servant had brought over.

'Your Grace is very kind,' said Nicholas, grateful that he'd been let off the hook so lightly. He enjoyed playing tennis, but preferably not after a ten-hour ride on a series of horses that had got progressively worse since he'd left his own horse, Harry, at Petworth. He drained his tankard and decided to make the first move whilst the King seemed in good humour. 'I'm delighted to be back at Court; but what was it you wanted to see me about, your Grace?'

'I always want to see you, Peverell,' said the King, putting an arm affectionately round Nicholas's shoulders. 'You ought to come to Court more often. The Queen was asking after you only last night. What keeps you away from us down in Sussex?'

'Your Grace, I have only been away three days. I have an estate to run, cases to hear, a murder enquiry to investigate . . .'

'It's time you relaxed, Peverell. I know what's wrong with you, it's time you married again. You're still young. It's time to take a bonny wife and rear a clutch of children. A man needs a wife, you know. Take a good look at me. See how happy I am now that my matrimonial difficulties have been sorted out. The Queen and I are like two turtle doves and soon, God willing, we'll have a son to bless our union. A brother to the Princess Elizabeth. He'll have my looks, my intelligence and my creative talents! What a royal prince he'll be. Good God, man, you don't know what you're missing without a wife. Calm down a bit, stop all this dashing around. Come and take your pick of our Court beauties tonight at dinner. We'll have some dancing later on. The Queen can't dance at the moment – she can't take any risks with the child she's carrying – but there are lots who will be only too pleased to frisk around with you. I've written some new canzonets, you know; I'd like your opinion on them. I've introduced some new harmonies. Bring you up to date a bit. You're wasting yourself vegetating in rural Sussex.'

'I look forward to hearing your compositions, your Grace, but I'm sure you didn't bring me all this way to lecture me about the new trends in music and my matrimonial prospects.'

'No, of course not, Peverell. I want to consult you about affairs of state. But not now, man. Hell's teeth, why are you always so eager? You've no sense of timing. You've only just got here. Relax, take it easy, find yourself a bed for the night; a comfortable one. You're going to be here for a few days. Then come and join us for dinner. Enjoy yourself. You look like an exhausted fox who's gone to earth. Keep a grip on yourself. You should get yourself fit, like me.'

He tapped Nicholas playfully on his shoulder with his racket and bounded off. It was always like this, thought Nicholas bitterly. The King's moods were as changeable as mercury. The same man who put his arm round you today could order you to the Tower tomorrow. Never be fooled by the King's charm, he thought, as he followed the servant to the room they'd prepared for him. He was most to be feared when most affectionate.

His room was at the top of a turreted tower at the far end of the great palace which Wolsey had built for his own use and had handed over to the King as a peace-offering only a few years ago. The King had accepted the house and turned it into a royal palace, but its founder was now mouldering away in his grave a hundred miles away.

Once in his room, Nicholas threw his cloak down on the narrow bed, and looked out of the window into the court-yard below. He thought of Wolsey and then of Sir Thomas More in the Tower about to be executed; both had been the King's friends. Would he be the next one to follow in their footsteps? Not if he could help it.

That night, Nicholas feasted in the great hall, which had only just been completed. A never-ending stream of servants carried in course after course: haunches of venison, huge pies containing succulent young rabbits seethed in onions, whole spring lambs and an endless stream of chickens and ducks, and fish from the royal stews. As soon as his goblet was empty a servant re-filled it and soon Nicholas found his senses reeling, and his eyes seemed to gravitate towards the plump white bosom of the lady sitting opposite him, Lady Frances Bonville, one of the Queen's ladies-in-waiting and strategically placed there by royal command.

The Queen was seated next to the King at the top of the table and whatever rumours were flying around that the King was tiring of her, that night they looked the perfect loving couple. Queen Anne still retained her dark-eyed beauty, and the elegant head-dress covered in the lustrous pearls that so suited her olive complexion framed her oval face to perfection. That night she was lively and vivacious and Nicholas could see how she had enthralled the King to such an extent that their affair had rocked both Church and State. There were also shadows under her eyes and when the dancing started she got up and kissed the King and said she was retiring for the night. She was still as slim as a willow wand and the child she was carrying hardly showed, but Nicholas could see how anxious she was and he realised how desperately she wanted their child to be a son, and he feared the consequences if once again the King was disap-pointed.

81

Lady Frances smiled at him invitingly across the table, and he rose unsteadily to his feet and took her hand and together they danced an elegant gavotte that brought the house down. But Lady Frances was duty-bound to follow Queen Anne and Nicholas was free to drink the King's health in endless goblets of fine Bordeaux and listen to the music of William Cornish and the songs which the King himself had written.

It wasn't long before the King retired and Nicholas was able to go to his room. A hunt was arranged for tomorrow. How long, he thought, as he threw himself down on his bed, was he expected to stay at Court? Why had the King summoned him? Not to play tennis and flirt with Lady Frances, that was for sure. As he fell asleep his mind was filled with an image of another woman, someone who beckoned him and then turned away contemptuously.

It wasn't until Sunday, after Mass in the royal chapel that the King sent a message to Nicholas that he was to come immediately to his private study. When he got there, the King was standing looking out of the window, and when he turned to greet Nicholas, his face was stern. Playtime was over.

'Peverell, isn't it time you returned to your duties in Sussex?'

'Your Grace, I have enjoyed your excellent hospitality but I am aware that I have work waiting for me back home.'

'You have indeed got work to do. You're becoming idle, Peverell. Too much soft living. Too much dalliance with Lady Frances Bonville.'

'Lady Frances is indeed a beautiful woman,' said Nicholas evenly, wondering when the King would stop all this preliminary fencing and get to the point. 'However, your Grace knows that my wife Mary still holds chief place in my affections and I am not yet ready to seek other company.'

'Yes, yes, I know all that. But I didn't summon you all

this way to talk about affairs of the heart. I wonder if you have any idea that the part of Sussex you live in has become a nest of traitors? Conspirators, Peverell, that would have me off the throne. Do I take you by surprise?' he said as Nicholas stared at him in astonishment.

'You seem much better informed than I am, your Grace.'

'Of course I am,' the King roared. 'Damn it, man, do you take me for a fool? It's my business to know what's going on in my kingdom, and let me tell you that I don't like what I see, neither do I like what's going on under your nose in Sussex. Fortunately I have people in strategic places who send me reports. My loyal Southampton assiduously watches the ports in your county and intercepts messages. We have enemies everywhere, Peverell, and whilst you tend that garden of yours and dine with that fat Prior, my enemies plot to remove me from the throne and put one of those damn relatives of my late, beloved mother on it. Yes, yes, Peverell, it's time you knew you were living next door to Yorkist traitors who were actually corresponding with that accursed priest, Reginald Pole and his brother. Those two are the bane of my life. Reginald Pole is over on the Continent drumming up support for his base ambitions, and your neighbour keeps in touch regularly. But little did he know that all his diabolical letters have been read by my loyal Southampton. It was a flash of real genius when I made him Lord Admiral of the Fleet.'

'My neighbour, your Grace?'

'Yes, you're a fool, Peverell. A blind fool; you and that Sheriff of Marchester. You seem to live in a different world from the rest of us. It doesn't do to be a dreamer, Peverell. The conspiracy's common knowledge – it's even got a name – Day of Wrath – and you know nothing about it. Its leader, Roger Mortimer, lived next door to you, and you saw nothing and heard nothing.'

'I see little of Sir Roger, your Grace. He lives a quiet life.'

'Lived, Peverell, lived. He's under arrest, and also that

83

Yorkist wife of his. They're on their way to the Tower, and will be interrogated. I've flushed out the conspiracy before it's really begun, and all we need now is for Mortimer to name names. That's only a matter of time. Not many people remain silent after a spell in the Tower.'

'Your Grace, I am astounded. Mortimer's been arrested whilst I've been up here and I wasn't even consulted?'

'Why should you be? Southampton's got me the evidence we needed. If I'd asked you you'd only raise objections, tell me what a good fellow he was, how much his wife loves him and I should think about his family.'

'I would certainly ask your Grace to spare his family. One of his children is a babe in arms.'

'I'm not a cruel man, Peverell. Of course the children will be spared. They can go back to his wife's family. But I need his wife. He's more likely to talk if she's around.'

He turned away to look out of the window, and Nicholas felt sickened. He'd never had much in common with Sir Roger, but he didn't deserve what was going to happen to him. No human being should suffer like that. He hoped desperately for the Mortimers' sake that the impending interrogation would come to a speedy conclusion. But he had his doubts. Sir Roger was a fanatic, and a stubborn one at that.

'Well, Peverell,' said the King, turning round to look at Nicholas. 'Do you still think I'm lacking in compassion? No, don't answer. I see that look on your face. You always were too soft. It will be your downfall. There's no place in this country for weakness. It's my destiny to be a strong ruler. This country needs me. And nothing is going to deter me. The Mortimers of this world must be eliminated. This continual plotting must stop.

'I'm surprised at you, Nicholas,' he said, coming over and putting an arm round Nicholas's shoulders. 'I didn't think there was any love between you and Sir Roger. After all, he had your steward killed. A good man, I believe.'

'Your Grace has heard that?'

'It's my business to hear everything. And this business of your steward has interested me greatly. Hayward overheard Mortimer's infernal plotting with Fitzroy. Fortunately Fitzroy valued his life, and would have nothing to do with it. But Hayward was discovered and had to be got rid of. Your servant, Giles Yelman, was Mortimer's agent and arranged his murder. Now, Nicholas, my loyal subject, what do you think of that? You've been living all this time in the midst of a den of vipers, and you didn't suspect anything. Well, it's over now. Yelman was caught by the Sheriff on the Portsmouth road soon after you left to come here, and it didn't take much to make him confess. But this is all by the by. We've caught the ringleader. It's only a matter of time before Mortimer confesses, so you can go home and sleep in peace. There, what do you think of a King who solves all your problems, Nicholas?'

'I am amazed at your Grace's perceptiveness,' said Nicholas, wishing the King would release him from his embrace. And the efficiency of your intelligence network is truly amazing, he thought.

'It's my wish to be your friend, Nicholas. And friends look after one another, don't they?' said the King, tightening his grip on Nicholas's shoulder. 'And now it's your turn to look after me. I know you're loyal. The Peverells always have been. After all, you've fought our battles for us down the ages; one of your ancestors was governor of Dover Castle when the first William was on the throne. And you've not a drop of treachery in you.'

'Then what does your Grace want of me?' said Nicholas, as the King released him and walked back to the window.

'The conspiracy known as the Day of Wrath has been destroyed. Mortimer will give us more names. One of those treacherous priests at Marchester Cathedral, the Precentor, of all people, Rodney Catchpole, has been arrested with Mortimer; they were as thick as thieves, you know. They plotted to get the Bishop of Rome reinstated in this country. But there will be others; you may be sure of that. And your

85

county seems to be particularly prone to treasonable activities. Too many of my mother's relatives live there, and I can't eliminate them all. Now I want you to keep an eye on things down there, Peverell. Watch Fitzroy. So far he's kept his nose clean. He likes his castle in Arundel. He's not a fool like Mortimer. But he might be tempted. Watch him, Peverell. And send your reports to me. You and my loyal Southampton will be my ears and eyes. You're going to help me clean up your county. I don't want this country plunged back into civil war. My father ended all that on the field of Bosworth, and it will never happen again as long as I live. I hope you share my sentiments, Peverell.'

'Indeed I do, your Grace; and I hope to God that those times never happen again.'

'Then live up to your family's motto and I'll not forget you. I'm not ungrateful, you know. I look after my friends.'

'I shall never be disloyal, but I don't like the idea of spying on my friends.'

'Oh, but you must, Peverell,' said the King, coming over and putting his face very close to Nicholas's so that he could feel his soft, red-gold beard brushing his own. 'To have friends is a luxury we can't afford in these times. Don't trust anyone, Peverell. You're naive, but you will change. Everyone does who works for me. Otherwise they don't last long. I want you as one of my spies. And I won't forget you. I might even consider that Priory of yours. Have a word with Thomas Cromwell before you go. He'll sort it out for you. I know you'll be loyal, but I also know how much you value that chantry chapel of yours. With luck you may still be buried in it. Now get back to your manor. Oh yes, it's my fancy at the moment, now that the weather's warm and pleasant, to come and visit you in your rural solitude. You'd like that, wouldn't you, Peverell? How do you feel about entertaining me and my Queen? I'll not stay long. Only a night or two. I might even stay with Fitzroy on my way back to London. No ceremony, now.

I'm a simple man. Just light meals, some exercise. Do the Queen good. Oh yes, you're short of a steward aren't you? I'll send one of my own and a few servants to help prepare the meals,' he said, grinning enthusiastically at Nicholas. 'See how thoughtful I am. I never want to inconvenience my friends. You see, I think it's time I went to see my fleet at Portsmouth – sometime in early June. It's my wish to build the fleet up into a fine fighting force. Got to keep invaders at bay, Peverell. Enemies at home and abroad – that's my lot. Fix it up with Cromwell; he knows my timetable. Now be off with you, and remember, you are my eyes and ears in Sussex. See that you live up to your family's motto.'

Nicholas bowed, and left the King. He was appalled at what he'd been told. Mortimer arrested; and Rodney Catchpole. Giles Yelman caught and interrogated, and the King coming to pay him a visit. And now for Thomas Cromwell.

Chapter Eight

Thomas Cromwell, Secretary of State, Chancellor of the Exchequer and Privy Councillor, was never far away from his royal master. He was sitting behind his desk in the anteroom to the King's private sanctuary, a plain, stocky figure dressed in a sombre grey robe over his doublet and hose, and, despite the warmth of the spring weather, a log crackled in the fireplace and two chairs were drawn up cosily on either side to catch the heat. Cromwell got up when Nicholas came in and went across to the fire. He stood there warming his back and rubbing his hands together in the nervous gesture of someone who was not quite at ease in his surroundings. However, he hid his lack of social graces with a bluff, slightly ingratiating manner which Nicholas found intensely irritating. But he was not blind to Cromwell's undoubted talents, which had been finely honed in the service of the great cardinal, and which King Henry had so promptly recognised and rewarded with high office. Nicholas knew it was fatal to underestimate him. Already people called him 'malleus monachorum', the hammer of the monks, and the fate of his Priory and his chantry was in this man's hands. He was the King's man through and through. Whatever King Henry wanted, Thomas Cromwell made it his business to provide him with it.

That morning, his plain, pale face creased into a genial smile. He looked what he was, a man of the marketplace, a manipulator of parliaments, a cynical manipulator of men.

'Welcome back to Court, Lord Nicholas. What can I do for you?'

'The King wants to visit my house in Sussex, Master Cromwell, and you, so I've been told, look after his engagement diary.'

'That is my privilege, my Lord. Now, let me see, he goes to Portsmouth on 7th June to review his fleet . . .'

'Then I can expect to see him on the 6th?'

'Yes, I can see no obstacle. An interview with the new legate from Constantinople on the 5th, but after that he's free. I must say, my Lord, I am most envious of you. Fancy owning a house so near the sea and yet so close to the Downs when the weather becomes intolerably hot.'

'Do you propose to come with him?'

'I might, my Lord, I might. It would be a good opportunity to meet my two Commissioners, who will be at your Priory by then. They'll be making their report and I can see for myself the Priory and that chantry chapel of yours which you seem so fond of.'

'My family have always been the Priory's patrons. The first Peverell was its founder.'

'Quite so, quite so. Somewhat diminished in size now, I understand. Only eighteen monks?'

'Seventeen. One is still a novice.'

'Still, quite small. Now about this chantry chapel – it's very beautiful, I suppose.'

'I hope so. I built it for my wife to rest there and I hope to join her when my time comes. I shall die in peace knowing that the monks will sing masses for my family in perpetuity.'

'In perpetuity, my Lord? Come now, that's a bit ambitious. Perhaps you haven't quite realised that the King has decided to put an end to such superstitious practices?'

'I think it's for me to judge whether they're superstitious or not, Master Cromwell.'

'Of course, everyone is entitled to his own private

opinions, my Lord, but we should not let them come between us and the King's policy. He wants the monks dismissed. He regards them as a bunch of useless parasites. They toil not, neither do they spin . . .'

'They pray for us, have you forgotten that,' Nicholas shouted, annoyed at Cromwell's cynicism.

'Oh prayers! Anyone can say those. You don't need a lot of idle fellows chanting prayers for your soul. We pray for the King and his ministers every Sunday, surely that's enough. Archbishop Cranmer is drawing up a new prayer book that will cover every aspect of our lives. We don't need the monks. They're out of date. The monks will have to go, my Lord, you can be sure of that. I am preparing the legislation. By this time next year the Act will be through parliament and will be law. Don't try to turn the clock back, my Lord. It's not worth the effort.'

'You call it progress to evict hundreds of innocent men and women to beg on the street?'

'Come, come, my Lord, don't be so melodramatic. We're not that heartless. All your monks will be given pensions, generous ones at that. The Court of Augmentations is talking about six pounds a year and they can take their beds and habits with them when they leave. Some will probably become local parish priests. Your Prior, if he's co-operative, as I'm sure he will be, could be offered the job of Precentor to Marchester Cathedral. You see, we think of everything.'

'And the Priory? What have you in mind for that?'

'Nothing as yet, my Lord. We haven't had the valuation. Of course the King will be entitled to the church furnishings, the bells will be melted down in the royal arsenal at Woolwich to make guns. Much more practical. The gold and silver plate will be sold, of course, to pay for the refurbishing of the King's fleet.'

Nicholas was appalled. This man had thought of everything: pensions, jobs, the church plate . . .

'Do you realise that these things you take so lightly were

90

given by my ancestors to the Priory to be used in the worship of God, not to be sold off to pay for guns and explosives and fund the navy?'

'Oh, we'll be reasonable, my Lord; we're not insensitive. We'll let you keep some of the church furnishings for future use. Of course,' Cromwell said, rubbing his hands together and looking keenly at Nicholas, 'there is one way you could still enjoy your church and retain your chantry chapel for future generations . . .'

So this was what it was all coming to, thought Nicholas bitterly. The marketplace haggle had started.

'Please state your terms, Master Cromwell.'

'Now, now, this is no time for cynicism, my Lord. We talk of serious matters and you talk like a jobbing lawyer. When the monks leave . . .'

'And are you so sure of that?' shouted Nicholas, angry that this man, who had started off as a jobbing lawyer in Putney, should adopt this patronising tone.

Cromwell looked pained. 'We administrators have to look ahead. There's no doubt that the monks will leave. As I said, I am in the process of drafting the legislation. I, personally, shall steer it through parliament. This time next year, these small monasteries will be closed down. Then we shall turn our attention to the great ones, like Glastonbury and Malmesbury. Now, let's be clear, what I am saying is this: all these buildings will become vacant, including your Priory. The King will no doubt put in stewards to look after the properties until they are sold. Yours, I think, will be offered to Fitzroy for safe keeping. But there's nothing to stop him from putting it up for sale. You could buy it, my Lord.'

'Buy it?' roared Nicholas. 'Sold like any common house or mill or farm?'

'My Lord, your attitude amazes me. Without the monks, the priories and abbeys are just buildings; some, admittedly, very fine. But they are buildings none the less. Take your Priory as an example. It could be sold for some pious

91

purpose, an extension of the parish church, or a theological college, or some other type of teaching establishment. Or it could simply be turned into a fine country house. Don't you understand what I'm saying, my Lord? Make the King an offer. I'll see that you get a good deal. Don't look so angry. Your Priory isn't one of the wealthy ones. I've been told it's only worth a couple of hundred pounds a year. I'm only saying that if you offered us a sum that was acceptable you could safeguard your chantry and that fine painted ceiling which your father commissioned. It should remain in your family. Think about it. You'll see the sense of it, I'm sure. If you don't buy it, others will. Fitzroy has already expressed an interest in it. As soon as the legislation is passed the monastic buildings will be sold off like hot cakes. And I'm trying to tell you that you'll be head of the queue, and still you look furious.'

'Yes, I am furious, Master Cromwell. And dumbfounded that all this has been planned without any consultation with the monks.'

'Consultation? Of course we're in consultation. My Commissioners are on their way to your Priory at this very moment.'

'You call that a consultation? It sounds like a *fait accompli* to me. They'll enjoy the Prior's hospitality, and leave with a list of trumped-up accusations of vice and corruption, all of which are untrue. Don't try to fool me, Master Cromwell. What you are doing is a disgrace. You are turning England upside down. We shall become a country where God has been pushed out and our churches turned into ruins.'

'We must move with the times, my Lord. The King wants the Pope brought to heel and the monks evicted. Their great estates will be the country houses of the future. I am only suggesting that you make the most of this opportunity.'

'I wouldn't dream of stealing what does not belong to me.'

92

'Not stealing, buying. What's wrong with that?'

'Because these buildings were built by people like my ancestors over four hundred years ago to be power-houses of prayer. You are going to strike a blow at God himself.'

'I see you are a man of principle, my Lord, and that's not a wise person to be at the moment – just look at Sir Thomas More; now there's a man of principle if ever there was one. Some would call him a fool. I just think he's an anachronism. But I respect a man who cares for his family and has high ideals, like you; as long as he's loyal. And I think you are such a person, Lord Nicholas. Your family have always been loyal, and you know where disloyalty can lead.'

'It can lead to civil war and the downfall of the lawful ruler. I hope I never have to go through the troubles that England went through fifty years ago like my father did.'

'Quite so, my Lord. May King Henry protect us against those times ever being repeated. Now sir, don't look so gloomy. I can see you have a high regard for your friends in the Priory. There's no need to despair. The King likes you and respects your integrity, and has told me to sort everything out so that we're all happy. It's my job as an administrator to minimise the inconveniences. I'll see to it that the monks get their pensions and I shall keep the job of Precentor open for your Prior until the time comes when he'll be looking for a job. For a small sum you can keep your Priory, the services will go on under the Vicar . . .'

'Master Cromwell, I'll listen to no more of this. I can't haggle over a building dedicated to God like a horse-dealer at a fair. I have a long journey ahead of me, and I must prepare for the King's visit. Good day to you.'

'Very well, Lord Nicholas. Everyone is entitled to his opinion. We shall meet again very soon. Oh by the way, we might have to ask you to come and speak to Mortimer soon.'

'Sir Roger?' said Nicholas aghast. 'What, in God's name can I say to him? He'll be more in need of a priest by the time I get to him.'

'We want Mortimer to name names. I don't share the King's optimism that the conspiracy codenamed the Day of Wrath is over. Mortimer hasn't the leadership qualities to turn honest men into rebels. He's just one of the pawns. There are others. And whilst they remain free, the King cannot sleep easily at night. Now you, Lord Nicholas, could be very persuasive.'

'I'll have nothing to do with your inhuman activities.'

'Inhuman? Surely you agree that Mortimer should be interrogated? It's the necessary fate of all traitors.'

'And may I point out that he hasn't been tried yet. Thank God no one in this country can be declared guilty before he's even been tried. This is England, not France.'

'Quite so. But there's no doubt he's guilty. We have letters to prove it. A trial will only be a mere formality. But he must tell us who the other conspirators are, and that's where you come in. You and his wife. Between you you'll make him talk.'

'Then I am mistaken. This isn't England. Master Cromwell, there's no doubt you make a brilliant administrator, but I wouldn't be in your shoes when the day comes that you can no longer please the King. And when you face your Maker, there will be no monks to pray for your soul.'

'I'll take the risk, my Lord. I'll take the risk.'

Chapter Nine

Early on Monday morning, Nicholas picked up Harry at the Three Horseshoes in Petworth and rode the last lap of the journey. Harry had been well fed and well treated at the inn where Nicholas was a regular visitor, and took the steep climb up Duncton Hill with nonchalant ease. At the top, Nicholas reined him in and paused to look across the flat coastal plain towards the sea, which shimmered on the horizon like a silver girdle. The early morning mist had cleared and he could see the spire of Marchester Cathedral and the five inlets of Marchester harbour stretched out like a giant's hand. This was his county, the county which his ancestors had settled in and served for four hundred years. The soil was fertile, the climate temperate, the sea teeming with fish and its people easy-going and prosperous. It was difficult to believe that anyone should contemplate treason here, but two men had been arrested and he felt sure others would follow.

Harry took the last few miles in his stride, and Nicholas was home by mid-morning. This time Geoffrey Lowe was ready for him and opened the main gate as soon as he heard him arrive. Simon led Harry away and Nicholas walked across the courtyard towards the house with Geoffrey, who looked very worried.

'What's up, Geoffrey? You look like a man going to a funeral. Cheer up and get me some ale, and a cut of beef, if you please. I've had a long night and only a couple of hours' sleep.'

'It's ready and waiting, my Lord. We were expecting you. Have you heard the dreadful news? Sir Roger's been arrested and carted off to London, him and his wife. We've all been knocked for six. Prior Thomas is hopping mad and says they've all made a horrible mistake. Fitzroy's come over from Arundel and put one of his stewards in Sir Roger's house, and the cook's going raving mad up there trying to please them all. Are you all right, sir? No chance of them coming to arrest you?'

'Not if I can help it. Yes, I know all about Mortimer. I'll get over to the Lodge as soon as I've sorted things out here. What's happened to his children?'

'They've gone off to Lady Margot's relations. Such a shrieking and a yelling, it was awful to see and I hope I never have to see it again. It's a terrible thing, sir, when children are torn away from their parents like that.'

A corner of the table in the main hall had been laid with a plate and a knife and Geoffrey filled the pewter tankard with ale and fetched cold beef and bread from the kitchen. Nicholas ate and drank quickly. Then he pushed his plate away and looked round the room. Despite the fire burning in the massive fireplace, the room felt chill and looked dark and gloomy. Why was it that, since Mary died, his house felt like a prison and not like a comfortable home? There was work to be done and not long to do it in.

'You've done well, Geoffrey, whilst I've been away. Keeping house isn't bailiff's work, is it?'

'I've tried to keep things ticking over now that Matthew's gone to God.'

'We'll have to get extra hands, Geoffrey. This place needs cleaning up, those windows are filthy. We've got to get beds aired, cellars stocked up, food brought in and lambs selected for the table.'

'Are you expecting guests, sir?' said Geoffrey, staring at Nicholas in horror.

96

'Yes, and soon. There's a lot to do.'

'May I ask who's coming, sir?'

'Let us just say some very important guests. They'll only be staying for a couple of nights, with any luck, but they'll expect a feast, and God help us, they'll probably want to go hunting.'

'Sir, we haven't the servants, we haven't a steward . . .'

'Don't worry, they'll be sending their own steward to give us a hand. You'll only have to hire servants, scullions, chambermaids, a cook, that sort of thing.'

'Lord help us,' said Geoffrey aghast. 'How many people are coming?'

'I don't know. About fifty, I suppose. Most of them can sleep up in the attic. We'll need extra beds brought in. The Prior'll help us out, I'm sure. Now, Geoffrey, one serious word. I don't want all this spread around the county, do you hear? Complete secrecy.'

'I'll do my best, sir, but when it gets to hiring servants and all the comings and goings up here, word's bound to get around. I'll not say a word, but I can't stop folk noticing.'

'Get servants you can trust. Start with people you know. Your own family for a start. They live in Marchester, isn't that right? Tell them it's vital they say nothing.'

'I'll certainly go and see them. But I can't guarantee they won't talk. How long have we got, sir, to get this place sorted out?'

'Two weeks. Maybe less.'

'God help us, sir.'

'Amen to that. Now let's get started. How many servants have we got at this moment?'

'I don't rightly know, sir. My job's with the field workers.'

'Well, you'll have to muster them together and allocate jobs until the steward comes and takes over. Cleaning first. Provisioning later.'

'Does this steward come from London, sir?'

'I've no idea. I suppose so. Don't worry, he'll know what's wanted.'

'I'm sure he will, but I'm not sure that I can take orders from a Londoner.'

'Oh get away with you, man, what does it matter where he comes from?'

At that moment, Simon, one of the grooms, came in, and came over to Nicholas.

'Mistress Warrener's here, sir. She says she wants to see you urgently, and she'll be waiting for you in the herb garden.'

'Now how did she know I'm here? I've only been back less than an hour.'

Simon looked astonished. 'Word gets round, sir. They all know you're back.'

She was standing by the wild rosebush and he watched as she leaned forward and buried her face in the delicate blooms. Suddenly she noticed him, her face flushed, and she studied the rose even more closely.

'So the King's dismissed you,' she said, without looking at him.

'For the moment, yes. And I can't tell you how pleased I am to be home. There's no joy being at Court. It's a place of intrigue, everyone out for what he can get. No one has friends at Court. Everyone's a rival. My heart is here, Jane, and at this moment it's in this garden. How well you look and how beautifully you set off my roses.'

'This isn't the time for compliments, Lord Nicholas. So much has happened since you went away. You've no doubt heard of Sir Roger's arrest?'

'The King himself told me.'

'Is it really true, then what they say? Is he a traitor?'

'Come over here and sit beside me on this bench, Jane. Do you remember once, not so long ago, you called me Nicholas? And that's how I like it. There's so much to tell you. But first, I must have your solemn word that whatever

I tell you will go no further. Pretend we are now standing in a court of law and you are asked to swear on the Holy Bible that you will never repeat our conversations to anyone. We live in desperate times. Mortimer's gone. Anyone could be next. Last week you said you wanted to be my ears and eyes. Do you still mean that? Can I count on your absolute discretion and your complete loyalty to the King? Swear to it, Jane, because I shall need your loyal partnership.'

They walked over to the wooden bench set beside a bed of lavender, and sat down. The scent filled the air with its relaxing fragrance and the endless drone of the bees was soothing. So peaceful, he thought, but he must not be lulled into a false sense of security. This house, this garden, could all be swept away if once the King's suspicions were aroused. It had happened to Wolsey, to Mortimer; it could certainly happen to him.

He waited for Jane's answer. It felt strange talking to a woman like this. Mary, his wife, had never once asked about affairs of state. Other women, like Lady Frances Bonville, cared only about dalliance and ensnaring a wealthy man to provide her with a great household. But Jane was different. She was intelligent, quick to learn, and compassionate, as her devotion to that old devil of a father proved.

Suddenly Jane swung round and faced him. 'Yes, I swear that I am loyal to the King and I will never repeat any of our conversations. The King is not infallible, but he keeps this country safe from the civil wars that so plagued us only fifty years ago. And if you remember it was I who told you about the conspiracy called Day of Wrath. You didn't believe me then, but I think you do now. Would I have reported all this if I wasn't loyal?'

'I see now that I should never have doubted you. The King knew all along about Mortimer's correspondence with Reginald Pole. His letters were intercepted by the Earl of Southampton, the King's Admiral of the Fleet. The King

99

and Cromwell are ahead in the game; and they have to be. They have a network of spies throughout the country, and as long as there are any descendants of the Yorkist King Edward IV alive and people think they have a better claim to the throne than the Tudors, there will always be conspiracies. The evidence against Sir Roger is overwhelming. Now we have to wait for him to name names, which he will do after interrogation, unless he's a man of superhuman courage.'

She shuddered and he longed to put his arms round her, but if she was to be his ally then there had to be a professional distance between them.

'Are you sure you want to be involved in all this, Jane? Treason is a nasty business. The penalties, if someone is found guilty, are unspeakable. Just say you don't want to go on with this, and I'll stop and then I can listen to your sweet voice and gaze at your beauty and enjoy your company.'

'We made an agreement, Nicholas, and I'm not going back now. But tell me one thing, why did they take away Lady Margot?'

'She comes from a Yorkist family, and they will use her to try and persuade her husband to give the names of his accomplices.'

She didn't flinch. 'And his children?'

'They will be safe with Lady Margot's relations.'

'And his house?'

'Confiscated. Fitzroy will put in one of his own stewards to keep the place running until the King decides what to do with it. It's not impossible that Lady Margot and her children will be reinstated. The King is not a monster. Once he's satisfied that the Day of Wrath is well and truly stamped out, he could be amenable to persuasion.'

'And was I right about Matthew? Was he murdered because he heard too much?'

'Mortimer ordered his death. Giles Yelman was under orders to open my gate to the murderers and showed them where to find Matthew. It had all been arranged.'

'How did you find out about Giles?'

'From the King, of course. The Sheriff picked him up on the Portsmouth road last Thursday night and he confessed before he was interrogated at Lewes.'

'Why do people get involved in conspiracy? Giles had everything going for him.'

'Giles was tempted by money and the promise of advancement. Mortimer believed he was doing the right thing. He wanted someone on the throne of England who was loyal to the Pope. He wanted to turn the clock back and the Pole family are the nearest Yorkist claimants and devoted to the traditional faith. But this is all over now, Jane. The conspiracy is broken. We can all sleep safely in our beds.'

'Then why did Bess Knowles die? You didn't know that, Nicholas, did you? She died on Saturday morning after Mortimer was arrested. She lies now in St John's chapel at the Priory, waiting to join Matthew tomorrow.'

Nicholas stared at her in horror. 'Jane, what are you saying? Bess dead? How? Why?'

'We don't know, that's the long and short of it. The Coroner thinks she died from natural causes. She was carrying Matthew's child and they say that the shock of Matthew's death badly affected the unborn child, and Bess's heart gave up. But I don't believe this. Bess was young and strong, and wanted this child. Yet slowly, over the last few days she slipped away from us. She wouldn't eat a thing, and we thought she was grieving for Matthew, but people don't usually die of grief. Finally, she was too weak to get out of bed and we found her dead on Saturday morning. I think that whoever wanted Matthew out of the way wanted Bess out of the way too. But they took longer about killing her.'

'But why should anyone want to kill her? She's a woman.'

Jane gave him a withering look. 'Women can see and

101

hear and talk, Lord Nicholas. We're human beings.'

'Jane, I'm sorry. I didn't mean that. Only that to kill a woman seems unbelievably wicked. Let me make this quite clear. I have a high regard for women, I love them, they think clearly, but I don't think they're interested in politics, and I hardly imagine Bess would talk to all and sundry about what she overheard with Matthew.'

'You mean she wouldn't have understood what she heard?'

'No, of course not. Don't twist my words. Not all women are as sharp as you, Jane. You're a one-off.'

'Thanks. That makes me a freak. I must say, Lord Nicholas, diplomacy's hardly your strong point. But the fact is, Bess is dead. She took a long time to die.'

'That suggests she was poisoned, or her body wasn't strong enough to bear the child. Some women don't take kindly to carrying children,' he said, thinking of Mary's troubled pregnancy.

'Nicholas,' said Jane, suddenly serious, 'Bess was as strong as a horse, and wanted that child. I think she could have been poisoned, but she didn't eat anything for days, and there were no symptoms of poisoning. I've checked with Mary the cook, who loved her as if she were her own daughter, but she says she couldn't persuade her to eat anything, not even the smallest drop of soup. The only things that passed her lips were sips of water, which she gave her from the big jug in the kitchen which the whole household used, and a few drops of the nourishing tonic which Brother Martin brought her from the monks' infirmary.'

'Then someone could easily have added something to the medicine. I'll get down to the infirmary and see what was in the medicine to start with.'

'Don't be too impetuous. You don't want to imply that you think the monks poisoned Bess.'

'Don't worry. I might not be a diplomat, but I am a member of the King's Council, and that requires a lot of tact if I'm going to survive. Now, I've got to go and see the Prior, so why don't we both go down to the Priory together and talk to Brother Martin. You can keep an eye on me and stop me from upsetting the Brothers. Did you come here on foot?'

'No, Melissa's outside, tied to the gatepost.'

'Then I'll pick up Merlin; Harry needs a rest.'

They left the garden, untethered Melissa and walked round to the stables where Simon, the under-groom, brought out Merlin, a big, bay gelding, used for heavy work. Jane, with a flash of white-stockinged legs, jumped up on Melissa and set off for the Priory. Nicholas followed more slowly, lost in thought. So the conspiracy wasn't over. But which direction would it now take? Bess, he felt sure, was the second victim. Who would be the next? He was vulnerable as he was known as the King's man. But he could look after himself. He was used to living with danger. But Jane? God forbid. He must do everything in his power not to get Jane incriminated.

The morning Mass was over and the monks' choir was deserted except for the hunched figure of Father John, the old priest, who was sitting by the body of Bess Knowles in the little side chapel of St John. Wrapped in a woollen shroud and placed on a wooden bier she looked like a marble effigy. Father John, his cowl pulled forward over his face, sat there motionless. There was no sound except for the distant chattering of the birds outside in the grave-yard, and the sound of the priest mumbling the Latin prayers for the dead.

Nicholas looked down at Bess's white face. She looked so calm; no signs of any grim struggle with death. He was conscious of Jane standing beside him, and he wondered what she was thinking. Bess looked so tranquil, so peaceful, that he half expected her to wake up. But her eyes remained closed, and after he'd said a prayer for the repose of her soul, he left her and walked out into the cloister,

103

where the monks were setting about their morning tasks. He waited for Jane to join him, and together they went over to the infirmary, where three elderly men were propped up in their truckle beds.

At the far end of the hospital ward was a small, high-ceilinged room with pointed lancet windows through which the sun streamed down on to rows of shelves packed with glass and pottery jars containing different coloured liquids. Brother Martin, the young fresh-faced monk who assisted Brother Michael, the Infirmarer, was making up a decoction by simmering various herbs over a small charcoal brazier. Another monk was stripping the leaves of some freshly picked sage, ready to steep in water to strain and press. The room was filled with the fragrance of herbs and the two monks looked peaceful and happy in their work.

Brother Martin glanced up at Nicholas but averted his eyes from Jane.

'Lord Nicholas, this is a great honour,' he stammered. 'What can we do for you?'

'We came to offer a prayer for Bess Knowles's soul and I thought I'd take a look at your apothecary's department. This is the right time for gathering herbs, I understand, Brother Martin? It's also the time for plagues and the sweating sickness so it's good that you are prepared.'

The monk crossed himself. 'May God protect us from such afflictions. I hope you and your household are well?'

'Thank you, yes. I heard you were called in to see Bess Knowles in her last hours, is that right?'

'Yes, and I'm sorry we could do nothing for her. I've seen nothing like her sickness before. It appeared like a rapid consumption, but there was no cough and no fever. Just a slipping away of her strength like the tide ebbing away.'

'Was there nothing you could do for her?'

'We tried. I made up a tonic for her under Brother Michael's instructions, of course. As there were no obvious symptoms we didn't know what to put in it, but feverfew is very effective if a fever had developed, and we added juniper berries in case she developed a cough. We macerated some camomile and the leaves of lemon balm and the oil from borage seeds – they're good for women in Bess Knowles's condition – then we added valerian for its sedative properties; and marigold, of course. This we mixed with a lot of honey, our special clover honey, and St John's Wort, which lifts the spirits.'

'Have you any left over?'

'To be sure. We've always got some in stock. It's an excellent fortifier for people who need building up. All our elderly and infirm monks take it twice a day. It gets them back on their feet. Would you like to try some, my Lord, and Mistress Warrener?'

He poured out a small measure in two pottery dishes and watched whilst they both drank it. The mixture was very sweet and the herbs gave it a delicate fragrance. It tasted good and Nicholas felt no strange effects; only a pleasant feeling of well-being and a lifting of the spirits.

'It's excellent. Are you quite sure this was the only medicine you gave Mistress Knowles?'

'Of course. What else could we have prescribed? What are you insinuating, my Lord?' said a deep voice behind them. Nicholas turned round and faced the tall figure of Brother Michael, a basket of herbs on his arm which he'd just gathered from the monastery herb garden. 'And Mistress Warrener, what brings you here? We don't usually allow women into our infirmary; it upsets the patients. You're welcome to come and sing ditties to the Prior after supper, but I'd prefer it if you stayed out in the gatehouse when you come here.'

'I'm sorry, Brother Michael, but Bess Knowles was my friend, a very dear friend, and Lord Nicholas and I are puzzled by her death.'

'It took us all by surprise, but we are not expert in women's diseases. The tincture which you have just tasted is a general tonic calculated to lift melancholy and therefore

105

often prescribed in cases of bereavement. But I'm sorry it was no use to her.'

It was obvious he wanted Jane to leave. He was nervously edging them both out of the apothecary's room into the main ward, where an old man with the closely shaven head of a monk raised his head as they walked past. His body, under the thin blanket, was skeletally thin, and his hands, lying on top of the blanket, were twisted and clawed like the twigs on a hazel tree in winter. But his eyes were bright and blue and he took in everything. Nicholas recognised him. He was Brother Wilfrid, who'd given him his first reading lessons. He stopped to give him a greeting, then followed Brother Michael and Jane down the long ward and out into the sunshine.

'Thank you for doing what you could for Mistress Knowles, Brother Michael,' Nicholas said as they turned to leave. 'She looks so young, lying in the chapel waiting for burial.'

'She's with God, Lord Nicholas, and His holy angels. May she rest in peace.'

They walked towards the gatehouse, where they'd left their horses. The gate stood open and a carriage swept in and the genial face of the Prior looked out at them from the window. He shouted to the driver to stop, and the horse came to a sudden halt, skidding back on his haunches.

'Lord Nicholas, welcome home. And Mistress Warrener, when are you coming to sing to us again?'

Jane bobbed a curtsy. 'I am at your bidding, my Lord Prior.'

'Good, good, that's what I like to hear. I'll arrange something soon. I've got visitors coming, Lord Nicholas. They're on their way from Lewes. Coming to see how we run our Priory. Well, well, we'll give them a good run for their money. They'll soon get fed up getting out of bed for Matins. But we'll feed them well. They'll not say they weren't welcome here. You'll come and dine with me tonight, my

Lord? It's not good to be up in that great house all on your own. Besides, I want to hear what the King said to you.'

'I shall look forward to it.'

'Good, good. By the way, what brings you here? Did you want anything in particular?'

'I wanted to arrange a time to speak to you, but I shall see you tonight. We've also seen all we wanted.'

'And what was that?'

'The body of Bess Knowles. A sad case.'

'A tragedy. I'm only sorry we couldn't help her. Well, I must be off. Tonight, about six.'

He rapped on the carriage roof, and it rumbled off. 'He's incorrigible,' said Nicholas. 'Inspectors from the King coming to report on his Priory and he doesn't give a damn.'

'They'll enjoy every minute of it,' said Jane. 'But now I must go and see Agnes Myles.'

'That old crone?'

'She might be getting on a bit, but she's the unofficial apothecary in these parts. Not so long ago, she delivered all the babies and laid out the dead; now she lives alone and makes her own herbal medicines. I want to ask her about the other sort of herbs, the bad ones, the dangerous ones.'

'A good idea, but it's not going to help us much in Bess Knowles's case. We've just sampled the medicine she was prescribed and we're both still standing.'

'She might know more than the monks when it comes to pregnant women. There might be some herbs that should never be prescribed in pregnancy.'

'That's possible. Well, you get off to your old witch, and I'll get over to Mortimer's place. Fitzroy's put one of his stewards in and I want to see if everything is in order.'

'What will happen if Mortimer is found guilty and executed?'

'The house will go to the King and he can dispose of it as he pleases. That's one of the penalties for treason; the whole family suffers.'

*

107

Two lay Brothers led out their horses and he watched as Jane mounted Melissa and rode up the street towards Agnes Myles's cottage. He felt uneasy about her. She already knew too much and if she continued to ask questions, she could be in real danger. But he couldn't keep her under lock and key; Jane had a mind of her own. Forcing himself to stop worrying about her, he jumped up on Merlin's solid back and turned his head towards Mortimer Lodge.

Chapter Ten

Jane had known Agnes Myles all her life. Agnes had brought her into the world, and helped her mother into the next. She knew how to cure most illnesses, how to alleviate stiff joints, prescribe soothing syrups for every type of cough. It was rumoured that she even knew how to cure the plague. Jane regarded her as a wise friend who possessed healing gifts; her enemies said she was a witch.

Jane tied Melissa to the gatepost of Agnes's cottage, which was at the end of a lane just off the main Marchester road. Most of the villagers lived in timber-framed houses with walls made of wattle and daub. The poor cottagers lived in houses made mostly of mud reinforced with wood and dung. Very few people could afford to live in a stone house. Agnes was one of these. She'd lived in Thyme Cottage as long as Jane could remember, and she knew very little about her past. Rumour had it that she'd been born the wrong side of the blanket; maybe she was a child of one of the clergy – the Dean of Marchester had been suggested – or one of the local gentry. Her mother had lived in Thyme Cottage and had never appeared short of money to buy bread and chickens and a clutch of geese, which the young Agnes had steered across the road and out on to the common land where they rooted around with the villagers' pigs.

Agnes was now in her sixties, a small, brisk figure

collecting eggs at the top of the garden. Jane walked along the stone path between the raised beds of lavender and hyssop and the sweet-smelling thyme bushes. The bed of marigolds glowed like a rich coverlet and all around the bees were joyfully collecting nectar, and the butterflies hovered like bits of brightly coloured mosaic. Ahead of her, she could see the small, white-capped head of Agnes bobbing over the herb bushes. At the end of the path, she watched as Agnes fussed over the hens, stroking one, looking closely at another who was coming to the end of her life. She was wearing a simple woollen dress with a white apron tied round her waist, and the wisps of hair which had escaped from the neat cap which framed her healthy, pink face, were white. She straightened up when she noticed Jane and smoothed down her apron.

'What brings you here, Jane? Not that father of yours again, I hope? He's had enough cough syrup to last him a lifetime. Take him some of these eggs – the hens are laying well – and there's nothing better than an egg to build up an ailing man.'

Her voice was soft and melodious with only a faint trace of the local accent. There was something different about her that set her apart from the other villagers – an air of refinement and contented self-sufficiency. Jane followed her into the cottage and once again marvelled at the cosiness and cleanliness of the living room, where brass and pewter pots and pans gleamed on the shelves, a fire crackled in the fireplace and a pot hung on a chain over it, bubbling and steaming and filling the room with a wonderful smell of boiled rabbit and onions.

'You'll take some refreshment?' she said to Jane, putting down the basket of eggs on the wooden dresser. 'There's a blackcurrant cordial, some syrup made from rose hips, or water from my well?'

She put a wooden scoop into the pot standing on the floor by the fire, and raised it to her mouth, drinking the water with a sigh of pleasure. Then she put the scoop back into the pot, filled it and offered it to Jane, who drank it grate-fully.

'Now what is it this time?' she said watching Jane closely with her bright, twinkling blue eyes. 'A wash for your hair? No, you don't need it. A love potion? Surely not. You'd have no need of that once you'd set your heart on someone. There, there, have I touched a raw spot? There's no need to blush; it's time you thought about marriage and raising a family. But take your time and don't rush into anything. Make the wrong choice, and you've a lifetime of pain ahead of you. But take no notice of me; I'm only an old woman. You'll choose well, I know. God's given you a good brain and you know how to use it.'

'I've not come here for a love potion, but I do need your advice; but not on matters of the heart.'

'I'll do my best. Come and sit down, my lovey.'

She pointed to the settle and sat at one end, patting the place next to her.

'So what's troubling you?'

'You know Bess Knowles has died?'

'I do, and I'm very surprised. The lass came to see me only a short while ago and I confirmed that she was carry-ing a child. She was fit and healthy and delighted with the news. She needed no potions and tinctures and I promised to be there when the child came into the world. All I can think of is that she went into a deep melancholy when Matthew died and lost the will to live.'

'Is that possible?'

'I've seen it happen with country folk but usually they are old and in pain and don't want to go on living any more. But I've never seen it happen to a young lass with everything to live for.'

'So you don't think there could be any suspicion of foul play?'

'Oh now I can't say that, can I? Everything's possible. But who on earth would want to kill Bess Knowles?'

'That's what they said about Matthew Hayward.'

111

'Aye, but he got in the way of thieves, so I've heard. Bess took to her bed and stayed there. Only there is one thing that is a bit odd, looking back, that is . . .'

'Yes, Agnes?'

'Well, when I heard she was poorly, I tried to go and see her. After all, I've tended Lady Margot when her children were born, and the cook, Mary Woodman, came to see and asked if I'd take a look at Bess. Well, when I got there the Mortimers said it wasn't necessary. I was a bit upset – well, you would be, wouldn't you? After all, I thought I was doing the family a good turn. But now I hear he's been taken off to London along with Lady Margot, and that he's in trouble with King Henry, and the children have all been sent to the St John Pearce's. He's in trouble and I feel sorry for him, and I suppose he was worrying about all these things when I wanted to see Bess and he refused to let me see her.

'But what are you thinking, Jane? You've got that look on your face which tells me you think you're on to something, and it won't go away until you've found the answer.'

'Agnes, I am worried, and now what you say about the Mortimers not letting you see Bess confirms my fears. I'm beginning to think that someone wanted to get rid of Bess, in the same way that someone wanted to kill Matthew. You see, Matthew and Bess were both together when they overheard something which they shouldn't have. We don't think Matthew was killed by thieves. That's what's been put around to hide the truth. I can't tell you any more because I don't want any harm to come to you, and the less you know the better. But, given that Matthew had to go, it follows that Bess also would have to be got rid of in case she told people what she had overheard with Matthew. I think she could have been poisoned. But she took no food for three days; just a sip of water which Mary brought up to her, and it's the same water which all the family drank.'

Agnes nodded, not taking her eyes off Jane's face.

'She took nothing else?'

'Only a medicinal drink which Brother Martin made up for her.'

'Then that's good. The monks are expert at making up tonics. After all, their infirmary is nearly always full of old and sick monks, monks who have just been bled, for instance, and need building up. Do you know what was in this concoction?'

'We've just been to see Brother Martin . . .'

'We?'

Jane hesitated. 'Lord Nicholas and I. He's interested in Bess's death. After all, she was going to marry his steward.'

'And did Brother Martin tell you what was in the potion?'

'He said there was feverfew, juniper berries and some lemon balm. Oh yes, borage seeds, valerian and marigold. They were mixed together with honey.'

'All quite harmless.'

'Yes, we both tasted it, and survived. But Agnes, you know all about herbs. There isn't one that you don't know the properties of. You have an apothecary's shed at the back of the house which is almost better stocked than the monks' place. Tell me about the bad herbs, Agnes; the ones you keep locked away; the ones that don't cure, but kill. Is there such a herb that, if added to a tonic would be unnoticed but would kill someone?'

Agnes looked keenly at Jane. 'Of course there is, but no herb is completely bad. It all depends on the quantity you give someone. Come outside and I'll show you what I mean.'

Jane followed Agnes out into the garden where, behind a low hedge, there was a wooden hut. By the side of the hut there was a row of beautiful pink and mauve foxgloves with their trumpet-like flowers blazing open.

'Foxgloves, Jane. A plant of great potency. Just a tiny dose and the heart of an old man can beat faster. Too much, and it stops altogether. Come inside.'

113

She opened the door and they went into the dim, aromatic interior. Hanging from the rafters were bunches of lavender, rosemary, thyme, hyssop, all recently gathered and tied neatly into bundles for drying out. On the far wall there were rows of shelves, each one stacked with bottles and bowls, all tightly stoppered. Agnes took down a bottle containing a dark, sticky liquid.

'This one is the king of all plants. I buy it in small quantities from a ship's captain who trades with the Levant. He brings me the heads of the plant and I extract the juice. Take a good look at it, Jane. One day you might have need of it. It brings relief to the dying and sleep to disturbed minds. It is the greatest plant God has given to us, but the deadliest when used improperly.'

'What is the name of the plant, Agnes?' said Jane holding the bottle up to the light.

'Why, 'tis the common poppy, Jane, but it doesn't come from this country. Our climate isn't right for it. It is called the opium poppy and the opiate which I extract brings relief to many people. I supply the monks, you know. Brother Michael uses it to ease the pain of someone suffering from a mortal disease. It is a blessed drug.'

'If it had been added to Bess's potion could it have killed her?'

'In the right quantity, certainly. But by the sound of it she doesn't appear to have had any signs of having taken opium. She would have drifted off into a profound sleep, and that wasn't the case, was it?'

'No, she remained mentally alert until the end. She was depressed, but that's not surprising as she could feel her strength going.'

'Then she didn't take any opium, because it lifts the spirits. There are other herbs which shouldn't be taken in large does, but Bess seemed to die with no obvious symptoms.'

'Agnes, are there any deadly medicines? Some that work quickly and without symptoms?'

114

'There are lots of deadly herbs, Jane, and many of the mushrooms and toadstools which I collect in the woods in autumn are also deadly. Amongst the poisonous herbs there is henbane, deadly nightshade, mandrake and hemlock. But all of these would bring on sensations of nausea, and convulsions. The poisonous toadstools would all bring on a violent attack of vomiting. No, I don't think Bess died through swallowing poison. Her death appeared to be painless and inexorable. I also think you shouldn't blame the monks for her death. Their knowledge of medicine is vast – they wouldn't make a mistake. Brother Michael knows far more than I do. I cannot, for the life of me, believe that they would want to harm Bess. I think we must assume she died of grief made worse by her pregnancy.'

Jane gave the bottle back to Agnes and glanced at the open book on the table. She turned the pages back to the front cover and read the title, *Banckes Herbal*. Agnes saw her glance, and picked the book up.

'Yes, this is a most useful book. It's a compilation of all the early books on herbs. Brother Michael procured a copy for me. He's very kind.'

'Do you see him very often?'

'Not often, but occasionally. We consult one another about difficult cases, and he's always raiding my supplies when his store runs low, especially in the winter time. Now look who's here! Ambrose, you're not allowed in here, you know that. No, don't jump up on the table. Jane can talk to you outside.'

Ambrose, a large and very black cat, took no notice. With one graceful leap he landed on the table, and from this vantage point he could curl himself around Jane's outstretched arm, purring loudly. She stroked his glossy fur and he flexed his claws appreciatively on the table, ignoring Agnes's cries of disapproval. Jane laughed.

'Ambrose is in fine form.'

'Yes, he likes this time of the year. The garden's full of

115

fledgings and the fields full of voles and mice. Come on, Ambrose, that's enough of that. Come and have some milk. You'll stay for a bite, Jane?'

'Thanks, but I must be off. My father will soon want his dinner.'

'Tell that father of yours to get his own dinner. You ought to have some time off.'

'That'll be the day. He'd sooner starve than get his own meal.'

Agnes walked with her to the gate, Ambrose, with twitching tail, leading the way.

'I'm sorry about Bess, Jane; and I'm sorry I haven't the knowledge to tell you what caused her death. Sometimes the Lord just takes back his own and it's not our business to question His ways. Now give my regards to Lord Nicholas and tell him from me that it's time he thought about taking another wife; and let it be soon.'

Jane untied Melissa and jumped up on to her back. With a flick of her tail, she trotted off. It was a lovely day and Jane decided not to go home just yet, but to give Melissa a gallop across the common. So she turned Melissa off the road and dug her heels into her sides. With a snort of indignation, Melissa raced off.

Merlin was heavy and cumbersome after Harry, and seemed reluctant to enter the wood. Merlin was, by nature, a lugubrious horse, safe, dependable but dull, and today he seemed to match Nicholas's mood. All around them the carpet of bluebells glowed in the dappled sunlight that streamed down through the canopy of beech leaves, but all Nicholas could think of was Bess Knowles's marble-white face and that still body lying before the altar in St John's chapel, with a monk praying for her soul. It didn't take much imagination to replace Bess's face with Jane's. He saw so clearly her heart-shaped face wrapped in its grave cloth and her beautiful hair shrouded from sight and her vivid blue eyes closed in death. Two innocent people had already died; pray God Jane wouldn't be the next.

Cromwell had seemed pretty certain that the conspiracy wasn't over yet; but where was it to reappear? And when? And who were the conspirators? Perhaps Mortimer would reveal more under interrogation, and then his way would become clear. But without more information, he felt he was groping in the dark.

With a heavy heart he arrived at Mortimer Lodge. The place looked deserted and an air of sadness hung like a black cloud over the courtyard where only days before he'd seen Sir Roger grooming Galliard. Now, no one came to take Merlin. He dismounted and tied him to a post. Then he walked over to the heavy, wooden front door and rang the bell. It was a long time before it was opened and a man whom he'd not seen before, peered out.

'No visitors. Sir Roger's not here,' the man said.

'I'm his neighbour, Lord Nicholas Peverell. Open this door at once. I've come to see that everything's in order here.' The door opened and a short, stocky man, dressed in a brown leather doublet and strong woollen hose, confronted him. His large, plain face was fringed with coarse black hair, and he looked coldly at Nicholas.

'You'd better come in, then. I'm Roland Seaward, steward to Lord Gilbert Fitzroy, and sent here to administer this property until His Majesty the King decides what to do with it. There's nothing to see, but come in if you must.'

It was unbelievable how much the house had altered since Sir Roger was arrested. There were no signs of life; no children playing and chattering; no Lady Margot going about her household tasks. Something had died when the Mortimers left. It felt as if the house had lost its soul. Only the cook, Mary, was still there in the kitchen. She was stirring a pot over the fire, and she looked up when Nicholas went in and promptly burst into tears.

'My Lord, you see what we've come to. Everyone's gone, and I'm left with this devil of a steward who expects me to cook for him three times a day. I'm ashamed to be here, but I've nowhere to go, and even if I had, Roland wouldn't let me leave.'

'Hush, Mary,' said Nicholas soothingly, 'you must stay here and look after the house until times become more settled. We don't know whether Lady Margot might return with the children. You must hope for that.'

'You really think they might come back here, my Lord? When I remember the faces of those poor children, shocked and bewildered they were, I thought I would never see them again. And God help me, at that moment I hated Sir Roger for letting his family suffer so.'

'He thought he was doing the right thing. Just think of his wife and children and think of better times. Did you see Bess Knowles in her last moments, Mary?'

'I did that. And that's another thing. Why should the poor lass die? She was never ill, not a day's illness as long as I've known her. I don't understand it. She wanted that poor child. She was all ready to marry Matthew; then he was taken and she just gave up and followed him.'

'Can you remember whether she took any food?'

'Not a morsel. It was almost as if she'd made up her mind to die, and die she did. A terrible thing to happen. Sometimes I think there's a curse on this house.'

Nicholas comforted her as best he could, and Roland took him round the house, showing him the deserted rooms. It was as if the house was in mourning; Sir Roger's desk was covered with a linen sheet; the beds were stripped, the shutters closed. Nicholas shuddered and decided there was nothing he could do there.

Shouting goodbye to Mary, he returned to Merlin, and mounted him. Using his whip, because Merlin seemed reluctant to move, he crossed the common and went into the wood. The sun had gone behind dark clouds, and Merlin was uneasy. Once in the wood, he refused to go along the woodland path and stopped, snorting uneasily.

'What's got into you, you old fool?' said Nicholas, urging him on with his heels and the whip. But it was no

118

use. Merlin began to play up, side-stepping over every fallen twig, and peering into every coppice. Then he stopped suddenly and refused to budge. The sun came out from behind a cloud and shone through the trees, creating a dappled effect on the ground. Then Nicholas saw something flit behind a tree; a dark, sinister figure, like a being from another world. He jumped and tried to look more closely, but the thing had disappeared. Then a twig cracked and that was enough for Merlin. With an almighty sideways leap, he shied away from the path and tore off through the thicket. Nicholas tried desperately to check him, but it was useless. Merlin was immensely strong. Too late, Nicholas saw the low branch ahead of him. Merlin made straight for it. The branch caught Nicholas across the chest and he fell heavily. Then he lost consciousness and Merlin, riderless, raced back to Peverell Manor.

Chapter Eleven

Nicholas didn't surface until Tuesday morning. He opened his eyes and heard the twittering of the birds greeting the dawn, but he had no recollection of where he was or why he was there. He moved his head but the pain hit him like a blow of the blacksmith's hammer, and he cursed and shut his eyes. Then he tried again. He moved his legs and found they still functioned; his arms and hands seemed normal. But when he tried to raise his head the hammers started again and his neck and shoulders were stiff and painful.

He sank back on his pillow and tried to concentrate, but it was no use, his memory wasn't functioning. Then he must have drifted off to sleep because when he next opened his eyes the sun was streaming into the room and the worried face of Geoffrey Lowe swam into view. A voice was speaking to him.

'Are you all right, my Lord?'

'I'll live,' he murmured, noting with interest that his voice appeared disembodied and seemed to come from a long way away.

Geoffrey's face relaxed. 'Thank God for that. You had a nasty fall, my Lord.'

Then he remembered. Merlin. The figure behind the tree.

'Who found me?'

'Mistress Warrener.'

He jumped in surprise and the hammers started up again. 'Jane Warrener? How?'

'She was out riding that mare of hers, and saw Merlin rushing along the path like a mad thing, and she guessed you'd had a fall. She went looking for you, found you lying up there in the woods, and came back here for help. Simon and the lads brought you home on a stretcher. But Lord, sir, we all thought you'd had it. Bloody great bruise on your head, blood all over your face from where a bit of tree stuck into you. We cleaned you up, put you in your bed, and waited for you to wake up.'

'Where's Jane Warrener now?'

'At home, I suppose. She took a good look at you, said you'd live and off she went. She's a clever wench, that one. Didn't think you'd broken any bones, and told us to let you sleep. She'll be back soon, I shouldn't wonder. Now sir, what can we do for you?'

'What happened to Merlin?'

'Oh he's as right as rain – eating his oats, rolling his eyes like he always does. But I don't understand how you came to have that fall, sir. There's not a more placid horse than Merlin. Now Harry ... I can understand if Harry threw you off his back. He's all nerves and muscle, but old Merlin's as safe as an old carthorse. That's what comes of losing his balls, I suppose.'

'He saw something in the woods – something he didn't like the look of. He took one look and galloped off. Unfortunately, a tree got in the way, and I couldn't turn him. He got under it, of course, but forgot he had me on his back.'

'That explains the bruises on your chest. Jane Warrener guessed that's what happened. Then you must have hit your head when you fell and ended up bruised and concussed. Now you'll have to rest up a bit.'

'Jane Warrener looked at my chest?'

'Aye, that she did, sir. I couldn't stop her. She took a look at other parts of you as well. She's a right determined

121

wench, that one, and doesn't care what people think.'

Somehow the idea of Jane running her hands over his body to see whether any bones were broken appealed to him immensely, and he began to feel better.

'Now get me some hot water, Geoffrey, and some food. Some eggs will do nicely, with bread and some honey.'

'Shall I bring it up here, sir?'

'Why not? I'll sit at that table. But first get me cleaned up, there's a good fellow. I can't have Mistress Warrener seeing me in this state.'

'She'll not care. She saw you in a worse state when they brought you home.'

An hour later, washed and fed, he staggered back to bed, his head still throbbing painfully. Suddenly, there was a knock at the door, and Jane came in with an anxious-looking Geoffrey behind her.

'I told her not to come up, my Lord, but she insisted.'

'Let her come in, Geoffrey. Nothing can stop Mistress Warrener when she's in a determined mood. No, don't you hang about,' he said seeing his bailiff standing there help-lessly, not knowing what to do. 'I'll give a shout when she leaves and you can escort her off the premises. Well, Jane,' he said, as Geoffrey, still with disapproval, backed out of the door. 'It appears you saved my life.'

He indicated a chair, and she sat down. 'I found you and went to get help. Anyone would have done the same thing, but it was lucky I decided to go up to the common before I went home. I hope you're feeling better?'

'Much better for seeing you. There's nothing wrong with me, just a bump on the head and a few bruises.'

'It looks painful, but probably it looks worse than it is. I'm glad to see you've been cleaned up.'

'Geoffrey sorted me out. What've you got in that basket, Jane? Have you brought me a present?'

'Some eggs,' she said, taking off the cloth that covered them. 'Agnes gave them to me. They were really for my

122

father, but I thought you might have more need of them.'

'Quite right. Why should that old devil have newly laid eggs?'

'Nicholas, stop calling my father names. He might be a bit outspoken, but he's kind.'

'Sorry. Like father, like daughter. Now tell me how did you get on with that old witch?'

'There you go again. She's a wise woman and a good friend, and there's nothing she doesn't know about herbs; but that doesn't make her a witch. I asked her about the poisonous herbs, and she said most of them would have side effects. Bess, as you know, died peacefully – no vomiting, no drowsiness, no convulsions. So we're no nearer to finding out why Bess died, and as her funeral is today, I suppose we never will. Another thing, what made Merlin bolt up there in the woods? I've always thought he seemed such a docile horse, a bit on the dull side really.'

'Of course he's dull. He's a carrier horse, just one stage removed from a carthorse. He's not supposed to be temperamental. Not like Harry. But thank God I wasn't riding him. He would've panicked and jumped around a lot more than Merlin when he saw it.'

'Saw what, Nicholas?'

'The thing, wraith, call it what you will; it came sliding out from behind a tree. Its face, if it had a face, was covered, and I've never seen anything so diabolical. Merlin sensed it long before he saw it. He stopped dead and refused to budge. Then when it glided out from behind the tree, he bolted.'

'Was it human or a beast?'

'I've no idea. Could've been the devil for all I know. Anyway, that's the reason why I was thrown off Merlin, and thank God you came along and found me.'

Suddenly, Jane leaned forward with a look of alarm on her face. 'Nicholas, you don't think . . .?'

'Yes, I do think. I think someone knew where I was going, and decided to remove me from the local scenery.

123

Thank God he didn't quite succeed.'

'Are you sure it was a "he"?'

'I didn't have time to notice its sex.'

'Don't joke. Someone tried to kill you.'

'Well, at least he picked on me. So far, no one's attacked you, thank God.'

'That's because I'm a girl, and not expected to know anything.'

'How wrong they are. Now what the hell ... Who's this?'

Someone knocked on the door, it opened and Brother Martin walked in, his good-natured face beaming with pleasure at the sight of Nicholas sitting up alive and well.

'Now what brings you here, Brother Martin?', said Nicholas, trying to control his irritation. 'Didn't Geoffrey tell you that I had company?'

'I'm not staying long, my Lord. We heard you'd had a fall and the Brothers send their best wishes for a speedy recovery. They will be pleased when I tell them that you are on the way to recovery. Brother Michael told me to tell you that a blow on the head must always be taken seriously, and he sends you this tonic.'

The monk rummaged about in the sleeve of his habit, and took out a small glass phial with a stopper. 'He sends you this healing potion. It will soothe your mind and heal the wound. Drink it and you'll be feeling better in no time at all.'

'Tell Brother Michael I appreciate his concern, but I don't need a tonic. I intend to get out of this bed as soon as Mistress Jane leaves.'

'You've been concussed, my Lord. Head wounds are always serious. Delayed shock is a serious risk after a fall from a horse. This is pleasant to take, and will get you on your feet again in only a few hours.'

'You'd better take it, Nicholas,' said Jane, looking at him steadily. 'The monks are great healers. You could drink it later.'

Brother Martin unscrewed the stopper of the bottle and handed it to Nicholas. Nicholas thanked him and put it casually on the table by the side of his bed.

'Thank you, Brother Martin, I'll take it when I need to sleep.'

'So you don't trust me. Well, let me show you it's quite harmless.'

Brother Martin picked up the phial and took a sip.

'Excellent, excellent. I can recommend it, my Lord.'

It would be churlish to refuse. Nicholas took the phial and drank down the contents. In seconds, he felt his body become suffused by a delicious languor. His head stopped throbbing and he felt as if he was lying on a bed of soft sheep's wool. Jane's face floated off out of sight, he sank back on his goose-feather pillow, closed his eyes, and sank into a deep void.

When Jane arrived home, her father was waiting for her by the front gate. She sensed trouble. His face was dark with disapproval and he was propping himself up on his stick as if he'd been waiting a long time.

'Where've you been, lass? People are talking.'

'You shouldn't listen to gossip, father. However, let's go inside, and you can tell me what they're saying.'

She handed Melissa over to Harold, the old gardener and handyman, who'd been with them as long as she could remember, and walked up the path into the house, her father following more slowly. Their house was stone-built, like Agnes's, but more substantial and built on a bigger plot of land. The window openings had recently been filled in with glass, which her father approved of, because now the openings let in the light but not the cold. She watched him making his way painfully up the path and realised that he was old and she should make allowances for him.

Once inside the bright, warm room, he sank down with a sigh of relief on to the wooden settle and propped his stick up against the side. The floor was covered with bright rugs, and bowls of flowers decorated the window-ledges. Guy Warrener was prosperous. The monks relied on him heavily when it came to selling their wool.

'Now, out with it, lass. Where've you been?'

'Up to the Manor to see how Lord Nicholas was getting on.'

'So they tell me. Seems you found him in the woods, is that right?'

'Yes, he fell off his horse. I went and got help and I wanted to know how he was this morning. There's no harm in that, is there?'

'No harm at all. But I advise you to keep away from the gentry, lass. I don't want your head turned. He's not for the likes of you. You might be bright and you're good-looking all right, but the likes of Lord Peverell don't marry the daughters of wool traders. He's charming, I'll give you that, but I'll kill him if any harm comes to you.'

'Now don't get excited, father. You do exaggerate. I only wanted to pay my respects. Geoffrey Lowe escorted me up to his bedroom . . .'

'You went up to his bedroom?' shouted Guy Warrener, trying to haul himself up from the sofa.

'Of course. That's where you usually go if you're not well.'

'Don't you smart-answer me, madam. You've no business going into men's bedrooms. The next time you go there he might not be so helpless, and then what'll you do?'

'I'll do what I please.'

'I'll not allow it. What pleases you could be the death of you. Believe me, he'll take advantage of you. They're all the same, the gentry. Love you and leave you; it's always been like that. And no one will ever look at you twice when you're one of Peverell's cast-offs.'

'You do talk rubbish, father,' said Jane, trying to control her exasperation. 'Now sit down for a minute, and try to calm down. Let me make you a hot drink. All this shouting's not good for you and I'll have you in bed next.'

126

'Now stop threating me as if I've got one foot in the grave. I'm good for many more years yet. I've spoiled you, Jane, I can see that,' he grumbled, but he did relax back again on the settle, and watched as she took hot water from the pot over the fire and mixed up a soothing drink of honey and lemon balm. 'I've watched you grow up into a beautiful wench; aye, with a brain, too. You can read Greek and Latin better than the monks. Yet you ride round on that horse of yours sitting up there like a boy, no saddle, showing those long legs of yours, and I've not said a word. But I can't abide watching you chasing after the gentry.'

'I won't have you saying that,' she said firmly. 'Lord Nicholas hardly knows me.'

'I daresay he doesn't,' he said as he accepted the herbal drink she offered him. 'But I've seen you talking to him, and I don't like the way he looks at you. Keep away from him, lass. He's up in London with the King and all those grand people. I hear he's bringing them all down to his house soon, so I've been told. All that cleaning and polishing and baking and brewing . . . Geoffrey Lowe says there's no end to it. He's at his wits' end with worry. Damn me, they even want to go hunting. Prior'll have to lend some of his horses, I shouldn't wonder, along with the contents of his cellar too.'

Jane stared at her father in consternation. 'What are you saying, father? Lord Nicholas has got some people coming to stay with him? Who told you this?'

'It's common knowledge. Geoffrey Lowe's been going round finding people to come and lend a hand with the cooking and the waiting at table. They're planning a great feast, I've heard. I'm sorry if I've upset you,' he said, noticing her stricken look, 'but I thought he would have told you. He'll no doubt want you to go up there and sing to all his noble friends. Now don't take it to heart, lass, it's all for the best. I don't want you upset by the likes of Lord Peverell. The gentry pleases itself, as it always does and always will do. Now, we ought to get ourselves ready for

127

poor Bess's funeral. You're coming, I take it?'

'Yes, father. We'll go together. Best to stick to one's own.'

'That's right, lass. You stick with me and you'll come to no harm.'

Late on Tuesday evening, Nicholas woke up. His head had stopped aching, he could think clearly, and when he sat up, his body no longer hurt. He got out of bed and pulled on his breeches. Quickly he splashed water on his face from the ewer which Geoffrey had placed ready for him, and turned to find the rest of his clothes. The door opened and Geoffrey came in, looking worried.

'I'm glad to see you're better, sir. There's a messenger downstairs, just arrived from the King. You've got to leave for London, sir. This time they've sent a coach, and after the horses have rested the man says he wants to leave. Oh my Lord, you're not . . .'

Nicholas sighed and finished dressing. 'No, I'm not being arrested, yet. Thank God there's not a drop of Yorkist blood in my veins. Now go and look after the coachman, see that his horses are fed and watered, and get some food ready. I could eat a good cut of beef nicely grilled over the fire, then pack my bags – I'll want some warm clothes as it'll be cold where I'm going. Oh, and Geoffrey . . .'

'Yes, my Lord,' he said with a long-suffering look. 'What else?'

'Did Mistress Jane come back?'

'After you went to sleep? No, my Lord. There's been no sign of her all day.'

'Now I wonder where she's gallivanted off to! I wanted to have a word with her. Never mind, it can't be helped. Now go along, Geoffrey. There's no time to lose.'

Chapter Twelve

'Peverell,' the letter began. The King had written the letter himself; the handwriting was unmistakable, elegant and clear. 'We want this tiresome disturbance in your part of the country obliterated; not one spark left to light another conflagration. To achieve this, we must get Mortimer to speak. We want you to persuade him to reveal the names of his fellow conspirators. We order you to proceed to our Tower in London and try to reason with him. So far, under the gentler tortures he has said nothing. When we proceed to the worst, he might weaken. His wife is with him in the Tower. If you think it necessary, take her with you when you go to see him. Her presence might just achieve the desired effect. Nothing can save him from eventual execution, but should he co-operate with us, we could release him from the full rigours of a traitor's death. When you've extracted the vital information, come to see us at Hampton Court on the way home. We are looking forward to a period of relaxation in the country when we come to visit your house in the very near future.

Yours Henry T.'

Nicholas read the letter again, then carefully placed it on the glowing log in the fireplace and watched it turn to ashes. Then he turned to Geoffrey Lowe.

'An extra cloak, Geoffrey.'

'It's done, my Lord.'

'Are the horses rested?' he asked the coachman, who was finishing off a plateful of bread, cheese and cold beef.

'Well enough,' he said, brushing the crumbs off his jacket. 'I picked up fresh horses at Duncton on the way down, they should get us to Merrow.'

'Then let's go. And Geoffrey . . .'

'My Lord?'

'I might be away longer than usual. See to it that this place is ready for guests by the time I come back. I'll want to see the stock cupboards full, the cellars replenished and the staff briefed.'

'Is it to Hampton Court you're going, my lord?'

'Not this time, Geoffrey. Where I'm going, there's no laughter, no dancing, no music. I'm going to hell, but God willing I won't be staying there long. I'll be back as soon as I can. Oh, and tell Mistress Jane to guard herself. Oh, one other thing . . .'

'My Lord?'

'Tell her I'll miss her.'

The maze of fetid streets and lanes, usually teeming with people, were strangely quiet that stiflingly hot day, as the coach made its way through the city and up Tower Hill. London was in the grip of the sweating sickness, the Court had moved to Hampton Court and most people either stayed indoors or took to the river. As the mighty postern gate swung open to receive them, Nicholas shuddered. When he heard it clang shut behind him he thought of those words of Dante's written over the entrance to hell – Abandon hope all ye who enter here.

The Lieutenant of the Tower, Sir Philip Digby, an elderly, military figure with thinning hair and grizzled beard, greeted him and personally conducted him to his room. At least, Nicholas thought, he hadn't had to arrive by the river entrance, the traitor's gate. That was reserved for the Mortimers of this world.

His room was at the top of one of the smaller towers in

the inner courtyard. It was a small room with immensely thick stone walls, small windows, with a narrow bed, a table with an ewer on it, and a chair. But at least there was a rug on the floor and the coverlet on the bed was clean.

'I trust you have everything you need here,' said Digby courteously. 'I'll send someone to light the fire for you. These rooms are always cold.'

Nicholas nodded. Yes, he thought, the sun's warmth would never penetrate these walls.

'Thomas Cromwell's just one floor below you, Lord Nicholas. His room's next to the council chamber, which we reserve for the use of the King's ministers. One of the guards will escort you to him when you're ready. I hope you'll come and dine with me later on when this grim business is over?'

'Thank you, Sir Philip, I should be delighted, but I doubt that I shall have much appetite.'

Digby left him, and he washed his face and hands, laid his two cloaks on the bed, and went out to meet Thomas Cromwell.

Cromwell was in his usual place, behind a desk. He looked up as Nicholas went in and his coarse, putty-coloured face with its bulbous nose, creased into a smile. He stood up, rubbing his hands together nervously as he always did. Dressed in a grey robe with a fur trimming at its neck, the front fastened with a silver brooch bearing the Tudor rose, he seemed to blend in perfectly with the sombre grey walls of the Tower.

'Come in, come in, Lord Nicholas,' he said with his usual *bonhomie*. 'It's good to see you again. I hope you had a good journey and everything here is to your satisfaction.'

'Apart from the inconvenience of being dragged up here when I could be at home working on my estate, yes.'

'Duty calls, my Lord. The King needs you at this moment,' said Cromwell, going over to kick up the logs on the fire, and lifting the back of his robe, he took up his

131

position with his back to the flames. 'Now let's not beat about the bush . . .'

'I appreciate that, Master Cromwell. The sooner I am given my instructions, the sooner I can leave this place.'

'Quite. You know, of course, we have a prisoner here – a neighbour of yours, I understand – who's guilty of the heinous crime of treason.'

'So, is it coming to this, that we now pass sentence on people without trial?'

'Of course he'll stand trial when the time comes, but the evidence against Sir Roger Mortimer is overwhelming. His signature is on several letters to Reginald Pole. Southampton, as you know, has been intercepting this correspondence for some time now, and the evidence has been piling up against Mortimer. But before he stands trial, it's imperative we extract information from him. As we said before, you nourish a nest of hornets in your part of the world. We've got the main ringleader, now we have to flush out the others.'

'Maybe there are no others. Maybe the conspiracy ends with Mortimer and Catchpole.'

'Don't live in a fool's paradise, my Lord. The conspiracy is not over. Mortimer was one of the instigators; Catchpole's a fool. He knows nothing, but he's a babbler and he refuses to recognise the King's lawful claim to be head of our Church. His name has never been found in any of the Pole correspondence. He'll end up at Tyburn. But Mortimer's a different kettle of fish. He was plotting with Pole to remove the King from the throne, and there are others who worked with him. And they are still out there. Just listen to this. I received it from Southampton two days ago. I'll only read the bit which concerns you.

'It's been brought to my attention that Lord Nicholas Peverell is soon going to entertain a great concourse of people from Court. Some say that the King himself is coming. Is this true? If it is, then I am deeply worried that his life could be in danger. My men have intercepted a

132

letter to Pole telling him, about these events, and the writer asks for instructions. He signs himself ULTOR.'

Cromwell looked up. 'How's your Latin, my Lord?'

'Good enough to know that *ultor* means avenger, punisher. Who the hell is this fellow?'

'That's for you to find out.'

'It's impossible.'

'Mortimer will know. Get him to tell you.'

'And if he doesn't?'

'Then you will have to face up to the prospect of having the King coming to stay with you and there's someone out there planning to assassinate him.'

'We don't know that for sure.'

'I think there's no doubt that that's what this Ultor's instructions will be. And may I remind you, my Lord, it's your fault we're in this mess.'

'What the hell do you mean? I didn't ask the King to come and stay with me.'

'No, but you let your servant babble to all and sundry and now everyone knows the King's coming to your place.'

'Now let's get this clear. I have never mentioned the King's name to anyone, not even to my bailiff. I told him to get the place ready, to hire servants, to stock up with food. And that's what he's been doing, and that's what everyone's been noticing. People aren't stupid and in a small village like Dean Peverell they notice everything. No one knows that the King's coming. The writer of that letter, this Ultor, isn't even sure.'

'No, but he suspects, and this puts the King in great danger. We shall hold you responsible for his safety when he's with you.'

'I live in a country house, Master Cromwell. It's not a fortress. I have no retainers to guard the King's person. You'll have to dissuade the King from coming.'

'If you think I can do that, then you don't know the King. He's set his heart on this visit. The fleet are expecting him. But out there in those woods and fields which

133

surround your house, an assassin lurks. You must find out who he is and deal with him before the King gets to you.' Only Mortimer knows his name, and you must make him give it to you.'

'If you think Mortimer will betray an accomplice, then you don't know Mortimer.'

'Don't be so sure. He's already had two days' torture with the manacles, and he's almost broken. A couple of turns on the rack and he'll be ready to tell us everything we need to know.'

'And if he still doesn't talk?'

'Well, if needs must, we have Lady Mortimer here in the Tower. We could bring her along to talk to her husband, and when he sees her he'll talk. They always do.'

'This is barbarous,' shouted Nicholas, appalled at the prospect of Lady Margot having to endure the sight of her husband being tortured.

'Maybe, but the law is the law. Treason is a hideous crime, the penalties must be severe. Now, if you're ready, perhaps you'd like to have a chat with Mortimer and see what you can do.'

Cromwell summoned the guard, and Nicholas was asked to follow him. Sick at heart, Nicholas followed him out to the great central keep, built by the first King William to defend London against invaders, and down steep, stone steps to the dungeons below.

At first, Nicholas didn't recognise him. Sir Roger had been starved, hung up by his hands from manacles fixed to the wall, which had torn his wrists, and the iron gauntlets, which he'd been forced to wear, had broken his hands. But he had not revealed the names of his fellow conspirators. Now, in the dungeon of the central keep of the Tower, he'd been stretched out upon a great oak frame which was raised from the ground. His wrists and ankles were attached by cords to rollers at each end of the frame. Two men wearing blood-splattered leather aprons stood by the levers which

134

turned the rollers and stretched the body on the rack until the bones cracked and arms and legs were dislocated, if necessary.

The low, vaulted room was dimly lit by guttering rush lights and the walls dripped with moisture on to the stone floor, as the dungeon was almost at the level of the Thames. The room stank of sweat and terror and unimaginable pain. Overwhelmed, Nicholas sank down on his knees by the side of Mortimer's ravaged face, which was almost obscured by the sweat-soaked dark hair. Where was the strong, middle-aged man he'd seen only last week polishing the gleaming chestnut-coloured flanks of his horse, Galliard? In a matter of days he'd been reduced to this ghastly wreck, a travesty of a human being.

'Sir Roger,' said Nicholas looking down into the dark eyes, glazed with pain and staring at him without comprehension. 'This is a terrible sight.'

'It could be ended,' said the voice of Digby, who had to be present at these occasions. 'Just tell us the names of your fellow conspirators and we can release you from this torment.'

Mortimer turned his head away, and said nothing. Digby nodded to the two men standing by the levers. They turned the rollers and gradually, inexorably, Mortimer's body was stretched so that his bones cracked. Mortimer screamed, an inhuman sound, like an animal torn to bits by the hounds. Nicholas covered his ears and Digby motioned the men to stop.

'For God's sake, Sir Roger, just give me the names. Why not end this pain? Think of your family, your children ...'

'I think of nothing else, Peverell,' said Mortimer in a faint whisper. 'I've been told my wife is here. She mustn't see me like this. Tell her I love her, and Peverell, if the worst should happen to me, you'll look after her, won't you? She knows nothing about all this and the children are innocent.'

135

'We just need one name, Sir Roger, and then you will be taken back to your cell. Who is Ultor?'

Mortimer's body twitched involuntarily and he groaned. Looking straight into Nicholas's face he said only one word. 'Never.'

The levers turned the rollers again, and Mortimer shrieked in torment, the sound reverberating around the room. Nicholas forced himself to look down into Mortimer's sweat-soaked face, now streaked in blood where he'd almost bitten his tongue off in agony.

'Just one word, Sir Roger. For Christ's sake, let us put an end to all this.'

Mortimer's eyes were glazing over and he was nearly unconscious. 'I cannot tell,' he managed to say, the words so faint that Nicholas had to lower his head towards those blood-smeared lips.

Nicholas got up and faced Sir Philip Digby. 'You must stop this barbarity,' he said. 'Sir Roger will never tell us what we want to know. Do you want him to expire on this fiendish instrument?'

'He'll not hold out much longer, my Lord. But I agree we mustn't lose him at this stage. Release him,' he said to the two men working the rollers. They untied the cords, lifted the limp body off the frame, and dowsed his face with a bucketful of cold water. 'We'll continue later. Take him back to his room. Now my Lord,' he said turning more cheerfully to Nicholas, 'we dine in two hours. Perhaps you'd like to freshen up, perhaps take a turn round the walls and get a breath of sweeter air from the river. Tomorrow, I'll take you to see Lady Margot, and we can go from there.'

Nicholas followed Digby up the stairs. Sickened and appalled by what he'd just witnessed, once back in his room, he flung himself down on his bed and tried to force the image of Mortimer's blood-soaked face and the sound of his cries out of his mind. And this was just the beginning.

136

Chapter Thirteen

That evening, Nicholas dined with Sir Philip Digby in the spacious apartment which had been allocated to him as Lieutenant of the Tower. Thomas Cromwell pleaded pressure of work and stayed in his room. Nicholas and Digby talked about everything except what they had witnessed that day, and as Nicholas had little appetite, he escaped to his own room as soon as possible.

Kicking off his boots and unfastening his doublet, he flung himself down on his bed. But sleep eluded him. A shaft of moonlight came through the narrow window and fell on his bed. He got up and looked out at the beautiful night sky, a canopy of velvety darkness punctuated by the brilliant dots of light from the stars. And illuminating everything with its mellow light, was the full moon. He breathed in the watery smell of the Thames, which he could just see in the distance, its surface lit by the twinkling lights from the lanterns of the ships riding at anchor. So much beauty, he thought, so much tranquillity; and yet, just a few yards away down in the dungeon of the great central keep, a man lay groaning in agony. Tomorrow his torment would increase until breaking point.

He shivered and went back to his bed. Dear God, he prayed, let Mortimer speak tomorrow. Then we can put an end to this diabolical torture.

He woke up just as the sun was rising over the marshes

of the Thames estuary. He washed and ran his fingers through his hair and beard. A servant brought his clean water and took away the night bucket. Another brought breakfast of boiled eggs and bread and a jug of small beer. He tried to eat but the food seemed to turn to gravel in his mouth. Then the guard came and escorted him down to that infernal place where, once again, Mortimer had been strapped to the rack.

It was obvious that Mortimer was very weak. Emaciated to the point where his bones almost protruded through his flesh, he looked like a bundle of old clothes, sweat-stained and streaked with blood, hardly human at all. His broken hands were now swollen with infection and he'd almost gone beyond pain as he turned his head when Nicholas came in and didn't make a sound. When he spoke, his voice was stronger and his brain seemed clear.

'So, my Lord, they've brought you here again. Now I wonder why that is? Are they warning you? Showing what could happen to you if you opposed the King? Not that you'd do that. You're too much of a time-server.'

'I'm the King's servant, just as all my family have been, and always will be. But, Sir Roger, you make a pitiful sight and I hope to God that you will make an end to this today. We only want one name; just one. Who is this Ultor? You must know him, because he speaks about you in his letters which Southampton has intercepted. Unless we know who he is, the King is in very great danger.'

'And I suppose they'll hold you responsible. But let me tell you this, Lord Nicholas, if they break every bone in this carcass of mine, I will never tell you the name of this man. Aaa ... '

The speech ended in a shriek of agony as Digby had arrived and had signalled to the two assistants to turn the rollers. Mortimer's body, already stretched to the point where broken blood vessels were oozing blood, seemed to disintegrate. He rolled his eyes in agony, and his breathing became short and laboured. But still he said nothing.

Digby turned in exasperation to Nicholas. 'This man is a stubborn fool. We haven't broken him yet, but, by God, we will. Get Lady Mortimer,' he said to the guard standing by the door.

His words revived Mortimer quicker than the bucket of water standing by the rack.

'No, no, for mercy's sake, spare me that.'

'It's up to you,' said Digby sternly. 'Give us just this one name and it will be over. Lady Mortimer can look after you. You know you can't take much more of this; do you want her to see you suffering *in extremis*? You, her husband and father of her children?'

'I cannot tell, but in the name of Christ, have mercy.'

'Mercy? I leave that to God. We've got a job to do.'

Nicholas heard footsteps coming down the stairs. He turned and she stood in the doorway, a tiny figure wrapped in a grey cloak. He went to meet her and her eyes when she looked up at him were dazed with terror. He tried to put an arm round her shoulders, but she shrank away from him.

'Lord Nicholas, what are you doing there?'

'For the same reason as you – to persuade Sir Roger to give us the names of his associates. We need only one name, but he will not co-operate.'

'He knows nothing. Oh God and His angels help us,' she said as she suddenly made out the figure on the rack. 'Husband, what are they doing to you?'

She tried to push her way forward but the guard restrained her. She fought him with the strength of a wild beast and he couldn't hold her. She ran forward and threw herself down on the floor beside her husband's body. She smoothed the matted hair back from his face and then collapsed over his body. Then two guards went over and pulled her away and she stood there sobbing.

'Tell your husband to give us the name we want and we can end this torture,' said Digby.

'Tell them, tell them,' she shrieked. 'Nothing in the world is worth dying for in such a way. Tell them for my sake and the sake of your children.'

He couldn't look at her. He closed his eyes, and his body was trembling and he was drenched in sweat.

'I cannot,' he said.

Then the assistants once again set about their task. This time there was a dreadful crack as both legs were dislocated under the tension. On the next turn, both arms would go.

Mortimer's scream was so terrible that even Digby recoiled. Lady Mortimer gave one cry and collapsed on the floor. The guards took hold of her and dragged her outside.

Then suddenly, it was quiet. Mortimer's body was limp on the rack. Nicholas went over to him and laid his head on the sweat-soaked chest. He felt nothing. The heart had stopped. Mortimer had made his own exit from that dungeon.

Nicholas stood up and crossed himself. 'He's gone,' he said to Digby, 'and may God have mercy on his soul.'

Digby turned to the two assistants. 'Stupid, clumsy fools. I told you not to be too strong.'

'Don't go blaming us, sir,' said the largest of the two men. 'Every man has his limits and this one's had a bad time. He was practically at his limit when you gave him to us. He's only human, flesh, blood and bones; and we can't stretch him forever like wool on the tenterhooks.'

'You should have given me a warning that he was getting to the end of his tether.'

'Not our job,' said the two simultaneously. 'You give the orders; we turn the levers.'

'It's terrible to die like this,' said Nicholas, appalled. 'No priest, no chance of making his peace with God. I must go to Lady Mortimer, Sir Philip. The sight she's just been forced to witness is enough to turn her mind.'

'The guards will see to her,' said Digby, his face still flushed with anger. 'You must look to yourself. The King's going to be in a right state when he hears about this. I wouldn't want to be in your shoes, my Lord. Take that man off that infernal machine,' he said to the men, 'and put him in the mortuary.'

'Let me take him home.'

'Home, my Lord? He hasn't got a home. He's a traitor, in case you've forgotten. He'll be buried here. We've a plot for the likes of him.'

'And Lady Mortimer?'

'That's for the King to decide. You'll have to speak to him. He'll be merciful, no doubt. She's done nothing. I expect she'll be sent to join her children back in her family home. Now, I'll order the coach to take you to Court.'

Feeling unspeakably wretched, Nicholas collected his things together. He asked to see Cromwell, but was told he was too busy to see him. He asked to see Lady Mortimer but they said she was still unconscious. The coach arrived and even the coachman didn't look at him. There was no Sir Philip to wish him God speed. The gatekeeper opened the postern gate, and the coach lumbered down Tower Hill. Despite everything, Nicholas breathed a sigh of relief. He'd escaped the Tower. This time.

The King was attending an archery competition in Richmond Park. There was no room prepared for Nicholas. He was shown into a small waiting room near the main gatehouse and told to stay there until someone sent for him. He asked for ale, and a servant brought a tankard of small beer and banged it down on the table resentfully. The writing was on the wall, thought Nicholas. Word had already got round and he was in disgrace.

Finally, another servant came and told him that the King would now see him. Outside, the coachman was waiting for him. He came up to Nicholas and stood there shuffling his feet as if uncertain how to begin.

'Out with it, man,' said Nicholas, not unkindly.

'It's nothing, really, my Lord, but I thought I ought to warn you. The King was beaten in the archery competition by the Earl of Surrey. He's in a very bad humour. Then, on the way home, his horse stumbled and he fell off in front of everybody. It wasn't a bad fall, just a blow on his shoulder, but it's put him in a right foul mood. Do you still want the horses stabled for the night?'

'By the sound of it, I'll not be long with the King. Give the horses a feed and I'll be with you soon. We'll put up at Merrow.'

'I'll see to it, my Lord. And . . . good luck.'

Feeling like a naughty schoolboy summoned to the head-master's study, and resenting every minute of it, Nicholas followed the servant into the King's presence. Why, he thought, hadn't he the courage to tell coachman John to bring round the coach immediately and drive home as fast as possible? Anything was better than this humiliating treat-ment for something he hadn't done.

Henry was still in his riding clothes. A servant was doing his best to tug off his long, leather riding boots slippery with mud. The King had unbuttoned his doublet and was roundly cursing everyone who tried to make him comfort-able. He glared at Nicholas with his small, piggy eyes, and continued berating the unfortunate servant, who was trying to get his undamaged arm out of the doublet.

'God's teeth, man, take care. My shoulder's as sore as hell. Do you want to kill me? Aaa . . .'

The man had removed one arm and was now eyeing the other apprehensively.

'Oh get out of here, you lumbering fool,' he shouted. 'Come here, Peverell, make yourself useful for once and get me out of this coat.'

The servant fled, and Nicholas approached the King. Gently he began to ease the coat over the King's shoulder.

'A nasty bruise you've got there, your Majesty.'

'That brute of a horse was all over the place. Take care, Peverell, it hurts.'

Then Nicholas had a flash of inspiration. 'Allow me,' he said. He took out his knife, which he always carried on a belt round his waist, and with one slash, cut away the mate-rial of the sleeve. The arm appeared as neatly as a sausage from its skin. The King looked at the two halves in aston-

142

ishment, then roared with laughed. 'So, you've cut the Gordian knot, Peverell. You're a right Alexander the Great. Mind you, you'll have to buy me a new coat.'

'Only one sleeve, your Grace.'

'One sleeve! Damn it, you've got a cheek. You've ruined the whole garment, you fool. You'll have to replace it for me.'

Nicholas bowed, mentally adding the cost of buying a new doublet to the already huge cost of entertaining the King. The servant eased off the boots, and the King stood up in his stockinged feet.

'Well, Peverell,' he said, turning to confront Nicholas. 'It seems you've been a disappointment to me.'

'Your Grace . . .'

'Oh, don't start making excuses, it's not your style. I've heard that Mortimer died under torture despite my express wish that he should live. A dead traitor who's kept his mouth shut is no use to me. That fool Digby . . .'

'Mortimer was very near the end, your Grace. His heart couldn't take any more. Four days of torture and starvation had weakened him too much.'

'Digby should've slowed down the last bit.'

'The last bit dislocated both legs.'

'Oh spare me the details, Peverell.'

'And it wasn't a good idea to bring in Lady Mortimer. She fainted, and Mortimer gave up at that point. He'd begged us not to let his wife see him in that condition. I fear that the memory of those last few minutes will haunt Lady Mortimer for the rest of her life.'

'Oh don't be so melodramatic, Peverell. Mortimer was a traitor. Unfortunately for you there are others out there and we don't know who they are.'

'I'll do my utmost to track them down.'

'You'd better, Peverell. Remember I'm coming to stay with you in ten days' time. You've got that time to catch the devils. Well, what are you waiting for? I'm ravenous and you've got a long journey ahead of you. You're

143

dismissed,' he shouted as Nicholas still stood there.

'Your Grace, Lady Mortimer ... will you allow her to return to her house? After all, she's done nothing.'

'That soft heart of yours will be the death of you, Peverell. What happens to Mortimer's house and his widow is entirely my business. But don't fret, man, you know I'm a merciful man. I'll send a coach to take her home to her family. They live in the other end of your county, I hear. She'll be reunited with her children, never fear. She might even marry again as she's still young. Now, don't mention this matter to me again. It bores me, and I can hardly concern myself with the fate of the wives and families of traitors. Now get away with you, man.'

Nicholas bowed and backed away from the King. Henry Tudor was a hard taskmaster, he thought. No offer of dinner, no accommodation, just a kick up the backside.

'Oh, and Peverell ...'

'Your Majesty?'

'Don't forget my new coat. See what the Marchester haberdashers can come up with. Green, I think, suitable for the country. Velvet, of course, with slashed sleeves. White silk lining. Just right for a summer idyll.'

'I'll do my best.'

'See that it's a good one. Oh, one other thing. I'll be bringing along a handful of my Yeomen of the Guard. See to it that they're given suitable accommodation. After all, with your county crawling with assassins, I shall need some protection.'

Cursing his luck, Peverell returned to the waiting coach. God damn them all, he thought as he ordered the coachman to drive off, he'd get a good dinner at Merrow if it was the last thing he'd do.

Chapter Fourteen

There they were again! Three women, outside the ale-house on the corner of the main street where it joined the main coast road. Usually Jane steered well clear of gossips. But that Friday morning there was an air of intensity about them that made her rein in Melissa and dismount. They were so engrossed in their discussion that they hadn't seen her ride up, until the ale-keeper's wife, Biddy Tomkins, turned round and noticed her. Biddy was a large, ungainly woman with a figure sagging from the birth of her seven children, four of whom were up in the churchyard. She wore her usual brown dress with a dirty apron fastened round her drooping belly. Her straggly grey hair was partly concealed under a grey cap, and her rugged face was criss-crossed with enlarged veins, the result of an over-enthusiastic sampling of her husband's brewing. When she recognised Jane her face broke into a deferential smile, revealing a row of blackened teeth which lurched round her mouth like ancient tombstones up in the graveyard.

'My, my, it's Mistress Warrener. To what do we owe the honour of your company?'

'To bid you good morning.'

'That's mighty courteous of you.'

'And find out what's new?'

'Well may you ask,' said one of the other women, an aged crone, her body almost bent double so that she had to turn her head sideways to look at Jane. Everyone called her Old Emily, and no one knew who her family was and how she'd come to live in Dean Peverell. 'There's lots of strange things going on around here. Too many for comfort, I think.'

'Really? Now what can they be, I wonder.'

'Well, for a start, my hen has stopped laying. Just once the old girl produced an egg, and then no more for two weeks now. Whilst her up there, now her hens are laying all the time.'

'Who are you talking about, Emily?'

'Why her, of course. Old Agnes Myles. That stuck-up old bitch who's too proud to come and talk to us,' said Biddy, her face flushing angrily.

'Agnes? Don't be so foolish. She's done you no harm. Her hens are always good layers, and anyway, at this time of the year, hens are always unpredictable. Just wait a day or two, and yours will be laying nineteen to the dozen.'

'My hens have given up, too,' said the third woman, the weaver's skinny wife; someone who Jane always tried to avoid. She had a small, pointed face, a bitter expression and a spiteful tongue. Her name was Matty; 'And there's another thing,' she said, 'Agnes Myles was there when Abigail Butcher's latest baby was born, and look what happened to him. He was all twisted and bent like a piece of old thorn bush and couldn't get his breath properly and he died hours later before they could get the priest to baptise him. Terrible it was. And who's fault was that, may I ask?'

'Babies often die,' said Jane impatiently, 'it's one of the facts of life. You can't blame Agnes for that.'

'You can, if she's a . . .' said Biddy ominously.

'A what?' said Jane, suddenly feeling a prickling of fear. 'What are you saying?'

'Why, she's a witch, Mistress Warrener. That's what we're saying. She's a nasty, evil old witch.'

'Stop this talk at once, all of you. You don't know what you're staying. Agnes is a healer. You've all benefited

146

from her treatment when you were ill.'

'She didn't cure my aching bones,' said Emily resentfully. 'She said there was nothing she could do for me. Gave me some ointment to rub on my back, and what happened? It got even more crooked.'

'That's got nothing to do with Agnes. She can't make you young again.'

'Now don't you start telling me what's right and what's wrong. We know, don't we,' Matty said, turning to the others for support. 'And we also know what went on up in the woods.'

'Oh, and what nonsense are you going to tell me, now?'

'It's not nonsense. It's a fact. They do say that witches can turn themselves into filthy demons if they've a mind to. Well, his Lordship was up there in the woods on his horse when out from behind a tree she pounced, disguised as a spirit from hell. Horrible it was. No wonder his Lordship's horse bolted and he fell off. It was a mercy he didn't kill himself.'

'That's rubbish. I found him and got help. He said it was a trick of the light on the leaves that frightened his horse. Spirits, demons, witches! You're all a poisonous lot of gossips.'

'And you, Mistress Warrener, are riding for a fall, too,' said Biddy. 'We all know what you're up to. You're always up at the Manor strolling around with his Lordship, even visiting him in his bedroom, so we've heard. Well, don't you come the high and mighty with us. His Lordship'll tire of you soon, and don't you come running to us when it all goes wrong. And where will you be, may I ask, when all the great lords and ladies come to his house? Do you think he'll want to walk out with you then? Oh no, you'll come creeping back to that old father of yours and no one will ever look at you again.'

'You've got a foul mind, Biddy Tomkins. There's no harm in me talking to Lord Nicholas.'

'Nothing at all, if it's only talking.'

147

The three of them cackled and spluttered and, impatiently, Jane turned to jump up on Melissa's back.

'That's right, you ride away on that horse of yours. But don't say we didn't warn you. There's changes coming to this village. They do say that the monks will be kicked out soon, Mortimer's gone and we don't know what'll happen to his place, and now they're saying the King's coming. Think of that. And we don't want any dirty old witch around here putting curses on his Highness.'

Jane turned and rounded on Biddy. 'Now what mischief are you saying? The King's coming here? Who told you that?'

'It's common knowledge, Mistress Warrener. You ought to talk to us a bit more. A bright girl like you ought to keep up with the news.'

Agnes was in the wooden hut at the end of her garden. She was tying fresh rosemary into bundles ready to hang up on the rafters for use next winter. The room was full of the pungent scent of herbs, like the church after Sunday's High Mass. She looked up as Jane came in.

'Come in, Jane. It's good to see you again.'

Jane walked over to the table and ran her fingers through the pile of herbs, smoothing out the grey-green spiky leaves of the rosemary. Gradually, the anger in her subsided. She picked up a bunch of rosemary and buried her face in it, inhaling deeply. 'Um, lovely. I envy you your healing talents.'

'It's nothing special. It's just a question of knowing which of God's plants is suitable for any particular ailment. I've studied them all my life, remember. Even the dangerous ones have a use if you know the right dosage. But what can I do for you?'

'You've heard the news, of course?'

'My dear, the village is buzzing like a beehive with news.'

'Do you know that a whole lot of people from Court are coming to the Manor?'

148

'Oh that! Yes, I've heard, and I feel sorry for Lord Nicholas. He's going to have his work cut out feeding and entertaining that mob. Master Lowe's been here and commandeered all my eggs for the next three weeks. Still, he says he'll give me a good price for them. Seems my hens are the best layers in the village. I hope his Lordship's coming home soon, otherwise Master Lowe's mind's going to give way under the worry of it all.'

'They say that the King's coming.'

Agnes put down the bundle of herbs and looked at Jane, suddenly serious.

'Best not to listen to gossip, Jane. Wait until Lord Nicholas tells you himself. There's all sorts of rumours flying around but no one knows for sure. Only his Lordship, of course. We'll all be glad if King Henry comes here, not that we'll see much of him, but it's best not too many people know about it. Master Lowe told me nothing and that's how it should be. The King's the King, and these are dangerous times. Now, I've nothing against Harry Tudor, but others might not agree with me. So steer clear of gossips, Jane.'

'Agnes, there's something else I must tell you.'

'Why, my dear, how serious you look. Come now, we've never kept things from each other, have we, so what is it?'

'I've just been talking to Biddy Tomkins . . .'

'Now what made you do that? Nothing good ever came out of Biddy Tomkin's mouth. She's nothing but a bawdy ale-house keeper's wife, a trouble-maker if ever there was one.'

Ambrose strolled in, rubbed himself round Jane's skirts, then sat down in a pool of sunshine in the doorway and proceeded to wash his face and whiskers with delicate precision.

'There are rumours going around . . .'

'There always are when Biddy Tomkins opens her mouth.'

149

'Abigail Butcher's child died recently.'

'I know. The poor, wee babe. But it was only to be expected with his spine twisted all over the place. There was no room in his chest for his breath. But the Lord gives, and the Lord taketh away, and it's not for us to question His ways. And I daresay it's better for the babe to be in Heaven with the angels with a good, strong body, than having to endure a wretched life down here with us.'

'You were there when he was born?'

'Yes. Abigail asked me to give the others a hand. It was a bitter labour. Jane, what are you saying?'

'It's not what I'm saying, it's what they're saying. People are also saying that it's strange that your hens are laying and theirs aren't.'

'That's because I feed them on corn and barley which I saved over the winter. Now what's all this about, my dear?' she said, as she wiped her hands on her apron and came over to put her arms round Jane's shoulders. 'Come on, look at me, and say what you have to say.'

'They say you're a witch, Agnes. That you cursed Abigail's child, turned yourself into a demon and frightened Lord Nicholas's horse up in the woods, and cursed all their hens so that they won't lay any eggs.'

Agnes threw back her head and laughed, a full-bodied, merry laugh that made Ambrose stop his ablutions and gaze at her disapprovingly with his huge, yellow eyes.

'I know it sounds preposterous. I know you're a healer, not a destroyer. I know you're one of the holiest people I've ever met, that you're on the side of the angels and wouldn't hurt a living soul. But the rumours are going round, like a fire in a field of dry hay and soon it'll be roaring through the village. Agnes, I'm afraid for you. Someone's started these rumours. Someone's got it in for you. Have you any idea who it could be? Anyone you've offended? Perhaps you turned someone away because you couldn't help him and he resented it. Think hard, Agnes, because we've got to put a stop to these rumours. There's nothing that excites the popular imagination as much as the cry of "witchcraft". It's but a short step towards the next cry "Hang the witch!" I feel that you're in real danger. Why don't you come and live with us for the time being? My father, as you know, is a bit cantankerous, but he won't tolerate any superstitious nonsense. You'll be safe with us.'

'Thank you for coming and warning me, Jane, but I'll stay here, if you don't mind. I know only too well what happens to witches. Up on Marchester Heath the bodies of two women condemned for witchcraft still hang from the gibbets. I expect that already they're saying that Ambrose here is my familiar. But I have a clear conscience. I wouldn't know how to cast a spell on anyone even if I wanted to, which I don't. People come here to ask me to help them. Some things I can't cure, and I always say so. I never give people wrong advice just to keep them happy. Even the holy monks come and consult me sometimes. Ask them if they think I'm a witch! As for babies dying and hens not laying eggs, that's all part of the natural world; and it's got nothing to do with me. I know how to prescribe a potion to make people with troubled minds go to sleep, and I know how to ease stiff joints and relieve coughs and fevers, but that's a gift which comes from God, not His adversary, the devil. Now don't you worry about me, my dear. Why don't you come inside and I'll make you a herbal drink with honey, and we'll forget all about these gossips.'

Jane left Agnes's cottage and rode up to the common to give Melissa a good gallop. She wanted to order her mind. Ahead of her was Mortimer Lodge, usually such a peaceful sight; but now an atmosphere of malevolence hung over it which seemed to contaminate the surrounding countryside. She avoided the wood. Something was going wrong in this little community, she thought. A family broken up through one man's treachery, two innocent people dying because they unwittingly overheard an incriminating conversation, and now a harmless old lady accused of witchcraft. But why pick on Agnes at this particular time? Agnes had always been held in high esteem. People called her a wise woman, even a holy woman. There'd never been a hint of witchcraft. What had she done? Had she, too, overheard something? Was someone trying to get rid of her?

Deeply perturbed, she turned Melissa back towards home. But first she had to see Prior Thomas. He wanted her to sing to his special guests who were due to arrive at any moment, and she wanted to look through the programme and maybe have a rehearsal with Brother Benedict.

Nicholas slept fitfully whilst the coach lurched and jolted over the rough roads of West Sussex. They reached home just as the servants were waking up and the labourers were setting off to work in the fields. Nicholas climbed stiffly out of the coach, dazed by tiredness, with his body aching from the rough journey and still sore from the fall he'd had in the woods.

A boy, sleepily rubbing his eyes and frantically trying to tie up the fastening on his trousers, opened the main gate. Nicholas had never seen him before.

'Who are you?'

'Anthony, sir. Geoffrey's nephew.'

'And where do you come from, and what are you doing here?'

'I live in Marchester, sir, and I've been offered a job as general servant. Geoffrey's had to take on a lot of new hands.'

At that moment, Geoffrey came running out to meet them. He, too, looked as if he needed a good night's sleep, although his worried face broke into a smile of relief when he saw Nicholas.

'Welcome home, my Lord. I don't know whether I'm coming or going at the moment, what with all the provisioning and the preparation of the rooms, I'm at my wits' end. I need you to guide me.'

'I'm sure you've got things well under control, but let me have something to eat, for God's sake, before we start on our domestic problems.'

Over a plateful of fried bacon and half a dozen eggs, Nicholas listened to Geoffrey's tale of woe: not enough beds, not enough servants, not enough food, not enough chairs ... Finally, just as Geoffrey seemed to be on the point of collapse, he blurted out, 'And they do say, my Lord, that the King's coming.'

Nicholas carefully mopped up the last drop of egg yolk with his bread, swung round and looked at Geoffrey.

'I suppose the whole world knows by now?'

'Bound to. The sailors talk about nothing else in the Portsmouth taverns. Seems he's going to look at the ships on the seventh so I suppose he'll be coming here on the sixth? It's too soon, my Lord. I'll never be ready.'

'Calm down, Geoffrey. I know there's a lot to do, but I daresay the Prior will come to our rescue. He can put up a whole lot of people on the top floor of the guest house, the servants, the valets. We'll have the most important people here, the King, of course, and his senior courtiers. Now listen carefully, Geoffrey. I know the problem you have of feeding this mob, but believe me it's nothing compared to the problem I'm going to have with guarding the King. He's a difficult man to keep under control and I don't want him wandering off anywhere on his own. He's bringing some of the Yeomen of the Guard – no, don't get alarmed,' he said as Geoffrey exclaimed in horror. 'They'll have to stay here with us, and we've got to put them up near the King. They'll have their instructions, of course, but I want you to co-operate with them one hundred per cent. Now, Geoffrey, I want you to swear that you won't go round prattling to everybody about this. Let people talk, but don't give them any information. It would be the most terrible thing if the King should come to any harm in my house. Remember our motto – always loyal.

'I shall need a list of everyone employed in this house;

153

their names and where they've come from. Anyone coming here to apply for a job must be turned away. Even if we're short-handed we must know who our servants are and we must be sure of their loyalty. Now I want that list immediately, as I shall have to check every person on it with you. I must insist on tight security at all times from now on, Geoffrey. If in doubt about anything, consult me. On the sixth of June, I want only those people known to us to be in this house. Anyone not on our list, or not on the King's list which I shall expect him to send down to me with his steward, is to be sent away. Is that clear? Don't worry about provisions; I'll see what the Prior's got in his store cupboard. But first I must go to Marchester and see Landstock.'

'But surely, my Lord, you should rest first.'

'No time for that. Get Harry saddled up. I can rest later.'

'But where's the King going to sleep?'

'The King? In my bed of course. Unless he brings his own bed with him.'

'And the Queen?'

'She'll have to have a room, I suppose.'

'How many meals?'

'For God's sake, Geoffrey, don't be such an old woman. I don't know. At least three feasts, I should think. One when they arrive, one on the seventh, unless Southampton's going to feed them, one after the hunt on the eighth.'

'And will they want entertainment?'

'Bound to. Something simple. Jane Warrener can sing to them with Brother Benedict. Some dancing, I suppose. Nothing vigorous, the Queen's not into dancing these days. The Prior and the Precentor can rustle up some musicians between them, I expect. Now off with you and get me Harry.'

Chapter Fifteen

'Ah, Lord Nicholas,' said Richard Landstock, jumping to his feet. 'I hoped you'd come today. You've become damned elusive. You're too much away at Court, my Lord. We need you here. Sit down, man, you look all in. Too much roistering, I suppose! Let me get you some ale.'

'Thanks,' said Nicholas accepting the tankard of ale which Landstock poured out for him from the jug on the table. 'God, that's good,' he said as he drank deeply, wiping away the line of froth along his top lip with the back of his hand. 'Now let's get this straight. I haven't been roistering, as you call it, but witnessing a barbaric interrogation sanctioned by our legal system.'

'There speaks the Justice of the Peace. I hope you're not going to turn soft on us, my Lord. Our safety depends on suspects owning up to their crimes. How else can we catch criminals? Or don't you want them caught? Perhaps you don't mind your barns raided and your stewards murdered?'

'Of course I want them caught. It's just sickening to watch someone under torture.'

'Teach the others a lesson, though. You'd think twice about raising a hand against the King once you've seen what you've just seen, wouldn't you?'

'I could no more lift my hand against the King than fly to the moon.'

'There you are, then. It worked. You'll stay loyal to the end of your life. But now, let me tell you what's been happening here. Whilst you've been away, I've been sorting out your affairs.'

'My affairs?'

'Concerning your steward, or rather your erstwhile steward, Matthew Hayward, or have you forgotten all about him?'

'I thought we'd cleared that up.'

'Not entirely. We know Giles Yelman let the killers in to your house. We've now got the killers. We sent Yelman to Lewes for interrogation, but fortunately, he's no hero. In fact, he named the killers as soon as he saw the manacles in Lewes prison. Now he's in custody waiting for the Assize judge to come. The hangman'll be the last man he'll see.'

'Who are the killers?'

'Two labourers who worked for Mortimer. They had a good alibi but we've cracked that. They said they were in the ale-house in the cattle market here in Marchester Monday of last week – the night Hayward was killed – but a witness says that he saw them walking along the road to your house. I checked with the ale-house keeper and his cronies, but no one could say for certain that the two men were there that night. Probably they didn't hand out enough free ale. You've got to be generous when you want someone to tell lies for you.'

'Where are they now?'

'Here in Marchester, in my prison. No need to send them to Lewes. They'll come up before you at Quarter Sessions in June.'

'You've done well, Richard. By the way, have you got any further with the investigation into Bess Knowles's death?'

'There is no investigation. Coroner was quite sure: death through natural causes. Aren't you satisfied?'

'I've got an open mind. She was Matthew's intended, as you know. She probably knew as much as Matthew about what was going on here.'

156

'That's as maybe. She's in the churchyard now, and that's the end of the road, unless new evidence comes forward. But any more news about Sir Roger? His arrest caused quite a stir, I can tell you.'

'He died yesterday in the Tower.'

'Are you sure of that, my Lord?'

'Quite sure. I was there; so was his wife.'

'What the hell did they do to him?'

'What do you expect? He died on the rack, under interrogation.'

'What was he accused of?'

'Treason. High treason.'

'Is that true?'

'Oh, quite true. His name was on letters addressed to Reginald Pole. Unfortunately for Mortimer, Southampton picked them up before they reached the Continent, read them and passed the information on to the King.'

'Do they know who else was in the conspiracy?'

'No. Mortimer wouldn't speak.'

'He wouldn't. He was too much of a fanatic. Now we've got the King coming, and we don't know for sure if the conspiracy's been well and truly stamped out. Someone might be out there ready to carry on where Mortimer left off. I don't envy you, my Lord.'

'Thanks for the sympathy. But we are not entirely in the dark. Mortimer wouldn't betray his accomplices, but we do know the code name of one of them, and the name of the conspiracy.'

'Which is?'

'It's called The Day of Wrath. The leader signs himself Ultor.'

'What the hell does that mean? Latin means nothing to me.'

'It means avenger, punisher.'

'Good God, to think this is all happening here in Marchester, a place where usually nothing happens except drunken brawling and petty theft.'

157

'Well, now you've got something to get your teeth into, Sheriff.'

'What I can't understand is why Mortimer should support Reginald Pole, for heaven's sake? I've heard he's more interested in a cardinal's hat than the King's crown.'

'You could be right, but it's more a case of who he is than what he wants. You know that the mother of the Pole brothers is the Countess of Salisbury, who, in turn is the daughter of George, brother to Edward IV, the King's grandfather. So they are the King's cousins and, more to the point, they're Yorkists through and through. If the Pole brothers aren't interested in the crown, then Lord Montague, their brother, would certainly risk his life for it. If the King doesn't stamp out this family, then they will be a constant thorn in his side. I can see the time coming when the Countess of Salisbury and two of her sons will all mount the scaffold on Tower Green. If Reginald Pole accepts a cardinal's hat and stays on the Continent until times change, he'll be the only one in that family to survive. The King, Richard, is not secure on his throne as long as there are any Yorkists left. And that's why Lady Mortimer will never be reinstated in her husband's house. Her family are all related to the Countess of Salisbury. The King promised to be merciful, though, and she'll go back to live with her children at the other end of the county.'

'A pity all these Yorkists chose to live around here. My God, Peverell, what are we going to do?'

'Protect the King; and find Ultor. And we start now. I want you to get your spies out. Get them into the ale-houses, particularly the Portsmouth ones, and tell them to pin their ears back. We've got just ten days to sort this lot out. Just think of the consequences if this Ultor gets the King.'

'You've got to guard your house well, my Lord.'

'I'll do my best. Henry Tudor isn't an easy man to guard. He'll be at his most vulnerable when he leaves me on the seventh of June to ride to Portsmouth Point. He's

158

bound to go on horseback as it isn't very far and he'll want to show himself off to his people. An admirable quality, but I'd be a lot happier if he decided to keep his Queen company in the royal coach. The Yeomen of the Guard can protect a coach, but not a man on a horse who wants to show off to the watching crowd.'

'I'll get the constables out . . .'

'That's a start. Get Fitzroy to raise a muster. At least we can line the Portsmouth road with bowmen. They'll have to check all travellers.'

'We could stop all traffic on the road until the King's clear.'

'He'll never allow that. As far as he's concerned, his subjects love him and he wants them to see him. I can just hear him – let no one be inconvenienced! Except me, that is.'

'I wouldn't change place with you, my Lord, even if they handed me Peverell Manor on a plate.'

'Play your cards right, Richard, and it just might happen. If I make one slip, then I, too, will end up in the Tower; and next time, I won't come out. Oh, and one other thing,' Nicholas said turning to go, 'who's the best haberdasher in Marchester, Richard?'

'You're not thinking of buying a new wardrobe for the King's visit? You've cut it a bit fine.'

'Someone needs a new coat. I said I'll see what I can do. Now, be a good friend, Richard, and find me a haberdasher. I want a green velvet coat, with slashed sleeves, and fine quality lining.'

Richard Landstock whistled. 'That'll cost you something.'

'Just a drop in the ocean,' Nicholas said wearily.

'Who's it for? Or shouldn't I ask?'

'You can ask, but I won't tell you. But tell this haberdasher friend of yours to come and see me. I've no time to go looking for him. Oh, and tell him to come soon – like today – and bring some samples of his best quality cloth.

159

He ought to start stitching immediately if it's to be finished by the sixth of June.'

'You're a man of many parts, Peverell. But I'll see what I can do. How big's this friend of yours?'

Nicholas looked Landstock up and down. 'Your size, a bit taller, I think, but certainly he's got your chest on him.'

'Sensible man. Can I order myself one too at your expense, of course? Sort of commission? After all, I shall have to be presented to the King. He always wants to see his Sheriffs.'

'And doesn't expect them to look fashionable. Order yourself a new coat, by all means, Richard; but don't send me the bill.'

Feeling relieved that he could rely on Richard Landstock, Nicholas rode back to Dean Peverell. The sun was already high in the sky so the main Mass of the day would be over and the Prior would probably be at work in the chapter house. Brother Ambrose opened the gate and one of the lay Brothers led Harry away to the Prior's stables.

'He's in the church, my Lord,' said Brother Ambrose deferentially. 'You'll almost certainly find him in the sacristy with Father Hubert.'

He thanked the elderly monk and went into the monks' church, a beautiful tall building rebuilt two hundred years ago, and paid for by one of his ancestors. He glanced up at the painted ceiling which he had commissioned as a memorial to his wife, and once again admired the design of heraldic shields entwined with some of the wild flowers which grew in the surrounding fields and hedgerows: succulent bunches of blackberries, delicate fritillaries, honeysuckle and wild roses. He felt a rush of emotion as he saw the sun streaming through the stained glass windows, falling on his chantry chapel, lighting up the sculptured figures of cherubs and angels clutching their lutes and harps. Whatever else happened, he thought, King Henry must never get his hands on this place.

160

The door of the sacristy was open and he heard the Prior's voice talking excitedly to Father Hubert.

'Now don't agitate yourself, Father, it'll do you no good in your condition. This all belongs to us. It was given to us over the years by our friends and patrons. The King's not going to rob us of all our sacred vessels.'

'If the King should see this . . .' he heard Father Hubert say in his distinctive nasal twang.

Nicholas forced himself to remove his eyes from the chantry chapel and walked over to the sacristy. He looked in. There on a footstool sat the Prior, and in front of him, laid out on a cloth, were the church treasures. The cupboard in the corner of the sacristy where all the things were kept was open, and Father Hubert was on his knees facing the Prior and cradling the beautiful gold chalice in his arms. There were tears in his red-rimmed eyes, which were sunken into his bony face, a result of too much fasting and a recent blood letting. Both looked up when they saw Nicholas, and Father Hubert clutched the chalice more closely to his chest as if Nicholas were King Henry himself about to wrench it from him.

'Welcome home, Lord Nicholas,' said the Prior, beaming broadly. 'We're just going through the inventory before our guests arrive to inspect us,' he said exploding with laughter. 'Well, they'll be welcome. We've got nothing to hide, though Father Hubert's a bit nervous about our altar furnishings. I've told him to relax; they can't just walk off with them, can they?'

'No, they'll simply write them down on a list and hand it over to Thomas Cromwell, who'll show it to the King.'

'Then there's nothing to worry about. Everything here belongs to us. It's all down in the inventories going back time immemorial. We've not pilfered anything.'

'Only that chalice and the icon,' said Nicholas evenly, 'but they were pilfered a long time ago from Constantinople – by one of my ancestors, as it happens.'

He picked up the jewel-encrusted icon and kissed it

161

reverently. The head of the Virgin was crowned with rubies, and the Christ-child was picked out in gold leaf.

'Oh that was centuries ago,' said the Prior dismissively. 'Besides, your ancestor was on a crusade – he was fighting the Infidel – of course he was going to do a bit of pilfering. They all did. If he hadn't picked it up, someone else would. Great heavens, my Lord, it might have ended up in some foreign church! At least it's got a good home here.'

'My ancestor might have fought against the Infidel, but there's no doubt that this icon came from a Christian church.'

'Christian?' roared the Prior, 'Don't be stupid. There are no Christians in Constantinople; they're Greeks!'

Nicholas said nothing. No use trying to argue with Prior Thomas. Father Hubert stood the chalice reverently on the floor. 'Whoever it belonged to,' he said softly, 'we've had it for three hundred years and Our Lord's blood is offered up in it every important feast day and holy day.'

Nicholas noticed how frail the Sacristan looked, how pale and emaciated his face was with the bones of his skull protruding like a death's head. The Prior noticed Nicholas's look of concern.

'Yes, he's gone too far this time. Look at his arms.' Nicholas saw the wizened arms, the wrists bound in blood-stained bandages. 'Too much fasting, and too much blood letting. You've hardly got any blood in that poor old body of yours, father,' he said, getting up off the stool. 'That Infirmarer of mine likes nothing better than to line us all up and extract our blood. I won't let him get his hands on me, though. God gives us our blood, and He means us to hold on to it. Hubert's given so much that he's had to have two days in the infirmary to get over it. Now God doesn't want you to make yourself ill, does He?'

'It's good to bring the body to order, Prior. I feel close to the Holy One after a blooding.'

'Of course you do, you old fool! You are nearer to God. One more drop out of that dried-out frame of yours and you'll be standing in front of His throne in His Heavenly Kingdom. Now let's put these things away and I'll go and talk to Lord Nicholas. I'm sure he hasn't come here just to admire the church furniture.'

'We could hide them, Prior,' said the Sacristan tentatively.

'Hide them? What on earth for?'

'So that they won't be listed on the inventory and the King won't know what we've got.'

'I've told you, Father, the King's not a common thief. Why should he take them?'

'Because these things are valuable,' said Nicholas, 'and he's short of money. The fleet, his pride and joy, is going to consume every penny in the Exchequer. Cromwell's already saying that with the sale of the monastic church furniture he can pay off the national debt.'

Father Hubert whimpered plaintively and picked up the chalice. 'Not this, oh not this. Not to fit out a fleet of war ships. It'll be sacrilege. Let me hide it, Prior.'

'Oh, put it back in that cupboard and let's hear no more of this. No one's going to sell something as precious as that chalice. The King can have the altar frontals; my cope, too, if necessary. That'll make him a fine cloak. Should keep him quiet for a bit.'

Leaving Father Hubert to lock away the church ornaments, the Prior and Nicholas walked back through the church and out into the cloister, where several monks were busily copying out manuscripts in their beautiful, elaborate handwriting.

'Now then, my Lord, what can I do for you? I've heard all sorts of rumours about the King coming to stay up in your house. I suppose he's bringing half the Court with him and there'll be feasting and all sorts of goings-on.'

'Not if I can help it. Already I'm beginning to think that I'll have to sell the high field to pay for all this. I suppose old Warrener'll be creeping up to me and offering to buy it off me for some knock-down price. The King's staying two

163

to three nights at the most, and I should be grateful, Prior, if you could help me out.'

'Well, out with it. What do you want?'

'Can you sleep some of the guests?'

'No problem. Send them down here and we can stick them up in the attic of my house. The floor'll take a hundred or so packed together. The nights are warm now and I'll get fresh straw down on the floor. Do you need help in your kitchen?'

'I could do with help in every department.'

'Then I'll send down my lay brothers. You can have Brother Cyril for a couple of days. I can manage on some cold cuts.'

'You're welcome to join us, Prior. You could then have a chance to talk to the King.'

'Good idea. I'll put him straight about what we do here. Have you got a good stock of wine and ale?'

'I've sent Geoffrey off to buy some . . .'

'Oh, he's got no idea about buying wine. Those Marchester merchants will rip you off something cruel. Help yourself to mine. I can always slip over to France and re-stock later in the summer. I could, of course, send Benedict back to Rivières to cadge some more wine from his abbot, but he might not let him come back. I'm only too pleased to help. After all, it was your ancestors who built our church and sent for the monks to come and start our community. You yourself have provided the money to have our ceiling painted and build the lovely chantry. It's the least I can do. Just leave things to me. Send Lowe along and we'll concoct some menus. I've got a barrel of lambs' tongues just arrived. Marvellous with a good pastry top and a rich gravy. My cook can rustle up some concoctions for puddings. Pity it's too early for grapes, but the strawberries! My Lord, you should take a look at the strawberries in my garden. I'll get the Brothers to cover the beds with straw and you take your pick.'

'Prior, I'm indebted to you.'

164

'No more than we're indebted to you and your family. I can also send Brother Benedict up to entertain the King with that lass of yours. By the way, they're both here at the moment, in my solarium rehearsing. I've got guests coming, you know, before yours. Great heavens, this is going to require some organisation. No lambs' tongues for my guests, though; they're only government officials. Roast lamb, that'll do for them. A good fat carp from our ponds. No strawberries, of course. Some custards; Cyril's good at custards.'

Deeply grateful that his catering arrangements were in such capable hands, Nicholas walked across to the gatehouse. The Prior called him back.

'Don't go yet,' he said. 'Don't you want to hear Mistress Jane and my Benedict sing? But before that, there's one act of Christian charity I want you to do before you relax and enjoy yourself. One of my old monks is drawing nearer to God and he's asked to see you. He's Brother Wilfrid, and I think you know him. He speaks often about you and a brief visit would make him very happy.'

Nicholas only half heard him. His mind was racing. Jane, here, with Benedict! It seemed ages since he'd seen her. Had she deserted him for the charms of a romantic-looking young monk?

'Of course I'll see him,' he managed to say.

'Good, good. Then come and join us afterwards. I'll get Cyril to send over some bread and cheese. You must be famished after all your gallivanting around the country on that horse of yours.'

Brother Wilfrid's bed was at the far end of the ward, near the apothecary's room. Nicholas walked up to him, nodding at the monk who was sitting at the foot of the bed, keeping vigil with him. Brother Wilfrid was lying quite still with his eyes closed. It was obvious he hadn't much longer to live. His body had shrunk down to the size of a child, and his skin was paper thin with no flesh underneath. When

165

Nicholas bent down to hear if his heart was still beating, there was the merest flutter and his breathing was just a faint sigh. He picked up one of the gnarled old hands which had written so many words and beaten out the rhythm of Latin words on his head when he was a boy resenting being in the monastery schoolroom rather than outside in the fresh air.

The attendant monk tactfully withdrew and Nicholas looked down with affection at the shrunken face of the old monk. He remembered how they'd laughed together over the antics of the classical gods which they'd read in the Latin texts, and how, once, the Prior had reprimanded Wilfrid for corrupting him, Nicholas, with stories of Jove's amorous pursuits. He'll not laugh any more, Nicholas thought. Only when he arrived in Heaven and then he could entertain St Peter and the angels.

Suddenly, Wilfrid's eyelids fluttered open and he stared at Nicholas. 'I'm not gone yet,' he whispered. 'It's good to see you Nicholas, my boy. You look fine. You always were a robust child, though you didn't like Latin, did you?'

'I took to it, though, when I was older, and we read all those stories together.'

The old eyes twinkled with appreciation. 'What stories they were! All nonsense, but harmless. I've grieved for you, Nicholas, when your wife died and the babe. You've had your share of sorrow.'

'It still seems only yesterday.'

'Don't go on grieving for ever, though. They're both with God and they'll want you to start living again. There's many a lass who'd have you . . .'

His voice tailed off and he screwed up his eyes as if he was trying to remember something. 'There's something I must tell you, but I can't recall it. Something recent. That's the trouble. I can remember our Latin lessons, but can't remember what happened yesterday. It's something that puzzled me at the time. Something not quite right.'

His eyes filled with tears of frustration and Nicholas

166

squeezed his hand. 'Hush, don't strain yourself. It'll come back to you soon. Now try to sleep. I'll come and see you again.'

'You'll be here when I pass on, Nicholas?'

'I'll be here.'

'Thank you. We'll say the last prayers together, shall we? In Latin, of course.'

A ghost of a smile flickered across his face. Nicholas let go of Brother Wilfrid's hand, and nodded to the monk who could resume his vigil. He was conscious that someone else had been listening to their conversation, but when he glanced round the ward there was no one there except the figures of the sick monks in the beds. He left the infirmary and made his way across the garden to the solarium which the Prior had built on to the southern end of his house a few years previously.

Chapter Sixteen

When he reached the solarium, Nicholas stopped and listened to the two voices. They were singing a duet and one of them was playing a lute in accompaniment. The plangent tone of the instrument set off the ethereal quality of their voices to perfection. They were singing an intricate song by William Cornish which he'd heard recently at Court. They didn't hear him open the door, and he went in quietly, not wanting to disturb them. He glanced round the room. It was spacious with a high, vaulted ceiling which made it especially suitable for musical performances. The sunlight was streaming in through the open window, casting a dazzling light on the beautiful tiled floor. Nicholas looked down at the images on the tiles which the monks had made in their own kilns. He saw griffins and unicorns, swans and a pelican piercing her breast to feed her young; and everywhere he saw the heraldic crest of his own family, a leopard's head, spitting a fleur-de-lys out of its mouth. Nicholas was very proud of his family's crest. It had been awarded to one of his ancestors after the Battle of Poitiers and he'd used it as a design in the ceiling and in the sculptures on his chantry in the monks' church.

Then he looked across at the two figures standing by the open window and immediately became enraptured. Jane had removed her cap and had let her bright, chestnut hair hang freely down her back. She stood there bathed in the sunlight, and together with Benedict, with his dark good looks and slim figure, they looked like a painting by one of the Flemish masters. They were both concentrating so hard that they didn't see him and the spell was broken only when the Prior came in with Brother Cyril, who was carrying a tray with a jug of ale and hunks of bread and chunks of cheese on it.

'Come now, that's enough music for today. Time for refreshments. Are you going to try our ale, Mistress Warrener, or shall I ask Brother Cyril to go and draw some fresh water out of the well?'

Then Jane turned and saw Nicholas and he watched her as her face flushed. She turned away, and Nicholas's heart sank. She was bored with him, that was obvious, and now she preferred the more entertaining company of Brother Benedict.

He wanted to leave, but it would have been churlish to refuse the Prior's hospitality, so he helped himself to the food, and the Prior poured him out some ale whilst Brother Cyril went to get Jane some water.

'Well, Lord Nicholas, what do you think of my two musicians? Don't their voices match perfectly? The King would be pleased to hear them, don't you think? I'll lend them to you, if you like. We'll get a little programme going and I'll have a word with the Bishop and see whether he can rustle up a few more musicians. The King will want to dance, I expect, and we ought to hire some instrumentalists to play us a galliard or two.'

'Will the King be staying long, my Lord?' said Jane, dropping him a full curtsy.

'Two nights, probably. It depends whether he'll want to hunt. I'm amazed at how quickly news spreads. I told the Prior not to mention the King's visit. Now I suppose it's general gossip.'

'My dear Peverell,' said the Prior indignantly, 'it's ale-house gossip. You can't keep news like that quiet. Best to let everyone talk about it until it's a seven-day wonder. But

169

some more cheese? It's very good, isn't it? Newly made from fresh curds.'

Nicholas helped himself, wondering desperately why Jane was being so unfriendly. He wanted to speak to her alone, but there was not much chance with the Prior around.

His opportunity came when one of the lay brothers came in and said Prior Thomas was wanted in the chapter house. Then Benedict decided he ought to get back to the work he was doing for the Precentor in the cloisters. He bowed to Nicholas and withdrew. The Prior finished his mouthful of bread and cheese, patted Nicholas affectionately on the back and went over to the door.

'Take your time, Lord Nicholas. I'm sure you would escort Mistress Warrener to her house. Remember to send your steward down to me soon or I might have second thoughts about the lambs' tongues.'

He went out, and Jane began to gather up the music manuscripts. Then she piled up her hair and began to tuck it under the pleated linen cap she wore. The silence was like a barrier between them, and Nicholas couldn't bear it any longer.

'Jane, what's wrong? Why won't you look at me? What have I done? Surely you haven't lost your heart to a young monk?'

She looked at him in astonishment, and then her face flushed with anger.

'How dare you even think of such a thing! Brother Benedict is a fully professed monk. We both love music, that's all. The Prior encourages us to sing together and there's no harm in that. Now if you please, my father has been left on his own far too long and I must get back to him.'

She made for the door. Nicholas couldn't let her go.

'Jane, stop. Don't you remember we are supposed to be a team? You said you'd be my spy and I've relied on you. Don't walk out on me now, just when I need you most. The

King's coming, as you heard, and the conspiracy which you alerted me to – remember? – isn't over yet. Jane, what is it? Have you tired of me? Has your father . . .?'

She stopped and whirled round to confront him. 'It's you who seem to have forgotten that we're supposed to be a team, my Lord. I thought that meant sharing everything. And then I learnt from common ale-house gossips that the King's coming to stay with you. Even my father knew about this visit before I did. Why didn't you tell me? Is it because you don't consider me important enough to take me into your confidence? A partnership is not one-sided, you know. How can I work with you if you won't tell me what's going on? Now let me pass, please.'

He reached out and grabbed her hand. She tried to pull it away, but he held on. Then he turned her head towards him, forcing her to look at him. She was so tense, and her eyes were so furious that he wanted to take her in his arms and smother her face with kisses, but he knew that he would be making a fatal mistake. Probably she'd never speak to him again. Probably she'd tell the whole village and his name would be mud.

'Jane, we must talk. So much has happened since I last saw you and I've only just got back from London. I watched Sir Roger die on the rack. I've seen his wife nearly out of her mind with the horror of it. She now waits in the Tower until the King decides her fate. I know that the conspiracy isn't over and that there's someone still at large who wants the King dead. I had to see the Sheriff about security arrangements and I have to see Southampton today about the King's protection when he goes to Portsmouth. Then I was going to see you. So do you understand? Of course I want our partnership to continue. I want you here in the village being my eyes and ears, because Mortimer's successor could be a local person. Now why don't we meet this afternoon – in the herb garden, our place? Come at three and I'll tell you my news, and you can tell me yours. Of course we must work together. I need you. Now I

171

promise not to mention Brother Benedict again, if you promise to trust me. If I go away again, it's because I'm needed urgently.'

She began to calm down and was looking at him now without resentment. 'All right, I'll come. But remember that there must be full co-operation between us. We've got to trust one another; only then can we make any progress. Now I think I ought to tell you that there are a lot of things going on in this village that you don't know about. I'm not easy about Bess Knowles's death and I think there's someone else who could be in grave danger.'

'Then you must tell me. I couldn't bear it, Jane, if we were not friends. I need your intuitive powers, your intelligence, and your local knowledge. So, until three, my dear friend, Jane.'

He kissed her lightly on the cheek and she didn't draw away. They left the solarium together and he watched her ride away on Melissa. Slowly he mounted Harry, which one of the lay brothers had fetched for him, and rode off towards his house. As he rode along the street, he noticed groups of people, mostly women because the men were working in the fields, standing around deep in conversation. They didn't look up as he went by and he could sense the atmosphere of suspicion and distrust. At the top of the street, clustered round the village well, there was the usual crowd of women. They always called out cheerful greetings as he went past, but not today. Something was going on, and he needed to know what it was.

'So that, Jane, is the whole sorry story. Am I forgiven for not briefing you sooner?'

They were sitting on the stone bench in the herb garden. Above them the sky was still cloudless; it was hot, and all around them the bees were frantically going about their summer tasks. The Tower and the rack seemed a long way away now, but Nicholas knew that it would be fatal to relax in a false sense of security. Time was running out.

'I can see that you've been a bit preoccupied, and yes, of course I forgive you. I'm sorry about Mortimer; and even more sorry for his wife. What makes people become traitors, I wonder?'

'Because they can't go along with the King's policy and think it's their duty to get rid of him.'

'And what makes them think they're right and everyone else is wrong? It sounds a bit arrogant to me. However, fortunately Mortimer didn't get very far; let's hope this Ultor gets no further. I can see now why Matthew had to go; and I still think Bess was an innocent victim, although we can't prove anything. And now there's another person who could be in danger, but I don't know whether she has any connection with the conspiracy or whether she's simply a victim of local prejudice.'

'Who is she, Jane?'

'The village is full of rumours – all ale-house gossip – about a harmless old woman: Agnes Myles.'

'What are they saying about her?'

'That she's a witch; that she puts curses on the hens so that they don't lay eggs, and babies are born with twisted backs when she looks at them; and now they're saying that she's responsible for your fall in the woods.'

Nicholas stared at her in amazement, then gave a great shout of laughter. Jane looked at him sharply.

'Don't laugh. You know how serious these charges can be. You've only got to ride over Marchester Heath and see the bodies swinging on the gibbets to know how many witches were hanged over the last few months. Probably, like Agnes Myles, their only crime was that they knew more about healing than other people. It doesn't do to be old, live on your own, and be clever.'

'Then, Jane, we must ensure that that fate doesn't happen to you.'

'Will you be serious, just for once. And don't think I'm being stupid. Agnes is in real danger. They say she can change her shape and that's what frightened Harry. What

173

he saw in the woods was an evil spectre.'

Nicholas threw back his head and laughed until tears came into his eyes. 'Stop glaring at me, Jane. What Harry saw in the woods was a trick of the light, a patch of shade that appeared to move. Don't listen to village gossip, Jane; you should be above that sort of thing, an intelligent girl like you. They'll soon come round to old Agnes when they fall sick with a fever or their joints stiffen up when it starts raining in the autumn.'

'If you're going to patronise me, Nicholas, then there's no point in me being here.'

To his surprise she stood up, shook out her skirt and walked off smartly towards the garden door. Nicholas jumped up and ran after her.

'Jane, stop. Don't take offence. I'm actually paying you a compliment when I said you were intelligent. And don't get annoyed because I can't share your concern over Agnes Myles. Just let the gossips get on with it. They'll soon get bored with the whole subject. Please don't go. I value you too much to let you walk away like this.'

The door handle was stiff and Jane tugged at it furiously; but it didn't budge. Nicholas took hold of her arm.

'Come back to our seat, Jane, and tell me why you think Agnes is in danger. I'm sorry I laughed at you, but it's a long way from local gossip to standing in front of the Justices at Quarter Sessions.'

'I'll come back as long as you take me seriously. I don't believe in witches; and I don't usually listen to gossips. But you asked me to be your eyes and ears in the village, and this is what I've been doing. And I don't like what I've been hearing. And it isn't just because Agnes is a friend of mine.'

She brushed his hand off her arm and they walked slowly back to the bench.

'I hope you're right in thinking that these rumours will die down. But doesn't it strike you as odd that people should pick on Agnes at this particular time? Matthew,

Bess. Is number three to be Agnes?'

'Jane, Matthew and Bess were witnesses to Mortimer's treachery. Why on earth should anyone want to silence Agnes?'

'Why indeed? That's what's bothering me.'

They sat in silence. Above them two larks poured out their spring song in rapture. Nicholas breathed a sigh of relief. He and Jane were once more a team. But he'd have to watch his step. He'd never met a girl like her before.

'You could be right, and there's only one way to find out. Get back to Agnes and talk to her. Make a note of everything she says and we can go over it later. Maybe a pattern will emerge. Let me know if anything occurs to you. I've got to go to Portsmouth today to see Southampton. He's the King's Admiral of the Fleet, and I must make sure he steps up his security arrangements. He'll need to have extra bowmen on duty and some of these new-fangled cannoneers. they fire hand-cannons, you know. The Germans use them a lot. They're a bit slow, and don't always hit their target but, by heaven, when a lump of lead or stone lands on a man it pierces his armour and makes a great hole in him.'

Now Jane began to smile. 'Are there really such men who carry cannons and hold on to them when they fire?'

'Oh yes. Soon every soldier will be equipped with one of these harquebuses as they're called. The longbow will be obsolete in a few years.'

'Has Southampton got any cannoneers?'

'Bound to. The King's all for these new inventions. Might help him to win more battles. But they've got to get them to fire with greater accuracy. I still think the longbow's best when speed matters. However, let's not waste time discussing modern warfare. You get back to Agnes Myles and find out who she's been seeing over the last few days, and I'll get off to Portsmouth.'

They got up and walked over to the door. This time, Nicholas opened it.

'How can I get in touch with you, Jane? Your father won't take kindly to me coming to your house.'

'He'll be rude and abusive. I'll try and report to you daily. I could leave a message with Geoffrey, but he's out and about so much that I might not catch him. I know – Brother Benedict – he can be our messenger boy. Because he's only a visitor he's not under such a strict Rule as the other monks are. I can send him up here with a message when I need to speak to you, and you can give him a message by return.'

It made sense, but even so, Nicholas had to fight down the now familiar twinge of jealousy. Had she got an ulterior motive in using Benedict?

She seemed to sense his hesitation. 'Don't worry about Benedict. He's a dear and a very talented musician; and his vocation to the monastic life is genuine. Probably one day he'll end up as abbot of a great monastery. But now he's free to come and go as he pleases. People are used to seeing him about and won't ask any questions.'

'I'm sure you know best. Yes, let's use him. You're a wonderful ally, Jane. I think the Sheriff could do with someone like you on his staff. Shall I suggest it when I next see him?'

'I'd do anything for you, Nicholas, but just steer me clear of Sheriff Landstock.'

She jumped up on Melissa and rode off. Nicholas took Harry round to the stables.

'Give him a good rub down,' he said to the stable boy. 'I'll be needing him soon.'

'You're not leaving us again, my Lord?'

'Just a short trip to Portsmouth.'

He went into the house. Geoffrey took his cloak. Suddenly tiredness hit him like a hammer. He tried to pull off his boots but had no strength. Geoffrey knelt down and began to ease them off.

'You look all in, my Lord.'

'I'm just a bit weary. Nothing that a short nap won't put

176

right. I think I'll get my head down for a few minutes. Incidentally, don't worry about the catering arrangements for the King's visit. The Prior's got it all under control.'

'Thank God for that. Will he let us use the guest house?'

'No problem. Says he can sleep a hundred people. Now let me get to my bed. Don't let me oversleep, though. I've got to see the Earl of Southampton before today's over.'

He went up to his bedroom and collapsed on his bed. In seconds he was asleep. After one hour, Geoffrey Lowe went to wake him up, but took one look at Nicholas's recumbent body and went away. Nicholas slept on for eleven more hours.

Chapter Seventeen

Agnes woke up in the early hours of Saturday morning. This was unusual. She always went to bed shortly after the sun went down and woke up when the first finger of daylight appeared. She lay there trying to accustom herself to the strange feeling of darkness pressing down all around her. The wind, she noted, had got up and one of the branches of the old lilac tree was tapping lightly on her bedroom window. She snuggled down under her warm coverlet and tried to go back to sleep.

Agnes enjoyed a comfortable life-style. Her bed was a solid four-poster with thick curtains which she could draw in the winter to keep out the draughts. Her windows were filled in with glass and she could open them in the summer to let in the sweet night air. Her bed linen was of good quality and smelt of lavender, and there were woollen rugs on the floor. All these things were the result of quarterly payments of money from an unknown donor presented to her by an attorney who came out from Marchester. They always drank a herbal infusion together and ate sweet cakes, and he asked her if there was anything she needed. She always said she had everything she wanted, so he nodded and went away, leaving a bag of money on the table. He never told her where the money came from and she assumed it was from someone who cared about her but who had never acknowledged her. Sometimes she wished she knew more about the mystery surrounding her birth, but obviously she would never find out now. When other people talked about their relatives she used to feel left out, but now she was glad she had no elderly parents to look after or aunts and uncles to visit. She felt as if she was floating in her own comfortable space where she could get on with the job of studying the properties of plants and healing people.

The tapping of the branch was preventing her returning to sleep so she got up, wrapped a shawl round her shoulders and went over to the window. She drew back the curtains. The weather had certainly changed. Dark clouds now scudded across the face of the waning moon and a summer storm was building up. Good, she thought. Her garden needed rain and the water butts would fill up nicely.

She went back to bed and drifted back into sleep. When she woke up the night had gone and the pale light of a troubled dawn illuminated the furniture in her bedroom. Unaccustomed to a disturbed night's sleep, she felt uneasy. Something was wrong. Something was missing. She splashed some water on her face from the bowl on the washstand, put up her hair under a neat white cap, and pulled on her dress. As she slipped her feet into her shoes, she realised what was missing. Ambrose hadn't come in. Usually he was inside the house well before the dawn. He always lapped up the plateful of milk she left out for him before padding up the stairs and jumping up on to her bed. There he'd curl up and sleep soundly until she stirred. Then, purring loudly, he'd come to her for his early morning welcome.

She went downstairs and saw he hadn't drank his milk. She wasn't particularly worried. He was a good hunting cat and maybe his hunting activities had taken him further afield than usual. At any moment, she thought, he'd come jumping in through the little window she always left open for him in all weathers.

She put some kindling wood on the fire and blew on the

smouldering log until it burst into flames. Then she heated some milk and poured it over some stale bread, adding honey. She sat down to eat it, but her appetite had gone. Was she sickening for something? In that case she would have to make herself a lemon balm infusion, which she knew had a calming effect on the body. The Prior had sent her down a bush which he'd brought back from France the previous year and she loved the delicious delicate flavour of its leaves. She pulled the shawl round her shoulders and went out into the garden to pick some sprigs.

Outside the wind was creating havoc in the flowerbeds and it caught hold of one end of her shawl and whipped it off. She ran down the path to retrieve it; and then she saw Ambrose. He was dangling from a length of rope tied to a branch of the rowan by the gate. With a cry of despair she ran to him. The rope was tied tightly round his neck and he hung stretched out like a rabbit caught in a snare. His eyes were staring wildly and his mouth was drawn back in a grimace of pain, revealing his sharp pointed teeth. Nailed to his soft, velvety underbelly was a piece of wood with letters scrawled on it. HANG THE CAT. HANG THE WITCH.

She tried to untie the knot round his neck but it was too tight. In a panic she ran back to the house and picked up a knife. With this, she cut him down. Then she sat down under the tree, cradling Ambrose in her arms like a child. For eight years he'd been her devoted companion. They had shared everything together. No human being had ever got as close to her as Ambrose had.

With tears streaming down her face, she got up and carried him into the house. She eased off the rope round his neck, flung the piece of wood with its evil message on the floor, and laid him out on the table on a clean cloth. Then she closed his staring eyes, pulled his mouth shut and stroked his beautiful velvety coat.

'Ambrose,' she whispered, 'my darling Ambrose. Who did this to you?'

Gradually time passed, the rain began to fall, gently at first, then with greater intensity. She wept for her cat, until she could weep no more. Slowly her grief gave way to anger. She didn't care what people thought about her. Let them call her a witch if they wanted to. They were all ignorant peasants, anyway. But why should anyone want to hurt a beautiful and harmless cat?

An hour later, Jane knocked at the door and found Agnes still stroking her dead cat. She gave a horrified cry and rushed over to her friend.

'Agnes, what's happened? When? How did it happen?'

Agnes looked up, her face distorted with grief. 'Go away, Jane, and let me be. The devil came here last night and killed Ambrose. He seized hold of him and hanged him up on a tree. What am I going to do without him?' And she rocked backwards and forwards, locked in her grief.

Jane put her arms round her, and Agnes didn't draw away. Then Jane looked down and saw the piece of wood on the floor. She bent down and picked it up.

'It wasn't the devil who did this; it was a human being. As far as I know the devil doesn't write messages. Agnes, you are in terrible danger. This is a warning. You must leave your house immediately. Come home with me. You'll be safe with my father. He has no time for witch-hunts. Let me get you your cloak.'

Agnes stopped rocking and stared at Jane. 'Nobody is going to frighten me into leaving my home. I am going to bury Ambrose, and then I shall carry on doing what I've always done – make up my herbal remedies. I won't be terrorised. I've done nothing. I know I'm not a regular churchgoer, but I have my own service books and I worship God in my own way. I go to Mass on the blessed feast of Christmas and on the day of Our Lord's resurrection. For the rest, I can't abide the ignorant, superstitious gossiping of the other members of the congregation. Does that make me a witch? I don't think so. I have no knowledge of the black arts, I have no truck with the devil. I lead a simple and, I hope, useful life. Why have I suddenly got so many enemies? Jane, I am going to find out who murdered Ambrose if it's the last thing I do; and I won't leave my house. Will you help me bury him?'

Together they dug a deep hole by the rosemary bushes. They lined it with the heads of marigolds and sprigs of sweet marjoram. Then they wrapped Ambrose in an embroidered linen pillow case and lowered him into the grave. With the wind tearing at their skirts and the rain splattering great heavy drops in their faces, they filled in the hole. Then Agnes tied two pieces of wood together and made a cross and set it up at the head of the grave. Together they stood there praying silently.

When they'd finished they went back to the house. Agnes built up the fire and they brushed the raindrops off their clothes.

'We've got to talk,' said Jane as she took the beaker of hot lemon balm infusion from Agnes. 'We've got to find out who's started this persecution. Can you remember who's been to see you over the last few days? Can you remember what they wanted? You must think carefully. Someone wants to get rid of you. All this witch nonsense is just a smokescreen.'

Agnes sat down wearily on the chair by the fire. 'Not now, Jane. My brain's not working properly. Leave me now to grieve in peace. Sit with me for just a little while and then get on your way. We can talk later, when I gather my wits together.'

Jane sat with her for a while, then seeing Agnes needed the peace and silence of her own fireside, she left her, telling her to lock her front door and shut all the windows. There was only one person who could persuade Agnes to leave her house. And that was Nicholas. She climbed up on to Melissa's wet back and rode up to Peverell Manor.

Nicholas woke up late on Saturday morning. He heard the

182

wind howling down the chimney and heard the rain splattering on the window-pane. Cursing Geoffrey, who'd let him sleep so long, he jumped out of bed and looked up at the storm-tossed sky and a reluctant sun. Realising it was late, he dressed hastily and went downstairs, where the servants were vigorously scrubbing the floors as if the King were coming that day.

Geoffrey appeared with a tankard of ale and a plate of bread and cold meats and stood there stolidly whilst Nicholas berated him for letting him sleep so long.

'You needed your rest, my Lord. A man can't go on for ever.'

It was true. He did feel restored. He drank down the ale and wolfed down the food.

'I needed that, too. Now fetch me my cloak, Geoffrey, and tell the grooms to get Harry ready. It's a good way to Portsmouth and it's likely to be a rough ride.'

Harry, too, was well rested, and raced along the Portsmouth road, passing the carts of farmers bringing their produce into the towns along the way. They were riding into the strong south-westerly wind and the rain had turned the surface of the road into a muddy swamp. Not that Harry cared. He galloped along, splashing mud everywhere, only snorting with disapproval when a particularly violent gust of wind hit him in the face. It took them two and a half hours to cover the twenty miles to Portsmouth and then they took the lower coastal road to the small castle at Southsea, which the Admiral of the Fleet used when he was in Portsmouth. The sea looked grey and angry that morning and very few fishing vessels had ventured out. But he knew that the King's fleet was anchored out at Spithead and he felt sorry for the men who were forced to remain on board and tend to the vessels.

At the castle, an old, crudely built stone keep, one of the army guards led Harry away to the stables. Then Nicholas was taken to a room on the ground floor where men in armour were clustered round the open fire. They stopped talking when he went in, and politely made a space for him to dry off in front of the fire. It wasn't long before he heard footsteps coming down the stone, newel staircase, and Sir Ralph Paget, Lord Admiral of the Fleet and recently created Earl of Southampton by the King, came into the room. He was a big, military-looking man, tough, vigorous, with a short, stumpy brown beard and hair cut short round his bullet head.

'You're welcome, Lord Nicholas. Come upstairs and we can talk in peace. Here, boy,' he said to one of the servants, 'take his Lordship's cloak and see that you dry it off properly. It's a foul day, both on land and sea. I pray God that those ships out there won't end up scattered all over the Solent.'

Nicholas followed Southampton upstairs to a small room. There was a bed in one corner and a rug on the floor, which made the room appear more comfortable. A log fire smouldered in the stone fireplace, and a servant came in with a tray of food and drink. Southampton kicked the logs into a blaze and invited Nicholas to stand in front of it and dry himself off. With steam rising from his clothes, Nicholas ate the food gratefully and drank deeply from the jug of ale.

'I suppose you're here in connection with the King's visit,' said Southampton when Nicholas had finished eating. 'I'm not at all happy about it myself. We hoped that with Mortimer out of the way that would mean the end of this conspiracy, but it seems that isn't so. We now have this new threat and I'm damned if I know what to do. It's all very well to clear the streets and increase the guard but what's the use if we don't know the name of the person we're after and where he's operating from.'

'You got on to Mortimer pretty promptly.'

'Yes, but we had a tip-off.'

'Who was that?'

'Fitzroy, of course. Lord Gilbert was approached by

Mortimer, who wanted him to join the conspiracy. But Fitzroy would have nothing to do with it. Too much to lose, I suppose. Mortimer was a fool to take Fitzroy into his confidence because Fitzroy went straight to the King and told him everything. Then, as soon as I intercepted the letters to Pole with Mortimer's signature on them, we could run him in. But as you know, Mortimer told us nothing, and Fitzroy says he doesn't know who Mortimer's accomplices are.'

'And you believe him?'

'Have to. Can't arrest every landowner in the county because we don't trust him. Have you in next, Peverell. After all, you lived next door to Mortimer and you must have discussed the King's policy with him.'

'We talked politics, not treason.'

'Amounts to the same thing these days. Keep your mouth shut, Peverell, and confine your conversation to estate management.'

'Thanks, I might take your advice. But what had Fitzroy got against Mortimer that he informed on him?'

'He had to, in order to save his own skin. Otherwise, as soon as the King heard he'd been talking to Mortimer, who'd been under suspicion for some time, he'd order his arrest. As it is, I wouldn't like to be in Fitzroy's shoes. He'll have a job keeping his nose clean. But as he's Lord Lieutenant of the county, he's needed to raise a muster when the King comes. I'm uneasy, though. These musters are not made up from trained soldiers. We haven't got a standing army, as you know. They're just ordinary citizens armed with pikes and harquebuses if they know how to fire them, which they don't. We don't know who they are and one of them could be this Ultor – what a damned stupid name that is! I think we'll have to confine Fitzroy's muster to your end of the county. I don't trust them poking their noses into everything round here.'

'The King's in just as much danger when he's with me, as when he's here with you.'

185

'It's not quite the same. You can at least confine him to your house. When he's reviewing the fleet he'll be at Domus Dei down on the Hard, right out in the open, standing around for an hour or more. Anyone could take a pot shot at him. I wish to God he'd come to Porchester instead of Portsmouth. He can't come here. It's only big enough for a handful of soldiers. Certainly nowhere to entertain the King. It's just a tower – there are plans afoot to rebuild it, but that's in the future – and he can't see the fleet from here. It'll be a nightmare trying to hold on to him down on Portsmouth Hard.'

'The King's got a mind of his own, and he'll not change it. God, man, if you think you've got a job keeping the King under control, just think of me. When I last saw him he was talking about going hunting!'

Southampton whistled. 'This is getting worse by the minute. I suppose he sneers at travelling in a coach and will want to ride here on horseback?'

'That's the general idea. Wants to show himself off to his loyal subjects, and ignores the fact that anyone not so loyal could shoot him down.'

'Then there's only one thing we must do, and that's find Ultor damn smartly. I wonder if the devil lives locally or is he only an infrequent visitor?'

'I'm sorry to say I think he lives in my area. Could be a Marchester man, of course. There's a nest of traitors in the cathedral as I'm sure that traitor, Catchpole, the Precentor, wasn't the only one to murmur against the King's policy. Let me remind you that my steward and his girlfriend overheard Mortimer talking to someone, probably Fitzroy, as it happens. The poor devils were in the wrong place at the wrong time. Hayward, my steward, was murdered. We know now that Mortimer ordered his death. But the girlfriend, Bess Knowles, died after Mortimer's arrest. This implies that someone else stepped into Mortimer's shoes and took over where he left off. And he's still at large.'

186

'So this Ultor took over straight away after Mortimer's arrest?'

'Yes, I'm sure he made a pact with Mortimer. Should Mortimer fall, his mantle would fall on Ultor's shoulders. But this is all speculation. So far we have no proof that Bess Knowles's death had any connection with her boyfriend's murder. She was pregnant. The Coroner said the death was due to natural causes.'

'Still, it's a coincidence. You'll have to keep a good eye on your patch. Get some spies out there, people you can trust, someone who can talk to everyone and not arouse suspicion.'

'I've got just the right person.'

'Good. Who is he? One of your servants?'

'No, a girl.'

'Good God, man, are you mad? Look here, Peverell, this is a serious matter. We're talking about high politics, not a church outing. Whatever made you think that a girl could be any use at all in espionage?'

'She's intelligent, well informed, independently minded. Gets around on her own horse, is liked by everyone, and no one suspects her. She's already investigating something that I admit is a bit far-fetched, but she thinks it's important and she might be right. After all, we have to keep an open mind if we're to find Ultor before the King comes.'

'I agree with you about that, Peverell, but a girl!' He looked keenly at Nicholas. 'I suppose she's in love with you; and by God, you're in love with her, aren't you? This is no time for romance, Peverell. You'll get nowhere with all this airy-fairy romantic nonsense. You always were too soft for your own good. Wake up, man. We're talking about the King's life here.'

'Love doesn't come into it, Sir Ralph. I like her, and she goes everywhere and reports to me. That's all.'

'Well, what is she investigating at the moment?'

'She wants to know why an old lady who's never done anyone any harm should suddenly be suspected of witchcraft.'

Southampton laughed derisively and slapped Nicholas on the back. 'Sometimes, Peverell, you drive me mad. You live right up in the clouds. Witches are two a penny. Apart from putting the old curse on someone, I've never known them to dabble in treason. Unless they put a curse on the King, of course, then we'd string them up.'

'She's done nothing. She's more of a local healer than a witch.'

'Then tell that girl of yours to stop wasting time on her. I say, Peverell, is she pretty?'

'I suppose she is, but that's not the point. She's as sharp as any man.'

'Well, good luck to you. If you're going to have a female spy it's just as well if she's pretty. No trouble in getting people to talk if you've got a pretty face. However, I think I'll place my bet on the Sheriff if we're going to find this Ultor. Wenches are all very well in their place but best kept away from politics. Now, if you've eaten sufficient, let's go through the security arrangements for the King's visit. You know you'll have to increase the number of guards on your house?'

'The King's sending down some of his yeomen.'

'Thank God for that. They, at least, can be trusted. Don't let anyone get near the King whom you don't know. Treat all strangers with suspicion. You can rest assured that no harm will come to the King when he's under my protection. I can't say the same when he's with you. Now let's get down to business. I've got a chart over there with all the King's movements mapped out on it. As far as I'm concerned he's not going to take one step outside proscribed limits. If I were you, I'd do the same.'

'I've just told you, my Lord, he wants to go hunting.'

'Then you must try to dissuade him, Peverell. Remember William Rufus.'

Jane arrived at Peverell Manor only to be told by Geoffrey that Nicholas had long been gone.

188

'Can I ask where he's gone to?'

'You can ask, but I can't tell you. More than my life's worth. Let's just say that he headed west.'

Then she remembered he'd said he had to see the Earl of Southampton. Well, she thought, there was nothing for it, she'd have to conduct her own investigations. Someone wanted Agnes out of the way and was setting about it in a devious way. But she was going to find him whether Nicholas helped her or not.

Chapter Eighteen

It was still raining when Jane arrived at Abigail Butcher's house. She lived in a tiny, timber-framed house, its walls made of a daub of clay and dung mixed with straw and twigs. A pig was rooting around in the piles of rubbish which littered the yard, and she scuttled off grunting and squealing when she saw Melissa. Jane tied her horse to a tree and went into the yard. The rickety front door was open and she peered into the dark interior where a woman was crouched in front of a smouldering log fire, stirring the contents of an iron pot. She looked up when Jane knocked and smiled. Jane was well known to her. The Butchers were one of the few really poor families in the village and Jane often dropped in a batch of eggs or some honey when she went past.

The wind was blowing the smoke back through the hole in the roof, and Jane could only just see the two boys and the girl, sitting on the damp mud floor watching the pot with hungry eyes, like three cats. Two chickens, perched on the wooden bed head, started up in surprise as she went in and flew out of the front door, squawking angrily. The children jumped up to welcome her. They were polite children, as Abigail was strict with them, and they tried not to look too eagerly at the pots of honey she'd brought with her. Jane hugged them all, and gave the eldest boy one of the pots.

'Here, Simon, go and share this with your brother and sister.'

Simon took the pot and they rushed to the table where they greedily scooped out the honey with their fingers, licking up every drop.

'Don't eat it all,' said their mother. 'Save some to put on your gruel when it's ready.'

They grinned across at her and went on eating. Jane went over the fire and looked closely at Abigail, who was still weak from childbirth. She was a young woman, still in her twenties, but already the strain of bearing four children in five years was beginning to show in her tired, worn face. Her long hair hung in lank strands round her face and her torn brown dress was mud-stained and hardly covered her body. However, she was pleased to see Jane and told her to bring up a stool and dry herself off.

'The fire's got the sulks today,' Abigail said, giving it a poke. 'It takes a long time to get the food cooked. It's good of you to come, Mistress Warrener. Just take a look at those three with the honey.'

Jane waved across at the children. 'How are you, Abigail? Are you getting a bit stronger after Daniel's birth?'

'Ah, the poor darling. He was just a wee bit of a thing. Didn't really know who we were or where he was. But the Lord gives, and the Lord takes away. Blessed be the name of the Lord.'

'You're not angry about his death?'

'Angry? Lord, Mistress, why should I be angry? These things happen; and it's best that it turned out the way it did. How could I cope with a child with a twisted body? He'll be up in Heaven now, with a beautiful straight body and a fine pair of wings on him. He was fair, you know; not like my three darlings over there. Daniel was meant to be an angel.'

'You don't blame the midwife who delivered him?'

'Oh no, she's not to blame. He was a bit upside down

when he was inside me and we had a struggle to get him out. But Mistress Agatha was very clever and Agnes Myles was very helpful too with her potions. At one stage, when the pains were real bad, she gave me something to drink which knocked me out. The next thing I remember Daniel was born. He's happy now, and that's an end to it. Some wicked people are saying that Agnes put a curse on him, but I don't believe that. She loves babies and has never harmed anyone. No, God wanted Daniel for his own.'

Jane stayed until the gruel was bubbling in the pot. Then she got up and went over to talk to the children, who were now extracting the final smears of honey from the jar. The two little boys were sturdy and lively and she asked if they were going to the monks' school. Abigail looked across at them.

'Yes, the Prior says they can start soon. I want them all to read and write. Neither Jack nor I can. Will you teach little Rose to read when she's a bit older?'

'Of course I will. It opens up a whole new world when you learn how to read.'

'I've told them that. It's the only way out of this dreary life we lead. Just think of all the people who live in this village. How many of them can read and write? Most people just scrape around for a living as best they can.'

Jane left the Butchers' house and untied Melissa. So that was that. She was quite sure that none of the Butcher family would harm Agnes Myles. But who, in the village, she thought as she jumped up on Melissa, could read and write? The priest, of course, the churchwarden, the monks Geoffrey Lowe. Not many people, but, of course, someone else could have written that message. Someone from outside the village. Lots of people could read and write in Marchester.

She rode off. Already it was time to see to her father's midday meal. Later, when he took his afternoon nap she'd go and see the churchwarden. Not that she could visualise

Edgar Pierrepoint skulking out in the middle of the night to string up a cat.

Edgar Pierrepoint was also taking an afternoon nap when Jane knocked on his door. He lived in a large, timber-framed house next to the church and, as a freeholder, he enjoyed a comfortable life-style. After a few minutes, he opened the door, recognised Jane and ushered her in to his front room. His wife, Phyllis, who was overweight and found it difficult to get about these days, was upstairs asleep. As Jane went in, a large tabby cat stood up on the settee where he'd been curled up asleep, arched his back, yawned and jumped down on to the floor where he proceeded to rub himself round Jane's legs, purring loudly.

'He's a beautiful cat,' she said as Edgar indicated a chair by the fire.

'Yes, he's got some fine markings on him. We're very fond of him, as you know. He's a good ratter. Getting on a bit, like us.'

'You've heard the news about what happened to poor Agnes Myles's cat?'

'Oh yes, I'm really angry about that. I've been down to see her and she's very cut up. There are wicked people around, Mistress Warrener. Who'd want to harm a cat who never bothered anyone, and who keeps down the vermin? Agnes might not be a regular churchgoer but she's a good Christian soul all the same. It's wicked what people are saying about her.'

'So you've heard the rumours too. Do you know who started them?'

'No, I don't. But I intend to find out. I'm going to start with the ale-house. A lot of rogues get together down there and there's always trouble after they've had a few jars. I'll get to the bottom of it even if it takes me the rest of the summer. I can't abide persecution of innocent people; and I can't abide cruelty to harmless animals. Don't you fret

193

yourself, Mistress Warrener, I'll sort this out.'

Once again, she'd drawn a blank. Pierrepoint and his wife would no more kill a cat than fly to the moon. Maybe he'd find out something from the ale-house regulars.

It was after dark when Nicholas got back to Peverell Manor. Geoffrey Lowe was waiting up for him. When he helped him off with his boots and brought him a tray of food, he told him about what had happened to Agnes Myles's cat.

'Mistress Warrener came looking for you this morning. I expect it was about this. It's a wicked thing to happen and I hope the devils who did it are found. Not much you can do tonight, sir,' he said, as Nicholas reached out for his boots. 'Master Warrener wouldn't take kindly to you bothering his daughter at this hour. Best go and see her tomorrow.'

Wearily, Nicholas went up to his room. He fell asleep as soon as his head touched the pillow. Just after midnight, he was woken up by a loud banging on the door and Geoffrey came in.

'Wake up, my Lord. There's a fire down in the village. You can see it from the gatehouse. Seems to be coming from the direction of Agnes Myles's house.'

Nicholas leapt out of bed and threw on some clothes. Then he went to the gatehouse and saw the flames which were lighting up the night sky over Agnes Myles's cottage. Already his servants were running down towards the blaze. Fire was everybody's dread, and everyone had a responsibility to try to put it out. Unfortunately the rain had stopped, but at least Agnes had her own well in her garden.

A groom brought round one of the other horses, and Nicholas mounted and galloped off down to the village.

Agnes's garden was full of dark figures, some, mostly his own servants, were already filling buckets of water from the well. Someone was trying to get people to form a

194

chain. Others did nothing. Nicholas jumped off his horse and shouted to them.

'Come on. Everyone's needed. Do you want to see her house go up in flames?'

It was the wooden shed which was burning furiously. Fortunately the wind had died down and the flames had not yet reached the house.

'She's an old witch,' said someone from the back of the crowd. 'She'll be the next one to burn, and serves her right.'

'Get hold of that man,' shouted Nicholas to Geoffrey, who'd joined them. 'And don't let him go. Now where's the old lady?'

'She's inside,' said a woman's voice. 'Mistress Warrener's with her.'

'Geoffrey, get this lot organised. Seize hold of anyone who won't co-operate. And get someone over to the Sheriff. Tell him he's needed urgently.'

He ran into the house, where Agnes Myles was sitting defiantly in her chair. Jane was on her knees in front of her. She looked up as Nicholas came in.

'She won't leave this house. She could have a bed with us. My father can't stand cruelty. Try and persuade her, Nicholas.'

Nicholas took hold of Agnes's hands. They were cold and she was shivering with shock.

'I want you to come with me, Agnes. There are evil people outside who want to harm you. Now I know somewhere where you can be safe until we've caught the people who want to harm you. There's a place in the Priory where she'll be safe, Jane,' he said. 'I don't want her staying with anyone in the village. It would be too dangerous both for her and the people she's staying with. Come, let me lift you up, Agnes. You'll be safe with me.'

Suddenly her body seemed to crumple and she fell forward. Before he could stop her she collapsed on the floor. The strain had been too much for her frail body, and she fainted with the horror of it all. He stooped down and picked her up in his arms and carried her outside, where already Geoffrey's organised team was bringing the fire under control. Some people cheered when they saw him. Others hissed. There were cries of 'Witch, witch, burn the witch,' but Nicholas took no notice. He carried Agnes to his horse, laid her carefully on its back, and led her down to the Priory. Jane walked with him, leading Melissa.

The frightened gatekeeper let them in and went to fetch the Prior, who'd just finished Matins. He came out straight away.

'What's this, my Lord? Am I expected to provide lodgings for all the old women in the village?'

'No, Prior. Agnes Myles needs a refuge. People are burning her property; they could start on her next. They are calling her a witch, and you know that's ridiculous.'

'Of course it is. Mistress Myles doesn't know anything about witchcraft. I know she's on our side, not the devil's. Brother Michael thinks the world of her. Some ignorant mischief-maker is spreading these rumours. I know, let's put her in the anchorite's cell. There's a bed in there and a chair, and we can lock the door.'

'And give me the key,' said Jane firmly. 'I'll be the only person who has access to her. I can bring her food every day, and see she has everything she wants.'

'Good idea. I can't have the monks looking after her. That wouldn't do at all.'

They carried Agnes round to the little hermit's cell, which had been built on the southern side of the priory. It was a small stone room, with a window cut into the wall of the Priory for the occupant to see Mass being celebrated on the high altar. It had been occupied for twenty years when the last occupant had died, but the bed was still firm and dry and there was a comfortable chair. Jane said she'd fetch some bed clothes and a rug for the floor. They laid Agnes down on the bed and Nicholas covered her with his cloak. She was still unconscious. They left her and went out, locking the door. Jane put the key in her pocket.

'Thank you, Prior,' she said. 'I wish everyone was as charitable as you.'

'I hate victimisation of innocent people,' he said. 'She'll be safe there as long as I'm head of this house.'

The Prior went off to his bed. Nicholas turned to Jane. 'You were right, Jane, as usual. I only wish I'd paid more attention to you before. Agnes knows something. Somebody wants rid of her, that's for sure. When she wakes up, see if she can remember the names of anyone who's been to see her recently. It doesn't matter if she doesn't think they're of any importance. We might think differently. Now I must go back to her house and see that the fire is put out. I've sent for the Sheriff and asked Geoffrey to keep hold of anyone who refused to co-operate in putting out the fire. Tomorrow, the Sheriff will start an investigation. Have you got any ideas yet about who killed her cat?'

'So you've already heard?'

'Geoffrey told me.'

'It was awful, Nicholas. They strung him up on a tree and hung an obscene notice round his neck. I've been to see two people today; one, the mother of the baby who died; she might have had it in for Agnes. The other was the churchwarden, who knows most things in the parish and can read and write. You see, whoever killed Ambrose knew how to write. But one thing's certain, Edgar Pierrepoint would never kill anybody's cat, not if it belonged to the devil himself, and Abigail had nothing but good to say about Agnes. Also, none of her family can read or write. However, Pierrepoint said he'd go down to the ale-house and talk to the regulars to see if they know anything. But at least Agnes is safe here. No one's going to burn down the Priory to get at her.'

He stared at her in admiration. 'Jane, what would I do without you? Local knowledge is vital if we're to fit all the pieces together. I go dashing round the county to talk to the Sheriffs and Southamptons of this world and you stay here and fill in the details. I always knew we'd make a wonderful team. Come and report to me tomorrow. Usual place. After your father's midday meal. Now I must be off to Agnes's house and see that it's made secure. We don't want thieves in to make the situation worse. Tomorrow I shall see the Sheriff. Jane, dear Jane, sleep well.'

Chapter Nineteen

'This is a pretty kettle of fish you've got landed with, Lord Nicholas,' said Sheriff Landstock, drawing a chair up to the kitchen table. It was Sunday morning and he'd just returned from checking out Agnes Myles's house. 'Who'd want to burn down an old woman's shed? Not her house, mind you, her shed. Thanks to your prompt action last night Agnes Myles has still got a house to come home to. Now, I suppose we ought to take a look at these two wretches you've hauled in. Who are they, by the way?'

'One's called Bovet, Tim Bovet. The other's a Will Perkins. Not from round here. Seem to be a couple of ne'er-do-wells. They earn a bit here and there and spend it in the taverns. They sleep where they can and help themselves to whatever they can lay their hands on and then move off before they get caught. However, that doesn't make them arsonists.'

'Why did you bring 'em in then?'

'Because neither of them lifted a finger to help put out the fire and both shouted insults at Agnes Myles.'

'Not enough to make an arrest. Do you want me to take them back to Marchester? I can hold them for questioning. They can cool off in my gaol and I can cross-examine them. If they've got anything to hide, we'll soon get it out of them.'

'That sounds the best idea. I can't hold them here for

ever in my cellar. Here, Richard, help yourself.' Nicholas pushed the jug of ale across the table.

'The thing is, my Lord,' said Sheriff Landstock, pouring himself out a tankard of ale, 'have these two got any connection with this fellow we're looking for? The traitor who's going to cause mayhem when the King arrives. The one with the damn silly name?'

'You mean Ultor? The answer is, I don't know. All I can say is that I'm uneasy about what's going on here. One murder – we know who was responsible for that – one suspected murder, and now a persecution of a harmless old woman who's never been threatened before. At the moment, I regard everyone as a possible suspect.'

'That's the best thing to do, but I can't, for the life of me, see any connection between setting an old lady's shed on fire and finding out who Ultor is. Sometimes people just gang up against someone for no particular reason. It takes just one rumour and the mob's ready for action. Very nasty. It mustn't be allowed to happen. We can't have mob rule.'

'Quite right, Richard. We must nip it in the bud.'

They drank their ale in silence, both men lost in thought. Suddenly, Sheriff Landstock looked up and glanced across at Nicholas.

'It's possible, of course – though I can scarcely believe it – that Agnes Myles could've been a witness?'

'It certainly is possible. I'm coming round to thinking that she might have seen or done or heard something that could incriminate Ultor. Once she loosens her tongue we might learn what it is. She needs protection and that's why I've put her in a safe place.'

'You said she's in the Priory. Is that safe enough?'

'I've put her in the anchorite's cell and Jane's got the key.'

'Jane?' The Sheriff raised a bushy, ginger eyebrow.

'My accomplice.'

'You've got an accomplice, and she's a woman? I'm

amazed, my Lord. You do like making things difficult for
yourself. Murder, treason, arson – these are not things a
woman ought to get involved in.'

'Jane Warrener's the best spy anyone could have. She
can go where none of your men could go. People talk to
her.'

'I can see that. But watch out she's not the next victim. If
she asks too many questions she'll end up face down in the
village pond.'

Nicholas winced. It was what he most feared. As soon as
possible he'd have her off the case; not that she'd take a
blind bit of notice, he thought ruefully.

'Anyway,' said Landstock, getting up and going over to
the fire, 'that's your affair, and I hope you know what
you're doing. But, back to Agnes Myles. If she really is a
witness, then why doesn't Ultor simply bump her off like
he did with the other witness, Bess Knowles, if you're right
about her? Why go through all this charade putting it about
that she's a witch? Why not burn her house down when
she's asleep? It's easy to make it look like an accident.'

'I've thought of that. I think that if Ultor's behind this,
he wants the mob to do his dirty work for him. If he did kill
Bess Knowles, he won't want to kill again too quickly.
We've got a cunning devil here, Sheriff. He knows he's
running out of time. It's only nine days before the King
arrives. He doesn't want the finger of suspicion pointing in
his direction. One old lady, who might have heard something that could incriminate him, could blow his cover sky
high. He'll be wanting the mob to take over and whilst
we're trying to restore law and order in the village the heat
will be taken off him.'

'God, let's hope that woman starts talking soon.'

'At the moment she's in such a state of terror that she's
still drifting in and out of consciousness. Jane's going to try
and get her to talk when she recovers. When she does, it
could take a long time before she gets her wits together. It's
more than likely that she'll have lost her memory. A shock

can do that, as you know. Also, she has a constant stream of people coming to her house for healing herbs and to ask advice about all sorts of problems. She's known all over the county. I doubt whether she'll remember who they all were.'

'If she can tell us anything it would help. At the moment it's all supposition. In the meantime, let's take a look at these two wretches you've got in your cellar. Maybe they can tell us something.'

They went over to the keep and Nicholas unlocked the door. Taking a lighted torch from the bracket on the wall, they went down a steep, spiral staircase to what had been the dungeons in the days when country houses had to double up as castles. Geoffrey Lowe now used the dungeons as cellars to store produce, but one of the rooms was too small and too damp to be much use as a food store. Nicholas unlocked the door and they went in. Lifting up his torch, as the room had no window, he saw the two men huddled together against the far wall on a layer of straw.

'Well, you two, here's the Sheriff come to see you. Now tell him why you wouldn't help us save Mistress Myles's shed last night? You know you've got a duty to help put out fires. And you also know it's an offence to slander a person without proof.'

'We don't need any proof,' said the older man, Will Perkins. 'Everyone knows she's an old witch.'

'Who said so?'

'Everyone says so.'

'Who's everyone?' said the Sheriff coming closer to peer at them.

'How should I know who they are? People you talk to in the ale-house, those sort of people.'

'Which ale-house?'

'One in Marchester. Down near the new cross they're building.'

'So why did you come to Dean Peverell?'

202

'We often come here, don't we, Tim,' Will Perkins said to the younger man, who was shivering on the straw next to him. 'There's work to do at this time of the year. The Prior lets us help with the lambs. We pick up pieces of wool from the shearing and the monks let us keep them. Comes in useful for covers for the winter. So we comes down here, drinks a few jars at the ale-house, and we sleep in one of the Prior's barns. Then we hears that there's a bit of a rumpus about an old woman down the road, and there might be a chance to see a bit of fun. Nothing like a good witch baiting. You should see them swing up on Marchester Heath with all their petticoats flying up over their heads in the wind. So we comes here and went along last night to join in the fun. But we don't help an old woman to save her shed where she makes up all those evil spells. We don't care if her house is burned down, and what's more, neither does anyone else. We weren't the only ones to stand back from the flames. If that old busy-body hadn't come along and got everyone organised with buckets of water the village would have been rid of its witch.'

'So you didn't go near the fire?' said Nicholas, going closer to the two men and shining the torch in their faces.

'Nope. Nothing to do with us. We got there after it was started.'

'So why is there a big scorch mark on your sleeve?' said Nicholas, indicating with his torch a large burnt area on the sleeve of the man's jacket.

Perkins peered at the patch. 'That's because I got too near to the blaze and nearly set myself on fire.'

'And yet you said you didn't go near the fire?'

'That was later, when that bossy fellow tried to get us organised. I did take a peek at it when we first got there. Now are you going to let us go? We've got nothing to tell, nothing to hide. We didn't see who started the fire. In fact I can't see why anyone would want to burn down her old shed. If you want to kill a witch, you burn down her house with her inside it. Now that's what I call fun. You've got to

203

let us go, you know. We've got our rights, haven't we, Tim?'

'Yes. We've got our rights,' echoed the younger man.

'Now don't start on about your rights,' said Sheriff Landstock impatiently. 'You didn't do your duty last night did you? You refused to help put out the fire and I'm going to take you into Marchester for further questioning. If you can tell us who started the fire, you'll be released and back in your taverns again by nightfall.'

The two men looked indignantly at the Sheriff. 'We don't know nothing. You can't take us in for not knowing nothing.'

'Yes, I can. Nothing easier. Now don't give us any trouble and you'll soon be off the hook.'

They left the two men protesting vociferously and went back up the stairs into the daylight. Nicholas put the torch back in its bracket.

'Think they're going to be any use?' he said to Landstock.

'Miserable-looking bastards. No, I can't see that they're going to be much help. But there is that burnt patch on that fellow's sleeve. He didn't give us a convincing explanation as to how he got it.'

'This all seems a far cry from our main task, to catch Ultor before the King gets here,' said Nicholas leading the way back towards the main house.

'If Agnes Myles talks or these two men give us the name of the person who started the fire, we could be home and dry sooner than you think.'

'I'd like to be able to share your optimism. But what bothers me is, is there any connection between Ultor, someone who's literate and writes letters to Reginald Pole, and two women living in a small Sussex village? Wait a minute . . .' Nicholas stopped.

'Well, what is it?'

'Let's try this for an idea. Just suppose that Ultor is Gilbert Fitzroy. No, don't look so surprised; it's not as way

204

out as it sounds. We know he went to see Mortimer. They discussed various treasonable activities. Then we know Fitzroy shopped Mortimer; the King himself told me that. Maybe he shopped Mortimer, whom he could see was doomed, in order to ingratiate himself with the King. Now we know Matthew and Bess Knowles overheard one of their conversations. That's why Matthew was murdered. Let's suppose that after Mortimer was arrested, Fitzroy, having made it quite clear that his sympathies were with the King, took over the leadership of the conspiracy. He called himself Ultor – the Avenger. Maybe he planned it all from the start. Maybe Mortimer was just his side-kick. Maybe he wanted Mortimer out of the way so that he could get his hands on his estate, and also be the power behind the throne if a Yorkist became King. He told the King he had nothing to do with Mortimer's scheming and it suited the King to believe him because Fitzroy, as Lord Lieutenant of the county, is important to him. Now, after Mortimer's arrest, Fitzroy would want Bess Knowles finished off. Perhaps he sent someone down to Agnes Myles to get a deadly potion to put in Bess's drink. He wouldn't go there in person, of course, but he could have sent one of his servants. And now he's got to get rid of Agnes before she remembers that servant coming to see her. She'd certainly remember one of Fitzroys' servants; and he'd have to tell her who he was because she wouldn't give her lethal potions to just anybody. Agnes has got to talk to us.'

'It's a good theory, my Lord, but too many "maybe's". You can't invent a plot and then arrange the facts to suit it. We know Fitzroy shopped Mortimer but the rest's just guesswork. Also, I just can't see Fitzroy getting involved with the Pole family. He's got everything to gain by remaining loyal to Harry Tudor. He's not a fanatic. He couldn't care less whether the monks go or stay, or if the King makes himself head of the Church. He's only interested in Fitzroy. I agree he might have wanted Mortimer out of the way so that he could buy his manor, but I can't see him as Ultor. He's not devious enough. And he hasn't one jot of imagination. And what makes you think Fitzroy's capable of carrying on a correspondence with Reginald Pole? I had to read a letter to him the other day and he had a job writing his signature.'

'Fitzroy must have his own clerks. He keeps a big household,' said Nicholas.

'Even so, Fitzroy's more interested in his hunting dogs than writing letters. But we ought to play safe. We'll keep him out of the King's way when he comes. He didn't say whether he intends to pay Fitzroy a visit on his way back to Hampton Court, did he?'

'No, he intends to go straight back to London. The Queen's expecting a child any time now. And he's quite sure this time it will be a boy and nothing must go wrong.'

'Good. As a matter of fact, I can't see the King wanting to pay Fitzroy a visit. I can't see him trusting him.'

'He doesn't trust anyone, Sheriff.'

'Oh yes he does. He trusts you, my Lord. He knows you'd never make a traitor. You haven't got the stomach for it.'

'Thanks for the compliment, Sheriff. You certainly know how to put a man down. However, you're right about me not being a traitor; but not because I'm a coward. With all his faults, King Henry will keep the country together. God knows what would happen if the Yorkists came back in power. We'd slip back into anarchy. Also, it's a relief to have an easy conscience. At least I can sleep soundly at night.'

Sheriff Landstock left after a hearty midday meal. His two assistants carted Perkins and Bovet away to Marchester. Geoffrey grumbled about how much they'd depleted his stocks of food which he was building up for the King's visit; and Nicholas thought about Jane's visit that afternoon.

*

206

They both arrived together at the gate leading into the gardens. Nicholas took her hand and led her into the inner garden where the fruit trees were in full blossom and the spring flowers made bright punctuation marks in the lush green meadow grass. Nicholas took her over to a stone seat under the fruit trees and they sat down. Yesterday's storm had passed away and the air was fresh and full of the scents of the newly washed plants. He looked at his beautiful assistant and once again felt that painful rush of fear at the thought that anything unpleasant could happen to her.

'Jane, I think you should let this case drop now. You've been very useful to me, but now I think things are getting dangerous. Let the Sheriff and me find out who this Ultor is.'

She stared at him in blank astonishment and her face flushed scarlet. 'I can't back out now, Nicholas. I'm just as much involved in this as you are. You've lost a steward. I've lost a friend and could lose another if we're not careful. Agnes is safe for the moment, but she can't stay there for ever.'

'She must stay there until we find Ultor. Have you been to see Agnes today?'

'Of course. What kind of person do you think I am? Do you think I would let an old woman go without food and bedding? The monks won't go near her, that's for sure, and the villagers think she should be dragged out and hanged. The rumours haven't stopped because the fire was put out. In fact they've got worse. People are now saying she started the fire herself to burn the evidence of her wicked spells. They think she's in league with the devil, and they blame the Prior for sheltering her.'

'Time's running out. There'll be no rest until we find Ultor. One thing's clear, that's for sure, he wants Agnes Myles silenced. And he's setting about it in a devious way. He wants other people to do his work for him. He could've burned down her house with her in it, but no, he sets her shed on fire. Now why? Did he know she kept something in there which could incriminate him? I wonder ... is the shed completely destroyed?'

'I could check on my way home.'

'I'll come with you, Jane. Has Agnes said anything to you, yet?'

'Of course not. The poor soul's been frightened out of her mind. She can't remember anything at the moment, except what happened to Ambrose and the fire. But I'll keep trying.'

'And Jane, take care. If it gets around that you are seeing Agnes regularly, then your life could be in real danger. I couldn't bear it if anything happened to you.'

He took hold of her hands and examined her slender fingers one by one. 'These hands are made to play the lute, not to put out fires. One day, when this is all over, Jane, you must come here and play just to me. And we will talk of music and dancing and love, and forget all these horrors.'

She flashed him a smile and withdrew her hands. 'I would love that, Nicholas, but there's just one small problem.'

'And what's that?'

'I've got an old and crabby father whom I happen to love, but who loathes the gentry. You'll have to get round him first before he'll let me come up here and play music to you. He's trying to find me a nice respectable wool merchant, someone he can gossip with; someone who won't make him feel inferior.'

'We can soon put a stop to all that. He can call me Nicholas like you do.'

'That'll be the day, my Lord,' she said, her eyes twinkling. 'Maybe he'll mellow as he gets older. But let's get down to Agnes's cottage.'

They rode together down to the village. Thyme Cottage hadn't been touched by the fire, but the shed was almost destroyed. Only a couple of corner posts were still standing looking like two blackened teeth. They picked their way over the charred wood and the smashed bottles, their contents spilled out and congealed on the floor. There was nothing here that they could salvage.

'I don't know what she kept in here. I don't think she ever made an inventory, but I think there was a row of pottery jars on a shelf over there. There's no sign of them now. Of course, Agnes could have rearranged her stock before the fire, but I think that someone knew what was in those jars and came back after the fire was over and took them away. Anyway, there's nothing left now.'

'It sounds like Ultor wanted to destroy the evidence in those bottles. Maybe he came back in the early hours of the morning. Maybe he hid somewhere until everyone had gone home. Damn, how stupid I've been! I should've put a guard on the house.'

'You weren't to know there was anything important to steal in the shed. After all, it was completely destroyed. I wonder if Agnes can remember anything about the contents of those jars. Nicholas, I pray to God that she's safe in her little room.'

'It must be the safest place in the county, Jane. She's in a strongly built room with no outside window, attached to a Priory. And you have the key.'

'You're quite right. I'll try not to worry about her. But I'm terrified he might strike again.'

They stood there looking at the blackened heap of rubbish that was once Agnes's apothecary's store. The shadows were creeping across the garden; evening was drawing in. Jane shivered.

'Who is this Ultor, Nicholas? He's clever, literate and ruthless. He'll not hesitate to get rid of an old woman who might be a witness.'

'And he's devious,' said Nicholas. 'And dangerous, Jane. He must never suspect you're involved in all this.'

'He'll not suspect a feeble woman. I'm only doing what all charitable women do – visiting the sick. No, I don't

209

think I'm in any danger. You are much more vulnerable.'

'He wants me alive, right enough. I'm necessary to his plans. After all, the King's coming to stay in my house. Of course if, God forbid, he succeeds in his plotting, he'll get rid of me later on.'

'We must find him, Nicholas. But where do we go from here?'

'You tell me, Jane.'

'Me? But I'm only a feeble woman. How should I know?'

Chapter Twenty

'Forty people!' exclaimed Geoffrey Lowe.

'At least,' said Nicholas looking at him impatiently. 'Oh stop panicking; you're acting like an old woman. Use your imagination. This is the King we're talking about. He'll have at least ten personal servants; the Queen about the same. She's expecting a child, remember, and will have extra ladies-in-waiting. Then there are the six yeomen, the King's personal bodyguard. We must invite the Prior, the Sheriff plus two of his side-kicks; and then there's Warrener. He'll have to be invited, I suppose.'

'Why the hell do we have to ask him?'

'Because his daughter's going to sing for us. Oh yes, that means Brother Benedict will have to come; and there'll be some musicians as well. Damn! That means we ought to ask the Bishop; but on second thoughts, no. There's been enough trouble in the cathedral lately. So get it into your head that there'll be at least forty people sitting down to dinner on the night of the seventh. Then don't forget the servants and the lay brothers; they'll want soup and small beer and cold meats.'

'My Lord, what about the night of the sixth? They won't expect a banquet surely?'

'No, with any luck, they'll all be tired. They'll need a good selection of roasts – the King's got a good appetite – nothing elaborate, mind. The Queen'll not want to stay up late.'

'What's the timetable for the seventh, my Lord? I'm not prying into matters that are none of my business,' he said, seeing Nicholas's look of surprise. 'I only want to know what time the King's going to want his dinner.'

'Don't worry. It hasn't occurred to me that you might be a spy. I'm afraid I can only give you an approximate time. It all depends on the King's whim. It's not unknown for him to order a banquet and then not turn up because something else has caught his fancy. But I think high water's around midday, and the fleet will only have a couple of hours to sail past before they'll have to make their offing.'

'A tight timetable, my Lord. The King'll be worn out.'

'King Harry? Exhausted? That'll be the day.'

'The Queen'll surely not want to go with him; the Portsmouth road is terrible after the recent storm.'

'Oh there you go again! Just stop worrying, Geoffrey. It's not going to happen until next week. The road'll dry out by then. Now tell me what you're going to feed us on and be quick as I've got work to do.'

'I've put aside ten lambs, still suckling. Six kids. Two oxen. A barrel of salt eels. We'll need half a dozen pigs, at least. Very useful they are when it comes to feeding large numbers. Mary makes good sausages, port meat, mixed with fresh herbs and stuffed into the pig's entrails ...'

'Mary?'

Geoffrey gave a guilty start and looked away. 'Mary Woodman – you know, Mortimer's cook. She's tired of looking after Roland, Fitzroy's steward, and she's offered to come over and help us. She's over here most days giving me a hand. She's a marvellous cook; great with fruit and honey desserts; we're lucky to have her.'

'Why not ask Fitzroy's steward to come over and help us out?'

'Not on your life, sir. We don't want the likes of him poking his nose into everything.'

A knock on the door, and Anthony, Geoffrey's nephew,

212

came in. He shuffled his feet nervously, not wanting to interrupt.

'Well, what is it?' said Nicholas.

'There's a man come to see you, my Lord. Says you sent for him.'

'Me? I haven't sent for anyone as far as I know. Well, did you ask his name?'

'He says he's Amos Cartwright.'

'Well, I don't know him.'

'He's the haberdasher, my Lord. You know, you asked me to find you one,' said Geoffrey.

Nicholas gave a start. Of course, the King's new doublet. How could he have forgotten it?

'Oh yes, now I remember. Well, tell him to come in.'

Anthony left the room, returning minutes later with one of the strangest men Nicholas had ever seen. He was tiny, with a neat, slim body, a sharp, pointed face, and a receding hairline. His skinny legs were encased in woollen stockings, brown with an orange pattern on them of trailing vines. A beautifully fitting jacket made of brown wool of the finest quality, the sleeves slashed to reveal a fine cream shirt underneath. A young man, with a long-suffering expression, staggering under the weight of several bales of cloth, accompanied him. They looked like a couple from elfin land, and Nicholas had a job to stop himself from bursting out laughing.

'Good morning, my Lord,' said the little man. 'Cartwright from Marchester. Tailor and haberdasher. This is my assistant, Christopher. You want me to make a jacket, I understand.'

'You're very welcome. Now, put those bales of cloth on the table, and we'll take a look at them. Stay with us, Geoffrey. We'll need you as a model.'

'Me, my Lord? I can't afford a jacket.'

'It's not for you. I owe the King a new doublet and he's not likely to forget. Now measure up my steward, Master Cartwright, whilst I take a look at the cloth. The King's about your size round the chest and belly,' he said, poking Geoffrey in the middle. 'He's a bit shorter than me. Now get it right, Master Cartwright. The King's very particular about his clothes.'

Cartwright was visibly shaken. He clutched hold of the back of a chair and gazed helplessly at Nicholas. 'The King, did you say?'

'That's right. Didn't you know? Don't panic, man. This is the chance of a lifetime. The King of England comes to Dean Peverell and you've been asked to make him a coat. It'll get you a royal warrant and your descendants will be the most envied tailors in the whole of Sussex.'

'My Lord, I'm not worthy . . .' babbled Cartwright. 'I'm overcome with the honour.'

'Oh, pull yourself together,' said Nicholas impatiently. 'It's only a coat. Let's get on with it.'

Whilst the two men set about measuring Geoffrey Lowe, Nicholas studied the bales of cloth. Eventually he chose a soft velvet fabric, the colour of fresh green leaves in spring. He held it up to the sunlight and shafts of light played over it, making it shimmer like a rainbow over a waterfall.

'This is the one. It'll go with his red hair. Good country colour. Make it fit Geoffrey. Have ties down the front so that it can give an inch or two if necessary. Make a good collar. The King likes collars.'

'When's the King coming, my Lord?' said Cartwright nervously.

'I'll need to have it here by the fifth. The King's got a habit of suddenly changing his plans.'

'But that only gives me eight days,' Cartwright wailed.

'Plenty of time. Now what are you waiting for? Hurry up and do your measuring. Give Master Cartwright and his assistant some beef and beer when they're finished, Geoffrey. Now I must get over to the stables and see to the horses.'

Anthony had slipped in quietly again and glanced across at Nicholas.

'A monk to see you, my Lord.'

'A monk! What sort of monk?'

'They all look the same to me.'

'Don't be a fool. Young? Old? Fat? Thin?'

'Young, my lord. Dark hair, thin.'

'Brother Benedict! Now what the devil does he want?'

'The Prior'd like to see you, Lord Nicholas,' said Brother Benedict, bowing deferentially.

'Did he say what he wants?'

Brother Benedict looked at him reproachfully. 'No, my Lord. It's not for me to know what's in the Prior's mind.'

'Well, I suppose I ought to get down to see what he wants. Did you come on horseback?'

'Me? Oh no. Monks don't ride horses.'

'Well, you can hitch a lift behind me if you like.'

'Oh I couldn't do that. What'll the Prior say if he sees me? I shall have to make a public penance in front of all the Brothers in the Chapter House.'

Nicholas shrugged his shoulders, collected Harry from the stables and rode down to the Priory, Benedict walking briskly behind him.

The Prior was waiting for them at the gatehouse. He looked his usual benevolent self, but Nicholas could sense an air of anxiety about him.

'How much longer do I have to put up with this old woman on my premises, Lord Nicholas? It won't do, you know. The brethren don't like it. Some of them think she's a witch. A very bad witch; in league with the devil. Mind you, I keep an open mind on such matters. I'm very tolerant, easy-going to a fault, I think. I need evidence before I condemn someone, and Agnes Myles seems quite harmless to me. But I'd still like her out of here.'

'What's bothering you, Prior? She's out of your way. Mistress Warrener's looking after her. She's harmless.'

'That remains to be seen. And that's another thing,

Mistress Jane's down here a bit too often for comfort. Some of the brothers are getting restless. She's upsetting them. Brother Martin's taken to sneaking out of the infirmary to wait for her. Brother Michael will have to start bleeding them again. Well, whilst we're here, we might as well take a look in the infirmary. Brother Wilfrid keeps asking for you, my Lord. He's taking a mighty long time to take his leave of us. Still, God knows when He wants Brother Wilfrid to join Him.'

They strolled over to the infirmary, which was close to the gatehouse. At the door, the Prior stopped suddenly and turned to face Nicholas. 'The Commissioners will be here tomorrow, my Lord. What am I going to do with 'em, eh? I'm told they're going to be here for two weeks. Two weeks! What the hell are they going to do in two weeks?'

'It'll take them that time to prepare the inventory,' said Nicholas, making a mental note to add them to the guest list.

'You really think it'll take them that long?'

'I'm sure it will. But don't worry, Prior. The King's coming and you can have a word with him. You'll come to dinner when he's here, won't you?'

'When have you ever known me to refuse a dinner, my Lord?'

So that was what was bothering the Prior, thought Nicholas. He was getting nervous about the inspection. And so he should. The Commissioners were going to look for faults; even where none existed. They were going to provide the King with a good excuse for destroying the monasteries, so that he could sleep at night with an easy conscience.

Inside the infirmary, the sun streamed in through the narrow, high windows and fell on the beds of the three sick, old men. Wilfrid was there, his shrunken face peaceful in sleep, his breathing shallow but regular. Nicholas picked up his gnarled hand, small and boney like a bird's claw. He shook it gently, but Wilfrid didn't wake up. He

216

was conscious that someone was standing behind him and turned round to see Brother Michael, the Infirmarer, standing there, his pale face twisted into a smile.

'It's good of you to come and see him, my Lord. He often asks for you.'

'Well, don't wake him up now. I'll drop in some other time.'

Brother Michael nodded and went back into the apothecary's room. Nicholas went out and joined the Prior, who'd been waiting for him.

'Come across and have a drink. I need your advice on what to do with these visitors. They've checked out Lewes Priory and now they're going to start on us. Then, I suppose they'll go to Marchester and check on the good friars there. This is a most appalling intrusion.'

As they walked through the cloisters, they met Father Hubert scurrying past them, holding a large wicker basket.

'That's right, Father,' the Prior said, his face lighting up with a smile of satisfaction, 'off you go. Make sure they're young and fresh, mind. None of your tough old leaves. He collects fresh sorrel and young nettles for me, my Lord, up in your woods.'

Nicholas stopped. 'Do you go every day?'

'No, my Lord, just sometimes. When the Prior says he needs fresh green leaves.'

'They're excellent, Lord Nicholas. Nothing like fresh nettles, simmered for just a few seconds in boiling water. Good for the bowels at this time of the year,' the Prior said, patting his substantial belly.

'Did you go up in the woods last week, Father Hubert?' said Nicholas. 'Let's say, the Monday of last week, in the afternoon? I think I might have seen you there.'

'You might have done, my Lord, but I can't remember. I still feel a bit weak . . .'

'I warned you. You'll addle your brain with all that bleeding. I expect he was up there, Lord Nicholas. He goes up most days.'

So that was one mystery solved, thought Nicholas as he followed the Prior into his house. Just harmless old Father Hubert gathering plants to ease the Prior's bowels. He'd look just like a patch of shade up under the trees. No wonder Merlin started. Nothing more sinister than that. He laughed with relief. How good it would be if everything could be solved as simply as that.

'Come and see me when you get back, Father,' said the Prior. 'I shall want all the silver cleaned for the Commissioners' inspection.'

Father Hubert stopped and looked at the Prior anxiously. 'I'll do my best. But I can't get everything cleaned before they come. Will they really want to see everything?'

'Everything. That's why they're coming. Now, my Lord, just tell me what I'm going to do with them. Bloody civil servants! I can't abide them.'

Nicholas rode slowly home, deep in thought. Much as he liked the Prior, he deplored his light-hearted attitude towards the imminent arrival of Thomas Cromwell's Commissioners. Didn't he realise that they meant business? he thought as he trotted up the deserted street. No longer were there groups of villagers shouting out greetings and swapping news. It was as if the events of the last few days had cast a deep gloom over the place. The arrival of Thomas Cromwell's men would unsettle everyone even more.

The Prior didn't seem to know what these men were capable of, he thought. They would pry into every nook and cranny of the Priory's affairs, study the account books, scrutinise the daily life of the monks, note down who attended services, who stayed away. They'd inspect the kitchens, raise eyebrows at the Prior's well-stocked cellar, gloat over the number of horses the Prior kept in his stables, exclaim over the carriage which the Prior used when visiting neighbouring parishes over which he had jurisdiction. They'd note the amount of lead on the church

218

roof, the number, weight and size of the bells, and the amount and value of the church furnishings.

And one thing was clear – the Commissioners would not take kindly to the harbouring of a suspected witch on the monastic premises. Maybe, he thought, as he turned in to his driveway, the Prior could pass her off as a holy anchoress. But the monks would object. No, time was running out for Agnes Myles, as it was running out for him. And that was just what Ultor was reckoning on. He'd framed Agnes, that was for sure. He wanted her disposed of; and he was setting about it very efficiently.

When he got back, Geoffrey was waiting for him with a message which had just arrived from the Sheriff. The messenger had left saying no answer was necessary.

'Lord Nicholas,' he read. 'I'm holding on to Bovet and Perkins for the time being. I'm sure they know more than they let on. They do admit that they often go to the ale-house in your village, so it might be useful if you could talk to the ale-house keeper and see if he overheard anything significant last Saturday night. Our two suspects could've been paid to start the fire, of course. The ale-house keeper could've seen money changing hands. There's still that burn mark on Perkins's sleeve not accounted for. Send for me if there's any more trouble. Landstock.'

Nicholas finished reading, and called for his horse again. He rode back down the street, arriving at the ale-house just as Josh Tomkins was getting ready for his afternoon nap. He was a big, florid-faced man, with sparse black hair, and a dirty apron tied round his enormous girth. Small, piggy eyes looked at Nicholas nervously as he ducked his head under the door lintel and went into the dim, smoked-filled interior.

'To what do I owe the honour of this visit, my Lord?' Tomkins said obsequiously. 'You know my licence is in order. There've been no complaints about the quality of my ale, I hope? I only use the best malt.'

'It's not your ale I'm interested in,' said Nicholas,

219

pushing aside two mongrels who were snarling over the bits dropped on the floor by the customers. Biddy Tomkins was famous for her boiled bacon hocks, which went down well with the travellers along the main coast road. Tomkins wiped over a table top with a corner of his apron, and pushed a chair over to Nicholas, who shook his head.

'A drink, my Lord?'

'No thanks. I'm not staying. You get a good crowd in here, don't you?'

'Most days we're full up.'

'People come here from Marchester?'

'Sometimes. Not often. They've got their own places to go to.'

'Do you know two men called Tim Bovet and Will Perkins?'

Tomkins looked shifty. 'Might do. They come here to give the monks a hand with the lambing. What've they been up to?'

'Were they in here last Saturday night? The night before the fire in Agnes Myles's shed?'

Again the cautious look. Careful now, thought Nicholas. Don't frighten him off. 'I can't remember,' said Tomkins, busily wiping down the tables. 'There are always lots of people here on Saturday nights.'

'Come on, man. It's not all that long ago. Think hard.'

'Well, I suppose they could've been. After all, they're regulars when they come to work here.'

'Did you hear them, or anyone else for that matter, talking about starting a fire?'

'Oh no, my Lord,' he said, polishing a table with unnecessary vigour. 'I never heard nothing like that. And if I did,' he said, standing up and looking at Nicholas indignantly, 'I would've chucked them out. We don't have such talk in here. Burning down other people's property indeed!'

'So you heard no talk of fire. And no one, in his cups, boasting about starting one?'

'I certainly did not. Ah, here comes Biddy. Come over

220

here a minute,' he said as Biddy Tomkins, flushed and perspiring, came in to collect the empty tankards. 'Lord Nicholas wants to know if we heard anyone talking about starting a fire up at old Agnes's house last Saturday night?'

Biddy came over and dropped a curtsy to Nicholas. 'I didn't hear anyone talk about a fire. It started well after we'd closed and Josh and me were tucked up in bed. We only woke up when one of the servants came hammering on our door and calling out "fire". We got up and went along to Agnes's house, but we were too late to help, of course.'

Nicholas cursed his luck. They were too glib. They'd had time to get their act together.

'You know Sheriff has Perkins and Bovet in custody?'

'We'd heard the rumour. What're they supposed to've done?' said Tomkins, trying to look unconcerned.

'They were reluctant to help put out a fire and they slandered Agnes Myles.'

'Well, that's only to be expected,' said Biddy indignantly. 'What right has a nasty old witch like her to expect people to help her put out a fire? It was only her shed, after all, that went up in smoke. Good riddance to it, I say. Put paid to all her spells for a bit. I can't see why you bother yourself with all this, my Lord. She oughtn't to be here. Best place for her is up on Marchester Heath.'

'And I say it's a monstrous injustice to accuse someone before they're proved guilty. Agnes Myles is a harmless old woman and most of the people around here have been grateful for her help. Didn't you go and see her, Tomkins, when your face sprouted boils last Christmas?'

'She said my blood needed cleaning,' he mumbled, not meeting Nicholas's gaze.

'And they all cleared up, if I remember rightly?'

'She gave me a herbal drink.'

'Well now, would a wicked witch do that?'

'Could've done,' put in Biddy. 'Witches are well known to be two-faced. Look how she frightened your horse up in the woods and nearly killed you.'

'Don't be such a fool and stop spreading such rumours. I had a fall, that's all. One of the monks was up in the woods collecting herbs and my horse was taken by surprise and shied, throwing me to the ground. But enough of this talk. Let's get back to Saturday night. So you heard no one talk about starting a fire?'

'No, my Lord. Just the usual crowd, out for a drink and a laugh.'

'And you saw nothing suspicious? No money changing hands, for instance?'

'Money? Oh no, my Lord, if there was any money around it would've come in my direction.'

'And no laughing about burning an old witch?'

'Oh no, we wouldn't have allowed such talk, would we Biddy?'

'Certainly not. Why waste breath on the likes of her?'

There was no point in probing any further, Nicholas thought as he turned to go. The two had closed ranks. They stood in the doorway watching him mount Harry, who swirled around impatiently. 'Well, let me know if you do hear anything. We want to know who started the fire. Someone must know. Bovet and Perkins might know and sooner or later they'll start talking. There's a reward, you know, for any information leading to the capture of the arsonists. I'll see that it's a good one.'

He pulled Harry round, and rode off. He didn't see the look which the Tomkinses exchanged with one another.

Chapter Twenty-One

'Just take a look at this lot, my Lord. Where's the money coming from?' said Geoffrey, hovering anxiously over Nicholas, who was sitting at a table with a pile of bills in front of him. Nicholas flipped through the pile, paused to read an invoice from the Prior for four butts of Burgundy, then he pushed them aside.

'Where's the money coming from? From me, of course. Who do you think's going to pay 'em? The King? But don't bother me with these now. If it means that I'll have to sell the top field, so be it. At least I know old Warrener'll snap it up, and I'll see he pays a good price for it. Now who the devil's this?'

A clatter of hooves in the courtyard; the sound of metal scraping on stone as a horse slithered to a halt; then Anthony burst in, breathless with excitement.

'A messenger, my Lord, from the Earl of Southampton,' he stammered.

'Well, don't keep him waiting. Just put these somewhere safe, Geoffrey,' he said, pushing the pile of bills towards him, 'and I'll see to them later.'

Geoffrey shuffled the pile together and fastened them with a cord. Anthony returned, followed by a young man in leather breeches and jerkin covered in dust. He handed Nicholas a leather pouch.

'From the Earl, my Lord. Shall I wait for a reply?'

'You'd better hang around. Geoffrey, fetch this young man some food and something to drink. Sit down and rest yourself.'

The young man sank down gratefully on the chair which Nicholas pushed towards him and Nicholas opened the bag and took out the message.

'Peverell,' he read. 'No more communications from Ultor. I don't like it. Either he's using another port, or he's gone to ground. That means he's feeling secure. He's made his plans and he's waiting for the right moment to strike. You must check on everyone; and I mean everyone. The King's coming next week, remember. Destroy this letter immediately. Paget.'

Nicholas cursed under his breath. He was sick and tired of people telling him what to do. And did Southampton take him for a fool? Of course he knew the King was coming. Hadn't he got a pile of bills to prove it?

He called for pen and a sheet of parchment and sat down and wrote.

'My Lord. I am well aware of the urgency of the situation. I also would like to see Ultor flushed out. Rest assured I will do all I can to ensure the King's safety. Would you send me more precise details of the King's timetable for the seventh, please. Are you planning to feed him after the review and put him up for the night? Peverell.'

Then he got up, gave his letter to the young man wolfing down a plateful of cold meats, and put the Earl's letter on the fire, kicking up the logs to make sure every scrap of it was destroyed.

Anthony had returned and was standing awkwardly by the door. 'Not you again,' Nicholas said, 'who is it this time?'

'That monk, my lord. The one who came before. He wants to see you.'

'Finish your food,' he said to the messenger as he left the room. 'Then get back to your master. I shall see you again soon.'

*

224

Nicholas went out into the courtyard where Brother Benedict was waiting for him. He bowed to Nicholas.

'A message from Mistress Warrener, my Lord. She wants to see you. Can she come straight away?'

'Tell her, yes. Tell her I'll meet her in the usual place.'

Benedict bowed and waited. 'What now?' said Nicholas impatiently.

'Prior says will you come and have supper with us tonight. He says he'd appreciate your help with his visitors.'

I'm sure he would, said Nicholas under his breath. 'Tell him I'll be delighted to come. What time?'

'Six. Just an informal supper, he says.'

That means only four courses, thought Nicholas as he watched Benedict leave the house. He paused for a moment, watching the retreating figure of the monk. He needed to speak with Jane, to mull over events, to use her sharp mind. There were so many possible suspects. Brother Benedict, for instance. What did anyone know about him? A visitor from France; always going backwards and forwards to his mother house. He could be in communication with Reginald Pole. He was allowed to roam freely round the village, was the Prior's favourite and probably knew what was in the Prior's mind. Could he be Ultor? Or, at least, could he be working for Ultor? So many suspects; so little time to find the right one.

Jane was waiting for him by the stone seat in the orchard. She came over to meet him.

'We must talk, Nicholas. It's Agnes.'

That name again, he thought. Somehow he knew instinctively that this old lady was going to lead them to Ultor. 'How is she, Jane?' he said.

'Still confused; but getting stronger. The isolation suits her. She's beginning to feel safe. But I am worried about her. She's a key witness, Nicholas. If she remembers the names of all the people who came to see her over the last two weeks and what they wanted, one of them could be the

225

person we're looking for – the person who killed Bess Knowles, who tried to kill you up in the woods, and is planning to kill again. Agnes could have supplied him with the means. He'll want her out of the way. And everyone knows where she is and it's only a matter of time before someone gets her out of that room. It's very strongly built, but it wouldn't be difficult to smoke her out or break down the door. And the Prior is under pressure to get rid of her.

'I know this, because something happened yesterday. I took her some food as usual. She was asleep so I shut the door and waited. Suddenly I heard voices. Now, as you know, there is a small window at the back of the cell so that the anchoress who used to live there could watch Mass being sung. Now I heard two of the Brothers talking. I stood on a chair and saw Father Hubert talking to Brother Michael and the upshot of it was that both said they wanted to get rid of Agnes. They called her names, old hag, dirty witch, and so on, and then went on to discuss the King's visitors who are coming today. They talked about ours being a godless society; you know how they witter on. Then they started talking about Agnes again and how she was putting a curse on the place and they would all be destroyed if they didn't throw her out. Utter nonsense, of course. Agnes isn't capable of cursing anyone, even if she knew how to.'

Nicholas stared intently at Jane. 'I wonder . . .' he began.

'You wonder what?'

'Perhaps we've not been concentrating on the right place. Perhaps we're being blind. Perhaps Ultor's here, in our community, in the Priory.'

'One of the monks? Surely not.'

'Why not, Jane? They might be holy, but they're human. And they're about to be sent packing. From the Prior downwards, they are all against the King's policy. And, by God, Jane, the Prior's coming to dine with us on the seventh. The Prior! If he's Ultor – and he's got the brains for it – there's his opportunity handed to him on a plate. All

226

he'd have to do would be to slip one of Brother Michael's concoctions into the King's drink.'

'Surely there's a royal taster?'

'That's true, but there would be an opportunity later on when everyone's relaxed. No, it's not as ridiculous as it seems. Just think of it, for a moment. He's literate. Everyone respects him. He has his own coach and travels round the county. He could be responsible for starting all these rumours against Agnes and everyone would believe him. I know he agreed to have her in his Priory, but that could just be a cover to put us off the scent.

'Now he could have consulted Agnes about which herbs were lethal, and of course, would want to shut her up. Yes, it makes sense. He might balk at the idea of killing her himself, but by spreading rumours that she's a witch, he can leave it to the community to take the law into its own hands.

'And Jane, don't you see that when she talks, she's going to talk to you, and that puts your life in danger.'

'Oh don't worry about me. As I said before, I'm only a woman, and therefore quite harmless.'

'I'm not so sure. If Ultor is my Lord Prior, he'll know you've got a mind as sharp as nails – equal to any man's.'

She gave him a sideways look, and he wondered what he'd said wrong. She bobbed him a curtsy. 'Thanks, Nicholas. I'm glad you've got confidence in me. But, just stop and think before we're carried away by supposition. The Prior! Nicholas, he's such a softy! He loves beautiful things: music, paintings, food and good-looking people. Ultor stands for all that's ugly, destructive. How can he be the Prior?'

'Jane, just because the Prior admires music doesn't rule out the fact that he could be deeply resentful that his Priory is going to be closed down and all his monks turned out, and his luxurious life-style would come to an end. Besides, he might also regret that he ever took the Oath of Supremacy and might seize any opportunity of getting rid

227

of the King. Jane, he could be the man we're looking for.'

'He could be, I suppose, Nicholas, but I don't believe you.'

'Well, maybe Agnes can help us.'

'If her memory comes back in time. But memories are strange things, and Agnes has had two severe shocks. Let's hope the Prior doesn't give in to popular pressure and evict her before her memory returns. She needs rest and quiet. To move her again would set us back days.'

'And we can't afford that. I'll make sure the Prior doesn't evict her. But all right, I take your point. The Prior looks, on the surface, too relaxed and easy-going to be our man. But now let's take a look at his monks. All of them could be involved in this conspiracy. All of them are against the King. But realistically, most of them are unaware of the trouble that's coming their way. They trust the Prior implicitly to look after them. But some of them could be more worldly and want to do something to put a stop to the King's policy. Brother Benedict, for instance – yes, I know it's unlikely,' he said noticing her astonishment, 'but what do we know about him? Not much. He frequently crosses the Channel, ostensibly to top up the Prior's cellar when it runs dry. It's a good excuse, isn't it? He could be under the Pope's orders to do anything he can to put a stop to the King's destruction of the monasteries. Then take Father Hubert, for instance. Yes, Jane, you may well look surprised, but he's just told me that he was up in the woods collecting herbs when my horse bolted, but, just think, he could have seen me and seized his opportunity to get rid of me. That branch could have caught me on the neck or round the chest and I wouldn't be here with you now. After all, I seem to have the reputation of being the King's favourite. A reluctant favourite, I must say! But all the same, my death could have been a warning to the King that if he doesn't give up his policy of closing down the monasteries, the same fate awaits him. I'm not saying

228

that Father Hubert is Ultor; but I am saying that he might know who he is, and be working for him. So, there are three people from the Priory whom we know about, who could be Ultor – if we count the Prior – or know who he is.'

'And I still think it's unlikely that any of them are involved in this. They're just not worldly enough. It needs a devious mind to plot the elimination of witnesses. Mind you, there are a lot of drunks from the ale-house ready to do any dirty work required,' said Jane. 'Although Pierrepoint, the churchwarden, says that none of them knew anything about the fire at Agnes's house. After all, it started after the ale-house had closed.'

'Yet I think, and so does the Sheriff,' said Nicholas, 'that the Tomkinses know more than they let on. Also the Sheriff's got the two men in custody whom he thinks started the fire. They were regulars at the ale-house. Sooner or later they're going to talk.'

'It seems to me that we're spending a lot of time waiting for people to talk,' Jane said bitterly.

'And we've not much time left. We've got to get back to our suspects. You to your spying; me to interviewing the monks.'

'Prior'll not permit it.'

'He will if I'm doing the interviewing. And if he doesn't, then he'll become the chief suspect and I can summon the Sheriff.'

He turned to go, but Jane paused, her face tense with concentration. 'You know, I still find it difficult to believe that the monks are involved in this conspiracy, Nicholas. I know they disapprove of the King, and it's understandable that they object to being ordered out of their own monastery, but they all took the Oath of Supremacy; there was no sign of rebellion then. This all smacks to me of a secular conspiracy.'

'I'm inclined to agree with you, Jane. Fitzroy's the obvious suspect. But monks are human beings. They have emotions just like us. They can love, hate, desire vengeance. We mustn't rule them out just because they seem unlikely suspects.'

The Sheriff and I did explore Fitzroy's possible role in this. Now, if you like, let's take another look at him. He's put his own steward, Roland Seaward, in Mortimer's house. Now Seaward could be doing Fitzroy's dirty work for him. He's in an excellent position to stir up trouble in the village against Agnes Myles, and prepare the way for when Fitzroy decides to strike.'

'And how's he going to do that?'

'He raises the muster for the county, remember. They are a band of loyal men, loyal to Fitzroy, that is. They are armed, ready to fight when he gives the order. Arundel is only an hour's ride away from here. Instead of coming here to guard the King, they could do just the opposite.'

Jane looked at him in horror. 'But that would be outright rebellion. You don't know this for certain, do you, Nicholas?'

'No, I don't. I'm just running through the possible suspects. Fitzroy's not to be trusted. His only loyalty is to himself. He's an unscrupulous rogue, only out for what he can get. He shopped Mortimer, remember, who trusted him, and look what happened – he put one of his own men in Mortimer's house. The only thing that makes me doubt he's Ultor is that the Sheriff doesn't think he's clever enough to be Ultor, and he's illiterate.'

'But maybe Roland Seaward writes his letters for him. Or someone else could.'

'Then I'll have to find out.'

'Also Mary Woodman might be able to help us. After all she worked up at Mortimer's place before your steward enticed her away.'

'Enticed? Surely not. Not Geoffrey!'

'What's so surprising about that? After all, Cupid's not fussy where he directs his arrows.'

'I didn't know you were an expert on Cupid, Jane. But

230

seriously, Mary might be able to tell us something. I wonder how many times over the last few weeks Fitzroy visited Mortimer's house. I know he said he denied any involvement with Mortimer's conspiracy, and that fits. He'd want to lead his own conspiracy, not let Mortimer call the shots.'

'You mean he betrayed Mortimer to the King, got his house, and then started plotting to get rid of the King, bring in one of the Yorkist claimants and so put himself in line for a fat reward? God in heaven, Nicholas, could a man be so evil?'

'He could and it's happened here before, not so long ago. After all, the Tudors have only been on the throne sixty years. They're relative newcomers. They can't afford to relax. But I'm quite sure the King's got the measure of Fitzroy. He's not mentioned to me that he wants him on the guest list.'

'But the trouble is, somehow I don't think Fitzroy's behind this. The time's not right for him. He's too obvious a suspect. I can't see him writing to Pole, who doesn't have, as far as I can see, any political ambitions at all. No, if Fitzroy's going to turn traitor, then he'll be doing so for his own ends and in his own time. However, I'll go and see Roland Seaward. And you, Jane, back to your squint window. And be careful. I couldn't bear it if anything happened to you.'

Roland Seaward was comfortably installed in Mortimer Lodge. He bemoaned the fact that he'd been left in the lurch by Mary Woodman, but he was able to roast lamb, and Mortimer's cellars were well stocked with casks of wine and beer. He seemed to be enjoying the life of a country gentleman and he hoped that if Lord Gilbert Fitzroy bought the house from the King for his new hunting lodge, then he could continue to run the place for him. No, he never went down to the ale-house. Why should he? He had everything he wanted closer to hand. No, he'd never

231

heard of Agnes Myles, and no, he couldn't read or write. He could count and that's all a steward needed to know. And he used an abacus for numbers over ten when he ran out of fingers. Does Lord Gilbert come and see him often? Nicholas asked. No, he doesn't, was the reply. Not once, since Mortimer was arrested. What was the point? He'd had his instructions. Look after the property and keep away thieves.

Nicholas rode slowly home. No, he couldn't see Seaward being involved in any plot to oust the King. Obviously he wouldn't do anything to jeopardise his own comfortable position. But that still didn't rule out Fitzroy. He could still be planning to attack the King whilst he was staying at his own manor house. Even if the King's Yeomen of the Guard would be more than a match for Fitzroy's collection of local layabouts, they would be heavily outnumbered. He knew that the yeomen were trained fighting men, but, even so, they would not be able to ward off an attack until help came from Southampton's soldiers. And, thank heavens, he thought, his house still had a strong keep and massively strong entrance gate.

Promptly at six, Nicholas presented himself at the Prior's house and was ushered upstairs by Brother Cyril, the Prior's steward, to the dining room. The table was laid for seven. Brother Cyril had put out a tray with eight fine Venetian glasses on it and a jug of malmsey wine. Brother Benedict poured Nicholas out a glass and offered it to him with a dazzling smile. Nicholas held the glass up to the light from one of the tapers and admired its translucency.

'The Prior's got exquisite taste in glass and porcelain,' said Brother Benedict conversationally.

He'd do better tonight if he'd used pewter and served a light beer, thought Nicholas, and then thought that the Prior seemed to be setting about his own extinction with remarkable efficiency.

At that moment, the Prior entered, followed by two dour-looking men. They were of medium height, stocky, strikingly similar in appearance to their master, Thomas Cromwell. They glanced around the room with their keen, observers' eyes, pausing to look at Brother Benedict and the tray of glasses. The Prior looked gratefully across at Nicholas and with false heartiness introduced the two men.

'My Lord Nicholas, come and meet our two distinguished visitors, Victor Laycock and Henry Wagstaff. They're a bit weary after their long ride, but I thought they would be ready for a good meal and chat with our noble patron. But first, come over to the fire and have some wine. This is a very fine malmsey, matured over five years. You'll take a glass, gentlemen, I hope? Brother Cyril, see that our glasses are topped up.

Wagstaff looked at the wine disapprovingly. 'Ale will suit me fine,' he said in a voice that had a strong London accent.

The Prior jumped as if he'd been stabbed in the back. 'Really? How extraordinary. Ale, at this time of night? How about you, Laycock?'

'Ale if you please, if it's no problem. Wine unsettles my stomach.'

Nicholas glanced across at the Prior, whose face presented a study in fleeting emotions. With difficulty he checked his urge to burst out laughing. This man was Ultor? No, the idea was preposterous.

'There's no problem,' interjected Brother Cyril. 'I'll just have to go down to the kitchen to get some.'

He came back, followed by the miniscule figure of Alfred Hobbes, the Vicar of the parish church, still dressed in his grimy cassock, and Father Hubert. Hobbes too, looked at the wine with distaste, and said he drank nothing but ale. Father Hubert said he preferred water. Nicholas drained his glass and, reaching for another, tried to smile reassuringly at the Prior. 'Come, a toast,' he said, after they'd taken their places at the table. 'To the King, gentlemen.'

233

'The King,' they said solemnly as they raised their glasses.

Nicholas did his best. He sat between Hobbes and Wagstaff and talked pleasantries. He ate a great deal of the Prior's giant pie made with the best beef and fresh ox kidneys. He drank quantities of Bordeaux wine and congratulated the Prior on the high standard of his cuisine. But he fought an uphill battle. Wagstaff and Laycock ate abstemiously, Father Hubert merely pecked at his food, but the meal was saved by Brother Benedict, who was in high spirits and prattled on regardless of the disapproving looks thrown in his direction.

When he'd finished, Nicholas pushed aside his plate. 'Well, gentlemen, what's the programme for tomorrow?'

Wagstaff, the more talkative of the two, looked up from his plate. 'Just a general inspection, my Lord. We'll attend a chapter meeting if that's all right with you, Prior, and then move on to the accounts.'

The Prior winced. 'You're welcome to see anything you like. But as to the accounts, you'll have to talk to Father Hubert about them. I never look at them myself. I never was any good at book-keeping.'

'It appears, Prior, that you keep a fairly liberal regime here.'

'Liberal? What the devil do you mean by that? I'm easy-going, yes. I like happy faces around me, people with strong digestions, wine drinkers, musicians. I can't abide kill-joys, parsimonious types with long faces. Father Hubert's one of the best treasurers we've had and I leave things to him.'

'And I suppose you have a general audit once a year?' said Wagstaff pleasantly.

'General audit? Never heard of such a thing. No I consult Father Hubert when we need anything, and he generally accommodates our needs.'

Laycock pursed his lips disapprovingly and pushed aside the last piece of meat on his plate. 'It's not good enough,

Prior. All institutions need a yearly audit.'

'How dare you call us an institution,' shouted the Prior, his face flushing alarmingly.

'What else can we call you?' said Laycock.

'We're a community. A community, I'll have you know, dedicated to the worship of God. I hope you've heard of Him!'

Nicholas felt it was time to intervene. 'What's next on your list, gentlemen, after the accounts?' he said evenly.

'The Treasury. We'll need to see all the plate. The King, we understand is coming next week, and he'll want to see an inventory.'

'You must give me time to clean it,' said Father Hubert who'd been darting hostile looks at the two Commissioners throughout the meal.

'Oh don't waste your time on cleaning it. We only want to estimate its value.'

'Its value! Do you realise that most of our plate is priceless? Some of it goes back centuries.'

'All the more reason for an inventory,' said Wagstaff. 'We're experienced in up-to-date prices.'

'I must object, Prior,' said Father Hubert, who was close to tears. 'These are sacred objects he's talking about. Master Wagstaff refers to them as if they were bits of junk bought at a Michaelmas Fair.'

'Calm yourself, Father Hubert, our guests only want to take a look,' said the Prior, who'd managed to get himself under control.

'I still regard it as sacrilege.'

'It seems to me that you regard everything as sacrilege,' put in Hobbes, who'd been sitting there quietly eating his supper and listening to everything. 'You won't lend me a cope for High Mass at Easter, and when the Bishop came you wouldn't let me borrow a thurible. You said it would be contaminated if I used it on the parish.'

'Quite right, too. We have our things; the parish has

theirs, Vicar. It's always been like that,' said Father Hubert crossly.

'And you don't think it's sacrilege to harbour an old witch on your premises?' said Hobbes.

'What's this?' said Wagstaff, suddenly alert. 'What old witch is this?'

'She's just a harmless old crone who's being persecuted by the village people – you know how superstitious they are – and the Prior is very generously giving her sanctuary,' said Nicholas.

'That's not what I heard,' said Hobbes vehemently. 'Some of the Brothers don't like it. Not one bit, so they tell me.'

'Who tells you?' said Nicholas.

'Why, all of 'em. Brother Martin doesn't approve, neither does Brother Michael, nor Father Hubert here. He was moaning on about her to me the other day.'

The Prior could bear it no longer. He carefully replaced his glass on the table mat put there by the fastidious Cyril, and swung round to face Hobbes.

'I'd be grateful if you'd leave the matter of Agnes Myles to my judgement, Vicar. She's on monastic premises and until I have good evidence that she's dabbling in the black arts she can stay here until the uproar dies down. If I were in your shoes, Vicar, I'd concentrate on preaching to the parishioners on Sundays. They seem to be letting their imaginations run away with them.'

'Still, witchcraft is a serious accusation, Prior,' said Wagstaff.

'Indeed it is. And if I have proof that she is indeed consorting with Satan I shall have her removed instantly to the Bishop's gaol. Now, Brother Cyril, have we any dessert? Or are you proposing to serve up yesterday's leftovers?'

Fresh strawberries, forced under cover in the Priory gardens, were brought in with a jug of thick cream, followed by fresh goat's cheese. The Commissioners were visibly mellowing.

236

'I've got a favour to ask of you,' said Hobbes suddenly. 'Mistress Jane says she'll come and sing to the congregation on Sunday. Will you lend me Brother Benedict to sing with her? I hear they go well together.'

'By all means, Vicar,' said the Prior amiably. 'As long as you don't think it'll be sacrilege.'

'Music can never be sacrilegious,' said Nicholas firmly.

'Music can incite unseemly passions,' said Father Hubert primly.

'Nonsense,' roared the Prior, 'what do you know about unseemly passions, Father Hubert? Of course you can borrow Brother Benedict,' he said, turning towards the Vicar. 'That's what he's here for; to entertain us.'

'Does your Rule permit this, Prior?' said Laycock. 'I thought St Benedict confined his monks to singing in choir, not going out to entertain the rough peasantry. And I'm sure he wouldn't approve of one of his monks singing with a woman! You should keep to the Rule, Prior.'

'And you, gentlemen,' said the Prior, getting to his feet, 'should mind your own business. Allow me to decide what the blessed St Benedict would approve of, or not approve of. Now, if you'll excuse me, I shall retire until I'm called to Matins. You, gentlemen can do as you please. Goodnight, Lord Nicholas.'

He bowed to Nicholas and stalked out. Nicholas looked helplessly at Brother Benedict, who shrugged his shoulders dismissively. 'You must forgive my Lord Prior,' he said to the company at large, 'he has much on his mind.'

And if he behaves like this, thought Nicholas, he'll have even more on his mind.

The Commissioners had only been here a few hours, he thought as he rode home, but already they'd collected enough evidence to damn the Prior out of hand; reluctance to show them the church plate; harbouring a suspect witch; enjoying rich and abundant food and fine wines; allowing one of his monks to sing in the parish church in front of a

237

secular congregation – and with a woman; and flying off the handle at the first hint of criticism. The best advice he could give to the monks now was to start packing immediately! And after his recent conversation with Jane, he felt certain he could put out of his head any idea that the Prior was Ultor. The Prior was a man of impulse and emotion; Ultor was devious and calculating. The two were incompatible. Unless the Prior was a very good actor indeed.

Chapter Twenty-Two

At four o'clock the following afternoon, Jane went down to the parish church to rehearse with Brother Benedict. She was in high spirits at the prospect of a pleasant hour making music. She pushed open the church's heavy wooden door and went in. Inside, it was cool and peaceful; the only sound came from the colony of jackdaws nesting in the tower. The straw on the floor of the nave crackled under her feet, and she jumped when a tiny field mouse scampered out from under the straw and bolted towards the daylight. The afternoon sun poured in through the door, lighting up the brightly coloured frescos which covered the walls of the church: above the door, a beautiful painting of the Holy Family fleeing into Egypt; the donkey, which carried Mary and her child, was huge with large, floppy ears and the expression on its face was one of resigned obedience. On the opposite side of the church a huge figure of the Angel Gabriel appearing to Mary smiled down at the congregation. At the east end, to the left of the altar, was the scene of the Crucifixion and to the right, the scene at the tomb on Easter morning. Jane loved the parish church with all its bright paintings, telling the story of Christ to the villagers who couldn't read it for themselves.

The door at the east end, which connected the monks' church to the parish church, opened, and Brother Benedict appeared. He looked his usual cheerful self, and after he'd greeted her, suggested they go up into the gallery under the tower where the Vicar wanted them to perform on Sunday.

He led the way up the narrow spiral staircase which went up into the gallery and then up again to the platform in the tower where the bellringer stood to ring the bell for Sunday Mass. The gallery was a sturdy, wooden structure built during the last century expressly for musical performances. There was no ceiling above it, just a view straight up into the bell tower, where the jackdaws were arguing vociferously over their nesting sites. The floor of the gallery was covered with their droppings and the twigs they'd relinquished in their constant battles. As they appeared in the gallery the birds set up a chorus of disapproval and Brother Benedict looked doubtfully at Jane.

'Too much competition?'

'Maybe they'll settle down once we start. It's strange they're noisier than usual today. I wonder what's upset them.'

'Nesting time?'

'They should've got over that. Now they should be settling down to feed their young. Anyway, let's start. What time does the Vicar want us here this Sunday?'

'About six. After Compline.'

'That's good. The birds'll be going to bed by then.'

'I hope so; otherwise no one's going to hear us. The Vicar, by the way, wants us to sing some of the Josquin chansons from the Ave Maria Stella. After all, May is the month of Mary.'

Benedict gave the note and looked at the manuscript he'd brought with him. Jane joined him for the first song. It was so wonderful to sing with someone as accomplished as Benedict that Jane forgot the jackdaws and neither of them saw the silent figure up in the tower who was watching them intently. Their voices echoed round the high vault and Jane felt her spirits soar. She hadn't felt so happy for a long time.

Although she knew most of the songs by heart, Jane

240

thought she'd be better off if she moved to the other side of Benedict so that she could see the notes more easily if she lost her place. It was at that precise moment, just when she moved, that a huge piece of masonry fell down from the tower and knocked her sideways, missing her head by inches. She fell, and Benedict gave a cry of horror and went down on his knees beside her. She was unconscious, but still breathing. Thank God, he thought, her guardian angel had been vigilant that afternoon. He went to the edge of the balcony and shouted for help. He should've been warned, he thought angrily. Surely the vicar would know if the tower was unsafe.

No one heard him, so checking that Jane was still breathing, he ran down the stairs and over to the little room that served as the priest's house as well as the vestry. He banged on the door and shouted for Hobbes, who eventually opened the door. Exclaiming in horror at the news, and calling to the Sexton, who was out in the graveyard, they ran back into the gallery. The Sexton puffed up the stairs after them, and, picking Jane up, they gently carried her downstairs and laid her on the straw.

'Quick,' Hobbes said to the Sexton, 'run and ask the Prior to send over Brother Michael or Martin. We'll carry her over to her house; her father's going to be horrified when he sees her. I can't imagine how it happened; the tower's been safe for as long as I can remember. There was no sign of faulty stonework when I last had a look at it with Pierrepoint.'

'Could be them birds,' said the Sexton as he got stiffly to his feet. 'Troublesome creatures they are. They will build their nests up there at this time of the year and it loosens the masonry. I'll get them out as soon as I can.'

'The jackdaws have always nested up there and have never given us any trouble.'

'Aye, but I always knew that one day something like this would happen. I'm sorry, though, that it was Mistress Jane who got in the way of that lump of stone.'

241

They carried Jane back to her father's house, where Guy Warrener hid his grief by ranting at the Vicar.

'You stupid fool, how dare you let my daughter go up into the gallery when you ought to've known it was dangerous. This is the last time I'll let her sing for you and those infernal monks.'

His diatribe was cut short by the arrival of Brother Martin, who took a good look at Jane and the place where the stone had landed between her shoulders. He looked at her father. 'Best to calm down, Master Warrener. There's no great harm done. She's concussed and her back'll be sore for a few days but nothing that a good sedative and a lotion for rubbing into the bruise won't put right. Now get her up to bed, and leave her to sleep. I'll come back later on and take another look at her. Would you like me to send for a goodwife from the village to keep an eye on her?' he said to Guy Warrener.

'Over my dead body,' he shouted. 'I can't do with any of those village crones around my house. I'll look after her. She's my own lass and I'll not have anyone else interfering.'

'Someone ought to tell Lord Nicholas,' said Brother Benedict gently. 'I'll get over to the manor. He's going to be very upset.'

'Don't bother,' said Guy Warrener, 'he's only interested in my lass's voice. She'll not be singing for the King now so he'll not bother to come and see her.'

'She'll be up and about soon,' said Brother Martin, packing away his phials. 'And have no fear, her voice will be as good as ever by next week.'

Nicholas stared at Brother Benedict in horror. His worst fears were now being realised. 'Jane? Unconscious? My God, what happened? Where is she?'

'Calm yourself, my Lord; she's in her father's house. Brother Martin has seen her and says that she'll soon be back on her feet. Best not to go and see her just yet. Her

242

father's raging at everyone and he'll not let you in. It was an accident, my Lord. The Sexton thinks the piece of masonry was dislodged by the nesting jackdaws.'

'That remains to be seen. Come on, I'll get my horse and you can tell me the details as we go along.'

'No visitors,' said Guy Warrener, standing in front of his door with his arms stretched out to fend off all comers. 'She's asleep; and it's best that she stays that way. I'll tell her you called,' he said, suddenly remembering his manners, 'when she wakes up. But, in the meantime, I'd appreciate it if you kept away.'

'I've no intention of waking her up. But I must see her and I want to see the place where the rock hit her. Now let me pass or I shall have to force my way in. I'm sorry, Warrener, but I have a huge respect for Jane.'

'You'll not see her. It's not decent.'

'Brother Benedict will come with me. Now let me pass. You can come too, for decency's sake, if that's what you're worried about,'

Much to Nicholas's relief, Guy Warrener put up only a token resistance. With Brother Benedict as chaperon, he led the way up to Jane's room, where she was lying on her bed, with her arms by her side, like a marble effigy in church. Her face was pale, but her breathing was regular.

'Where was she hit?'

'On her back. You'll not lay a finger on her, my Lord.'

Nicholas took no notice. Beckoning Brother Benedict to help him, they eased Jane over on to one side, and with Warrener grumbling his disapproval, he pulled down her dress and saw the great bruise that was just emerging out of the whiteness of her back. He stared down at her in horror. Horror that he should have exposed Jane to such danger, because he knew that this was no accident. Ultor couldn't get at Agnes Myles, but he could stop her talking to the one person she would trust, Jane. And he would strike again, he felt sure. He pulled up her dress and gently eased her on to her back. The sedative which Brother Martin had administered assured that she remained in a deep sleep.

He looked at her father. 'Guard her well, Master Warrener. She's very precious to me. See no one comes near her and tend her yourself. I shall come again soon and see how she is. If you need anything – anything at all – get Brother Benedict here to come and get me. But now I must see where the accident happened. Brother Benedict, would you show me the place.'

They went together to the parish church, where the Vicar was hovering anxiously at the front door, talking to a group of villagers who all fell silent and stared at Nicholas as he walked up the path.

He nodded to Hobbes, and went into the church with Brother Benedict, who led the way up into the gallery.

'There it is. It's still where it fell. We were standing here. Had Jane not moved just at that moment when the rock fell, she wouldn't be with us now.'

Nicholas looked at the big lump of masonry. It was a large piece, with rough-cut edges, and the mortar still looked as fresh as the day it was put there by the old craftsmen. There was no sign of crumbling.

'Let's go up into the tower,' he said when he'd finished examining the stone.

They climbed up the second flight of stairs and went out on to the bellringer's platform. He looked up into the huge space above him where the bells hung, and he saw where the jackdaws had built their nests on the embrasures in the wall which let in the daylight. The platform was littered with twigs and droppings, but there was no evidence that the birds had dislodged any of the stonework, which seemed to be in a good condition as far as he could see.

Brother Benedict nudged him and pointed out a place in the wall, level with the top of their heads, where a piece of masonry was missing. Nicholas went over and took a good look. The other blocks of stone around the hole were all firmly in position, the mortar intact.

244

'This was no accident, Brother Benedict,' he said, grimly. 'Someone prised that stone out of the wall and carried it to the edge of the platform and dropped it down. Now it couldn't dislodge itself and it couldn't make its own way down into the gallery. Someone was up here, Brother Benedict, when you and Jane started to rehearse. Someone chose his moment, but didn't reckon on Jane moving at that precise moment. Thank God she did.'

Brother Benedict started at Nicholas disbelievingly. 'Maybe one of the stonemasons removed it to replace the mortar and left it carelessly at the edge of the platform where it would only need a slight movement to dislodge it.'

'And where did that slight movement come from? Your voices? I hardly think so. From the birds? Of course not. However, let's take a look at the edge and see if there are any marks left by a piece of masonry being put down there.'

They went over and examined the edge of the platform. There were no marks. Just bits of twig and other rubbish jettisoned by the birds.

'Well, we shall have to check with the Vicar – he'll know if any stonemasons have been working on the tower recently. Did you see anyone up here when you came to rehearse with Jane? Think carefully now.'

Brother Benedict was staring at him with troubled eyes. 'No, we saw no one. But Jane did say that the birds seemed noisier than usual, which would've been the case if anyone was on their territory. Lord Nicholas, what are you saying? Is it possible that someone wanted to kill Jane? I can't believe that. What harm has she ever done?'

Nicholas looked thoughtfully at Brother Benedict. How much should he tell the young monk? How far could he trust him? He seemed genuinely upset over Jane's accident. He couldn't have been responsible. He was here with her, unless . . . No, he just couldn't imagine Brother Benedict agreeing to be a decoy.

Brother Benedict seemed to sense his dilemma. 'You

245

must trust me, my Lord. You see, I love Jane as much as it's possible for a monk to love anyone. She is a wonderful musician, a talented and intelligent girl. why should I want to harm her? If that's what you're thinking. Now take me into your confidence. Is it anything to do with Agnes Myles? I know Jane went to see her often and I guessed there was more to it than Christian duty towards an unfortunate old woman. Let me look after Agnes whilst Jane's recovering. I'd be only too pleased to help – but I would like to know what's going on.'

Nicholas deliberated for just a few seconds. He was going to need Brother Benedict now that Jane was out of action. He'd have to take the risk.

'I'd be relieved if you would look after Agnes, Brother Benedict. Jane has the key to her room. We ought to go and get it.

'Don't worry about that. Father Hubert will have a spare key. I'll get it off him.'

So there's more than one key, he thought. If Ultor was one of the monks, he could have got at Agnes any time. But perhaps it would be too risky, or perhaps he was just biding his time. As long as Agnes's mind remained confused, he was safe. But when her memory returned . . .

Again Brother Benedict seemed to read his thoughts. 'I'll have to ask the Prior's permission first, of course. We're not supposed to go into women's rooms. Already I've broken the Rule once today by coming up here with Jane and going to Jane's room at her home.'

'But that was necessary. If you hadn't come with me, Guy Warrener would never have let me go to see her. Now Brother Benedict, before we go and ask the Vicar about the stonemasons, I would like to ask you a few questions. What time were you up here with Jane?'

'Four o'clock.'

'Did you tell anyone you were coming?'

'Yes, Brother Oswald. He's the Precentor and likes to know what we're doing.'

'Anyone else?'

'No, but Brother Oswald's a bit of a chatterer. What's this all leading up to, my Lord? You must take me into your confidence if I'm to help you.'

'I'm hesitating because what I have to tell you is very serious. You see, Jane and I are working together to unmask a traitor who's out to murder the King, who, as I'm sure you know, is coming to stay with me in a few days time. Now Jane is my assistant; and look what happened to her! Do you think I want to put another person's life in danger? You could be taking a grave risk if anyone knows you're working for me. Do you want to take that risk?'

'Lord Nicholas, I want to – how do you say it – step into Jane's shoes. If she was your assistant, then I should be proud to replace her until she recovers her strength. Now tell me as much as I need to know.'

Later, Nicholas went to see Alfred Hobbes, the Vicar. He said that no stonemasons had been employed by him that spring. If the churchwarden had asked for work to be done in the tower, then he couldn't bring in stonemasons without consulting him first. Hobbes was worried and upset by Jane's accident, especially as it had occurred in his church where nothing like that had ever happened before.

Nicholas left the parish church and walked across to the Prior's house. He felt full of anxiety. Anxiety about Jane, and now Brother Benedict, who had so willingly agreed to look after Agnes, not fully understanding the risk he was taking. Nicholas knew that someone had been told that Jane and Brother Benedict would be up in the gallery at four o'clock, and that person had gone there with the intent to kill Jane. Thank God he hadn't succeeded, but he felt sure he'd try again. The Prior would now have to help him. He had to know where all his monks were at four o'clock that afternoon. And the Prior wouldn't like that at all; especially with Wagstaff and Laycock prowling around the premises.

247

Supper was almost ready, but Prior Thomas took one look at Nicholas's face and told Brother Cyril to delay the proceedings. He took Nicholas into the solarium and poured him out a generous glass of wine, which Nicholas accepted gratefully.

'You look as if you need it,' said the Prior. 'What's been going on?'

'You've not heard then?'

'I've not heard anything since Cromwell's minions arrived. We've been over the accounts. They think we spend too much on unnecessary luxuries. The infernal cheek of it! I can't see that what we spend is of any concern except to ourselves. We don't owe anybody anything.'

'I'm sorry they're giving you so much trouble, but now listen, Prior . . .'

Nicholas talked and Prior Thomas listened. When he'd finished, he refilled their glasses and sat down heavily in one of the armchairs.

'I'm so sorry that this happened to Mistress Warrener. Are you saying that you think this wasn't an accident?'

'I think that someone knew that Jane and Brother Benedict were going to rehearse in the parish church at four and attempted to kill her.'

'But why on earth would anyone want to do that? And, God help us, he could have killed Brother Benedict as well; and then what would I have said to his abbot?'

'Well, give thanks that only one of them was hurt. But as to why anyone should want to kill Jane is because she is the one person Agnes Myles would talk to when she recovers.'

'And you think Agnes Myles might be able to lead us to finding out who this traitor is. My God, Lord Nicholas, I thought we'd got rid of the conspirators when Mortimer was arrested, but now it appears that they're rearing their ugly heads again.'

'And, just in case you've forgotten, the King is coming to stay with me next week. Unless we find this traitor, his life could be in great danger.'

248

'And you really think this man is here with us in the village?'

'I'm saying more than that, Prior. I think he's right here, in your Priory, and cursing his luck at this very moment because he missed his chance to get rid of Jane.'

The Prior's eyebrows shot heavenwards and he stared in amazement at Nicholas. Then he jumped to his feet and confronted him, stabbing his podgy fingers into his chest.

'Now this really is sacrilege, my Lord. Are you telling me that this traitor could be one of us?'

'I think so, and I would like you now to assemble all the Brothers together and ask each one, under oath, where they were at four o'clock this afternoon. Brother Benedict and I will then check out their alibis.'

'You take the most appalling liberties, my Lord,' the Prior roared, his face flushing alarmingly. 'What's Brother Benedict got to do with this? He's our guest.'

'He's also agreed to be my assistant, until Jane recovers.'

'Your assistant? Over my dead body. Since when have monks been asked to assist in tracking down traitors?'

'Calm yourself, Prior. I'm sure there are precedents. Brother Benedict seems to think he's answerable only to his own abbot. But it's only for a short time. Jane will be on her feet very soon, I'm sure. Now, if you please, will you assemble all the brethren?'

'Certainly not. It doesn't please me at all. It's supper time, and I can't keep them waiting.'

'It won't take long. All I want you to ask them is where they all were at four this afternoon.'

'We don't have to go to all the trouble of calling an assembly. I know where they were at four. In the choir, of course, singing Vespers.'

Nicholas sighed. Another blind alley. 'Were they all present, Prior?'

'How should I know? I wasn't there. I was dealing with Wagstaff and Laycock.'

'Then who checked all the monks into choir?'

'Usually Father Hubert presides when I'm busy. But I sent him off to collect more young nettles. I can't do without them at the moment after a winter of salt meat and dry fish. So today, I asked Brother Oswald to lead them.'

'Then we must send for Brother Oswald and you'll soon be able to get to your table.'

Brother Oswald arrived looking flustered after this disruption to his routine. He looked nervously from Nicholas to the Prior.

'You want to speak to me, Prior?'

'Yes. You took Vespers this afternoon, I gather?'

'Yes, I always do when Father Hubert is otherwise engaged,' he said with a faint hint of disapproval in his voice.

'What time did you begin?' said Nicholas.

'The usual time, four o'clock,'

'Was everyone present?'

'Nearly everyone. Brother Benedict had been given permission to rehearse in the parish church. Father Hubert was up in the woods, and Brother Michael was visiting Old Eddie up in High Dean.'

'What's the matter with Old Eddie?' said Nicholas.

'He can scarcely draw breath, my lord, after all that smoke he's been breathing in all his life. It's the lot of char-coal burners to die before their time because their lungs give up. Brother Michael gives him something to ease the pain.'

'So there you are, my Lord,' said the Prior triumphantly. 'We're all accounted for. Now can I please ask Brother Cyril to serve supper. Oh, and by the way, send my regards to Mistress Warrener and I hope she soon recovers.'

Nicholas collected Harry from the gatekeeper, who had brought him over from Warrener's house. He mounted and trotted off up the street towards the woods and the neighbouring village of High Dean.

250

The charcoal burner lived in a clearing in the woods, in a beehive shaped house made of wattles. Beside the house, the great kiln which slowly reduced the wood to charcoal, smouldered and crackled, belching out smoke which hung over the clearing like a heavy pall. Harry sneezed and backed away from the furnace, and Nicholas dismounted, tied him to a tree, and went across the glade to the cottage. Inside, he saw, in the far corner, a dim figure lying on a mat. He went across and spoke quietly to Eddie, whose breath was coming in huge laboured gasps which racked his body.

'Eddie. It's Nicholas Peverell. Can you speak?'

'I'm sorry, my Lord. My lungs are playing me up,' came the wheezing reply.

'I'm sorry to see you like this. Can I bring you anything to help?'

'Thank you, my Lord. But one of the monks has been with some medicine. It'll soon make me feel a lot better. Don't worry about me, I'll soon be up and about. When this lot of wood's done, I'll let the kiln go out for a bit, and then my breathing comes easy.'

'Do you remember which of the monks came to see you?'

'The same one who's been before. Brother Michael, the miserable-looking one. But he knows how to make people feel better.'

'Do you know what time it was when he came?'

'Oh Lord, how should I know? Everyday's the same to me. The sun rises, and I gets up, or tries to. When it's overhead I eats a bit of bread and cheese, if I'm up to it. I goes to sleep when the sun does. That's my day. He came, if you really want to know, after the time when I usually eats my dinner, and before bed time. About two hours ago, I suppose.'

A terrible burst of coughing stopped him from saying any more. He tried to sit up, and Nicholas handed him the little jar of medicine which stood by the mattress and removed

251

the stopper. Eddie drank a mouthful with a sigh of relief and sank back on to his bed and shut his eyes. It would be cruel to ask him any more questions, so Nicholas left him and walked back to where he'd tethered Harry. So Brother Michael had been to see Eddie; but what time it was was anybody's guess.

Chapter Twenty-Three

'I can't hang on to 'em for ever, my Lord,' said Sheriff Landstock tersely. 'They keep moaning about their rights; and they have every reason to. I haven't arrested them yet because a burn on a sleeve of a jacket's not enough evidence and unless we have a witness who comes forward and says that they actually saw Bovet and Perkins start the fire I can't hold them for questioning much longer. I can't make 'em talk, you know.'

'I thought you had ways of making people talk,' said Nicholas, who was standing at the window of the Sheriff's office in Marchester watching the crowds surging round the nearly completed market cross.

'I've done what I can, within the law. I've kept them in the dark and starved 'em. I can threaten them with the manacles but I can't move them to Lewes to use them. We need some proper evidence. What about the ale-house keeper and his wife? Any joy from them?'

'None at all. But I'm sure they know something, and in time, they will probably come out with it. But not yet. Everyone seems frightened; everyone's clammed up. You know how it is. Who are all those people out there, Sheriff?' said Nicholas, leaning forward to get a better look at the crowd outside.

'God knows. They come to look at the cross, I suppose. They make a lot of work for us – thieves, vagabonds, muggers – ale-houses working all hours; more trouble when they close and the drunks roam the streets. People have heard that the King's coming and rumours are flying around that he's coming here to Marchester. What do you think, my Lord?'

'I'm quite sure he'll be giving Marchester a wide berth. All that business with the cathedral Precentor, Rodney Catchpole, has put him off coming here for a long time. Besides, we're running a tight schedule. Because of the dangerous security situation, Southampton wants him off his territory as quickly as possible. I think we'll get him to leave most of his retinue behind and ride to Portsmouth with just a handful of people he can trust. The King's quite capable of riding the twenty miles to Portsmouth and back on fast horses. It's probably safer keeping him moving than letting him lumber along in a coach where he could be ambushed. I know Southampton says he's providing soldiers to line the route, but he hasn't enough men to cover every square inch of the way. There's bound to be gaps.'

'Fitzroy wants to bring his men here. Says we'll need extra men to guard the King. What do you feel about that?'

'Tell Fitzroy to stay where he is until we need him. I don't trust him; and neither does the King.'

'My sentiments exactly. Southampton'll give us enough men. He's edgy enough as it is and wants to put bowmen all along the route and cannoneers at Portsmouth Point; much good they'll be!'

'They can be deadly if the ball lands in the right place.'

'Let's hope the beggars know how to aim straight. In any case the King won't be standing on his own for long. He wants to see the fleet sail past – God willing. Let's hope the wind changes direction by this time next week – it's coming from the east at this moment, and that's hopeless. Let's hope, too, that it doesn't give up altogether, or work itself up into a storm and scatter the fleet all over the Solent.'

'Cheer up, Sheriff, I didn't know you were such a pessimist.'

254

'A pessimist? Aye, that's the right word. It's because I'm losing sleep over this visit. I don't like it one little bit. The sooner next Thursday's over, the happier I shall be. Then it's back to the thieves and muggers again – child's play! Oh, by the way,' he went on, looking across at Nicholas sympathetically. 'I'm sorry about this lass of yours. I hope she's not too badly hurt. A pretty girl, if I remember rightly.'

'Yes, she is. It was a wretched business; and what's more, I don't think it was an accident. Someone tried to kill her, Sheriff.'

'Now that's a bit far-fetched, isn't it? No one takes a wench seriously.'

'They do if she's the one person a key witness is likely to talk to.'

'You mean that old witch of yours. I thought you put her safely out of harm's way.'

'She's under lock and key, but it now appears there's more than one key, so she's not entirely safe. Fortunately she's still confused, but when she comes to her senses, it'll be Jane she'll talk to – provided nothing happens to her in the meantime.'

'Better keep an eye on both of 'em then; just like I do with Bovet and Perkins. How is the lass?'

'She'll recover. I'm going to see her after I leave here, provided that old bear of a father lets me in. Now Sheriff, I've got something to tell you that's going to shock you. But just hold still until I'm finished.'

'Shock me? Sheriff of Marchester? Never. I've seen everything. Mind you, I was pretty shocked when Mortimer was arrested.'

'Then you'll be even more shocked when I tell you that I am beginning to think that our traitor, who took over when Mortimer was arrested, could be one of the monks.'

The Sheriff whistled. 'Now that does take a bit of swallowing. And I hope to God, Lord Nicholas, you know what you're doing. But you've got a good head on those

255

shoulders of yours, even if you're not too keen on using it. Now what makes you think that this fellow with the damn silly Latin name is one of the holy monks?'

'Because, in the first place, they've got a motive. They've got a grudge against the King. Secondly they're all literate and quite capable of carrying on a correspondence with Reginald Pole. They know Latin. They know the King's coming, and they're on the spot. And they know how to poison people with harmless-looking herbs, and they know they are above suspicion.'

'And they're also enclosed behind the monastic walls.'

'Not all the time. The Prior's very lax. They visit the sick, collect herbs in the woods, and one of them runs messages for me.'

'Let's hope it's not the Prior?'

'It's possible, but I don't think so. I don't think he's capable of murder. He's far too easy-going. This Ultor, like Mortimer, is a ruthless fanatic. He's not afraid to die if he's caught in the attempt to murder the King. In fact, he's probably training up someone else to take over should he get caught before the King arrives.'

'This is bad, my Lord. And very worrying. Damn me, it's time we got some good ale down our throats.'

He called for a servant who came with a jug and two tankards in hand. Both men drank in silence.

'If you're saying that our Latin friend is one of the monks, then why would he want to get rid of Agnes Myles? Bess Knowles, I understand. The poor lass was a witness. But Agnes Myles? Come off it, Lord Nicholas!'

'Agnes Myles is a holy woman, a healer. She makes potions, balms for the whole village. She also knows about poisons. She buys valuable medicinal products from a merchant in Portsmouth. Everyone comes to her for some sort of healing. Now if anyone came to her for something a bit out of the ordinary, she'd remember. Then she might tell us if we jog her memory. And that person could be Ultor.'

'Yes, I'm with you. But I don't think Ultor would visit Agnes Myles on his own. He'd send someone else, surely?'

'He wouldn't if he's well known to Agnes. And I think Ultor works alone. He does the planning, but uses others to do his dirty work. He also knows human nature, and knows how to work on the prejudices of the local people.'

'But there's no evidence that he is a monk. Hell's teeth, Lord Nicholas, I can only work with evidence; not supposition.'

Nicholas sighed and drained his tankard. 'No, no evidence at all. Just a hunch. However, anything can happen, and I want to be there when it does. Now I must be off. I've got to check up on Jane.'

'I hope she's soon better. And, by God, Lord Nicholas, I hope this fellow is one of your monks – he'll be outside my jurisdiction until the Bishop passes him over to me for hanging!'

When Nicholas arrived at Jane's house, she was out of bed and sitting in an armchair in the main living room, impatiently stabbing at a piece of embroidery with a needle. She got to her feet when Nicholas went in and he saw her wince with pain. He also saw her face flush with pleasure and thought how marvellous it was to be given such a welcome.

'Thank God you've come, Nicholas. I was worried about you.'

'There's no need. I take good care of myself. More than you do, I see. Shouldn't you be up in bed resting?'

'Resting? I've done enough of that. How's Agnes? How's Benedict? Have you seen the Sheriff? What's the news?'

'Hold on, Jane, you've got to take life quietly.' He kissed her lightly on the forehead and firmly pushed her down into the chair. 'Agnes is fine; Benedict's looking after her. And you must rest, otherwise you'll not be well enough to sing to the King.'

'And you, Lord Nicholas, can leave my house immediately,'

257

said an angry voice behind him. 'It's bad enough having a daughter who won't stay in bed without you coming along and talking to her about singing to the King. She's still frail. And you're not helping her, my Lord.'

'Father, don't be such an old woman. Of course I'll be well enough. My back's a bit sore, but that'll soon go. Now please leave us; we've important things to talk about.'

'Oh? Since when have you and Lord Nicholas had important things to discuss? Get on with your embroidery, lass. As soon as Brother Martin comes, we'll get you back into bed.'

'I refuse to go.'

'You will, my wench, even if I have to carry you up there myself.'

Nicholas smiled at Jane's furious face. 'Don't worry, Jane; we'll talk later. Go carefully, now. You're safe in here. And I must ask you to lock your door, Master Warrener,' he said, turning to look at Jane's father, who was scowling at him like an angry boar. 'We don't want any intruders in here.'

'I've never locked my door in the daytime, and I'm not going to start locking it now,' said Warrener, walking across to the door and flinging it wide open.

'I'm sorry, Nicholas, he means well. But do you think this really was an accident?' said Jane softly.

'I'm sure it wasn't,' Nicholas said, glancing across at Warrener, who was getting increasingly impatient for him to leave.

'Don't worry,' she said, 'he's very deaf. Listen, I think there was someone up in the tower when we were there. Now I didn't see anyone but the birds were more restless than usual. Did you come across anything when you looked round?'

'I found the place where the stone was removed. It was very neatly prised out of the wall. It was carried to the edge of the platform and dropped on you. Thank God you moved when you did. There was no evidence that the stone had

258

been accidentally dislodged. In fact I would say that it couldn't have been. Now stay here and get strong and I'll come back when there's anything to report.' He bent down to kiss her and she lifted her face to his embrace.

'And God go with you, Nicholas. And take care. You're in more danger than all of us.'

Nicholas rode home through the silent village. No groups of chattering women. No one sitting outside enjoying the sunshine. Front doors tightly shut. No one setting off to walk to Marchester. Everyone had turned inward, frightened to leave their cottages. It was as if the plague had struck; the same atmosphere of suspicion and fear. Fear of the unknown; fear of the supernatural.

Geoffrey was waiting for Nicholas when he rode up to his main gate.

'My Lord, he's come, he's here,' said Geoffrey, looking white-faced and tense. 'He drove into our courtyard without a by-your-leave, and he's making himself at home checking everything. The cheek of it!'

'Who's come?' said Nicholas patiently, as he dismounted and summoned over a groom to take Harry away.

'Why the Frenchie fellow. The King's sent him, so he says. Calls himself a steward. He's in our kitchen already taking the lids off our pots and telling Mary she doesn't know how to make proper custard. He's upset us all. He's got his own carriage. Look over there. Just look at all those arty drawings on it. He's got a fine strong horse, though.'

Nicholas glanced across the courtyard and saw a small, lightly built coach, designed to hold just one person. It was made of painted wood with long shafts and a seat for a coachman. The door panels were decorated with angels and cherubs, picked out in gold paint and blowing trumpets and playing harps.

'Very pretty and very nippy. Now what's this Frenchman's name?'

259

'Pierre Lamontagne,' said a soft, heavily accented voice behind him.

Nicholas turned round and saw a small, slightly built man with a shrewd face, twinkling eyes, curly dark hair and a small, perfectly trimmed beard. He wore fashionable clothes, a dark blue doublet with sleeves slashed to reveal a silk shirt underneath, blue slashed breeches, and a neat pair of soft leather shoes on his small feet, each shoe decorated with a blue rose on the front. He removed his blue, soft woollen hat with its curling feather and bowed gracefully. 'At your service, my Lord. The King sent me to help with the arrangements. This man,' he said pointing a contemptuous finger at Geoffrey, 'will not co-operate. The woman, now she's different. She'll be very useful, in time, when I've tamed her.'

'Tame Mary,' roared Geoffrey, 'just you try. You'll not tame an English lass with your foreign ways. I'm steward here. Getting ready for the King's my business.'

'And just in case you've forgotten,' said Nicholas, fighting back a smile, 'this happens to be my house, and I'll give the orders. Now Monsieur Pierre, we'll show you your room – I take it your coachman can look after himself – rest yourself, and come and join us for dinner tonight. Why not taste what we can provide, and then tomorrow you can show us some of your recipes.'

Monsieur Pierre bowed low and allowed himself to be led away. Nicholas went into the kitchen where Mary was in her usual place by the fire, stirring a pot. But today she looked different. She was smiling.

'Mary,' Nicholas said, with a bowl of soup in his hand, 'I want you to forget, just for a moment, the charming Monsieur Pierre and think back to when you were over at Mortimer's place.'

'Those days are over and done with, my Lord. I'd much rather work here. Me and Monsieur Pierre will get on famously. He knows how to treat a woman. Geoffrey treats

260

me like one of his servants. Now I'm to teach Monsieur Pierre some of our English recipes and he says he'll teach me how to make some real fancy dishes which the King likes. I've forgotten all about Sir Roger Mortimer – wicked man that he was; although he always seemed so holy.'

'Holy? I didn't think he went to church regularly?'

'He'd not go down to the church, not with all those common people. He had his own chapel, didn't he? Father Hubert came and said Mass for the family. If he couldn't come then the Prior'd send another priest. Even the old one who sits by people when they're dying. Sir Roger liked the monks. He said they were the real holy ones, nearer to God than the Vicar.'

'So Father Hubert used to come and see him? Who else came from the Priory, Mary?'

'Oh lots of them. I don't know all their names. The old one, I think he's called Father John, then Brother Martin came with his tonics and purges when any of the servants got bunged up.'

'Anyone else?'

'Someone came after dark. Real sinister it was. I never knew his name because he always pulled his cowl over his face. He'd come to say the night prayers with Sir Roger. Prayer, that's a laugh, isn't it? Much good it did him when he was hauled away to London. I only hope to God Lady Margot's all right; and the children. They say she's returned to her family the other side of the county. Let's hope she's left in peace. I still can't get over Sir Roger. Wicked he was. Much he cared about his family.'

Nicholas finished his soup and went into his study. Now, he thought, he was making progress. Several monks had visited Mortimer's house. Now he had to find out who the night visitor was – the one with the cowl pulled over his face. Mary made him sound sinister. But he knew that, unfortunately, all the monks covered their faces when they went out.

Chapter Twenty-Four

Nicholas's temper wasn't improved on Friday morning, after a disturbed night's sleep, by the sight of Monsieur Pierre hovering over him as he ate his breakfast.

'My Lord, today is the first of June. We have six days, six days, to get this . . .' he paused as he looked contemptuously round the great hall of Peverell Manor. 'This – barnyard cleared out,' he finished on a note of triumph.

Nicholas, who had become accustomed to living in a corner of the hall nearest the fire and had neglected the rest of the house, stared at him in astonishment. 'Barnyard? I see no animals.'

'See this straw?' said Pierre, kicking aside a scattering of straw which covered the cold flagstones of the floor. 'Look, it crawls with animals. When did Monsieur Lowe last put down clean straw?'

Nicholas shuffled the straw under his feet. As far as he could remember, the straw hadn't been changed since Mary died. What was the point? It never got wet; it served its purpose well enough. Then, much to Pierre's delight, a mouse scampered out from under Nicholas's feet, immediately pounced upon by the family of cats who had taken up residence by the fire.

'See, animals!' he said. And then, 'Poof! The odour, my Lord. How can you stand it?'

Sure enough, in disturbing the straw Nicholas had

released various sinister smells. Nicholas glared at Pierre. 'Oh come now, it's not that bad,' he said as Pierre drew out an elegant handkerchief from his pocket and held it to his nose.

'Bad? It's terrible. And I'll have you know the King does not like bad smells. Nor does he like animals under his feet.'

'Well, what do you suggest?'

'We replace it all. Now is the time for fresh herbs and flowers. The fields are full of them. Your barns must be stuffed with last autumn's straw for the animals. Well, get it out. Clean out this ordure,' he said waving his arms theatrically, 'and put down fresh straw. But first you must scrub the floor. Then, just before the King arrives, we gather fresh herbs and lay them down for the King to crush under his feet. In this way, his Majesty's nostrils will be assailed by sweet smells, not this foul stench. The King tells me he wants no fuss, just simple bucolic pleasures. But simplicity, my Lord, is difficult to achieve. It means using only the best materials. Now where is Monsieur Lowe? He has much work to do.'

And so the whirlwind struck. The great hall was cleared of all its debris. The floor was scrubbed, fresh straw laid down. The cats were banished, the dogs kicked out. Then it was the turn of the sleeping quarters. The bedroom floors were scrubbed, the woodwork polished. The tapestries which had hung on the walls and over the doors to keep out the draughts for as long as Nicholas could remember, were taken down, hung out on posts in the yard at the back of the house, and beaten black and blue. Many of them were so worn that in some places the daylight came through, and then Geoffrey Lowe was sent off to find women from the village who knew how to sew valuable materials.

Then Pierre wanted to inspect the store cupboards and cellars, and Geoffrey, white-faced with anger, led the way. Pierre, with a slate in one hand and a piece of chalk in the other, wrote down a list of what was needed: more pigs, especially the newly born suckling piglets, wild boar, venison for pies, fowl of every sort, woodcock, duck, chickens, swans, larks and other song birds. 'And then,' said Pierre looking triumphantly at Nicholas, who had joined them in the cellars, 'we must have a surprise pie. The King expressly wishes to have a surprise pie.'

'And what the hell's that?' said Geoffrey irritably.

'Why Monsieur Lowe, you call yourself a steward and yet you don't know what a surprise pie is?'

'Once upon a time, I was a mere bailiff. That suited me well enough until I got involved with Frenchmen and their fancy menus.'

'Now, now, Monsieur Lowe, no tantrums please. A surprise pie, is a great pie, made with suet, and divided into compartments. In each compartment there is a different sort of meat. Now one of the compartments is left blank, and just before the pie is served, you add something spectacular. Once we put two live blackbirds in the empty compartment and that made the King laugh because he said it reminded him of the monks. We could put anything you like in it – one of those kittens, for instance; that will make the ladies laugh.'

'We'll put a dove in it,' said Nicholas firmly. 'A symbol of peace.'

'Very clever, my Lord. The King will be delighted.'

And I feel like Noah, thought Nicholas, stocking up the Ark.

When he'd finished his inspection, Pierre turned to Geoffrey. 'And now, Monsieur Lowe, we go to market. When we come back, Mary will make us all an omelette; like I showed you,' he said to Mary, who'd joined them on their rounds. 'Remember, twelve eggs,' he added, treating her to one of his dazzling smiles, 'and keep it soft. As soft as a woman's breast.'

Mary blushed and curtsied. Geoffrey clenched his fists. Then, much to Nicholas's relief, Pierre set off for the courtyard, calling out that they would go in his carriage, and there was room for Geoffrey if he didn't mind squashing up beside him.

Nicholas took one look at his house being torn to pieces by his servants, and felt very much in the way. He decided to go and see the Prior.

At the Priory, he found very much the same situation. Cromwell's Commissioners were into everything. The services were disrupted, the Prior had to be always on hand to receive complaints about the account books or the sumptuous nature of his store cupboard. He was too bothered to talk to Nicholas, so there was nothing for it but to go home. Maybe he could find peace in his herb garden, Nicholas thought, before it was denuded of herbs to strew on the floors.

A messenger was waiting for him when he got back. It was the same young man who'd come before. He was in the kitchen eating the fresh bread and cheese Mary had given him and he jumped up when Nicholas went in.

'From my Lord of Southampton,' the young man said, handing Nicholas the leather pouch which held a letter. Nicholas took it over to the window and took out the contents.

'Peverell,' he read. 'We have intercepted a letter at the Port of Littlehampton. It was written to Reginald Pole and signed Ultor. He says that the Day of Wrath is at hand. In fact he gives the day a date. The seventh of June. I think he's getting over-confident. Almost boastful, don't you think? I don't have to tell you how serious this is. It means that Ultor has not given up. We must not let the King out of our sight all the time he is with us. I've sent a message to him advising him not to come, and I think you should do the same. But I'm not hopeful. He never changes his plans. As to your letter, of course I don't want him staying the night with me. He wants to stay with you and find out how much your Priory's worth. I'll send him packing as soon as I decently can. Burn this letter, and be vigilant. Take no risks. Remember you must have all his food tasted before it gets to him. Paget.

265

N.B. We caught the messenger – he was one of Mortimer's servants – but he jumped over the side of the ship and got away. The tide swept him along the coast, but Fitzroy's confident he'll be picked up.'

Nicholas swore under his breath. The stupid fools – to get the letter, to lose the messenger. Terrible news indeed, he thought as he burned the letter. Ultor still with them, and getting ready to strike in six days' time. And he still didn't know who they were looking for.

Matins, the first service of the new day, came to an end, the monks filed out of their choir and climbed up the night stair to their dormitory over the chapter house. They entered through a small door high up in the north transept. It was a warm night, the air still and oppressive with a hint of thunder around. Each monk went to his own cubicle, separated from the others by a low wooden partition. They took off their night shoes, and lay down on the rough straw pallet on their truckle beds. In seconds, they were all asleep.

But Brother Benedict couldn't sleep. His mind wouldn't relax. Highly sensitive, he couldn't get the images out of his mind of Jane singing with her clear, bell-like voice, the noise of the jackdaws and the sound of the falling stone. He relived the shock he felt when he saw Jane fall to the floor when the stone hit her and the anguish he felt when he saw her lying white-faced in her bed. He knew he couldn't love her like a man loves a woman, he'd renounced all that when he took his vows, but Jane was special. Not only was she beautiful, but she was blessed with an independent mind and intelligence, like the women he'd heard about at the Burgundian Court. It was madness, he thought, to involve her in politics. This was a serious situation: a conspiracy, no less, against the King himself. Lord Nicholas should know better.

He grew even more awake as time passed, and soon it would be time for Prime. But someone else was awake. As he looked down the rows of cubicles, he saw someone get up, bend down to put on his night shoes, and then go towards the night stair. It was Father Hubert, who always slept in the bed nearest the stairs because, as Sacristan, he would have to ring the bell to wake the monks up and lead them down to the choir for the next service.

At first Benedict thought nothing of it. Father Hubert was elderly, he'd been much weakened through bleeding, and maybe he wanted the latrines. Perhaps, Benedict thought with growing concern, he wasn't feeling well and might need help. He got out of bed, put on his shoes, and silently made his way past the sleeping brethren and followed Father Hubert. Not wanting to embarrass him if he wanted to use the latrines, Benedict paused half-way down the stairs, and watched where Hubert was going. Much to his surprise, he didn't go out into the cloisters, which he would have done if he needed to relieve himself, but instead he went to the sacristy and opened the door. Benedict came down the stairs and hid behind one of the pillars in the north transept. Moments later, Hubert emerged carrying something which was hidden under a piece of cloth. He then walked past Benedict and went out into the cloister by the little door in the west end of the north transept.

Much disturbed, Benedict wondered whether he should follow him, but not wanting to be seen stalking a senior member of the community who had every right to visit the sacristy even if it was in the middle of the night, he went back up the stairs and lay down on his bed. This time he fell into a deep sleep which lasted until Father Hubert rang the bell for Prime.

Late on Saturday morning, after another disturbed night's sleep, Nicholas decided to go and see Sheriff Landstock again. Everything seemed to have come to a dead end. Tomkins and his wife weren't talking, Bovet and Perkins weren't talking either, Agnes Myles couldn't collect her

267

wits, and Ultor's messenger was drifting around in the sea somewhere along the south coast. Someone, soon, would have to talk. Much as he hated cruelty of all kinds, he knew he would have to recommend sterner measures to the Sheriff if they were ever going to break the stalemate.

As he went to get Harry from the stables, Monsieur Pierre's little coach, drawn by a sturdy, piebald cob, came hurtling into the courtyard. Nicholas paused, then went over to meet him.

'Good morning, Monsieur Pierre, any progress in your department?'

Monsieur Pierre grimaced. 'Not good. I get up at dawn to seek out the best produce but everything is too dear. It's as if they know who I am and whom I'm buying for, and they want to cheat me. There's also a shortage of song birds, but I'm glad to say I've bought some barrels of live eels. We can do something with those. Some hot eel pies on the night the King arrives might go down well, I think.'

'Sounds perfect. Now listen carefully to me, Monsieur Pierre, I'm sure you understand that we have to take every precaution to ensure the King's safety when he's here with us.'

'Of course. I'm here to see that security arrangements are fully carried out.'

'We'll do our best to see that they are. Now, one other thing, we shall also have to see that everything the King eats will be tasted beforehand.'

Monsieur Pierre gave Nicholas a withering look. 'My Lord,' he said with an elaborate bow. 'I am the King's taster. That's why he sent me here.'

And with that, he stalked off. Nicholas watched him go. So the King was no fool, he thought. He knew all the risks, and yet he still wanted to come. Was he really interested in reviewing the fleet? he wondered. He could do that at any time. Why now, when he knew there was still a conspiracy at large? Did he really want to discuss south coast defences with Southampton, or was he coming deliberately to draw out Mortimer's successor? He was brave indeed to put his head in the noose. Brave? Or foolish? But Nicholas knew that it didn't do to underestimate the King. He'd probably weighed up the risks and decided that between the Sheriff, Nicholas, and Southampton, he would be in safe hands. Still, it was a fearsome responsibility.

He collected Harry, who, newly groomed with his coat shining like jet in the strong sunlight, was in fine form. He led him back into the courtyard and was just about to mount when Brother Benedict came in through the main gate. Nicholas felt a sudden surge of fear. Jane? Had anything happened to her? He almost ran to meet the young monk.

'The Prior sends for you, my Lord. Can you come at once?'

'What's happened? Is it Jane . . .?'

'Calm yourself. Mistress Jane is recovering rapidly. No, it's one of the old monks. He's near death – he's already received the last rites – and wants to see you.'

'Brother Wilfrid?'

'That's right. He approaches his end quite calmly but keeps asking for you. Can you come?'

'I'll come straight away.' After all, Nicholas thought, as he set off for the Priory, Landstock's not going anywhere and Brother Wilfrid won't be with us much longer.

Leaving Harry with the gatekeeper, Nicholas walked over to the infirmary. Inside, all was peaceful. Two monks stood on either side of Brother Wilfrid's bed, reciting the office for the Dying. Wilfrid's eyes were closed, his hands folded on a crucifix placed on his chest. Nicholas looked down at the tiny, parchment-yellow face, and was glad that Wilfrid's passing was so serene. He bent down to listen to his breathing, which was so faint that it scarcely lifted his chest.

'Brother Wilfrid,' he said softly, 'it's me, Nicholas. I've come to thank you for everything you taught me when I was

269

a child. Now go to God; He's waiting for you.'

Wilfrid opened his eyes, which, although clouded over by death, were still surprisingly blue. He turned his head to look at Nicholas.

'Thank you,' he said, his voice just the merest whisper. 'Those were happy days. Pity about the lass.'

For a moment Nicholas thought he was talking about Jane. But Wilfrid went on. 'They did their best for her. Brother Martin made the potions and took it to her. It was strange, though, when the other monk added something; it was later, after Brother Martin had gone inside. It wasn't right, was it? Why be so secretive if it was harmless? The next thing, she was dead. I saw it. It worries me . . .'

His voice faded, and Nicholas, with growing agitation, bent down to listen.

'Which monk? Brother Wilfrid, try to remember.'

'Which monk? Why the old one . . .'

And then he stopped. He tried to take another gasp of air, but the effort was too much. When Nicholas put his head to the old man's chest, his heart had stopped.

Chapter Twenty-Five

On Sunday morning, Jane went to Mass as usual. She still ached all over and her head felt woozy, but she was determined to get back to normal as quickly as possible. After Mass was over and she'd managed to extract herself from the congregation, who were fussing and exclaiming over her, she went to see Agnes.

She had her own key to the cell, and after knocking, she let herself in. Agnes was up and dressed, her hair knotted neatly at the back of her head, and she'd washed her face and hands from the clean water in the pail by her bed. She beamed with pleasure when Jane went in.

'I'm so glad you're better, my dear. Brother Benedict, what a nice young man he is, told me about your accident. You really shouldn't go climbing around in these old buildings, they're very unstable.'

'I'll live. I'm just a bit stiff. But some of that oil of peppermint which you gave me to rub on my father's legs will soon loosen me up. Are you being well looked after?'

'Couldn't be better. Brother Benedict's been very kind. But I'd like to go home now, if you please. I ought to be out in the garden gathering up the herbs for next winter; this is the best time to pick them, as you know. And I must see to Ambrose.'

Jane's heart sank. Agnes was still confused. Would her brain ever function normally? She knew that deep shock

271

could wipe out the recent past. Of course, Agnes couldn't go home; not yet, not until she was ready to face up to reality. And not until they'd caught Ultor.

'You see, Jane,' Agnes went on, 'I don't know if anyone has been feeding Ambrose properly. You've been laid up, and I can hardly ask Brother Benedict to feed a cat. Ambrose does so enjoy a good dinner, although no real harm can come to him as he's a good mouse-catcher. But he'll miss not coming up on my bed in the mornings, and he does so like taking a little nap on my lap before he goes out at night. It's nice of you to give me this holiday, but it's really time I went home.'

Jane stood the basket she was carrying on the table, and lifted the cloth which covered it. The smell of chicken and fresh bread and new cheese filled the room and Agnes exclaimed with pleasure. Jane took out an earthenware jug and poured out a beaker of milk, which she handed to Agnes.

'Don't talk about going home yet, Agnes. I'll see to Ambrose and make sure he's all right. Now come and eat some dinner and tell me something about yourself. We've not had a talk for ages, have we?'

'I don't know what I've done to deserve such treatment,' Agnes said, as she accepted a plateful of food. 'I've had such a wonderful rest here. Listen, you can hear the monks chanting. I watched them say Mass this morning and I hear them chanting the night offices. It's very soothing. I know most of the monks, you know. They used to come and visit me at Thyme Cottage and ask for advice when they had to treat difficult cases. I wish I could understand Latin so that I could follow the words of the singing.'

'Then you might find this useful,' said Jane, taking out a small leather-bound book from her pocket. It was a small, beautifully made Book of Hours, illustrated with some very fine hand-painted pictures. 'My father gave me this on my sixteenth birthday. He bought it from a London bookseller and it's got all the monks' services in it, and some prayers

272

and readings from the Bible.'

Agnes took the book and began to turn the pages. 'What a treasure! I shall so much enjoy reading it and studying the pictures. I shall keep it safe until I go home. Thank you, my dear.'

'You said you know most of the monks,' said Jane conversationally as Agnes put the book under her pillow. 'Which ones come to you frequently?'

'Oh Father Hubert, of course. He always calls on me when he goes up to the woods to collect sorrel. He exchanges some of the sorrel for my parsley, which grows very easily in my garden but the monks for some reason or other find it difficult to cultivate. He often wants some of my foxglove tincture. It's marvellous for the treatment of elderly hearts. There is an old man in the infirmary who was kept going for a long time with a daily dose of foxglove.'

'Is he a frequent visitor?'

'Oh yes. He's getting on a bit, you see, not strong, and sometimes the walk up into the woods is more than he can cope with without a rest. He's a nice man, very gentle. I like talking to him. Ambrose loves him.'

This wasn't the image of a ruthless killer, thought Jane, as she arranged the rest of the food on one of the plates and put it on the table for Agnes's next meal. 'Do many people come from the village to see you?' she asked.

'Oh occasionally, when they wanted my services. Abigail Butcher came to see me when she was worried about the baby she was carrying. Poor little thing. I knew it wasn't right when I felt him in her womb. But God wanted him for Himself. Then old Tomkins came to see me when his face was covered with that rash. The Prior often sent down for something when his stomach was troubling him. Sometimes the Bishop would send one of his servants to buy one of my special potions. And Brother Martin came for the opiate. Brother Michael used to send him when he was too busy to come himself.'

'What would he want with an opiate?'

'It's the greatest medicine of all. Everyone wants my opiate; but it's very precious and I can't let just everyone have it. You see it eases the pain of the dying, and brings relief to the living. The monks use it in their infirmary, but they run out from time to time, and I always let them have some of mine. I keep it at the back of the shed, as you know, in some pottery jars with good stoppers set in wax. The monks always returned the jars and paid me for the opiate. It's very expensive as you know.'

'Does he come to see you very often?'

'Oh no, my dear. Once or twice a year, when my stocks run low and I have to send a message to him by the carrier.'

Then Jane remembered. There was no sign of the jars when she went down to Agnes's last Sunday, with Nicholas, to see what damage the fire had done. So someone had stolen them, but before, or after the fire?

Agnes had finished her meal, washed her fingers in the bowl of water and leaned back on her bed.

'It's strange,' she said. 'I feel quite tired. Perhaps I should stay here after all. Everything suddenly goes blurred, as if my brain was clouded over with fog. I think I'll take a nap. You will look after Ambrose, won't you?'

'Of course I will. Don't worry about anything.'

Jane covered her over with the rug and left her in peace. The monks had stopped chanting. They, too, were eating their midday meal. It was time to see to her father's meal, too. She wanted to see Nicholas. But how was she to get there? She wasn't yet ready to ride Melissa. Suddenly, she felt weary, and it was as much as she could do to walk back to her father's house.

Late on Sunday evening, as the shadows lengthened, and the colony of rooks in the old elm trees which marked the boundary of the graveyard, began to settle down for the night, Edgar Pierrepoint, Churchwarden of the parish of

274

Dean Peverell, made his rounds before saying goodnight to the Vicar and making sure that the church was locked up. It was what he did every Sunday evening, and sometimes the Vicar would produce a jug of ale, and they'd talk over the week's events, and count up the Mass pence.

That evening, Edgar was troubled. Things were not the same in the parish, not since the witch came. He looked across to the little room, stuck on the side of the monks' church like a boil on a thumb, and thought of her sitting there thinking up her next piece of wickedness.

Too many things had happened to give him peace of mind: Lord Nicholas's steward murdered, so it was said, then the lass from up in Mortimer's place, Bess Knowles, dying in mysterious circumstances, and now Mistress Warrener nearly killed in his church, and he knew that the gallery was perfectly sound – he'd only inspected it and the tower a week before the accident happened. And he knew an unsafe piece of masonry when he saw one. So it must have been some diabolical influence which made a stone dislodge itself and fall on Mistress Warrener. And if there was a diabolical influence about, he knew where it was coming from – that little room. Then there was that business of Abigail Butcher's baby and the shadowy figure up in the woods which had frightened Lord Nicholas's horse, and the murder of the cat and the burning down of the witch's shed. It was all very unsettling. Edgar Pierrepoint was a sensible, God-fearing man, and he was no more superstitious than anyone else in the village, but he had to admit that so many unpleasant events happening over such a short time, a mere three weeks, meant only one thing – there was a witch in their midst. A wicked witch, in league with the devil. And as he looked at the little room attached to the monks' church, he crossed himself and said the Our Father, twice. Then he continued to walk round the graveyard to make sure that the sexton had started to scythe down the long grass before the graves got completely covered.

At that time of the year, the mounds of earth which

275

marked the graves were covered with a blanket of daisies and buttercups. On some, the families had placed posies of herbs and flowers gathered from their own gardens. In the far corner, under the great yew tree which had been there since the Conqueror, there were the graves of the wealthier parishioners whose relatives had marked the last resting place of their loved ones with a stone cross, or maybe a stone slab with the details of the person's life engraved on it. It was very dark under the yew tree, the air soft and warm. It was going to be a beautiful summer night. Suddenly, he stopped. On one of the larger tombstones, old Eleanor Hammond's, he caught a glimpse of bright blue that didn't seem like the colour of flowers. He walked over to take a look. The Hammond family were one of the wealthiest families in the parish, freeholders and sheep farmers. Old Eleanor was ninety-six when she died, and it was right that her family should have given her such a fine tomb. From a hawthorn bush near the tomb a nightingale began to practise a few runs as a warm-up before the real concert began.

The blue wasn't from a posy of flowers. It was the blue of a linen dress, and it was on a small girl who was laid out on the slab, her dress neatly arranged and her fair hair unbound. Edgar stopped and clutched his heart, which began to beat wildly. He knew the little girl. She was Eleanor Hammond's great granddaughter, Katharine Hammond, aged six, the apple of John Hammond's eye. Edgar braced himself and walked over to the child. Her face was deathly pale and when he peered closer because his eyesight wasn't too good, he noticed that both of her eyes had been closed with what he thought were two coins, like the pennies the old people put in the eyes of their dead to pay the ferryman to row them across the River Styx. But they weren't pennies. They were communion wafers. Then he saw the marks around her slender neck and he realised that Katharine Hammond had been vilely murdered whilst she came to visit the tomb of her great grandmother – her little posy lay on the grass where it had fallen when she'd been attacked. This was the devil's work, he thought. Only the devil would commit such a sacrilege as to put communion wafers on his victim's eyes. And there was only one person who was conversant with the black arts – the witch! With a shout of horror Edgar ran back to the church and banged on the Vicar's door.

'Murder, sacrilege! Open up quickly, the devil's been here. Murder, murder,' he continued to scream when Alfred Hobbes opened the door, and together they ran back to the place where Katharine Hammond was lying.

News travels fast. Nicholas was given a detailed account of Katharine's death from Geoffrey Lowe, and by the time he'd sent an urgent message to the Sheriff, and ridden down to the church, a crowd had gathered, led by John Hammond, Katharine's father. They were carrying lighted torches and were crowding round Agnes's room, screaming for vengeance.

'Burn the witch, kill the witch before she kills all our children.'

Nicholas pushed his way through the crowd and flattened himself against the door of the cell.

'Stop! I'll arrest the first person who takes one step nearer this door.'

'Don't you stick up for the old hag, Lord Nicholas,' said a rough voice from the crowd. 'We'll burn her here and now and get rid of her. Don't you know what she's done to Kate Hammond?'

'I know Katharine's dead, and I grieve for her parents, but we don't know Agnes killed her. How could she? She's locked up in here and she hasn't got a key. She can't get out, you fools.'

'She don't need no keys,' said the same voice. 'Them witches know how to spirit themselves through doors. Don't you stand up for her, Lord Nicholas.'

Such was the respect that the villagers had for Nicholas

277

that no one took a step nearer. He stared at the crowd with their flaming torches, he saw the darkness settle down on the scene, and knew who was responsible for this. Ultor had struck again. Ultor was getting desperate. Agnes could soon recover her wits. Agnes had to be silenced. What better way to arouse the fury of the mob than to murder a young child and make it look like the malevolent action of a witch, one of the devil's emissaries.

The crowd would not be pacified, and some threw their torches at Nicholas in defiance, and by the time the Sheriff arrived with his men, they were almost out of control. Order was soon restored, and the crowd pushed back from Agnes's room. Then the Prior came panting up to Nicholas.

'This is terrible, my Lord. An abomination. The Sheriff must take Agnes Myles away immediately. We can't keep her here. The mob will tear us to pieces. Let her go to Marchester where the Bishop will know how to deal with her.'

'Stop, Prior. Think. There's no evidence that Agnes killed Katharine. Don't be swayed by this mob. Use your reason. She can't get out of this room. She's too old to murder a little girl. And how, in God's name, Prior, could she have got hold of communion wafers?'

'She's right,' said a clear, firm voice from the crowd. It was Jane, who'd just arrived and was pushing her way forward to stand by Nicholas. 'Whoever killed Katharine knew how to get hold of communion wafers. Now who could do that? Someone from the parish – the Vicar uses communion wafers, of course – someone from further afield who stole wafers from a church, or someone from this community. Which one of your monks has access to the sacred vessels and the communion wafers?'

Nicholas looked at Jane in admiration. He had underestimated her strength. The Prior gasped, and, all of a sudden, seemed to crumble. He looked desperately at Jane, then at Nicholas, and finally at the Sheriff. The crowd had fallen silent.

'Send these people home, Sheriff. Bring Katharine into our church, where we'll see that the prayers of the dead will be said over her body. And let's go over to my house and sort this out.'

'And meanwhile, Prior,' said Sheriff Landstock, 'let none of your monks leave these premises. Shut the gate. Assemble all the brethren in the chapter house and let none of them leave until I say so. My men will guard them and I shall put a guard over Agnes Myles's room.'

'Oh what a dreadful thing, what a scandal,' said the Prior as he led the way over to his house. 'What sacrilege – and the King's Commissioners here too. What will they think of us?'

'And Katharine's family, Prior, think of them,' said Nicholas.

'Oh I am, I am, Lord Nicholas,' said the Prior. 'It's a terrible tragedy for them. But why, oh why, should anyone want to murder a little girl in such a diabolical way?'

As they walked over to the Prior's house, the great bell of the Priory tolled out, bringing the monks down from their dormitory and into the chapter house. The crowd slowly dispersed. Two men stood guard over Agnes Myles.

Chapter Twenty-Six

'This is no place for a woman, Mistress Warrener,' said the Prior, once they were up in his study. 'I must ask you to leave.'

There were five of them present: the Prior, Nicholas, the Sheriff and his secretary, and Jane. 'I have to be here, Prior,' she said firmly, 'Don't you see I'm involved in all of this? Someone, maybe the same person who killed Katharine, tried to kill me. I have been in Lord Nicholas's confidence since his steward was murdered and I have been talking to Agnes Myles, our key witness, who will, I'm sure, lead us to the murderer.'

'It's still not suitable . . .' said the Prior, glaring at Jane as if the presence of a woman was the most important part of the proceedings.

'Oh let her be, Prior,' said Landstock, 'she's here, she has a right to be here, she can stay as far as I'm concerned.'

'And I insist she stays here,' said Nicholas. 'She's been a valuable assistant to me over the last weeks, and she knows as much as the Sheriff and I do.'

'Oh very well, let her be. But tell me, Peverell, why, in heaven's name do you still protect the old witch? Just look at her – there she is, locked away on my premises, muttering to herself, hatching up all sorts of wickedness.'

'Prior, I didn't think you, of all people, would succumb

to popular prejudice. Sit down, and try to think rationally, or else another monstrous injustice is going to be enacted on your premises. The person who killed Katharine Hammond knows his way round churches. He knows where the communion wafers are kept. He also knows that putting the wafers on Katharine's eyes would seem like an act of witchcraft – I'm sure you know about the rituals used in the black arts – and all eyes would turn to Agnes Myles. And he's succeeded, hasn't he, Prior? He wants Agnes Myles out of the way. And why does he take so much trouble over an old woman? Because he knows that she knows who he is; and one day she'll give us his name. Jane visits Agnes. Jane knows that one day the old lady'll recover her wits. This is why Agnes must be protected. So don't play into the murderer's hands, Prior. Let the Sheriff and I tackle this in the time-honoured way. Now who do you think is our prime suspect, Sheriff?'

'Whoever has access to the communion wafers, Lord Nicholas,' said the Sheriff.

'And that means Father Hubert,' said the Prior aghast.

'Anyone else?'

'Only me; I have the master key.'

'What about the Vicar?' said the Sheriff. 'He uses communion wafers to celebrate the Mass.'

'Yes, and he gets them from us. Mind you, we do give him several at a time, and presumably he keeps them in his sacristy.'

'So Hobbes could have murdered the child?' said the Prior, happy to grasp at any straw.

'He could, but what's his motive? He grumbles about Agnes Myles, but has never once wanted to put her to death, and I can't see him going to elaborate lengths to incriminate her. Where is he now, by the way?' said the Sheriff.

'He went off with Katharine's parents. He'll probably stay with them for the rest of the night,' said Jane.

Suddenly, there was a knock on the door and Brother

281

Benedict came in, his face tired and anxious.

'What is it, Brother Benedict?' said the Prior, jumping to his feet. 'You look worried to death.'

'There's something I have to tell you, Prior. Early on Saturday morning, after Matins, I saw Father Hubert get up and go down to the sacristy. Thinking he might be unwell, I followed him. He went in to the sacristy, and returned carrying something hidden under a cloth. He then went out into the cloisters by the north door. Not thinking too much about it, I returned to bed and slept until Prime. But now I think it could be important.'

'It's very important,' said the Prior gravely. 'It seems you might be right, my Lord,' he said turning to Nicholas, 'that one of my community could just possibly have murdered the child. And Father Hubert, of all people! What unspeakable wickedness!'

'Don't jump to conclusions too quickly,' said Nicholas. 'Father Hubert might have been doing something quite harmless for all we know.'

'Harmless? Then why sculk around in the dead of night?' roared the Prior.

'Agnes also told me that Father Hubert came to her for a tincture of foxglove. He uses it to stimulate the hearts of elderly patients. Used with care it is a life-saver. Too much, it can kill,' said Jane quietly. 'It could've been added to Bess Knowles's potion – she was a witness too, remember? – and it would have killed her without leaving any traces.'

'And Brother Wilfrid was going to tell me the name of the person who added something to Bess's drink,' said Nicholas with growing excitement, 'But, unfortunately, he died before he could give me that name. But he did say, "the old one". It could've been Father Hubert.'

'Then we must send for him at once. Have him brought here, Brother Benedict.'

'And take one of my men to bring him here,' said the Sheriff. 'And don't let him escape.'

282

Minutes later, Father Hubert was brought in. He looked frailer than ever with his pale face drawn with anxiety, the sprinkling of grey hair round his tonsure, and his bandaged wrists. Nicholas simply couldn't see in this pathetic old man the cunning traitor who called himself Ultor. However, he certainly looked terrified, and when the Prior accused him of going down to the sacristy in the middle of the night, he began to shake with fear.

'My Lord Prior,' he said, in a voice so low that the Prior had to bend down to hear him, 'yes, I did go to the sacristy after Matins.'

'And what for?' said the Prior looking at him in astonishment.

'I wanted to get the chalice.'

'The chalice? What unspeakable abomination were you going to commit with our holy chalice?'

'No abomination, Prior, I only wanted to hide it.'

'Worse and worse! Has the devil got into you too? That chalice belongs on the high altar of our church when we celebrate important feast days. What right do you think you've got to hide it?'

'Because I didn't want the inspectors to see it.'

'And where have you put it?'

'I'd rather not say; not until those two men have gone. You might make me give it to them.'

'Enough of this,' said the Sheriff roughly. 'This sounds like a pack of lies to conceal the real reason for visiting the sacristy in the dead of night. You wanted to help yourself to some communion wafers, didn't you, for your infernal murder of that innocent child?'

'My Lord, have mercy, don't let him say such things. Why should I want to harm a child?'

'To throw the blame on Agnes Myles so that she'll be put on trial for witchcraft; then she'll denounce you, and that would put an end to your scheming.'

'But why? Why?' said the old man, weeping. 'What am I supposed to have done?'

283

'You want Agnes Myles out of the way,' went on the Sheriff remorselessly, 'because she knows you went to her to get some tincture of foxglove to kill Bess Knowles.'

'Yes, I did get some tincture of foxglove from Agnes,' said Father Hubert trembling uncontrollably. 'I gave it to Brother Martin; he's the one who asked me to collect it from Agnes's house. Why should I want to kill Bess Knowles? She never did me any harm.'

'No, but she was a witness to a conversation when Sir Roger Mortimer was plotting against the King. He'd want to get rid of Bess Knowles and hired you to do his dirty work for him.'

'Lord Prior, Lord Nicholas, have mercy! Tell the Sheriff it's not true. He's making a dreadful mistake. I only gave the foxglove to Brother Martin. Why not ask him?'

'We've only got your word for it. And there's the matter of the communion wafers. That's going to take a lot of explaining away. Now Prior, I shall have to arrest this man and take him to Marchester for further questioning.'

Father Hubert uttered a cry of despair and threw himself down at the Prior's feet. 'Lord Prior, don't let them do this to me. I've done nothing. It's all a terrible mistake.'

'Get up, Father,' said the Prior not unkindly, 'if you've nothing to hide, you've nothing to fear. Now go with the Sheriff and answer his questions and you'll soon be back with us again. Just remember to tell the truth.'

The Sheriff's men led Father Hubert away to the Sheriff's carriage. Nicholas turned to the Prior. 'I hope to God we've not made a dreadful mistake.'

'I still can't believe it, poison, murder, sacrilege. Not Father Hubert,' said the Prior. 'Not unless the devil's got into him and given him supernatural strength.'

There was another knock on the door and Brother Cyril, the Prior's steward, came in.

'There are two people here to see you. Biddy and Josh Tomkins. They say it's urgent.'

Nicholas looked triumphantly at Jane. 'At last,' he said,

'we're getting somewhere. The rats are leaving the sinking ship.'

'Well, what do you want?' he said as the pair came in, looking nervously round the unfamiliar surroundings.

'We saw you taking away the old monk,' began Josh, 'and I said to Biddy, we've got to tell Lord Nicholas. You see, when we saw the little girl, and I know how much the parents are going to grieve, I knew I must tell someone what happened in our house a few days ago.

'Perkins and Bovet were drinking ale, a bit too much as it happened, and the talk went round to witches and deformed babies and then Perkins said how he'd strung up the witch's cat, and he said he was glad as it only brought harm to the village. The next thing, a strange fellow comes into the house, calling himself a visiting lay brother. Well, we've certainly never seen him before, and we've not seen him since. Then he puts down some money on the counter, and says that's for anyone who'd burn down the witch's shed, because he couldn't abide witches, and neither could his master. Then he says, "I want it done tonight" – he means Sunday morning by that time. Then off he goes. We didn't ask him who his master was because Bovet and Perkins had their eye on the money and I was anxious to get my cut. So we shared the money, the two men went off and you know what happened, and we thought no more about it until now when poor little Katharine was murdered and we saw the monk taken off.'

'What did this – lay brother – look like?' said the Prior.

'A monk's a monk, sir, if you know what I mean. They all look the same to me. But he did say he was a lay brother and I suppose he meant by that that he wasn't a proper monk.'

'Was he young or old?'

'Oh, they all look old to me. This one wasn't tonsured, but what hair he had didn't look grey; not that I looked too closely.'

'Well, let me summon all the lay brothers and you can

point him out to me.' said the Prior.

'I wouldn't bother, sir, if you'll excuse me saying so. You see he said he was only visiting.'

'Only visiting? What diabolical nonsense is this? If he's a visitor, he stays here with me in my house. And we don't have visiting lay brothers. They stay where they are and help to run their monasteries. No, the man's a fraud. And he did say, if I heard correctly, that he was working for a master? Could it be, my Lord, that Father Hubert employed this lay brother to do his work for him? After all, Father Hubert's not strong; he'd need help. And he does travel around a lot and would've met lots of people, wandering lay brothers included.'

'It's a good theory,' said Jane, who'd been following the conversation intently, 'except, for the life of me, I can't see Father Hubert as a devious plotter, willing to go to any lengths to carry out his main aim, the death of the King. Can you, Nicholas?'

'No, it seems highly unlikely. But he is fanatically opposed to the King's policies. You've seen how he admitted to hiding the chalice. With the help of a younger man, he probably thought he could succeed.'

'Lord Nicholas,' boomed the Prior, 'we're all opposed to the King's policy. We're all going to be thrown out of here in the very near future. Wagstaff and Laycock will see to that. But that doesn't mean that we're all fanatical killers, does it? We simply bow to a higher authority, and hope that an even Higher Authority will look after us.'

Nicholas left the Prior and rode straight into Marchester, where he stayed for the rest of the day with the Sheriff. Father Hubert, deeply shocked, was locked in the Archdeacon's prison. Bovet and Perkins confirmed the Tomkinses story. Yes, Perkins had killed the witch's cat, yes, they'd been paid to start the fire – only the shed, mind, just to get rid of the witch's potions. Yes, they'd seen money change hands between the monk, who wasn't really

286

a monk, and the Tomkinses. No, they didn't get a good look at the monk – they all looked the same anyway. Miserable lot!

Late on Monday evening, Nicholas rode home. One man arrested. His accomplice still at large. Finding a tall monk who wasn't a proper monk was going to be very difficult. Monks were two a penny; and probably he'd come from a distance any way, because he'd not been seen since the burning down of the shed.

He felt he shouldn't be so depressed. The Sheriff was positively ebullient now that Father Hubert was under lock and key. But Nicholas was uneasy. He felt, instinctively, that they hadn't got the right man. This was just what Ultor wanted. He wanted everyone off the scent. With the hunt called off, he could plot his next bit of devilry. And that meant that the guard on Agnes Myles must not be relaxed. And he must do his utmost to dissuade the King from going to Portsmouth. The King! Nicholas urged Harry forward. He would be here just the day after tomorrow!

Chapter Twenty-Seven

The arrival of Amos Cartwright on Tuesday morning brought home the imminence of the King's visit. He triumphantly showed the doublet to Nicholas, who had to admit that it was indeed a work of art. It was made of a sturdy but soft green cloth with lacings down the front to ensure a flexible fit. The sleeves were slashed to reveal a white satin lining. But the collar was the masterpiece. Stiffened, and embroidered with tiny seed pearls arranged to form tiny Tudor roses, it would frame the King's face to perfection. The cuffs were embroidered with the same pattern, and tiny Tudor roses were embroidered down the front of the jacket with the eyes for the laces fitting exactly in the centre of each rose. Even Monsieur Pierre gasped with pleasure when he saw it, and Nicholas took in a sharp breath when he read the bill. Twelve pounds! Twelve pounds just for a coat! There was no doubt about it, the King's visit was going to bankrupt him.

From then onwards, Monsieur Pierre was determined not to be upstaged by a haberdasher. He was going to provide a banquet that would outshine the new doublet. Everywhere there were sounds of cattle lowing, and pigs grunting, whilst geese fluttered round Nicholas's feet when he went out into the courtyard. From a pen erected at the back of the house, two swans glared at him balefully.

He was glad to escape and see Jane. He found her at the

Priory, having just taken food to Agnes.

'How is the old lady?' he asked.

'Getting stronger by the minute. Nicholas, I'm glad to see you. I've been uneasy about Father Hubert.'

'I share your concern, but unless he can give us some satisfactory answers to our questions, he still remains our prime suspect.'

'But he's not got the qualities to be the "master" whom the lay brother referred to. There's not a jot of ruthlessness in him. He's a gentle, kind old man, who wants to do what he's always done, look after the Priory's treasures. No, I'm sure, Nicholas, that Ultor's still at large. And until we're satisfied that we've really caught him, I'll not let Agnes go home.'

'And keep on talking to her, won't you? And meanwhile I hope you'll practise some songs with Brother Benedict – in a safe place, like the Prior's solarium.'

'Don't worry. We'll do our best to keep the King entertained. Provided that is, that nothing happens to the King before supper time!'

On Wednesday morning, Nicholas woke to find his house transformed: clean rushes and straw on the floors; tapestries, revealing intricacies of designs hidden for years under layers of dirt, hung on the walls, and everywhere was the heavy scent of herbs, culled from the garden and strewn on the straw. Huge garlands of roses and wild flowers hung from the rafters. The stables were cleaned, the horses groomed to sleek perfection. Messengers continually rushed backwards and forwards between the Priory and his house; and Monsieur Pierre was everywhere, from the kitchen, where he tasted soups and stews, to the great hall, where he sniffed the air appreciatively, to the bedchambers, where he checked the sheets and pillows.

Then, in the late afternoon, there was the sound of hunting horns, and the clatter of hooves, and the vanguard had arrived. Nicholas had just managed to put on a clean

289

shirt and fasten the laces on his doublet, when he heard the commotion. He dashed down into the courtyard and came face to face with King Henry, sitting on a great chestnut horse, covered in sweat. The King sprang lightly down from his mount and grinned at Nicholas.

'Well, here we are, Peverell. On time, you see. The Queen's following in her coach, but I thought I'd surprise you. Now what's that steward of mine cooked up for us? We're all famished.'

Monsieur Pierre, bowing deferentially at every step, advanced towards the King. Geoffrey, who'd lost at least five pounds off his stocky frame through all the worry of the last few days, hung back, until Nicholas dragged him forward and introduced him.

From that moment on, Nicholas was no longer master of his own house. Monsieur Pierre took it upon himself to be Master of Ceremonies, Geoffrey was butler, and Mary queened it in the kitchen. Dinner was served early, as the Queen, in the last stages of pregnancy, was tired and wanted to retire early. The King insisted that the first meal should be a modest one: eels stewed in ale, a roast bullock, a quantity of delicious fowl, and a splendid dessert, provided by the Prior, and made with cake, almonds and raisins, custard and fresh cream.

The Bishop had sent four musicians to play during the meal, and it was after the dessert had been cleared away and bowls of nuts and dried fruit were placed on the table that the King turned to Nicholas.

'Well, Peverell. A fine meal. A fine house; everything for our comfort. But haven't you forgotten one thing?'

Nicholas groaned. What had gone wrong?

'My coat,' the King roared, clapping Nicholas on the back. 'Don't you remember, you cut a great hole in my coat when you came to Court, and you promised me a replacement. And you've forgotten, haven't you?'

'Sire,' said a voice behind them, 'Lord Nicholas wishes you to accept this coat, with his compliments.'

It was Monsieur Pierre, carrying the great doublet on a silver salver. The King stared at it in astonishment, then exclaimed with pleasure as he stroked the beautiful cloth and ran his fingers over the intricate embroidery.

'This is wonderful, Peverell. You've excelled yourself. We shall wear it tomorrow at the great feast.'

There was no dancing that night due to the Queen's fatigue, and after the meal was over, the King asked Nicholas to take a stroll with him in the gardens. The moon hung like a lantern overhead, lighting the way, and the warm air was heavy with the scent of flowers. Henry was in fine humour.

'You look worried, Peverell. It doesn't suit you. Now what's up? Don't you want me here?'

'Your Grace, I'm honoured to have you here. I'm delighted that you find everything to your satisfaction, but the fact remains that you are in grave danger. You know we're not sure we've caught this traitor who calls himself Ultor.'

'Rubbish. I thought you'd caught the man. A monk, I hear. Bears a grudge against me – I can't think why!'

'We've arrested someone but I'm not one hundred per cent sure he's the man we're looking for.'

'Well, we'll soon find out, won't we? And if it's a monk out to get me, then I'm not in the least bit worried.'

'Shouldn't your Grace seriously consider cancelling your visit to Portsmouth tomorrow?'

'Cancel my visit to Portsmouth? What nonsense is this? I'm not a bit worried by a demented monk. I intend to rise early, leave the Queen here – Monsieur Pierre will look after her – and you and I, Peverell, will ride together to Portsmouth. I want to build a castle there, you know – a good strong one to replace that feeble tower at Southsea. Porchester's too far away. Got to defend the realm – we need more defences along the south coast. Damned French are stirring up trouble again. So I must see Southampton, and set a few things in motion. Besides, think of the scene,

291

Peverell, my ships sailing past me, dipping their flags in salute. Will it not be a brave sight?'

'It will indeed. But there's just one problem . . .'

'Which is?'

'Look around you, sir. Is it not a beautiful night?'

'Wonderful. If the Queen were feeling better, I'd have her out here dancing on this velvety grass.'

'But what's missing?'

'Nothing's missing, you great worrier, Peverell. This is just what I wanted, simple, rustic pleasures.'

'There's no wind, your Grace. Not a breath of it. No wind expected tomorrow. So how is the fleet to sail past?'

'Oh, don't be such an old woman! Those fellows can row their damn ships past me. Or I can be rowed out to them, like we do on the Thames at Hampton Court. I'll get Southampton to rustle up a barge or two. Just get this into that thick head of yours, Peverell, nothing's going to deter me from visiting my fleet. Especially not an absence of wind.'

Jane woke early on Thursday morning. She hadn't slept well. The King was here, she'd seen the commotion, heard the hunting horns. She knew Nicholas shared the same doubts as she did, and she knew that if Ultor was going to strike, today was the day. The Day of Wrath he'd called it. Dies Irae. She had to have another talk with Agnes. She knew she'd be awake early as she liked to listen to the monks chanting Prime.

She crept out into the garden where the birds were singing their dawn chorus as the sun appeared over the horizon. She walked down to the Priory and went round to the little room at the back. All was quiet. She knocked gently and unlocked the door. She went in and put down the jug of milk she'd brought for Agnes's breakfast on the table. Agnes was just waking up. She sat up and smiled at Jane.

'Have you come to listen to Prime, Jane? How strange,

292

the monks haven't come down yet. They always do at sunrise, you know. Let me take a look.'

She climbed up on the bed and looked through the tiny window. Then she turned and looked at Jane. 'No sign of them. Well, well, not like them to be late.'

She drank the beaker of milk Jane handed her and sat on the edge of the bed.

'Agnes, tell me once again the names of those people who came to see you just before the fire. Try to remember. It's very important. Can you remember the fire? Is it coming back to you? We also want to find out who killed Ambrose. You see, he's not with us any more. Someone murdered him. Someone strung him up on a tree. Try to remember, Agnes. We are relying on you.'

Suddenly Agnes bowed her head and began to cry bitterly with great sobs that racked her frail body. 'Oh yes, my darling Ambrose,' she sobbed. 'He's gone, hasn't he? And that little girl, too. Brother Benedict told me what had happened. All that noise and shouting, it was quite horrible. I felt sure that any moment the mob would break down that door.'

'Lord Nicholas wouldn't let that happen. Now try to think, Agnes. Who came to see you recently, just before the fire? Please, please, try to remember.'

Suddenly, Agnes stopped crying. She lifted her head and looked intently at Jane. There was something different about her; a new strength which showed itself in the keenness of her gaze.

'Well, I've told you about Father Hubert – poor man, do you really think he could have killed my Ambrose? Then there was Brother Martin who worked in the Infirmary with Brother Michael. Now he used to come often.'

'What did he want, Agnes?'

'Oh, he always wanted my opiates. I kept them in the shed, in a special place. Brother Michael sometimes came, and used to help himself. He bought up a lot of my stock just before dear Ambrose died.'

Brother Michael, thought Jane with growing excitement; the tall, intense Infirmarer, with his ugly face and bald head. Yes, it was just possible.

Telling Agnes to rest quietly, Jane went out, locking the cell door. She ran over to the gatehouse. The door was locked. There was no sign of the gatehouse keeper. The sun had now risen and still there was no sound from the monks' choir. Something was wrong.

She ran round to the parish church and hammered on the Vicar's door. Hobbes was an early riser and opened the door immediately. He gazed in astonishment when he recognised Jane.

'Why, Mistress Warrener, what's happened?'

'There's something wrong in the Priory. The monks haven't come down for Prime, and there's no one in the gatehouse.'

'Not yet sung Prime? Good heavens, they must've overslept. Come into the church and wait here. I'll see what's up.'

He opened one of the connecting doors and disappeared. Minutes later he came running back. 'Quick, quick, fetch the Prior. They're all there, asleep in their beds. I can't wake them up.'

'They're not . . .?'

'Oh no, they're breathing all right. Some of them snoring.'

They went across to the Prior's house, where he was up and grumbling at the disturbance of having an extra twenty people to feed at breakfast. He stared in astonishment when he saw Jane and the Vicar.

'Not up for Prime?' he said when he'd listened to them. 'Things always go wrong when I'm especially busy. I gave instructions to Brother Michael to fill in whilst Father Hubert's away. Well, you'd better take me to them, Vicar, and I'll wake them up all right.'

Together they went back to the Priory church. The Prior dashed up the night stairs into the dormitory and came

294

down looking very angry. 'They're all asleep, and I can't wake them up. Someone's given them something lethal to drink last night. And the devil of it is, Brother Michael's not with them. His bed's empty.'

Then Jane knew that she had to warn Nicholas. She ran home to fetch Melissa, and rode up the street, past Edgar Pierrepoint's house. He was standing at his front door, scratching his head and filling his lungs with fresh, morning air. He waved when he saw her.

'What's the hurry, Mistress Warrener? You're the second person I've seen up at the crack of dawn today.'

She reined in Melissa. 'Who else have you seen?'

'Why, the ugly old devil, that Infirmarer. I had to get up early this morning, for natural reasons, you know – I'm not as young as I used to be – and I heard the sound of horses' hooves and ran to the window to take a look. And there he was, riding one of the Prior's horses as if the devil himself were after him.'

'How long ago was this?'

'Well before first light. Two hours ago, I suppose. He took the Portsmouth road.'

Worse and worse. Jane galloped up to the manor. The courtyard was seething with horses and dogs, and in the middle of it all, sat King Henry on Nicholas's horse, Harry. Nicholas, looking furious, was mounted on a bay stallion, the prime mount from the Prior's stable.

She pulled Melissa to a halt. Nicholas came over.

'Jane, what is it? What's happened?'

She told him the news. 'Brother Michael's had a head start. He's well mounted and he took the Portsmouth road. Tell the King he mustn't go to Portsmouth.'

'And who's this wench that says King Harry mustn't go to Portsmouth?' said the King, who'd ridden over to join them.

'Mistress Jane Warrener, your Grace. You'll hear her sing tonight. But she brings bad news. You can't go to Portsmouth, Sire.'

'Can't go? You tell your King that he can't review his fleet? Just because a disgruntled monk's after him? It's too late, Peverell. This is a fine horse you've lent me. Come, I intend to race you to Portsmouth. We'll get fresh horses from Southampton to bring us back. Mistress Jane, my compliments, I look forward to making your acquaintance tonight.'

He blew her a kiss, Harry pawed the ground restlessly, and without waiting for Nicholas, the King set off down the road towards the village and the main coast road. Nicholas, with a despairing look at Jane, followed. He had no choice.

They reached Portsmouth at midday. Both horses were exhausted, but not King Henry. He rode up to the gate-house of Domus Dei, the hospital, founded three hundred years previously for the relief of pilgrims going to Canterbury, Winchester and Chichester, now run by twelve brethren under the control of a warden. Since its foundation it had accumulated wealth with which the brethren had built extra buildings – a brewery, a forge, a smithy, a captain's chamber and a great chamber, a pigeon house, and a house for visiting dignitaries. This complex stood near the Hard, where, out across the blue waters of Portsmouth Harbour, tucked away in the lee of the western shore, King Henry's warships placidly sat on the still water, with not a drop of wind to fill their sails. Southampton had ordered out the towing boats to drag the vessels nearer the shore, but the great wooden tubs hardly moved despite the frantic efforts of the crews.

Unperturbed, King Henry made himself comfortable in the presence chamber of the visitors' house and ate game pie and cold chicken and quaffed flagons of ale.

'This is a damnable state of affairs,' he said to Nicholas, who was breathing a sigh of relief that, with no wind, the King would have to look at his ships from the comparative safety of the visitors' house. 'You said there'd be no wind, and no wind it is. Never mind,' he said turning to

Southampton. 'Get the Admiral's barge ready, and whilst we're waiting we can go through those plans I sent you for the castle I want built to the east of here, and some forts along the entrance to the harbour.'

Whilst the King pored over the plans, Nicholas had a word with the Captain of the Guard. 'Keep a good look-out for a tall, bald-headed monk,' he said.

The Captain laughed and shrugged his shoulders dismissively. 'The place is full of monks, my Lord. This is a resting place for pilgrims, you know. We've got every kind of monk – French ones, Spanish, and even Italian monks. And what's more, they all pull those hoods over their faces when they go out, so how the devil are we going to find out if they've got bald heads or not? Don't worry, sir, if the King stays here, we'll take him up on top of the gatehouse when he wants to see his ships, and he'll be as safe as houses. No one can get in here. Everyone's been checked out.'

Reassured, Nicholas began to relax. The King could discuss his plans with Southampton, refresh himself, take a look at his ships, then, with fresh horses, they could ride back to Dean Peverell and get there in good time for supper. It was all going to plan.

A continuous stream of messengers was coming and going from the hospital. Southampton read the despatches and passed them over to his secretary for a reply, if that were necessary. But one despatch held his attention. He came over to Nicholas.

'Here we are, Lord Nicholas. We've got the messenger we lost at Littlehampton. One of Fitzroy's men found him in a barn at Shoreham. He was in a bad state so it didn't take Fitzroy long to get the information out of him. He said he was employed by a monk – one of your monks, it seems. He said his name was Brother Michael, the Infirmarer. Seems this Brother Michael is a formidable character. His messenger calls him the Avenging Angel and says that he took over Mortimer's work when he was arrested. So now, at least, we know who we're looking for.'

Brother Michael, how blind he'd been. He should have guessed long ago. Sour, fanatical, familiar with all the Infirmarer's potions. Passionately against the King and his policies; why had they overlooked him? Passion was the key word, Nicholas thought. All the monks were against the King's policies, but only Brother Michael had the passion to do anything about it. Then recently all the evidence had pointed to Father Hubert, and that was probably just what Brother Michael had planned. But where was he now? Had he realised that, with the capture of his messenger, the game was up and he'd fled the country? Somehow Nicholas didn't think Brother Michael was the type to give up so easily.

'The messenger?' he said to Southampton. 'What was he like?'

'Tall, not tonsured. Called himself a lay brother. Apparently he'd worked for Mortimer and Brother Michael had taken him on. Infernal devil! He cursed the King, my Lord, even as they dragged him away. God, how I hate these fanatical types. They give us all a lot of trouble.'

The King folded away the charts, finished his ale, and stared out of the window. Then he strode across to Nicholas.

'Come on, Peverell, stop looking so miserable. I thought that ride would've cheered you up a bit. Now, is the barge ready, Paget?'

Nicholas started. He'd forgotten the barge.

'It's ready and waiting, Sire,' said Southampton.

'Good. If the ships can't get to us, we'll have to go out to them, eh, Paget? Do us good – rowing on the Thames; do the sailors good too, to see their King.'

'Your Grace, stop. This isn't the Thames. We can't guard you on open water,' said Nicholas with growing panic.

'Don't be a fool, Peverell. Do you think I'm afraid of a miserable monk who wants to take a swipe at me? Of course you can guard me. Are you telling me that all those bowmen and cannoneers are useless? Come on now, let's be off.'

He walked swiftly out of the presence chamber, went through the gatehouse, where the guards were too astonished to stop him, and out on to the Hard. The three sally ports were just four hundred yards away. Outside Domus Dei the crowds had gathered. The whole of Portsmouth had come to see its King. The crowd was good-humoured and people were chatting cheerfully with the guards who held them back. On top of the gatehouse stood several bowmen with bows drawn back at the ready. On the Hard itself, lined up against the sea wall, were the cannoneers with their clumsy hand-held cannons, and matches at the ready. Nicholas measured the distance to the first of the sally ports, where the top of the royal ensign on the Admiral's barge could just be seen hanging limply in the still air.

The King, with a wave of a hand to the crowd, who roared their appreciation, set off towards the sally port. With his heart beating wildly, hardly aware of what he was doing, Nicholas drew his sword.

Just then, as they almost reached the sally port, a tall figure ran straight out of the crowd. His hood had fallen back and Nicholas caught a glimpse of a pale face, contorted with hatred.

'Death,' the man shouted, 'Death to Anti-Christ!'

He held a dagger in his hand and he launched himself at the King. But Nicholas was there before him, and just as the monk was about to strike, Nicholas knocked him sideways and struck him across the arm and shoulders with his sword. Immediately arrows fell all around them. There was the sound of an explosion and a puff of smoke came out of one of the cannons.

'Don't kill him, Peverell,' said Southampton's voice behind him. 'We need him to talk. Take him away, and keep him alive,' he said to the guard, who was starting to drag the monk away, Brother Michael turned his head to glare at Nicholas, who recoiled from his look of concentrated malevolence.

'Why? Why have you risked everything?' Nicholas said.

'Because we've lost everything,' Brother Michael answered.

The King drew a deep breath and put his arm round Nicholas's shoulders. 'Well done, Peverell. Remarkably quick of you to spot that fellow. Now that you've got your man, let's take a look at these ships of ours.'

Twilight was falling when they arrived back at Dean Peverell. Wearily, they trooped up the drive and into the courtyard, where waiting grooms seized the horses and led them away for a much-needed rest. Nicholas felt a pang of remorse that Harry had been left behind in Portsmouth to be collected later, but King Henry had ridden him hard, and he'd beaten them all in the race to Portsmouth Hard.

The King, for once, looked weary as he walked stiffly into the great hall, his arm draped familiarly across Nicholas's shoulders. Once inside, Nicholas came to a sudden halt. The house was unrecognisable. The air smelt fresh and clean, the wild flowers and herbs strewn on the rushes on the floor had released their heady scents. Monsieur Pierre, dressed in a doublet of many colours, advanced and bowed low.

'Welcome home, Sire,' he said, 'welcome home, my Lord.'

Henry glanced round. 'Seems you've done us well, Pierre. Now I must freshen myself up, then we'll be down to see what you've concocted for us. A special meal tonight,' he said, raising his voice so that all the servants could hear, 'because your master saved your King's life. Now that's some news for you, isn't it?' he said, smiling at the row of astonished faces. 'Now I hope you've ordered some hot water, Pierre. I need a full tub with sprigs of fresh rosemary in it. You've got a damn fine house here, Peverell, and that stallion of yours is a damn fine horse.

Pity we had to leave him with Southampton. I might have made you an offer for him.'

Thanking his lucky stars that Harry was out of reach of the King, Nicholas went up to his own tiny room, wedged under the eaves, and put on a clean doublet and hose. Then he combed his hair and went down to meet the guests.

The Sheriff was the first to arrive. He looked relaxed and cheerful and thumped Nicholas heartily on the back.

'Well you got the devil, I hear.'

'News travels fast, it seems,'

'Everyone in Marchester knows how you saved the King. You know, I nearly beat you to it. Father Hubert, we can release him now, admitted to the Archdeacon that Brother Michael had covered for him in the sacristy last week after he'd been blooded. That's when the devil must've helped himself to the wafers. Also, it seems, Brother Michael regularly went up into the woods to gather herbs. That's when he must've seen you and decided to lie in ambush. He didn't reckon on the hardness of your head, did he? But by this time, it was too late to send a message to Portsmouth. I reckoned you'd caught him. By the way, Father Hubert says he's hidden the chalice. And what's more he's not telling anyone where it is until those two Commissioners have gone. You'll have a job extracting the information out of him because we can't.'

The Prior arrived, accompanied by Wagstaff and Laycock, dressed in suitably sombre clothes, as befitted the King's servants.

'My God, Lord Peverell, am I glad to see you. All my monks are as dozy as a lot of dormice. Take them days to get over this. It appears Brother Michael, may his name be cursed, laced their drinks yesterday with a tincture of opium. Mistress Warrener found out from Agnes Myles, who can be released now, I suppose, that Michael bought up most of her supplies of the stuff so he must've been planning this for some time. We think he might well have come down to her shed and cleared out all the bottles of the

301

stuff before Bovet and Perkins set fire to the place. I should've known, of course. He always was a sullen devil. Hated wine, by the way. Never trust a man who doesn't drink wine, eh, Wagstaff? By the way, I've sent my coach back to pick up Mistress Jane and that surly devil of a father. Benedict says he'll come with them.'

Nicholas was glad to see the Prior looking so happy. He'd sit him next to the King. The King liked robust conversation at mealtimes.

Then Jane arrived looking dazzlingly beautiful in her green velvet dress, heavily embroidered with gold thread, and her long hair loose down her back. She wore a garland of flowers in her hair, marigolds, wild white roses and sweet-smelling pinks. Brother Benedict, with his dark looks, made a perfect contrast. Her father, not the slightest bit overawed by the grand surroundings, shook Nicholas's hand enthusiastically and offered Nicholas his congratulations.

As Nicholas went to greet Jane, she dropped him a curtsy. 'So, you're safe, Nicholas. What a relief! Now Agnes can go home.'

'My dear Jane, it was entirely due to you that we caught him. Without your speedy intervention this morning we would've been living in a fool's paradise.'

The King's trumpeters blared out the arrival of the royal couple. The King, resplendent in his new doublet, Queen Anne, elegant in dark-blue velvet cut very low in the front, her dark hair covered by a head-dress studded with seed pearls. The baby she was carrying hardly showed, and her face was pale and drawn with fatigue.

The King was in expansive mood. He signalled for the Prior to say grace, the musicians to start playing, and the first course to be served without delay.

Course after course arrived, from steaming vats of beef soup laced with beer, through fish and game and the royal swans. The King was in fine form, repeatedly putting his arm affectionately round Nicholas's shoulders. Finally, a great shout went up as the surprise pie was carried in by four servants. Then a hush descended, and the King looked at Nicholas.

'So, you've made me a surprise pie. I didn't expect it of you, Peverell. You're too much of a worrier, not enough imagination. Now what's in it? Come along, Pierre, chop it up, let's see its innards.'

As the steward plunged his knife into the first compartment, rich smells wafted up into the rafters. There was venison, cooked in red wine, in one compartment, rabbit, cooked with baby onions and wild mushrooms in another, tiny song birds cooked in madeira in a third, larks' tongues in another, and finally he came to the last section. Pierre asked the King to raise the cover. King Henry leaned forward and lifted the pastry lid. Two doves, indignant over their last-minute imprisonment, flew out and upwards, where they came to rest on one of the roof beams. Amidst the laughter and applause, Nicholas signalled to the musicians to start up a lively galliard.

But the King had other ideas. He stood up, forcing Nicholas to stand up with him. Then, with an arm round Nicholas, he called for silence.

'Come, a toast. To Lord Nicholas Peverell, who saved my life today. From now on he is my friend, my Companion of Honour, and I shall treat his house as my own.'

Nicholas, thinking this sounded a doubtful honour, turned to the King. 'You honour me with your praise, your Grace, but the real honour should go to Mistress Jane Warrener, my friend and accomplice, without whom, had she not acted so promptly this morning we would not be here now to celebrate this occasion.'

Jane stood up, and, urged on by her father, approached the King, and, blushing, dropped him a deep curtsy. 'Great Heavens, Peverell, you've got a good-looking lass to act as your accomplice! Come here, my dear, and sit next to me. Out of the way, Peverell, Mistress Jane can tell me herself why I must be grateful to her.'

After a few minutes, Nicholas decided that enough was enough. The King was getting a bit too enthusiastic, and Queen Anne's eyes were shooting daggers at him. He extracted Jane away from the King's clutches, and led her towards the stage which had been erected at one end of the hall. Then, oblivious to the fact that all eyes were on them, he held on to her hand and gently turned her round to face him.

'Jane, you've been my loyal friend for so long, now will you honour me by becoming my wife? Just think of it, you will be the mistress of Dean Peverell.'

She looked startled, withdrew her hand, and dropped him a curtsy. 'Lord Nicholas, I'm overcome. But just at this moment, the King is looking at us, my father is glaring at me, and Brother Benedict is waiting to sing with me. Besides, being mistress of Dean Peverell means nothing to me. I would only ever consider marrying the man I love and who, I know, loves me. Ask me another time, when we are not so public.'

'Jane, don't be so contrary. You know I love you. Just say "yes". The King's in the mood to give us his blessing.'

'First things first, my Lord. And just at this moment, music is my priority.'

She turned to where Brother Benedict was waiting for her on the stage, and took her place beside him. Then they sang, to the delight of the guests. They sang songs about love and happiness and the pleasures of the countryside. When Jane sang one of the King's own compositions called, 'Pastime with Good Company', the King rose to his feet in delight.

'By God, Prior,' he said, 'Tell me, who's the good-looking monk singing with Mistress Warrener? Don't they make a fine couple? Tell him to pack his bags and I'll take him back to Court with me. He can entertain the French Ambassador.'

The Prior looked the King straight in the face. 'Sire, you

304

have every right to govern your kingdom as you think fit. Allow me to govern my Priory in my own way. Brother Benedict stays with me until his abbot recalls him to France.'

'Well said, Prior, you'll make a good diplomat. You're quite right, of course. None of my business what you do with your monks. Now, Peverell, come and take a turn with me in that garden of yours. I want a word in your ear. Let the dancing commence,' he said as they went out, 'if the Queen's got a mind to it.'

He linked his arm in Nicholas's and strolled outside into the garden, where the night air was warm and velvety and, in the background they heard the sweet sounds of the lutes and shawms coming from the house.

'You know, Peverell, I'm damn grateful we've put an end to all these treasonable goings-on down here. I love this place, and I've much work to do in Portsmouth. I can see that I'll be a regular visitor here in the future. I could appropriate Mortimer house, but I don't fancy it, somehow. Treason contaminates the atmosphere. Also I've a mind one day to reinstate Lady Mortimer there with her children. I'm a merciful man, am I not, Peverell, when the occasion demands it?'

'Of course you are, your Grace; I've never doubted it.'

'And you're a good friend, Peverell. Now, why not marry that lass of yours? Don't mind the father, he'll come round to you when you sire his first grandchild. The wench will agree, I'm sure, and it will be good to see her at Court. She can sing to me when affairs of state get me down. I could compose some songs for her. Matrimony's a fine institution. I can heartily recommend it. Mind you, the Queen's not well at the moment, not well at all. I hope she can stand the journey tomorrow.'

'Tomorrow, your Grace? You leave so soon?'

'There's work to do, Peverell. I've got a kingdom to govern. And the Queen's baby could arrive at any moment. Pray God it's a fine son to carry on my name.'

305

'Amen to that, your Grace.'

'Now, Peverell, what are we going to do about you? You've got a fine house, a fine wench – I know, you want your Priory, don't you? Well, this time next year, Cromwell will have got the legislation through Parliament, and the monks will have to go. Don't worry, I'll fix that Prior of yours up with a good position somewhere. By the way, he's a nice fellow. I could do with someone like him around at Court. He could make a second Wolsey. But no monks. No monks at Court. I've had enough of them. But you can have your Priory, then, and get yourself buried, when the time comes, in that chantry chapel you were telling me about. Mind you, it'll cost you something . . .'

N.B.—Nicholas bought his Priory off the King for £125.13.4d, of which £40.00.0d was paid immediately, with the balance due the following Michaelmas and Easter.

The proceeds from the Priory brought £276.10.11d into the King's coffers. It was the most profitable disposal of ecclesiastical property in West Sussex. There was no mention of the chalice in the inventory.